WHERE THE
SHADE ENDS

MEGAN MEREDITH

WHERE THE SHADE ENDS

Copyright © 2016 Megan Meredith

Cover design by Tim Logan

Photography by Jared Sluyter

A Herald's Megaphone Publishing Ltd. Co.
ISBN: 978-0692923993

For KP.

Thank you for letting me dream about this for twelve years and for being the guy I want to write about.

Thank you to many people.

Thank you to Nathan, Brad, and Caleb for answering my random and incessant questions about horses and cowboys. Thank you, Zak, for lending your expertise on the film industry. Kristin, who had been there since the beginning, you read the birthing of this story so long ago in the studio and encouraged me that it could be something one day— thank you for that.

To those who must remain nameless, thank you for being brave and telling me your story.

To my friends who are just as excited about this book as I am, thank you for the continual support and encouragement. I am grateful to do life with you.

Thank you to the city of Chicago for being dreamy.

To my editor, thank you for being flexible and gracious, even when computers sabotage us. Thank you for being more than just an editor but also a sounding board and a friend.

Thank you to my Father who entrusts me with a voice and stories to tell. Thank You for setting the ultimate example of telling truth through fiction and talking about hard things but doing it with massive amounts of love and mercy. Thank You for chasing me down and changing my story.

PROLOGUE:
A MAN AND THE OPEN THROTTLE

A feeling started between fourth and fifth gear, something that formed in the gear shaft and jolted the nerves all the way up to my shoulder, making me feel good by the time I threw it into fifth. I was getting the hang of driving a manual, and I could shift through the gears in less than a minute. In second and third gear, I could feel limits, and I hated limits. I could appreciate the feel of fourth because I knew the throttle was almost wide open, but once in fifth gear, I felt as if I could fly—and I mean really fly. Tonight I was loving the open throttle, and I was planning on flying close to 95 miles per hour the whole way home because I had movie contracts waiting in California.

I had been driving in the dark for about three hours, and I was glad to have GPS. Out in the middle of nowhere, my mind wandered to why I was on the road, but that train of thought lasted only long enough for me to get angry and blow past those thoughts like the car rocketing by the highway road signs.

I loved the growl of the engine, adding my own growl along with it. It was just me and my machine…only the car wasn't actually mine. I had taken JJ's Jag and told him to find another way back to L.A. I had given myself about a block and half to learn how to drive a stick, and then I hit the interstate.

I had been snaking my way across this dark map of roads for a while, and I knew I would need to stop soon to refuel both the car and myself. I floored the gas as I rounded a tight curve and listened to the engine whine. I passed a city limits sign quicker than I could read, and I threw the car into neutral and coasted down a hill. Before I reached the first intersection in the town, I saw smoke leak from under the hood and heard a loud crack, a long hiss, and then a fatal clank. I let out a string of expletives and hit my fist against the wheel. I stalled just feet from the vacant intersection in a silent, dark Texas town.

1: TRAFFIC LIGHTS AND SHORTCAKES
TEXAS, PRESENT DAY

The traffic lights blinked in a predictable rotation. Annie's morning always started with the same slow, methodical changing of the lights outside the large front windows of the bakery. *Vacant intersections and ironic crossroads,* she thought to herself, sitting down to put on some music. As soft tones poured from the speakers, she smiled at how the notes filled the tranquil space, and she looked out at the street and the changing lights.

Red to green.

She straightened yesterday's mail before carrying the coffee carafe to the sink.

Green to yellow.

She listened to the water as it pooled in the bottom of the glass carafe. It sloshed up the sides and swirled in the middle. When it was full and heavy, she carried it to the large coffee machine that sat against the wall by the register counter. The machine was black and chrome, and although it looked retro at first glance, a closer inspection revealed that the modern appliance might possibly launch into outer space if she pushed the right series of buttons. As she started the coffee, she looked back out the large window.

Yellow to red.

Just about all her days began the same way, but methodical and predictable were things she could handle.

Productive and quiet, she moved about the room, sometimes matching time with the rhythm of the music. The coffee brewed and filled the air with the inviting smell that would saturate her senses throughout the day. She paused and closed her eyes, delighted by the smell. She took a moment to pour herself a cup of coffee, even before the coffee pot finished brewing. Though she rarely had to force herself to slow down, she did have to remind herself to indulge in her favorite things. She knew that savoring was what life was about these days.

Seven years ago, life had moved her to this warmer climate and different pace, which she welcomed, but the charm of this new life wasn't in the climate; it was in the people and the solitude of a small town. The preserved historic buildings and town square could put a natural Western swagger in anyone's step.

Even now, with coffee in hand, Annie remembered how she had strolled down the timeless streets on one of her first days in town, taking in each corner, peering through windows, and admiring heavy ornate wooden doors. As she wandered around town, wondering what would be in store for her here, she had stopped at a corner. Adjacent to the corner drugstore had been a boarded-up storefront that used to be a barbershop. The red and white cylindrical barber's pole still hung outside even though the windows had been carefully protected with wooden planks. A sign hung on the door said, "FOR SALE."

Now, seven years later, the slow, casual pace of the town set the perfect tone for her bakery. She served coffee and pastries in the morning and a daily special, which consisted of whatever she was in the mood for. Everything was fresh and always drizzled with glaze or garnished with fruit to perfection.

People came in mostly for morning coffee and pastries, but the conversations had become just as much of a sweet craving. Later in the day, her only employee, Mandy, helped her serve cake, pie, and small delicacies such as truffles and éclairs. Annie hardly ever took special orders. She made what her heart desired, and everyone came in asking what she was making that day. She liked being on her own schedule and rarely ever rushing to meet demands of disappointed customers.

She had escaped her past life and been gladly reborn into Texan culture.

I never have to go back my old life, she thought as she watched the coffee finish brewing. *I can happily spend my days covered in flour and smelling of buttercream and oatmeal.*

A knock at the door broke her free from her thoughts. She set the coffee down and walked to the door, feeling the lasso of panic begin to tighten around her stomach, causing a lump of fear to rise in her throat. She hesitantly cracked the door slightly.

"Can I help you?"

A man's silhouette filled the doorway. She opened the door a little more so she could see his face but not so much that it would seem like an invitation. The man held up his cell phone and shook it from side to side, trying to animate that it didn't work.

The glow from the lamp outside illuminated the side of his face. There was something familiar about the slant of his nose and his perfectly square chin. His face didn't have a single crease or wrinkle even though his cheeks were a flawless shade of tanned

2

bronze. He towered over her with his broad shoulders and slim frame. He wore a tux with an untucked white shirt, and a bow tie hung lifelessly around his collar. His face was mostly in shadow, but it didn't matter since she had figured out who he was.

Quit staring at him, she told herself. *You're staring at him. What's he doing here, and what does he want? What should I say? I want to slam the door. God, help me. Say something!*

"I tried to use my cell, but I must not get reception out here in the great state of Texas," he said, poking fun at the rural surroundings. He turned slightly and pointed at the silver Jaguar in the road, hazard lights flashing with the hood propped open. "I seem to have stalled or something. May I use your phone? I mean, you do have one, right? Are there any repair shops in this...town?"

She looked up at the sky and said, "None open at this hour." The stars still lingered at five in the morning. "You can use the phone to call Randy's shop around eight, but we should get your car out of the road until then. I can help you move it in front of my shop."

"That must make you Antoinette?" he asked, looking up at the bakery's signage. He didn't look at her when he asked the question, nor did he wait for her answer. He only studied his reflection in the large front window.

She cocked an eyebrow at him and pointed at the sign. "Name's on the sign, ain't it?" she said, thinking he seemed too interested in himself to be a danger to her. The lasso of panic and fear around her stomach loosened enough so she could breathe easily.

"So, eight, you said?" He brought up his wrist and looked at his watch. It sat largely on his wrist with a face that had several gadgets on it, but for now, all he paid attention to was the time—5:15 a.m.

He looks like a spy with that watch, she thought to herself, trying to lighten her thoughts and loosen the lasso a little further. *I bet James Bond never got stranded.* The thought made her chuckle in her mind. *Plus, Bond is older and nicer...and he looks better in a suit. However, I suppose Bond couldn't always be trusted. Oh boy...Jesus, help me.*

The man let out several cuss words and then cut his eyes to her.

"I'll have to tell JJ about the car. He'll be pissed but...what can I do, right?" He shrugged at her.

She stepped outside, closing the door behind her, and then moved around him, brushing past his arrogance and language, and moved to his car. He trailed behind her.

3

"Let's see if we can push the car out of the road." She stood inside the driver's side door and pushed on the top of the doorframe while pulling the steering wheel to the left.

"Push?" he asked, looking even less charming with his mouth agape with surprise.

She just mirrored his expression, irritated.

"Oh, right. Push," he said. He set his whole weight against the trunk of the car and pushed. The car began to roll slowly. She yanked the wheel hard to the left. They got it across the street and halfway in two parking spaces, and Annie decided that would have to do. She let the hood down, grabbed the keys from the ignition for him, and then handed them to him. He flipped them around his index finger and into his right hand.

Fancy, she thought fastidiously, then wondered if she truly felt irritated with him or was just unsettled by the break in her usual morning routine. *Maybe it's the lack of coffee. Should I be hospitable to him, Lord? Help me not be fearful.*

"Thanks for helping with that," he said, flipping his keys again. "I'm Mace, by the way." He extended his other hand.

She already knew who he was. He was Mace Harlen, the Hollywood actor.

"I know," she said as she briefly shook his hand but then quickly released it. "And no problem, I..." She paused, thinking, *Am I really supposed to let him stay here? I can't believe I'm about to say this...*"I guess you can come in and sit if you'd like to wait until Randy opens, or you can sit out here." She opened the door, not waiting to see what he decided. "I just brewed a pot, if you drink it strong."

"Coffee would be great. I just need to call my agent real quick if you don't mind," he said, holding up his phone and pointing to hers inside the shop on the counter. "If I can use your phone, that is. I can call out, can't I?"

She could feel herself scowl at him before she could look away. *Call out? What does he think this is? An international call?*

They walked inside, and she went to retrieve the phone from behind the register. Mace stood just inside the door and surveyed the room.

The black and white tile floor led his eyes around the room to the old barbershop chairs. They were green leather chairs, facing outward instead of toward the mirrors behind them. Side tables sat next to each chair. Across the room from the green chairs were several small cafe tables, each set with vintage appliances. Old electric table fans, toasters, and rotary phones served as centerpieces.

The originality of the space surprised Mace, but he quickly forgot his complimentary thoughts as she handed him the phone. *What is it about her that irritates me—her curves, her unruly hair, or her plain clothes? On the other hand, is it the cautiousness in her eyes?*

"Thanks," he said, taking the phone. "I'll take this outside. JJ can get a little manic, especially this early."

"Okay," she said, conveying her disinterest though her stomach flopped with unrest. *God, help me relate to him the way I should...* she replayed her prayers again. He held up the phone the same way he had before and shook it slightly. *That is already getting old*, she thought, smoothing her shirt, realizing she didn't even have her apron on yet.

Her morning routine was off completely now, and she stood staring at the door after he had closed it behind him, wondering where to start with her busy to do list. She knew that Randy wouldn't be in until later and that it was long shot to get engine work done fast around here. The nearest airport was close to two hours away. *What should I do with him? Should I let him stay here until that car gets fixed?* She walked over to her worktable, trying to think about something other than the stranger—the *famous* stranger—at her bakery.

She decided that, despite how things had started out, it was a shortcake kind of morning and maybe a fruit tart kind of afternoon. The farmers market was open later, and she knew she could get fresh peaches from Mr. Jenkins.

Outside the shop, Mace slid out of his tux jacket and set it on the hood of the car. He tapped JJ's contact number into the phone. It began to ring as he unbuttoned another button on his dress shirt. *Man, it's hot in Texas*, he thought, *even in the forsaken hours of the morning.* He was glad when the phone went to JJ's voicemail.

"JJ—it's Mace. Look, I'm sure you're pissed, but we can hash that later." He leaned against the red brick wall. "I'm a little off schedule. Your car broke down, and I'm stranded in some small town in Texas, which serves you right or maybe it serves us both right but...whatever. My cell is no good around here. I'll be in touch."

JJ had been his agent for the past five years, helping Mace get his first major break in film roles. Everything came easily after that. Now everyone was saying he was the next big thing. JJ was aggressive and demanding, but that's what made him good at what he did. Knowing JJ, he would be ranting and calling his cell phone every two minutes. Mace felt relief that he wouldn't be on his case.

Mace looked around. It was still dark out, and he noticed the stars. He had never seen them so bright. Somehow, noticing the stars helped him not think back to the series of events that landed him here when he'd rather be landing at home. He pushed off the wall and turned back toward the door. *What am I going to do until the car is fixed? I hope JJ can get me out of here soon.* He raised his fist to knock on the door again and noticed his watch. *Seriously, it's only been thirty minutes?* He threw his head back in frustration and then knocked on the door.

"It's open," Mace heard from inside, but he hesitated to open it, wishing for a camera on the other side with a director behind it. *I could close the door behind myself and cross the room to frame in the woman.* Of course, there was no camera or director. He was on his own. He needed to manufacture confidence, casual conversation, and witty remarks without a writer or director's help. He finally opened the heavy black door that had a long glass pane in the center.

Annie was tying her apron behind her waist as she turned around to see him come through the door. She smiled hesitantly and caught herself thinking that his smile was perfect. *Maybe too perfect...it's rather arrogant*, she thought. He held up the phone again, and she knew she was growing tired of his *one* prop.

"Got his voicemail, which is good and bad." He laid the phone on the counter, scratched his head, and then gestured toward her with an open hand. "Listen…"

She interrupted him. "You're welcome to stay here until you get things worked out. I have a lot to do, but there's hot coffee and a place to sit."

"Oh...are you sure?" He hesitated. "I guess that'll have to do. I'm hoping JJ has studio jet time and can come get me soon."

"So...you're an actor?" She said it like a question.

"Yeah." He laughed slightly as if she was being sarcastic, but he noticed her face was unpretentious. Maybe it actually had been a question. "Man, this town is small," he laughed. *Ridiculous,* he thought.

She was measuring something into a bowl when she looked up confused. He had cornflower blue eyes that were offset by his bronzed, olive skin and dark hair. *I'm sure I would have seen you in movies or all over the entertainment news if I had time for such thing*, she thought but then tried to be sincere. "I'm sorry. I thought I recognized you, but you know, what are the odds?"

"Right." He laughed as he looked back over to the green barber chairs. Though they were almost a putrid shade of green, he began to study them. *This place is motley*, he thought, *but it would make a great set. The barbershop bakery*, he said to himself. The woman seemed eclectic and creative, but she was also cautious and guarded. He alternated between studying the decor and her, careful to not get caught watching her.

She was behind a worktable, dumping dry ingredients into a large bowl. Grabbing a large spatula, she began to stir, making wide sweeps of the entire bowl. After each one, she would tap the spatula on the side of the bowl. Her movements nagged at something in him further, so he sat down. With every tap of her spatula, he cringed internally at the dull drumbeat sound it made. He shifted several times, rubbed his head, popped his knuckles, and tried to ignore her, but he gave up.

"Will it bother you if I talk? I guess I have ADD. I can't stand silence," he commented, studying her movements. She stirred clockwise and scraped the edge of the large red mixing bowl, almost predictably counterclockwise every seventh stir. He wondered if she knew that.

"Talk to me?" she asked, looking up from the bowl and suddenly feeling flour on her cheek. She tried to wipe it with the back of her forearm, but she knew she just made it worse. Feeling nervous, she shook her head and said, "Sorry, that's obvious. No, I don't mind as long as you don't care if I'm distracted. I have a lot to get started for the day." *Keep it light. Talking too much makes you too familiar. That is trouble. He could be trouble, so keep it light*, she lectured herself.

"What are you working on right there?" He pointed to the bowl.

"This is the base for the shortcake," she said, occupied. She didn't even look up from the recipe. She ran her index finger across the page, following the print. She nodded to herself and pivoted quickly to the shelves behind her. She lifted several other ingredients off the shelves and piled them on the table. She did this all so quickly that Mace added the words *light* and *agile* to his ongoing assessment of her.

"What makes shortcake...uh, short?" he asked, and she could tell he was trying to be funny.

She chuckled a bit, thinking that he was naive and young. *And possibly narcissistic. See? He's trouble,* she scolded.

"You've never had shortcake, I take it?" She put her hands in her apron pockets and looked at him. "It's quite definitive actually. There are several ways to make shortcakes, but the way I prefer calls for biscuit mix or starting with scratch biscuits. You have had biscuits before, right?" He nodded, sensing that she was playing along with his joke. "Well, shortcake is a sweeter version of a biscuit. It's fluffy and somewhat light but dense, so it doesn't bake up real tall. People typically top it with fruit and cream."

"Hmm," he said carelessly, clearly not paying much attention to her explanation. "How long have you worked here?"

He moved so quickly from one subject to another she knew he didn't really care what she said. *He's just making conversation. Play along,* she thought.

"I don't just work here. I own the place," she answered. "I opened about six and a half years ago." Annie went back to stirring methodically for a minute before she walked slightly out of his line of sight to the sink. He heard the water running. When she came back into view, she put her hands into the bowl and folded the doughy mixture twice before dumping it onto the table. She separated the dough into small, equal portions.

"So you are here by yourself every day?" he asked vacantly, his eyes wandering away from her.

Annie's spatula hesitated, and she couldn't seem to make it move. She tried to take a deep breath, reminding herself, *He is just making conversation. He's undoubtedly trouble, but you don't know he's dangerous.* She calmly checked off her mental list: cell phone, pepper spray, .22. She finally regained control of her spatula and managed to answer him, hoping he hadn't noticed her pause.

"For a few hours in the morning. I have one employee who comes in when I need her and in the afternoons. I have customers that filter in and out every day—regulars and some who just pass through. Sam should be in before too long."

"People *actually* pass through here on purpose?" He looked around the room as if he was surveying the entire town inside one room. He sank down into the chair, put both hands behind his head, and clasped his fingers together.

"Didn't you?" she questioned.

His surprise showed in his arched eyebrows and his mouth hanging open. Memories blurred together in his mind: his girlfriend's black dress, the party, the fight, the drinking, JJ, the car...the open road. "No, not directly. I mean, I was following the GPS, and the car just died on me," he recounted. "Believe me—I didn't intend to stop here."

Her face was surprised and comical. "You probably would have been better off turning around. I don't know where you're headed, but we're not exactly 'on the way' to anywhere."

"Yeah, maybe that British lady voice on the GPS was leading me astray."

"Might explain it," she commented. "So what were you doing driving cross-country?"

He sighed and rubbed the stubble forming on his jawline. "Ugh. It all sounds so dumb now that I am going to say it out loud. We had gone to this huge preview event, and my on-again, off-again L.A. girlfriend and I broke up on the way to the after party, which is ridiculous and stupid. She hooked up with some guys at the bar. We ended up at the loft JJ keeps in Austin. He had invited some big producer execs to talk about some new projects and a film festival. I started talking to them about wanting to direct. JJ was more than a little inebriated, and he started laughing at me in front of everyone. I was so furious that I gave him my left hook, snagged his keys, hopped in his car, and sped down the highway. That's how I got here, broken down in nowhere. Sob story, huh?"

"Yeah, I guess so." Annie didn't really know what to say. *Shouldn't he have his own helicopter or something? Bond would.* She lifted the baking sheet with the shortcakes and walked to the oven. She opened the doors and placed the tray inside.

Mace looked around the room again. *This is going to be a long day,* he thought as he moved to the farthest barber chair by the window and grabbed a stack of magazines. He settled in the chair with his back slightly to her now.

He looked out the window every few pages as he flipped through a travel magazine. Barbados, Jamaica, and New Zealand—he could be anywhere else but in some small town in Texas, sitting in a bakery with a stranger. He stared at the pages. He could feel the sun, hear the waves, and taste the drinks if he just closed his eyes.

Megan Meredith

10

2. SAM AND RUM MUFFINS

Annie peeked around the counter, thinking that Mace hadn't spoken for at least ten minutes. He was slumped down in the chair with his head propped up in his right hand. His lips were slightly parted, and his breathing was heavy and slow. Her shoulders relaxed at the thought that he wouldn't talk for a while. *Too many questions could be dangerous, and small talk is difficult.* Her customers told her all about their families and their opinions, but people rarely asked about her life. Her privacy was expensive as walnuts but just as highly valued.

Turning back toward the oven and feeling her auburn curls falling around her face, she restrung her hair up on the top of her head into a pile. *Maybe it will stay there this time,* she thought as she checked on the shortcakes, whose tops were just getting golden. She opened the doors and slipped on oven mitts to retrieve the tray. The warm, buttery smell burst from the oven and filled the room.

Annie took a deep breath. She had a usual rhythm that started with the traffic lights, and their predictability set the pace of the rest of her day. Home to shop. Mixing bowl to oven. Oven to case. Customer to customer. Morning to lunch. Lunch to afternoon. Work to home.

Another predictable part of her day was Sam. Sam would be in by seven, so she needed to start the muffins. Sam was her most loyal customer, though, really, he was family. He loved her rum muffins and coffee every morning. He came in at seven to talk and keep her company before she really opened at eight when his buddies came and played poker in the back room. Every day, Dale, Tom, and Gus came in at eight. *Eight. That's when Randy opens,* she thought, *though he'll probably notice the car before we've even called him. I'm sure he'll give me grief about it.*

Her life was at least well-adjusted and relatively simple here. Her afternoons were filled with community projects and volunteering. Nightlife was a rare thing in this town, and Sam didn't do much past four o'clock. Her evenings were quiet and uneventful, much like her mornings. That was why she came here seven years ago. This small, predictable town offered uneventful solace.

Just as she pulled the muffins from the oven, Sam knocked on the door. "He's early today." She wiped her hands out of habit and

11

walked to the door, glancing over at Mace, still slumped in the chair. She opened the door to Sam's familiar 5-foot, 3-inch frame and leathery skin. He handed her his hat, revealing his silver waves on his round head. He wore his farm uniform, as he called it, every day, and it always consisted of some plaid shirt, jeans, and boots. Annie adored that it had been his standard attire for eighty years.

"Did you forget how to open the door?"

"Morning, Sam. Getting a head start today, are you?" She smiled at him.

Sam toddled past Annie and surveyed the room. He spotted Mace by the window. "There's a man in here," he said as if he were enlightening her.

"No, Sam. I just made that. He's breakfast." She nudged him as they stood there looking at Mace.

"I'd rather have a muffin. Stick to the muffins, Annie. He looks toasted." He looked at her over his bifocals.

"You're not impressed, eh? Then a muffin it is," she retorted as she removed a rum muffin from pan and set it on a plate. She handed it to him as he sat at the farthest table from Mace.

Sam picked at the warm muffin and watched Annie cross to the coffee station. She poured him his cup, refilled her own, and sat down across from him at one of the cafe tables.

"How'd he get here?"

"In a car." She avoided his glare and changed the subject. "Did you sleep well, Sam?"

"Get to it, Annie. How'd he get here, who is he, and why can't he park better than I can?"

Typical Sam, she thought to herself. He was protective of her; although given her past, his protectiveness had been earned.

"His car broke down in the street, so we pushed it over here. You can blame me for the slant. His name is Mace, and he's a famous movie star. That's all I know." She quickly ticked off the facts.

"That's all, huh?" He sipped his coffee, eyeing her over the top lip of his cup, letting all the information settle. "What's he got to stay here for?"

"Sam, he knocked on the door at five. No one else was open or even up yet. It was the decent thing to do."

"Annie." He shook his head at her. "Decent is...well, it's been so long, I can't remember what decent is, but you shouldn't be decent anymore, especially to men."

She had heard this speech before and commented, "Not with you around." He smiled at her. "Plus, I could break his nose if I had to."

"If you can reach it." Sam glanced at Mace and pointed at the ceiling. "He looks huge." She tried not to laugh as she took a sip of her coffee. The scent of the muffins reminded her that she needed to start the tarts. She needed peaches for them, and she could just walk to the market from here.

Should I wait until after we take the car to Randy's? Maybe I could just go now and be back in time.

Sam interrupted her musing. "What are we making today?"

"I made shortcakes, and I'm going to start some peach tarts. Actually, I need to walk over to the market and buy some fresh ones. Would you mind staying here until he wakes up? He needs to call Randy at eight so we can get the car in first thing."

Sam groaned and rolled his eyes. Annie ignored it and patted him on the shoulder.

"Thank you, Sam. I'll just be gone a few minutes. He may not even wake up before I get back." She grabbed some cash and walked toward the door. "Besides, the guys will get here, and if you need to, you could rough him up a bit. Just don't kill him," she said jokingly.

Sam buried himself in the sports section and groaned again. As she opened the door, she could hear him saying something, and she knew it wasn't just about the Rangers' score from last night's game.

"What's that, Sam?" she asked, knowing he wouldn't repeat it.

"Love you, Annie."

"Love you, Sam," she said as she shut the door behind her.

The sky was barely breaking into blue as she stepped outside. Half of it was still fighting off night as the horizon faded into a color that told her they would have a beautiful morning if the rain held off. The farmers market was a block away and across the railroad tracks. She followed the sidewalk to the tracks and crossed over. The market was set up in what used to be the town square. The funny part to Annie was that the square was a circular courtyard that served as a town monument now. *A square that's a circle*—the thought always made her smile.

Once at the farmers market, she meandered past booths with squash, cucumbers, fresh peanuts, and jalapenos. The smell of Mrs. Cottonworth's herbs and spices always caused her to stop. She savored the aromas of thyme and rosemary, and it was a special delight when mint and tarragon were available. She approached Mr. Jenkins' booth, where he typically had apples by the bushel, plums that weren't always quite ripe, and mouthwatering peaches and cherries when they were in season. She handled several peaches, turning them over in her hand and breathing them in. The sweet, ripe smell was wonderful; she couldn't wait to cut into them.

"They're perfect today, Mr. Jenkins."

Mr. Jenkins looped his thumbs through the straps of his overalls and nodded at her. "Sure are, Annie. What are you making today?"

"Peach tarts, so I'll need about two dozen."

He handed her two buckets, saying, "Pick what you need."

After getting her peaches, Annie began making her way back to the shop. Just down the street from the market were the beauty parlor, a grocery store, a hardware store, a hotel, a western clothing and boot store, a theater, a church, three restaurants, and Annie's shop.

Taking the long way back, she saw some magazines stacked outside *BeBe's Hair Stylings* on a bench. *Wouldn't you know? Mace is on the front cover*, she thought as she set the buckets down and grabbed one of the magazines. She propped herself up on the bench and began to flip through the magazine as the clouds started to roll in.

Storm's moving in…sooner than I thought.

3. ENGINES AND PEACH TARTS

Waking up slowly, Mace adjusted his eyes to the light streaming past the letters on the window. He noticed the letters on the windows matched the sign outside. *Redundant,* he thought.

Mace stretched his neck, regretting falling asleep in the chair. *How long have I been asleep?* He looked around the room, seeing no one in sight. *What was that woman's name again? Antoinette?* He had a hard time believing that was her name. She didn't really look like an Antoinette; plus, it sounded so formal. He mouthed it to himself. *Antoinette.*

"Annie will be back in a minute."

He jumped in the seat at the sound of a man's voice and then shifted to the left to see where it came from. The elderly man by the counter held a coffee cup in one hand and motioned outside with the other. Mace followed his motion out the window toward the street. *There's nothing there*, Mace thought, looking back at him and shrugging.

"She just stepped out. I'm Sam. I'll be in the back with the guys; we're playing poker. She said you needed to call Randy." Sam gestured toward the phone as he headed past the counter, between the butcher-block worktables toward the back of the room, and then through a green screen door.

Half asleep, Mace turned back toward the window and stared for a minute. *The old guy called her Annie. I guess that's her name. Is it short for Antoinette? Oh—what do I care?*

He replayed the early morning in his head as he wiped his mouth with the back of his hand, paranoid he'd been drooling in his sleep. He stood and walked toward the counter where he had seen her get the phone. Beside the phone was a small note. She had good handwriting, and it slightly resembled the whimsical letters on the sign and on the window.

"Randy's Repairs. Tell him the car is here, and I told you to call." A phone number was scribbled underneath. Mace sighed. He still couldn't believe he was stranded here. He was annoyed, tired, and hungry.

Geez, JJ!

It had been almost three hours since he left the man a message, and he hadn't heard from him. Mace sighed again and dialed the number Annie had left. A voice with a distinct twang picked up on the other end.

"Randy's. What can I do ya for?"

Mace was annoyed again. *What a redneck! Probably doesn't even know how to fix a Jag.*

"My car's broken down over here at Antoinette's, and she told me to call you. She said you could get the car fixed."

"You're over at Annie's place, you say? I need a sweet fix anyhow. I'll be right over and get you towed back. We'll see what we can do."

"All right, thanks."

Mace hung up the phone and then dialed JJ's number. It rang twice.

"Mace! Where the heck are you, man?"

"JJ, listen to your messages much?" Mace's voice was tense.

"Hey, man, I'm the one who got your left hook to the face, but I'm sorry about the car. I had no idea it would do that, or I wouldn't have *let* you take—"

Mace interrupted him. "JJ, I'm on a borrowed phone. I don't have a lot of time to chat; we'll talk about that later. Have you heard from Lithgow? Is he willing to meet us in L.A.? Will he have the contracts?"

"Yeah, Mace, everything is a go, but we need to get you here as soon as we can. Lithgow likes to change things last minute. You need to be ready for the meeting."

"I've got it. Don't worry about that part. When can you get me?" Mace asked agitatedly.

"I'm using some connections. I'm working on it, and I think I could have you in L.A. by sundown."

L.A. by sundown. Mace repeated it in his head.

"Can you find a place to sit tight until I can get to you?"

Mace scanned the room and laughed. "I found a place, but don't take too long. I risk becoming one of them."

JJ's laugh bellowed through the phone as they said their goodbyes and hung up. Mace immediately longed for coffee.

"I just made some fresh coffee." The old man must have come back in while he was on the phone. "I will tell you, though, Annie makes it better."

Mace grunted, making Sam laugh.

"So, how'd you end up here?" Sam asked, pouring steaming hot coffee in his cup and then turning to Mace and offering the pot to him. He took it. The coffee was thick and darker than chocolate.

"Long story," he said as he grabbed a nearby coffee cup.

Sam raised his eyebrows and looked around. "You got somewhere to be?"

"No, I guess not."

"Does it look like I have plans?"

Mace chuckled. "No, I guess not." Mace recounted his story, walking back to the barber chair. It was almost summer, but Mace imagined Sam probably always wore a button-up western shirt, jeans, and boots no matter the weather.

"So, how'd you end up at Annie's?"

"I saw her through the window, and it was the only light on in town."

"Yep, she brings up the sun, saves the day, and feeds us all by noon."

Mace momentarily drifted into a daydream and imagined it in his head: a woman with wild hair holding the burning sun up with one hand and a mixing bowl in the other. If a woman really could be strong enough to bring up the sun, she'd probably need to wear an outfit similar to Wonder Woman in order to do that and save the world. He thought maybe he would like Annie more in Wonder Woman's outfit. He let his mind linger on that thought for a moment.

"Saves the day, huh?" he mumbled mindlessly.

"Yes, sir, one dessert at a time," Sam chuckled.

For a brief minute, Mace wasn't annoyed that he was stranded. Sam was witty and dry, which Mace liked. He pictured the newspaper as a script and the two of them reading a scene together. Mace also pictured himself behind the camera guiding the scene. Then, the more they talked, the more Mace realized even if this were a scene, it was too slow.

He needed JJ to get him out of here. Mace preferred action, but this sleepy, bare town was filled with lackluster people. He continued to file away harsh assessment and jagged criticisms, thinking he was being a realist, observing his current situation with an objective and creative eye.

Someone knocked on the door.

"That'll be Randy," Sam said matter-of-factly.

Mace looked at Sam. "How do you know? I didn't see anyone walk up."

"This is a small town. It doesn't take long to drive across it. Besides, Annie takes her time at the market. She'll be back after a while." Sam walked to the door, assisting himself along the wall.

"Randy, come on in!"

A man walked through the door, shaking Sam's hand. "That smell always gets me. What's she making today?" he asked, breathing in the scent of baked goods.

"Does it matter? It's Annie. It'll be worth eating."

"That's true," Randy said and eagerly looked around the room. "Where is that girl?"

"Farmers market. She'll be back in a minute."

Mace stood and crossed his arms, irritated that Randy seemed more interested in Annie than getting his car to the shop. He'd watched Randy's shoulders drop when Sam told him that she was at the market. As he finally turned to Mace and extended his hand toward him, three older guys busted through the screen door in the back, arguing about aces and hearts in Sam's direction. Mace had forgotten Sam mentioned the men were in the back. They must have arrived while he'd been sleeping in the chair. Mace rubbed his neck again, reminded of the stiffness that lingered.

Not even sparing a glance at Mace, one of the older men, barked, "If I cheated, you would know, Gus, you blind bat, because I would have taken all your money."

"No, Dale, cheaters never win—and you just lost, so you cheated," Gus retorted, waving plump fingers at him.

Sam chuckled, "You both will lose next round, so pipe down."

The other guys looked away from each other to see Mace and Randy standing there. They started laughing and poking each other with their elbows. They took turns shaking Randy's hand and nudging Sam. Then everyone turned and looked at Mace.

"Hey, guys, I'm Mace. My car is broken down outside. I was just passing through."

Dale, a tall, lanky man, introduced himself. He wore a denim shirt tied off at the top with an arrowhead bolo tie. He was bony with deep crow's feet at the corner of his eyes. He nudged the shorter man with thick salt and pepper hair and glasses that sat atop his abrupt nose with a full mustache underneath.

"That one is Gus. I'm Dale, and this here is Tom," he introduced himself and then pointed to the dark-complected man standing behind him. Tom was muscular for an older guy, Mace noticed. He had long black hair with a single silver streak in the front.

"I'm Cherokee. I own a tomahawk. Watch yourself, sport," Tom said.

"Don't mind him. He's got low blood sugar. He gets cranky when he needs a snack," Dale said.

"Sam here let it slip that you're famous or some such nonsense."

"All right, boys, get back to your lair," Sam interjected.

"Yeah, man...the car," Randy finally chimed in. "Let's get a look at that and see if we can get you towed." He slapped his glove across his other hand and walked toward the door. "Fellas, no cheating now. Word will get around, and no one will want to play tomorrow night. Ya hear?"

The guys all chuckled and lifted their "scout's honor" fingers.

"We'll play fair so that we can win your money fair!"

Sam followed Mace and Randy outside, leaving the other guys inside. At the car, Randy propped the hood up, checked the oil dipstick, took off the air filter, and dusted it off. He wiggled the cables to the battery connectors, scowling at some slight corrosion. He disappeared underneath for a brief moment but quickly returned, facing Mace with a scowl on his grungy face.

"Is this your car?"

"No, it's my agent's car. Why?"

"Looks like you have a blown transmission, and the oil hasn't been changed...ever."

"Glad that's not on me," Mace said, throwing his hands up. "I've got people to do that for me. JJ's an idiot."

"I'll tow it back to the shop, run some numbers, and call you with an estimate. Maybe I can cut you a deal since you're a friend of Annie's."

"Money's not really a problem. My agent will pay for it. I'm not really a friend of Annie's, so don't feel like you have to do me any favors." He didn't know why he felt the need to say that, but he did.

Randy gave Mace a half smile when he said that they weren't friends. Mace closed himself off again with his arms crossed, knowing no one would notice. He was slightly annoyed Randy was making it so obvious he was only here for Annie. Mace could feel Sam looking at him as Randy got busy hooking up the car to the

19

tow truck. They watched him for a minute before he came around the back of the truck, arm extended to shake Mace's hand.

"Nice to meet you, man." He moved on to Sam, shaking his hand too. "Sam, good to see you again. Tell Annie I stopped by."

Sam nodded politely. Randy walked back to the truck and hopped up into the cab. He fired up the truck and then stuck his head out the window, raising his voice to say, "I'll call you after a while!" Sam and Mace nodded and waved. He drove off.

"I can't decide what drives you crazier—that people love Annie or that people don't know who you are." Sam was studying Mace again.

Mace couldn't believe this old guy had the nerve to talk to him that way.

"Don't think I didn't notice all your huffy arm crossing and such. You're very subtle, you know. I almost couldn't tell that you detest everything but yourself." Sam turned to walk back toward the door.

Mace looked at his watch, cursed the time, the day, the town, and the old man under his breath. After he was done stringing expletives together, he looked at his watch again. *This most definitely is going to be a long day,* he thought.

Sam turned back toward Mace, thinking maybe he should try being nice to the kid. Annie would want him to, though he didn't know why. "The guys and I go eat lunch at the senior center. Since Annie isn't back and Mandy isn't here yet, I'll have to lock up. Maybe you want to tag along with us old guys?"

Senior Center? Lunch? It isn't even 10:00!

"Nah, I think I'll just take a walk and take in some sightseeing," Mace said sarcastically.

"Suit yourself, kid. Looks like it might rain. Don't get caught in the storm or get lost. We'd sure hate to lose such a treasure like yourself," Sam said, gazing at him over the rim of his bifocals and pointing toward the horizon.

There were a few spindly, gray clouds clumping together. *So threatening.* Mace thought, feeling his irritation shift into something else. *Yeah, looks like a perfect storm, old man.* He shoved his hands into his pockets. Sam went in the door but left it open. A moment later, he reappeared with the other three guys behind him.

"Well, we're off. Have a nice walk."

"Don't get wet." Dale jabbed at him and pointed to the wisps of gray.

"If you do, you can borrow some clothes," Gus offered, smiling.

"Yours would never fit him. You're too robust." Tom patted Gus's bursting belly.

"Keep that in mind when the storm hits." Dale shook his fat finger at Mace playfully.

"Got it," Mace muttered under his breath as he turned toward the railroad tracks. *It doesn't even look like rain. What do those old guys know? They probably need to turn on their hearing aids.*

He glanced back to see all four of them piling into an old green Ford pickup. They poked and pushed each other as if they were young guys, joking and making fun of each other.

He crossed the tracks, trying to picture something classic like James Dean walking broodingly along the tracks, but he knew nothing would reverse his compounding irritation. The retro buildings drew closer. They were all in good condition, to his surprise. No paint was chipping or canopies falling in. He had half expected a ghost town. There were about two blocks in each direction of two-story brick buildings, all with big front display windows and colored canopies. There were small park benches in front of most shops, ferns, or flowers in big planters. It was quaint and picturesque.

About a block to the left, a marquee sign caught his eye. The old, yellow aluminum, arrow-shaped marquee glinted in the sun through the clouds. The name *ARROW* stood vertically in red letters and pointed downward to the marquee below. Mace began to walk toward it. The marquee stuck out over the sidewalk, covering the old box office. In black block letters, it read, "Upstage: Enrolling now."

He wondered what Upstage was. *Whatever it is, it probably could use a better name,* he critiqued. He passed an antique store and a dance studio. He looked down the street in the opposite direction. No cars appeared, which he assumed was normal. He crossed the street toward the theater.

Mace had studied stage acting when he went to college for two years back before he got cast in the role that put him on the map. After that, he dropped out, always thinking he'd have time to finish later, but he never did.

As he approached the box office, he could see his reflection in the polished brass around the window. He wasn't surprised to see dark circles underneath his eyes.

Through the box office window, he could see a red velvet chair sitting behind the box office counter looking preserved in time, perfect and statuesque. A sign in the window repeated what the marquee said. Walking toward the large sets of double doors, he pulled the heavy brass handles. Finding it locked, he cupped his hands around his eyes, trying to look inside, but he couldn't see past his own reflection in the glass into the dark lobby beyond.

Maybe Annie knows who owns it, Mace thought to himself. He tried to make a mental note to ask her later. He walked by the "Now Showing" posters, which were all old musicals. He touched the frames as he walked by and tapped the last one. He was facing the street again and saw someone on the opposite sidewalk holding a couple buckets.

The girl was looking at him as a clap of thunder startled them both. She looked up. The light gray that had crept along the horizon earlier now filled the sky. It had begun to rain, but Mace had been so curious about the theater he hadn't noticed the dark clouds rolling in over the ridges beyond the town. The streets glossed over as the rain began, and the black pavement became a shiny reflection of the threatening sky. He was safe from the rain under the extension of the marquee. The girl grabbed a newspaper off the bench, held it above her head, and stepped out to run across the street. As she ran, he noticed her wavy auburn hair. *It must be Annie*, he thought as his eyes followed her across the street. She shook the newspaper out and then did the same to her hair. It had grown larger. *She looks ridiculous*, he thought and laughed to himself.

She touched the outline of her hair and smiled back at him. "Yeah, it grows when wet, just like a chia pet."

He laughed again, thinking she was funny in a simple way as if maybe she didn't know it.

She looked back toward the street and shrugged. "Who knows how long this will last—might as well set these down," she said, setting her peaches down and lowering herself to the concrete where she leaned against the wall, kicking out her legs in front of her and crossing her boots at the ankles. They watched the rain for a few moments before a clap of thunder broke their trance. She pulled out a cellphone, which surprised Mace. Dialing a number, she let it ring and continued to watch the storm.

"Hey, Sam," she said and waited while he answered amidst the cackling she could hear in the background. "Did you lock up?"

"Yes, I always do, dear. You stuck in the rain somewhere?"

"Yes, we're underneath the Arrow's overhang, waiting out the rain."

"Okay—we're headed to lunch. We'll be back in a bit. Mandy coming in soon?"

"Yes," Annie started, "I may see if she is on her way. I don't know that I'll be back very soon."

"We'll see you later then."

"See you soon."

As they hung up, she sent a text that Mace assumed was to Mandy. She received a text back and then stowed the phone away and turned her head toward Mace.

"Tell me, Mace. How famous would you say you are?"

"Are you kidding me? I mean, I'm kind of a big deal." Mace laughed.

Annie knew he was joking, but she also assumed he was as narcissistic as he sounded. Mace took three steps backward and propped himself against the box office. He shoved his hands in his pockets. He knew it was possible he had misread his own irritation with her. It was more nervousness than irritation. Something about her made him *nervous*. He didn't want her to notice.

"I'm on the map, JJ says, but I don't have the street cred to be as big as we want me to be yet. That's why I need this movie with Lithgow." He smiled and looked down, trying hard to be confident. It was strange that she did this to him. No one really ever made him nervous, not even the most talked about director or actor. He could always take it in stride and conjure up *calm*, but there was something about her voice and casual mannerisms that made him fidget. "I guess I'm pretty famous already. A lot of people out there know my name or my face, but that doesn't make me worth knowing." It was false modesty, and he knew it. His face burned, and he knew she could tell he was trying too hard. If he could hit himself in the mouth right now, he would, but she moved flawlessly through his stupidity.

"Well, I'm sure you love what you do. That's great."

He nodded. "It's a great career. I always knew I'd be acting. I'm hoping to land some prominent roles this year."

"You must have started young, huh?" She wanted to know just how young he still was.

"I'm 27 now, and my first gig was when I was 20."

"That's cool," she said awkwardly, realizing how much older 32 felt at the moment. She tried to mask her awkwardness by asking another question. "Who are some people that you hope to work with that I may know?"

"Let's see. That's harder than you think, considering you didn't know me..." He trailed off while she smiled and shrugged, and he continued. "There are so many guys that are big right now. If I could get work with any of the likes of Judi Dench or Johnny Depp, it would be epic."

"Yeah, okay. I may know them."

"Yeah, okay." He smirked at her. *She probably doesn't know them,* he thought. "So, I take it this theater doesn't show movies?"

She looked up underneath the marquee as if she forgot where they were. "Nope. This is a privately owned theater. The owner has an after-school program but no movies. The nearest movie theater is in Austin, I'm afraid."

"Oh." He didn't know Texas, but he knew that was hours away. "Do you know who owns it?"

"Yes, I do, and like everything in this town, it's owned by a small-town type," she retorted, slightly defensive.

"Oh, I didn't mean anything by it," he said, holding up his hands. "I'm actually really impressed. Whoever owns it really did a bang-up job. It looks pretty much restored."

It was probably the first time he hadn't had cynicism and judgment in his eyes since she met him, she noticed.

"You've got a good eye. It is almost back to its former glory. It was pretty much a pile of rust and rubble before they took it on. There was a lot to restore."

"How long did it take them?"

She hesitated, her face searching the ceiling and then the glass doors.

"They started it just after I got to town, so about six years, I suppose."

"Wow, big undertaking. I bet that was cool to watch."

"Yeah, it was. It was quite the transformation..." she trailed off, wondering how much to tell him. She looked out to the street. "Hey! It's stopped raining for the moment, so I should head back toward the shop. This storm will probably pick up again soon, so as long as we have a break..."

Even though he found himself wanting her to keep talking, he guessed she was right, although he really wanted to get inside the theater. Mace couldn't tell if she meant to change the subject or not. He followed her gaze out to the glossy street. For a moment, while they had talked, he had forgotten that he was stranded in a strange town. Thinking about going back to the bakery and spending the day slumped in the green barber's chair all day while waiting to hear from JJ made him edgy and annoyed.

"Yeah, okay," he complied.

Megan Meredith

4: POKER AND A RUEBEN

They walked along the sidewalk beside each other.

He seems disappointed that the rain stopped, and his disapproval of the town is all over his face, Annie thought. *I can only imagine how awkward it must be to be stranded in some strange town with some strange girl he couldn't be less enamored with. I feel like I should apologize or something,* she mused. They turned the corner and could see her shop just beyond the railroad tracks.

"So, Randy picked up the car, then?" she asked, trying to break the awkwardness.

"He did and said he'd call later, though it already was bad news. JJ says he's going to get me out by tonight; we've got a big meeting tomorrow."

"I'm sorry you are stuck here...even for a while." She wasn't sure why that came out of her mouth.

They walked past a beauty parlor that looked like it was stuck in the 1950's, and he could see that they were headed back toward the center of the town. He kept his hands secure in his pockets and resisted that feeling of nervousness creeping in. He looked at her from the side.

"No, it's cool. It's not so bad around here."

"Maybe it's not too bad, but it's not L.A. It's not even Austin. There's nothing even remotely close to probably what *you'd* call civilization."

"That's a little unfair. Civilized, maybe. Familiar, no." He smiled at her; he was relaxing, which made Annie want to relax.

Her defenses were solid, she knew. She was safe behind her manufactured walls. She wasn't uneasy or scared being around him, but her reality stayed the same: even if she felt relaxed, no one could be trusted.

The rain made the street shiny and sticky with the humidity. Leaves seemed glued to the asphalt. There was a distinct smell that Mace noticed. He couldn't quite recognize it. It was much fresher than when it rained in L.A., yet the air was so thick and heavy that it was hard for him to breathe. The air seemed to hang on his skin.

"I can run you by Randy's at lunch to check on the car if you want."

"That'd be great. I need to get out of here as soon as possible."

Annie laughed. "I thought it wasn't too bad."

He looked at her with a startled look. "Oh, sorry. That's not what I meant. I just have been at meetings in Chicago and then Austin. We have some big stuff going on, and I'm anxious to get back."

Annie's mind went blank for a moment. She felt like the cement in the sidewalk had melted and was sucking her down, sliding deeper into the cracks. She was stuck on the word "Chicago." Her mind circled around it for a moment like a vulture. *Chicago. Chicago.* Everything was fuzzy and beginning to swirl. She tried to pull her focus from it, but fainting was becoming more alluring. Then his voice startled her.

"Are you all right?" Mace was looking at Annie as if she were insane. She hadn't realized she had stopped walking.

She tried hard to focus on his face. "Yes, I'm sorry. I just got a little lightheaded...I guess I just need some lunch or something."

"I could use some food myself. I suppose that you guys have a diner or something around here?"

"We do. Max's." She hesitated and waited for some sort of reaction from him. She wasn't sure what expression she was expecting, but she waited. His eyebrows lightened and then lifted. *So now we're having lunch?*

"And then we can head over the Randy's," she added.

"I'm good with that." He shrugged again.

"Let me get this fruit in the fridge so I don't get flies and make sure Mandy is all set. Then we can take my truck."

"Since my car...is..." He smiled and lifted his eyebrows, trying to be funny.

"You and JJ should learn to change the oil," she crushed his efforts to be charming.

They walked back into the shop, and Annie put the fruit away. She called after Mandy toward the back.

"Here," said a thin, wispy-haired older woman as she popped her head through the screen door. She wore a purple apron and thick brown clogs. Annie adored that she looked Swedish most of the time, though Annie didn't actually know where she was from.

"I'm going to go grab some lunch. I'll see you in about an hour. Can you finish the shortcakes?"

"No problem, dear. I'll see you then." With a slight hop, Mandy disappeared back through the screen door.

Annie grabbed her keys and her purse. Mace followed her out the door and over to the truck.

"This is yours?" Mace gawked at the large pickup.

Annie smiled. "Yeah, Sammy and I live on a ranch. I haul stuff around."

"Cool," he said, acting interested. "You've got horses and stuff then?"

"Yeah, horses and a large garden. Sam used to have cows and a few chickens, but I didn't want to take care of all that and him too."

"When you say you and Sammy...Sam is your...?"

"Sammy?" She stumbled over the name. *Did I say Sammy?* Biting her lip to regain control, she clarified, "Sam is my uncle."

"Right. Your uncle," he repeated, not noticing her slight misstep.

They pulled up to Max's, a fully restored, silver, streamline diner. It had all its original fixtures and mismatched curtains and booths that had been collected from other diners around the state. It was old and eclectic, just like Annie's bakery. It had a revolving door decorated with homemade lost and found signs and garage sale signs.

Max yelled Annie's name as they walked in, and a group of high school girls in a corner booth started giggling and whispering. One looked as though she might hyperventilate. They recognized Mace and couldn't finish their lunches because they were too busy scrambling in their purses, trying to find phones to take pictures or pieces of paper for autographs. They all checked their hair in the small mirrors from their compacts and applied too many layers of glittery gloss to their lips.

Annie smiled and continued toward the bar.

She seems completely unaffected by me. Mace couldn't decide if he felt irritated or challenged by her.

"Hey, Max!" Annie called across the room to the black-haired Italian-looking man with a wide face and long nose. He wore black frame glasses and white diner hat. His apron was smothered in grease and ketchup. He waved his spatula at her, signaling her to come over to the counter. She and Mace picked swiveling stools and sat down.

"Max, this is Mace. He's just passing through, and we need some lunch."

"Mace, you've come to the right-a place-a!" Max said in a fake Italian accent that then switched to Spanish as he turned to Annie, "Choo need some soostunance?"

Annie laughed, pointed at Max, and said to Mace, "*He* is why I come here."

"Best place in town to get diner food from an international, I'm sure." Mace laughed with her.

"Dori, get the girl some menus, please, and some sweet tea!" Max yelled across the counter to a petite older woman wearing a hair net.

"Thanks, Max."

The woman handed Annie the single-page menus. After studying her menu for a minute, Annie ordered the Reuben sandwich with coleslaw, and Mace ordered the barbecue burger with fries. They chatted about the fixtures around the diner and the uniqueness of small towns as they waited for their food. Annie reminded herself to keep it light, and Mace reminded himself to be objective in his observations.

"I think we're about to hear some squeals," Annie said, taking a sip of her sweet tea. "I bet you get this all the time everywhere you go."

Mace spotted the girls in the corner booth again. They were piling out and heading toward them. Mace nodded and turned around to face the oncoming girls before they arrived at the counter. They stopped and giggled.

"Come on. I won't bite," he said to them.

He is actually being pretty decent, she thought but remembered her conversation about decency with Sam earlier, which made her smile. She guessed that it might be possible for Mace to be as nice as James Bond; if she were honest, she knew that Bond was actually a selfish womanizer rather than a decent gentleman. She wasn't sure if the similarity between the two men said more about Mace or James Bond.

Dori brought their plates just before the teenage groupies came scampering toward him, thrusting napkins and whatever they had in their purses at him to autograph. He signed each one and took more pictures than any one man should have to. The girls got halfway to the door, turned, and waved again, but this time, they squealed, "Bye, Miss Annie," and then ran out the door.

"I'm sure the whole school will be on lockdown first thing tomorrow morning; otherwise, there will be a stampede." Annie laughed. "You just gave those girls glory for the whole female population of Penumbra to be insanely jealous of. That was nice of you."

"Penumbra? Is that where we are?"

"Yep, you're here."

"Well, yeah, but you get my point. That's the strangest name for a town that I've heard of."

"Well, nobody asked me either," she shrugged, feeling dangerously close to comfortable.

"And, *Miss Annie*? Are you a high school teacher too?"

"Um…no, more like a mentor."

"Oh, like a tutor? Or what?"

"Yeah, I guess you could say, like a tutor."

"Cool," he said, not asking anything further. They ate in silence.

"Well, I'm done here. How about you?" Annie tossed her napkin on the counter and tucked a twenty-dollar bill under her cup. "I should get back to the shop. I have something this afternoon, and I still haven't finished those tarts."

"I'm good. That was delicious."

"It was. Max, thanks!"

"Yes, Max, it was truly a soostaining experience!" Mace said, mimicking the same accent Max had used earlier.

Max roared back, laughing behind the counter. Annie waved goodbye, and they walked back to the truck. They drove a few streets up from the diner and took a left, made their way a couple more blocks from the main part of the small town, and then pulled in the parking lot of Randy's garage. The large brown metal building had an oversized orange sign that advertised "Randy's Repair Garage."

"Randy's probably under a car. I'll just run in and ask him how long he thinks it'll be," Annie offered, hopping out of the truck.

"It's fine. I mean either way JJ's going to—" He stopped himself. "I'll just stay put." He felt reiterating that he was leaving was rude since she was trying to help him.

"Suit yourself. I'll be back."

Mace watched her walk into the garage bay and yell something toward a rusted '57 Chevy.

Randy came sliding out from under the truck, and Annie leaned on the side fender and talked down to him as he remained on the floor.

"I've been trying to call you," he said agitatedly.

"We grabbed some lunch over at Max's."

"Oh, I get it. Off gallivanting with the famous guy, huh?" he said, frustration coming through in his thick Southern vowels.

"How did you know he was famous? I can't believe you know who he is. I'm impressed."

"I looked him up on the, uh, that internet."

"You have internet?" Annie asked, shocked.

"Yeah, just got it with the new cable last week. You can email me if you like. Do you want my email address?"

"We're standing here talking now, so why would I email you?"

"Just saying, in the future."

"Well, we'll see. Anyways, how much longer do you think?

"Into the future?"

"No, Randy. How much longer will Mace's car take?"

"I had to send Rickie to Austin to get the parts I didn't have. It may be tomorrow."

"Will you check in with Mace by the end of the day and let him know? I think he's pretty antsy, and he's got a chopper in route."

"What? With a drop dead gorgeous woman like yourself showing him around, I think if that were me, I'd move here or something."

Annie pushed off the Chevy with her elbow and moved toward the entrance of the bay. "All right, Randy, it's getting a bit thick in here, so I'm going to get on back. We'll talk to you later."

"Yep...oh hey. Where do you think he'll stay?"

"He's not staying," she started but didn't finish explaining, already turning to walk back to the truck. Stopping just before the truck, she yelled back, "Goodbye, Randy!"

As Annie climbed up into the truck, she commented to Mace, "He said it may be tomorrow. He had to send out for parts. I asked him to check in with you by the end of the day."

"Thanks," Mace said rather dully.

"No problem."

"Not that it matters. I'll be gone. I'm not sure how JJ will get it, but I guess he'll figure it out."

Annie's face did not reveal her contempt for his reply. *Is he really just going to leave his agent's car broken down in Texas and let him figure it out?* She knew she shouldn't be surprised, but there were brief moments when he seemed to care about more than just himself. They drove the short distance back across town and pulled into the shop parking lot. The green truck was back, and that meant the old guys were in the back playing poker.

"Why did Randy want to know where I was staying?"

Annie laughed.

"I didn't know if you heard that." She turned off the truck. "Let's just say that Randy assumes every guy is like him, and if every guy is like him, then they propose to me on the second day after meeting me."

"He proposed?"

"The day after I moved here."

"Whoa!"

"That's Randy. He's a little possessive. Anyway, I have to get those tarts done, and then I have an appointment at 4:00. You're welcome to stay here. You can play poker with Sam and the boys if you'd like, or there's a hotel a block down from the theater if you want to check in there until JJ rescues you."

"Maybe I'll play one game. I bet that will be all they can handle of Mace." He had a cocky smile again.

"I wouldn't be too cocky around Sam and the boys. They'll mop the floor with you."

"We'll see about that."

They both walked through the shop door and saw the men sitting around Annie's worktable, eating shortcakes. They all looked up at once, with faces like deer in headlights. Sam didn't even try to hide the shortcake that was halfway to his open mouth.

"Sam!"

"Well, Annie." Sam shrugged. "You shouldn't just leave this stuff out. All they had at the cafeteria for dessert was lime Jell-O. Lime Jell-O! It's not our fault."

Annie laughed, shaking her head. "All right, boys, scoot. I've got stuff to do. I've got you a fifth poker player, so go get playing."

The men looked at Mace and then looked at each other and cackled in a chorus round.

"Oh, the youngster wants to play!" Tom said.

"He wants to come up to the big leagues," Dale echoed.

"He thinks he can play with the big boys!" Gus bellowed in mocking laughter.

"We'll mop the floor with this one," Sam announced.

Annie shot a look to Mace. "Told you."

With that, all the men, including Mace, disappeared through the screen door.

Annie sighed as she tied her apron around her small waist and readjusted her hair, spotting her coffee that sat right where she left it, still full but now cold. Annie dumped it down the sink, poured another cup, and sat down on a stool to start peeling peaches. They were perfectly ripe, bright, and juicy. She cut the skins off into a bowl, thinking she could use them for something else. She shot the pits into the trashcan like a three-point shot across the room. Only three of them made it.

She dumped all the peaches into one bowl and rolled out several crusts, neatly pinching the edges around the pie plates. She tossed the peaches in light syrup and then overlapped the slices in the crusts, arranging them to fan in a circle. She then poured the leftover syrup over the top of the peaches. She put them in the oven and came back to the worktable to clean up the half-eaten shortcakes.

After everything was clean and she had checked on the tarts, she sat down with her reheated coffee, grabbed a cookbook, and flipped through it. She stopped on a caramel soufflé, admiring the picture, and then read through the ingredients for a citrus flan. Twenty minutes later, she pulled the tarts from the oven and left them to cool on the racks beside the oven. Sam had helped her build the red cooling racks made of wooden frames with shelving slats for baking trays. She wrote a small note for the boys that read, "DO NOT EAT," and stuck it on the rack. She knew there was little chance that they would respect the sign, but she needed proof that she had tried when they would surely argue about it later. It was almost four o'clock.

"Mandy?" Annie called out.

Mandy appeared through the screen door. "Yes?" she answered sweetly.

"I've just pulled the tarts. Don't let the men eat them. I'm out for the afternoon. Are you good to close up?"

"No problem, Annie."

"Thank you for coming in early. Today has not been at all what I thought it was going to be."

"I love being here, Annie. It's no problem."

Annie smiled at Mandy, slung her purse over a shoulder, grabbed a clipboard off the counter, and headed out the door.

5: REHEARSALS AND BUBBLE GUM

"Okay, okay—listen up!" Annie stood up from her seat and turned to face the teenagers sitting in the seats behind her.

No one was listening because all the kids were laughing and passing around a cell phone. The girls were squealing, and the boys were rolling their eyes and mimicking the girls' swooning expressions.

"People!" Annie yelled. Everyone froze. Annie was now standing on a chair. "Listen up. Yes, I'm aware that you are excited about the rumors going around town."

"I hate to tell you this, but they're not rumors. You were there," said a sassy blonde in the back row who had been at the diner. "Half the rumors are about you."

Annie breathed in slowly. "Okay, we are not discussing that right now. We are still going to rehearse, even with someone famous in town. You are still going to give me 100% of your attention, even with a famous person in town. I am going to confiscate that phone until the end of rehearsal. Okay?" A petite brunette girl in the front row sheepishly handed Annie the phone. "Thank you. We have a show going up in six weeks, and we have a lot to do."

A senior in the back row raised his hand. He was broad shouldered with a handsome, sharp jawline, and today, Annie noticed, he wore a fresh bruise under his right eye.

"Yes, Colby?"

"Miss Annie, why didn't you bring said famous person with you?"

Everyone perked up and started nodding. "Because, Colby, he doesn't know we're here. I didn't feel the need to tell him because we don't know anything about him. He is merely a passerby. Can we all just forget that Mace Harlen is here for at least an hour and a half, please?" Annie pleaded. Everyone nodded reluctantly.

"Okay. Now, status reports. Where are we with the backdrop and the lights?"

A thin boy with freckles and strawberry hair flipped through a legal pad and then looked up at Annie, saying, "We will put the finishing touches on the backdrop this week and next. The lighting cues are ready, and I have a list for you of the color gels that I need ordered."

"Excellent work. How is your paint crew?"

The boy gestured that it was just so-so.

"Do you need an extra person for help to finish up?"

"No, it's tight quarters. We already have to referee fights enough as it is."

"Good. It's good to know your limitations," Annie said, scanning the crowd with her eyes. "That's a good lesson. Everybody, it's good to know when to ask for help and when to just do it yourself to avoid conflict."

Almost everyone nodded, and a few of the kids pointed toward the front row at a girl who was chewing on her pencil. She had a short nose and wavy hair that was black and shiny like a crow's feathers.

She popped her gum loudly and looked around. "What? I didn't start that, and all of you know it."

"All right, all right—moving on," Annie said, pointing to the back row of snickering girls.

She waited until she could see compliance on their faces. "Biannca, how are the posters coming along? Have you thought of ideas for advertising or fundraisers?"

The sassy blonde from the back row stood up and smoothed her skirt. "The homecoming parade is coming up. I thought it would be cool if we put together a float to enter, and some of the play's characters could be on the float. We can make signs and stuff."

"That's a very good idea. What else?"

"I've got Colby doing some artwork for the posters, and Kristin said that we could stage a photo shoot. I thought it would look good to have some of the actors on the poster; people are more likely to come if they are supporting someone in the play. As far as the fundraiser goes, some of us were thinking we could auction some people off." Biannca winced a bit.

"I don't think Mace Harlen will be around for that," Annie said, knowing whom Biannca was referring to. Everyone's shoulders dropped, but Annie continued, "The auction is still a great idea. Biannca, you are doing a wonderful job. I like the way you have utilized others' talents to help get your projects done." Annie turned toward Colby. "Colby, I didn't know you were an artist."

He held up two fingers to signify a little bit. Annie nodded and pointed to his bruised eye, saying, "Talk to me about that later, okay?" She gave him a look of stern concern but quickly moved on.

"Lastly, but certainly not least." Annie pointed toward a girl sitting out in the middle of the auditorium. "If it weren't for her, we'd all look awful. Kristin, how are costumes and makeup?"

Kristin was a striking blonde sitting off by herself, mainly because she was holding a hoop skirt covering two chairs in each direction. She had needle and thread pinned between her teeth, and she was battling yards of fabric. She looked up and scrambled to get the thread out of her mouth.

"We're doing good. I'd say we're on schedule. I could use new makeup...all of that is fairly old and cakey."

"Is Jason still dancing with the mannequin?" Annie asked, giving Jason a look of suspicion.

Kristin nodded, not wanting to say anything or look Jason's direction.

"Are you still trying to get chiffon?"

Kristin nodded.

"And were actors in the costume closet again?"

Kristin didn't move. There was silence except for the loud pop of gum again. Annie shot the black-haired girl a look, and the girl's eyes widened.

"I'll take that as a yes, and so it goes—a day in the life of the costume designer. Everyone, please cooperate with Kristin. She may have one of the hardest jobs here. She has to get all of you to look like you're more than a bunch of crack-ups."

Everyone laughed.

"All right, let's get into places. We're going to run Act 1 scene 5. You know who you are and where you're supposed to be, yes?"

Everyone scattered and scurried off behind the curtains. The lights were cued, and the curtains ascended. Annie moved back a couple rows and sat in the seat where she always sat to observe plays. She loved this place—the noise the curtain made as it went up, the smell of the theater seats, and the cold air on her face in the dark as she waited for the first lighting cue to come up—but more than any of that, she loved these kids.

A blue light hit the black-haired girl standing center stage. She had flawless skin that glowed in any lighting cue that they made. She ate, drank, and slept theater, and she was the center of the drama at all times, on stage and off. She was a very good actress for only being a sophomore at Penumbra High School, and she somehow managed to snag Colby as a boyfriend. Annie hoped Colby would let go of that relationship before he graduated. The gum popped again from the stage, and Annie jumped up from her seat, irritated.

"Excuse me! Gum."

The girl cringed and looked around for a trash can. She shrugged and pulled the gum out of her mouth, extending it to Annie. Annie scoffed but then realized the girl was seriously trying to hand her the chewed bubble gum.

"No," Annie said and pointed backstage. "Go."

As the girl skulked off stage, Annie returned and tried to resettle back into her chair.

The teens had been studying classic literature this semester, and since Upstage was an after-school educational program, Annie thought it would be good for them to continue that literature onto the stage. Collectively they had adapted the Jane Austen novel *Northanger Abbey* into a '50s-style drama with a little mystery and intrigue. Annie showed them how to tease out the universal themes in the book and transfer them into another time period. Annie then held auditions for the parts and had everyone also sign up for a work project for the play. She felt that doing so taught the kids to be responsible for the success of the play and how to enlist their friends' help for something worthwhile.

Annie had bought the theater with an inheritance her father had left her. She hired a preservationist to come in and restore most of the original fixtures and adornments. She also enlisted help from guys Randy's age to do most of the construction. They had replaced the stage floor and put in lighting tracks.

From the historical documents that she could find at the courthouse, the Arrow originally served as a saloon during the 1800s, was converted into a small playhouse in the 1920s, and then finally was added on to in the late 1940s to make what was the current Arrow Theater. Annie remembered coming here as a little girl when she would come visit Sam. They used to have open mic night, and the whole town would come and listen to bands play bluegrass and sing gospel hymns. It had closed in 1991 when Earl Pumphrey, the fifth generation owner, died. He was the last of his family, and no one else in town could afford to keep it running.

Annie had finally finished the remodeling this year. It had been her dream to do theater again after she left Chicago. After living and working in Penumbra for the last several years, she realized that she needed to use the theater to give the kids of the town something to do and something to feel proud of.

It had taken almost a full seven years, but she was finally starting to feel proud of herself.

6: AUDIENCE OF ONE AND LIME JELLO

"All right, boys, I'm just about out. You've sucked me dry," Mace said. The men were sitting in lawn chairs around a poker table made of a large wooden spool used for metal cable.

"I'll go all in if the pretty boy can answer me something," said Dale.

"What is this? Trivial pursuit poker?" Gus jabbed.

"I'll see you all in and raise you my lime Jell-O tomorrow," Dale retorted.

"Oh pish, you don't even like lime Jell-O. You only get it because you don't have the gumption to tell Sally and her hairnet no," Sam cackled.

"Don't start on the dames with me, Sam. Everyone knows you want to help Mandy clean her dentures."

"Place your bets, boys, and prepare to read 'em and weep." Mace ended their argument with his interruption.

"All right, boys, of all the acts, who is the greatest team television has ever seen?" Dale asked.

Mace pretended to ponder, looking at his cards and looking at the table.

"I got this...Batman and Robin," Mace said as he slid down in his chair and smiled.

"Batman and Robin? Are you crazy, boy? The Rat Pack, son, the Rat Pack!" Dale barked.

"Ah ha! We knew you were bluffing." Gus pointed his finger at Mace like he was Watson to an elderly Holmes.

"You're not rich, and you're not famous. You're just bad at poker," Dale said while smoothing his fluffy mustache. "And apparently, you don't know anything."

"Annie told you we'd mop the floor with you." Sam shrugged.

Mace laughed. "All right, boys, you got me. I'm done. You've taken all my cash, and you've worn me out. If you'll excuse me, I'm going to go check into the small town hotel and take a nap until my ride gets here."

Sam stood up with him and put his hand on Mace's shoulder. "Seriously, son, you have to mop the floor now. We made a mess earlier, and Annie will kill us if we don't mop the floor with you. Now run along."

The other men cackled as they all stood up and followed Sam and Mace out into the shop. They noticed everything was clean and realized they'd forgotten what time it was. Annie and Mandy were already gone. They saw the tarts and the sign.

"Does she ever really think that we won't eat them?" Dale pouted.

Sam retorted, "No, but she hopes." Sam patted Mace on the back. "Can you find your way to the hotel?"

"I think so. Annie said it was just past that old theater."

"Yep, just past and around the corner. It's called the Statehouse Inn."

"All right, boys, nice to meet you! Thank you again for taking all my money," Mace announced, realizing the poker game was the first time he'd felt jovial since he arrived.

"Anytime, youngster," they all called after him as he walked out the door.

"Might storm again, so watch out," Sam said after him. Mace looked up that ever-darkening sky.

"You'll believe me this time, won't you?"

Mace flashed him a smile and pointed up. "This time."

Gus chimed as he heard Mace leave through the front door, "He's nice...once you beat him."

Mace crossed the railroad tracks and walked the same street he had earlier that day. Only this time, as he grew closer to the theater, he could see the lights were on.

It began to drizzle again, so he jogged to the corner and then crossed the street. The theater doors were open, and he could faintly see people down by the stage. He stepped inside. He noticed that everything was shades of gold and pale yellow with deep red velvet ropes and chair rails. Mahogany trim ran along all the baseboards and doorways. The carpet was the same deep red as the velvet ropes. There were counters to the left and the right of the lobby that looked like original concession booths. Directly in front of him were two open double doors that led to into the large theater. He took in a deep breath, thinking the theater was incredible.

What is something this ornate doing in such a nothing town? He wondered. He stood just inside the doorway and watched what was going on onstage.

They're just a bunch of kids. What are they doing here?

A black-haired girl stood center stage with a boy approaching on her left. He was taller than she was and very muscular for a teenager. The girl was in the middle of a speech as the boy approached when they both froze.

Annie stood up from her chair. "What is it?"

Mace recognized Annie from the back. *Annie? What is she doing here?*

A few more kids peeked out from behind the curtain but also immediately froze. "What is going on? I did not stop the scene. Jason, what is wrong?"

Jason, the boy on stage, simply lifted a finger and pointed to the back of the auditorium where Mace stood in the doorway. Annie followed his finger and turned around to see Mace. She groaned loud enough that Mace heard her and yelled at the top of her voice, "EVERYBODY, FREEZE! DO NOT MOVE!"

Everyone froze like mimes, half of them pointing to the back. Annie walked up the aisle toward Mace. Mace took a few steps and met her. She had tucked her lips in, looking agitated, and had her arms folded across her chest.

"I was just heading to the hotel, and I saw the lights on," Mace offered. "What is this?"

"A rehearsal," Annie said frankly. *He's invading. Be careful,* she thought hyper-defensively.

"I can see that." Mace squinted at Annie and cocked his head. He couldn't understand why she had avoided him so intently. "Do you own this? Why would you lie—"

She put her hands up toward him to interrupt him. "Look, I'm not going to apologize for lying to you because I didn't actually lie...I just left out a few descriptive pronouns."

Why is she so guarded and defensive? What is her deal? He wondered but said, "Well, that's fair enough."

"Thanks." Annie eyed him, thinking that she saw through his nonchalant answer but turned her head instead to look at the kids. "I'd better get back and let them unfreeze."

"Can I stay?"

"I don't know if that is such a—"

"I promise I won't interfere or disrupt. You won't even know I'm here."

"It's not me I'm worried about," she said, lying. "It's them…they'll be worthless."

"I can take a hint; I'll just head back." He turned to head out.

"Hang on." Annie stopped him, feeling guilty for the way she as acting. "Give me a minute." She turned and jogged down to the stage and up the side stairs. She clapped her hands three times and shouted, "Can I get everyone out on stage please?"

There were a dozen pairs of different shoes heard scuffling around backstage, and in a matter of seconds, all the kids were fidgeting out on stage.

"Freeze," she commanded.

Everyone froze again.

"I'm going to say a few things, and if you can contain yourselves, we will continue. However, if any of you so much as snickers or blinks when I say what I'm about to say, it will not happen, and you will stay frozen for the remainder of rehearsal. Is that clear?"

No one moved.

"Good." Annie crossed her arms and watched the kids very closely. She began to speak very softly and slowly. "Mr. Mace Harlen would like to stay and watch our rehearsal." She paused to see if anyone moved. No one did. She was impressed.

"If you can be mature about this, I will allow him to stay. If you cannot, I will ask him to leave. Is that understood?"

No one moved.

"Okay. You may slowly unfreeze, but go straight back to your positions and do not speak. Yes?"

The kids acted like butterflies slowly coming out of cocoons as they unfroze from their poses. Each one of them walked by Annie and softly whispered, "Thank you, Miss Annie."

As soon as all the kids were off the stage and the lights went down again, three girls behind the curtain squealed in unison,
"We love you, Mace!"

"Oh, this should be good!" Annie mumbled as Mace sat down a row behind her. "I know who that was, and you'll hear about it later!" Annie yelled from her chair. "Let's cue up scene six, please."

Everyone got to their places.

A boy came out on stage with a cardboard cutout of an old convertible. He got out of the car and knocked on a freestanding door. A female voice could be heard off stage, saying, "I'll get it, Mother." The girl then ran on stage and pretended to smooth her checkered skirt before opening the door. The boy leaned on the doorframe.

"Hey, doll face. Ready to go for that ride?"

Mace leaned up and over the seat next to Annie.

"So far, so good?"

"Well, they've only done one scene, but yes...I heard no giggling backstage."

"That freeze thing was pretty impressive."

Annie turned her head and looked at him skeptically. He was being nice, and she couldn't tell why. She whispered, "Thanks, we spent the first three weeks of the program working on that. It's hard to get this age group to listen, so this is how we do it. We make it sort of a game, and it works most of the time."

"How long have you been doing this?"

"I just opened the program this year. The theater wasn't finished until about three months ago, but I've been doing workshops with the kids at the school gym for about five months."

"Do you do this every day?"

"No, just twice a week after school. Then the weekend before we open, we'll have three days of dress rehearsals."

"This whole scene here is very attractive." He actually sounded honest and sincere.

"We might be small town, but I highly doubt we're boring," Annie said, smiling. Then she turned back toward the stage.

Mace settled into his seat and folded his arms across his chest. The scene ended, the curtain came down, and the auditorium lights came up. It was quiet backstage.

Annie stood up, cupped her hands around her mouth, and called, "Okay, everyone to the edge of the stage for notes, please."

The kids scurried out from behind the curtain to the edge of the stage and sat down. Some folded their legs up under them, and some let their feet dangle off the side.

Annie said, "First, remember what I said about kicking the stage, please." They nodded. "Second, thank you. You were all very mature about our guest's presence here. I appreciate that. You may all say hello now."

47

It an overwhelming chorus of "hello" and "oh-my-gosh" as the kids finally let out their excitement. Mace laughed, stood up in a casual, collected manner, and replied, "It was my pleasure to sit in on your rehearsal. Thank you."

The girls all sighed in unison. The boys laughed. Annie was surprised by Mace; she half expected a snide or condescending comment.

"Let's get through the notes, and then you can all go post about this on social media."

They sat up straight, and all eyes were on Annie for the next five minutes.

"Really quick, lights? Lights, are you still up there?" She turned to look up at the balcony.

"No, Miss Annie, I'm over here." The redhead with square glasses was sitting on the far left.

"Oh, sorry. Let's move can #4 over to center, I'm not getting enough light on the car, and it needs to be lit completely when it's parked. Other than that, we look good."

"Dancers at the sock hop, raise your hands."

Four girls and three guys raised their hands.

"I need a good rotation all the way around the stage. You are cutting into the middle too much, and I want to show off the footwork, right up here in the front, okay? Who are my wallflowers?"

Four other girls raise their hands.

"I need you to be in constant mode. Do you know what I mean by that? You need to be constantly whispering and swaying, drinking your punch, etcetera. Never stop acting just because you are in the background. Then when you get asked to dance, change your facial expressions—a boy just asked you to dance, and that is what you've wanted your whole life."

All the dancers nodded.

"Lastly, my leading lady." The black-haired girl perked up as if surprised Annie had notes for her. "When he comes to the door, he is charming, but he is not the guy you wish was at the door. Right? You need to reluctantly go for a ride with him because you suspect that Colby's character might call while you are gone. You were way too eager to get in that car with him."

"All right, that wraps up rehearsal for today, and that's all we have time for. I need to get you all home before this storm picks up momentum. Anybody have questions?"

Three girls raised their hands, waving them intently. One of them was the lead girl.

"Could we get any notes from Mace, I mean, Mr. Harlen?"

Annie turned to Mace and signaled for him to come up. He hopped over the seat and stood beside her, feeling a strange sensation to get on this woman's good side. He had tried to find the worst in this town and in her all day, but after watching her direct, he filed away a new adjective for her: *intriguing.*

"I have nothing better to say than what your wonderful director has said to you. You guys are great. I would love a backstage tour and a group picture if your director would allow it." He looked at Annie. She laughed and agreed. All the kids scrambled to their feet and practically stampeded Mace backstage.

Annie was gathering her things when a student walked up quietly behind her.

"Miss Annie?"

Annie turned around. "Biannca, you did great today. What's up?"

"Our first fundraiser is coming up. Some of the other girls and I thought we could ask Mr. Harlen to be a part of that? Maybe we could auction him off?"

"It's a good idea to be sure, Biannca, but I'm sure he has to get permission from his agent and publicists to do that sort of thing. I doubt they would go for that, sweetie."

"Do you think that it would hurt to ask?"

Annie smiled sweetly at her. "I doubt it would hurt, but I really doubt that it will do any good. He won't be around for that, sweetie. He's leaving as soon as he can."

"But he seems to like us a lot, and he liked our rehearsal a lot. Maybe he'd come back for it."

Annie led her to a seat, and they both sat down.

"Listen, Biannca, he is an actor, and he's very good at what he does. Okay?"

Biannca lowered her eyes and nodded slowly. The realization of what Annie was implying was settling in.

"I don't want you to be disappointed. If you want to go ask, then go ask, but don't be crushed if he says no."

"All right, but I *can* ask?"

Annie nodded.

The girl jumped up and ran up the stairs to the stage. She met Mace and several of the other kids as they were coming out from behind the curtain. Annie stood up to watch her talk to Mace. She watched as Biannca explained her proposition and used her hands a lot. Mace pretended to be deep in thought and then made the girls huddle around him as if they were scheming. When they released from the huddle, Biannca turned around to face Annie and stepped to the front of the stage.

"We've decided that auctioning off Mr. Harlen would be too much of a copycat of that movie *Win a Date with Tad Hamilton*, so it would be a better idea to be original and auction off you, Miss Annie."

"Oh, do you now?" Annie flashed Mace a glare. "We'll talk about it at the next rehearsal. Okay?"

"Okay," the girls said together.

"Lights out, please. Time to go home," Annie called.

All the kids filed out the aisle and through the front doors. Annie flipped off the lobby lights and locked the door. Mace was standing nearby. Colby and the lead boy walked by and gave him high-fives.

"High-fives are back!" Colby yelled into the street as he and the other boy disappeared around the corner. It was pouring down rain. Annie called after them, but they couldn't hear. She was sure that she would hear from the lead boy's mom about why they had been cavorting in the rain, and she hoped someone was home at Colby's house.

"That was nice of you, what you did for that girl," she said awkwardly.

"What do you mean?"

"Not embarrassing her by letting her down easy."

"I'm not following you," he said blankly.

"Mace, come on. These kids might be able to act on stage, but they don't know how to tell if you are acting in real life. They have you on a pedestal, and they think you are a certain type of person."

"While you clearly think I'm the furthest thing from that person."

"No, that's my point. None of us knows you, and you don't know us. It's kind of clear that you could care less about any of this, but those kids THINK they know you. They thought if they asked you to fly back from L.A. to be auctioned off for their small town theater fundraiser, that you would be Johnny-on-the-spot for them."

"I see what you are saying." Her intensity was unsettling, and now it was clear he was still on her bad side. Again he wondered why he had the urge to change that. "Mostly I just wanted it to be her idea, but it'll be better this way."

"Yes," she said aloud. *Fair enough*, she thought to herself.

They looked around; all the kids had gone home, and they were, once again, alone under the marquee.

There were torrents of rain now, and the thunder began to sound like a tympani roll. The wind swept through the rain like a curtain in an open window.

"Thanks for letting me sit in on your rehearsal. That was very cool to watch."

"You're welcome," she said, looking at him and wondering if his demeanor had changed since he'd been with Sam playing poker.

"I've had younger co-stars, but youth stage theater is a whole different game. The way they are so responsible for the show is quite unique. You've started an amazing thing here."

"Did Mace Harlen just find something to compliment in our small town of Penumbra?"

Mace smiled, slightly embarrassed. "Maybe just one."

"Well, don't make it a habit. We can't have you going back to L.A. thinking that we're a nice place to visit."

"Trust me. That would not happen." He laughed. "Plus, I've just come from Chicago, and I've got big shoes to fill there."

Chicago. Chicago. The word echoed in her ears again. She fumbled her keys and dropped them on the pavement.

"Whoops!" Mace picked them up and noticed her face. It was the same pale as it had been earlier in the day, and he remembered that he had mentioned Chicago then as well.

What is it about Chicago that makes her she freeze up? He wondered, but he decided not to make an issue out of it. "Are you okay?"

"Oh, yeah...it's nothing. I should run by the shop and grab my phone in case Sam calls. Maybe I should head that way and check on him."

"Shouldn't you just get on your CB or two-way radio for that?"

She knew he was making fun of her. "Can't reach all the way out to the house on that. I've got one in the truck if you want to play on it." She poked back. "Did you want to check into the Statehouse Inn? Have you heard from JJ when you're leaving?"

"No, I was going to call him when I got to the hotel, but I never made it there."

"Is he sending a chopper, or will he just beam you up?"

"You hide your disdain for me so well." He ran his hands through his hair. "Yes, he's sending a chopper most likely." *L.A. by sundown*, Mace repeated JJ's words to himself, *not that we can tell when that is since it's so dark from the rain.*

"You're welcome to have him land it out at the house. It would probably be a good place. You can just ride along with me." *All in one day he's hung out at your bakery and had lunch with you, and now you're bringing him out to the ranch, Annie? You're losing it.*

"Yeah, I'll come. What else am I going to do, sit alone on a twin bed in the hotel and watch black and white TV?"

"Very funny."

They drove over to the bakery, and Annie hurried inside and reappeared with the phone.

"That took like 15 seconds, and I'm already soaked. Good grief!" Annie exclaimed.

"It's really picking up," Mace noted, looking out the window at the very spot he'd stalled the Jag that morning.

"I bet Sam is worried," Annie said softly.

"About you?"

"Yeah, he worries about me."

"You've got several overprotective men around you, don't you?" he stated but then continued jokingly. "I doubt anything could get to you in this monster of a truck." Mace chuckled.

"They have their reasons, I suppose," she said, hoping that would satisfy. "How did poker with the guys go?"

"Let's just say I'm not as good as I thought I was. Those guys are ruthless!"

"I tried to tell you," she said, shaking her head.

The rain was so heavy the windshield wipers couldn't keep up. It was dark outside even though it wasn't very late in the day. Annie's face was illuminated by the lights on the dash. She intently watched the road and the oncoming cars. She slowed down considerably. They rode in silence for a while; Mace noticed a serious clench in her jaw. It flinched every time they drove through a flooded area.

He took his mind off the storm by calling JJ. "Hey! It's storming badly here. Can you still get the chopper for me?"

"Yeah, man. It's already on its way," Mace heard him say through the phone.

"Perfect, thanks. Sorry it's loud in here, it's really coming down."

"No problem, Mace. We'll be there in about an hour. You'll just need to tell us where to land."

Mace shot Annie a look, and she motioned for the phone and proceeded to give JJ directions to the ranch and the best place to land. She quickly gave the phone back to Mace, and JJ said goodbye. As they drove in the battering rain and wind, Mace thought through all the unexpected things from today. He finally landed on the image of Annie standing under the marquee facing him as the wind twisted around on the street beyond. He turned to look at her.

"So, Miss Annie, what in the world brought you here to Penumbra? I mean you bake, you direct…"

A breathy laugh barely escaped as she smiled. "That's a long story, a saga really, but I suppose the cliff notes version is that I moved here for change. I bake because I love it, and I love to make things others enjoy. I direct because it's what I feel like God called me to do."

"Called?" He landed on that word and questioned it. *God called her?*

She glanced at him to search his expression, and when she saw sincere questioning there, she smiled at him and continued, "You know—when something is part of you, like DNA. It's like you can't get away from it even if you wanted to. Theater is just something I can't get away from."

As they pulled onto a muddy gravel road, Mace let her words soak into him like the heavy rain soaking into the earth around them. *It's like you can't get away from it even if you wanted to.*

7: BRAINSTORMS AND CAKE ROLLS
LOS ANGELES, SIX MONTHS LATER

Mace slouched on the couch. His best friend Chuck sat on the adjacent couch with his head in his hands. Faint melodies came from the other room. The coffee table was covered in legal pads, crumpled pieces of paper, and pens. Mace looked at his watch, thinking, *We've been brainstorming for six hours now.* They had been through a box of doughnuts, Ping-Ping takeout, and a whole box of cake rolls. They thought they needed brain food, but it turned out they were just bored. The food didn't help. Chuck kept coming back to the same idea, but Mace couldn't see it.

"I've got it!" Chuck sat up.

"Chuck, I just don't think that it can go anywhere."

"The idea of it is compelling. It could go any number of directions. What did Lithgow say? You need to have something *gritty and brilliant*. This is it. We need to explore this. What do you have the rest of the week?"

"Nothing." Mace inquired hesitantly, "What are you planning?"

"Hear me out, Harlen. What if we explore this script in person?"

"What do you mean? Go there? Why?

Mace pictured Annie. The bakery, the theater, the rain, the truck, and the chopper—it all flashed sequentially. He shook his head.

"Yes, this is it, Mace. This is the movie I want to write, but I need a vision quest. Also, we'll need her help. We'll need her perspective to write some of the scenes. We'll need to study her. Can we get her on board?"

"I don't know that she'll go for it, Chuck. I told you, she's guarded and cautious."

"How can you say that when you haven't even asked her?"

"It just seems like a stretch."

Chuck jumped up from the couch and began to pace around. "Now, here it is. You call her out of the blue. She is surprised but thrilled to hear from you. You chat and catch up. She can't believe you are calling her. You pitch her the idea, and she faints. *Mace Harlen* wants to see her again. We go to her; we visit the places you went. She tells us her life story, maybe more develops between you two. We write a killer ending and boom! Done."

Feeling like he would be exploiting Annie, Mace hung his head, but he didn't see any other way to shake off writer's block. "Okay." Agreeing to it was painful. "Let's call her."

Chuck bounced around the room like spring, punched the air, and played his air guitar before finally flopping down on the couch next to Mace and flashing him a "rock on" gesture. Mace shoved him and told him to grow up and settle down.

"Dude, I'm chill. Dial her up."

"I can't promise how this is going to go, but I know she's not enamored with me. I guess we can call and ask her what she thinks. Believe me, she'll tell us."

"Now we're getting somewhere," Chuck said, handing Mace the phone. "Put her on speaker. I want to hear what she says."

"All right, but if she doesn't go for it, don't say I didn't warn you."

"Come on! If Mace Harlen called me on the phone, I'd do whatever he wanted." Chuck swooned.

"She's not affected."

"Maybe you've lost your wooing skills, but now practice your dialing skills."

"I'm dialing, I'm dialing." Mace scrolled through the numbers on his phone and dialed the bakery's number. He set the phone on speaker and put it down on the table. It was ringing. "It's not like that with us. I didn't try to get with her. I've still got skills."

"Oh, she's not up to the Harlen standards then."

"Shut up, Chuck."

This is a bad idea, Mace thought, noticing that his heart was thumping in his ears. "Maybe she's not in yet."

"I thought you told me that you rolled in at five in the morning, and she was already there."

"Yes, Chuck. Good for you, a man of annoying details. I haven't talked to her since then, so she might have changed her routine." Mace hung up the phone.

"Harlen, I don't get you sometimes. You tell me that this woman practically changed your life, but then you act as if you couldn't care less about her. What is that about?"

"Chuck, you can be such a pain in the…I never said she changed my life."

"Hey now!"

"Chuck, sometimes…you… I really shouldn't have told you any of this."

"Really? What were you going to say? I haven't heard you cuss in weeks. I thought there was some sort of reformation going on, but it seems that one mention of this Annie woman and you're all agitated and back to your old self."

Mace kicked the table jokingly and threw a legal pad at Chuck. Chuck ducked and pretended to fall on the floor. He started coughing and convulsing. Mace laughed.

"I hate you, Chuck. You're so annoying."

"Yes, and it's what I do best." Chuck was just lying on the floor. "Why don't you try her again?"

Mace dialed again.

8: A PHONE CALL AND APPLE PIE

There is something refreshing about starting over each day. If every day just ran into another day without night, it would be a miserable existence, Annie thought as she drove to work with the windows down, the breeze crisp and the sun shining. The seasons were "thinking about changing," as Sam liked to say. She turned the radio off and listened to the road beneath the truck's wheels. She knew it was going to be a beautiful day. It felt like an apple pie day, which she was certain Sam would enjoy.

A few minutes later, as she unlocked the bakery door, she could hear the phone ringing inside. She threw her purse down and hurriedly fumbled for the phone, but she missed the call. The number was a strange one, not from Texas. She figured whoever it was would leave a message. She straightened things up at her desk and around the register. She got out some apples bought the day before, starting to peel and slice them for the pies. The phone rang again. It was the same number as before. Annie answered it, dreading the automated voice of a telemarketing call.

"Antoinette's, this is Annie," she said, faking the usually chipper tone she used to answer the phone.

"Annie? Hi, it's Mace."

"Mace?" She hung her mouth open after she got his name out and then stammered, "Hi."

"Hi. How are you?"

"I'm fine," Annie said awkwardly, wondering why he was calling. "How are you?"

"I'm good. Listen, I need to talk to you about something. You got a minute?"

"Sure." Annie tried to sound open and warm without sounding eager. *I wonder what he could possibly want to talk about.*

"I'm sitting here with a writer and producer of mine, Chuck, and we've got you on speaker, okay? We've got an idea we want to pitch to you."

Annie felt confused. "Okay," she muttered, knowing she sounded hesitant.

"It's just us, I promise. No big deal, really."

"All right."

"Chuck and I have been brainstorming. We're working on some new projects, and we've had some late nights. I told him the story of how I met you and Sam. He loves it and thinks it could be a great screenplay. He wants to collaborate and write it." He paused and then continued, "I know it may not sound like a compelling story or even have an ending, but Chuck thinks it's worth the time to explore it. Would you be up for that?" He was trying too hard, and he hoped she wouldn't notice. "If you are not okay with that, it's all right to say so, Annie. It won't offend us."

"Yes, it will," Chuck commented jokingly in the background.

"He's kidding," Mace said.

Annie stood in the center of the bakery, playing with her necklace and staring out the window. The streetlight cycled through two red lights, and then finally, on a green light, she spoke. "I'm not really sure I understand what you want from me. I don't think that you need my permission to come to town. I don't own the place." Her answer was calculated and had a certain duality to it. "But Mace?" She paused, her voice going breathy.

"Yeah?" he answered, feeling uncertain and exposed with just one word.

"There's still a lot of my history I can't share with you. You told Chuck that right?"

"I did. Chuck just wants to experience places firsthand. We'll visit the shop, the theater, Billy's, the ranch, stuff like that. Then we'll just flesh out some of the ideas we had for the script together. The story isn't so much about your history as it is about us," Mace explained.

Us? There's not really an us... She tripped over the word but managed to say, "That sounds fine. When do you think you will come?"

"Tomorrow!" shouted Chuck in the background. "Annie, it's Chuck. I'm Mace's best friend. He left off that word. Best. I am the BEST, but enough about me. What do you have tomorrow?"

"Tomorrow?" Mace and Annie both asked in unison.

"What? Do you need more time?"

Annie was confused.

Back in L.A., Mace covered the phone's receiver with his hand and shot Chuck a frown.

"What?" Chuck asked. "She was there. Don't you think that she knows how things ended?"

"Oh my gosh, Chuck. Shut up!" Mace shoved Chuck, who pretended to fall off the couch. Mace lifted his hand off the phone.

"Mace?" Annie asked.

"Sorry about that," he said.

"It's okay, Mace. Tomorrow is fine. It's sooner than I thought you would say, but it's fine with me. Are you coming by chopper or a private plane? Will you need a ride from Austin or Dallas? Do you think that you'll just rent a car?" Annie scolded herself for asking so many questions.

"You don't need to pick us up. We'll rent a car."

"I guess I'll see you tomorrow then."

"Thanks for doing this, Annie," Mace leaned in closer to the phone.

"Not at all. It could be interesting." Annie tried to sound detached.

"Thanks, Annie!" Chuck yelled as he stood up on the couch and jumped off like a rock star jumping off the stage.

Annie laughed and said, "Okay, guys. I'll talk to you tomorrow."

"All right, bye."

Annie hung up the phone but continued to stand in the middle of the room, staring out the window. Sam toddled through the door toward her and stopped just short of her boots. He put a hand on her shoulder.

"Annie? What is it?"

Annie snapped out of her trance and smiled honestly at Sam. "You won't believe who was on the phone."

"I bet you I might."

"You're right. You might, but it's still crazy."

"Spit it out, dear. I waste away just waiting on this kind of suspense!" He poked her in the side, jokingly.

"It was Mace Harlen."

Sam's eyes lit up, but he controlled his face and voice, simply saying, "Oh yeah?"

"It's the craziest thing. I almost missed his call this morning. Actually, I did miss it the first time. Anyway, he and this producer friend of his, Chuck something or other, are apparently writing a screenplay and want to write about Mace's time here. They asked me to help, I think. They are coming to town tomorrow so Chuck

61

can do research and such." She spoke very quickly, showing her apprehension.

Sam laughed at her and said, "Deep breaths, girl. Now, let's talk about this. Are you nervous?"

"Actually, Sam, I think talking about it will make me nervous. I need to just act like everything is normal. He's normal, life is back to normal, and tomorrow is just a normal day. Okay?"

"Have it your way. I suppose we have a lot to do today. We'll need to clean the house up a bit."

Annie looked at him, surprised. "What happened to normal?"

"They're staying with us, aren't they? We'll need to make up some extra beds, which means we'll need to clean up and rearrange a bit."

"I hadn't thought about that. I guess that would be the hospitable thing to do."

"Yes, it would. I'm going to go back and clean up the barn a bit. You bring me one of those apple pies, you hear?"

"Got it. I'll see you later this afternoon."

After Sam left, Annie stood alone for a long time. She shifted her weight back and forth and pushed receipts and bills around the counter until she put them right back where they were originally. She picked up a pen and tapped on the counter in different patterns. She put the pen down and twirled a tendril of her curls around her finger. She picked at her nails and picked at a piece of tape that was stuck to the counter.

Finally, she slapped the counter. "Okay…I'm nervous," she admitted to herself.

9: STORMS AND FUDGE BROWNIES

Mace sat on the end of his bed, staring at the empty suitcase on the floor. He didn't know what to put in it. He punched the bed beside him. Chuck called to him as he came up the stairs.

"Mace! Dude, are you ready?"

Mace kicked the suitcase closed and against the wall. "No."

Chuck leaned on the doorframe of Mace's bedroom. "I can't believe it."

"What?" Mace fired back defensively.

"You're nervous!" Chuck accused.

"Shut up, Chuck." Mace lay back on the bed. "I just think this is a bad idea."

Chuck disappeared in Mace's closet. Clothes started flying out of the closet and landing on or near the suitcase. A candy bar flew out and almost hit Mace in the head. He picked it up and began to eat it rather than packing the clothes Chuck was throwing at him.

"What is it about this woman? It's as if she put some spell on you or something. You can't figure out what you think about her or what you want with her. She's like an evil goddess or something."

"It's not like that. It's just that stuff happened while I was there. It was between strangers...yeah I guess you're right, I can't shake it."

"Remind me of the stuff," Chuck said, kicking shoes toward Mace.

"What?"

"What happened that has you both like this?"

"Both?"

"Mace, she was there too, wasn't she? Tell me about it on the way."

"On the way?"

"I just packed for you. Now let's go. Our plane leaves in an hour."

Chuck pushed Mace toward the stairs and threw his suitcase down after him. Mace caught it over his shoulders as it barely missed his face.

"You're a jerk. Why are we even friends?"

"Just go get in the car."

Once at the car, Mace slid into the passenger seat. He slouched in the seat and propped his arm on the door.

"Okay, start talking. By the time we get to Texas, you need to be back to your old self and relaxed. You should see yourself right now."

Mace looked in the side mirror. *That's the problem, I can see myself,* he thought. He rubbed his head and sighed. Chuck was right. He needed to relax and think. He needed to get back there in his mind. They were going to write this, and he wanted to be serious about this project. They would be there shortly, and he needed his mind right before they got there.

"Let's wait until we're on the plane," Mace said. Chuck agreed, weaving his way through L.A. traffic. Once at the airport, they checked in, made their way through security, and arrived at the gate just in time for boarding.

As they settled into their seats on the plane, Mace asked, "Where should we start?"

Chuck pulled out a recorder and turned it on. "When would you say that the two strangers were no longer strangers?"

"It's hard to pinpoint. There were a lot of little things that piled up, almost like a crash, if that even makes sense."

"That's good—two worlds colliding, crashing, a pile up of emotions. I like it. What was the first moment in the pile, as it were?"

"I don't know. I need to think first."

Chuck rolled his eyes as Mace leaned his head back against the headrest and closed his eyes. He could see her face, her wild wavy hair, and her boots, and he felt his whole body sink into the seat.

It was raining in his mind. He could still smell the distinctive scent of the Texas rain. The storm surrounded the truck.

We pulled up to a red gate that sat on the edge of a tree line. Just beyond the tree line, I could see a wide dirt road wind across the field until it disappeared on the other side. There were dips in the road that were small bridges, she told me, but tonight I could see they were completely washed out. It looked as though there were several small tributaries now flowing across the field and converging somewhere in the valley to our right.

It had started to rain torrentially about an hour ago while we were still in town, and the closer we got to the ranch, the harder it rained. The wind had picked up and was leaning trees over and howling.

"Want me to get the gate?" I offered as she craned her neck over the dash as if she were looking all the way to the other side of the field.

"No, I'll get it. I just hope we can make it through all that."

"Have you seen the size of your truck?"

"Big doesn't always matter to the mud," she said, laughing.

"True," I said, shrugging. After all, what did I know about trucks?

She pushed down her sleeves and tucked her jeans into her boots.

"Here I go, I guess," she said as she hopped out of the truck's cab. In the few seconds it took her to jump out of the cab and get to the gate, I could see through the headlights that she was already drenched. She pushed on the gate. Nothing happened. She shoved her body against it and pushed harder. It was stuck in the mud. She leaned her head on the gate in defeat, turned and shrugged in my direction.

"Need a hand?" I shouted over the rain, sliding out of the truck.

"Nope, I need a forklift."

"Well, in that case..." I pretended to walk back to the truck.

My clothes were heavy with rain, and it was pouring so hard I could barely see beyond the gate. The clouds were so dense and saturated they looked like a solid charcoal blanket over us. I tried to wedge one of my legs between the post and the gate so that I was straddling the gate. I put both hands under one of the rails and tried to lift it. I could hear the suction of the mud. It budged only a little.

"Push!" I yelled.

Annie leaned against the gate forcefully. Nothing happened. She put both hands on the bars and pushed as hard as she could. Maybe it moved an inch. She looked up at me and said, "I think we're stuck even before we got stuck."

"I guess so. Do you have a shovel or something?"

"Maybe. I'll check." She walked to the back of the truck, climbed up the wheel well, and hopped over the side. She opened up the tool chest and rummaged around until her head popped up from behind the truck and she proudly held up a tire jack and a crowbar. Setting them on the side of the truck bed, she hopped down.

"*Hear me out,*" *she said, walking up and standing extremely close, so that I could hear her over the rain.* "*If you can get the gate up with the crowbar far enough so that I can wedge the jack under there, we can pump it up far enough out of the mud and then push it off and open. Yes?*" *She nodded at me, looking for agreement.*

"*I'm open to anything at this point,*" *I said.*

"*No kidding,*" *she said, handing the crowbar to me. I struggled with the gate and the crowbar, and with both our feet sinking in the mud, we put as much force into the gate as we could. Once I got the gate up far enough, she maneuvered the jack under it. Then we switched positions, and I tried pumping the jack up.*

"*One more time. I think she's almost free!*" *I yelled.*

"*Okay. One! Two! Three!*"

I pumped the jack, and she pushed with all her weight, holding the crowbar in her hands. I felt my shoes slipping in the mud, and I heard the jack snap before I could yell out. We both lurched down into the mud. Annie let out a high-pitched yelp, and I cussed out loud, now covered in mud.

We sat there defeated as the rain pelted us and began to wash some of the mud off us, which made Annie laugh. She hung her head but couldn't stop the trickle of laughter. I watched her lift her head toward the rain as she let the rain run off her cheeks and down her neck. My eyes couldn't help but follow the rain all the way down her.

She looked over at me with makeup now bleeding down her face and smiled. "*Well?*" *she asked simply.*

I shrugged, actually enjoying the wet sight of her, this stranger I'd never see again. I felt oddly guilty for it, but I let myself enjoy the sight for a moment before I pointed back at the truck, suggesting we at least get back in.

Once we trudged back to the truck, she flipped on the brights and stood up on the runner. The headlights blasted brightly through the wet darkness, barely revealing that the bridge was completely invisible and water as tall as the tires rushed over it.

"*Bridge is out anyway. I'm going to head us back over to Billy's to get dry. There's another place for JJ to land out behind Billy's,*" *she said as she ducked back in the truck. I couldn't help but notice that her clothes now hung loosely on her; they were no longer suctioned to her frame as they had been when we tried to open the gate. Around her face, small curls were plastered to her skin. The rain ran off the end of her nose and dripped on her shirt.*

"Billy's?" I asked, surveying all the mud in the truck.

"Billy's Roadhouse." She put the truck in reverse and turned to look out the back glass as she backed up. She put her arm up on the seat, and her hand briefly touched my shoulder. I pretended not to notice the heat that rippled down my arm. Before I could say more, her phone was ringing on the dash.

"Sam," she answered, "the gate's stuck, and the bridge is washed out...I know, we are headed back toward Billy's...No, I'm fine, just wet. His ride is on the way, but it may be too wet for them to land. I'll let you know...Love you too."

Stowing the phone in the cup holder, she suggested I call JJ with our change of plans. After I talked to JJ briefly and let her give him directions to the landing site, she sighed deeply and said that she was sorry.

"I doubt this torrential downpour has anything to do with you."

"Well, no, but you're stuck in a storm with a stranger, soaking wet. It's nobody's idea of hospitality."

"I don't know about that...I mean this is a nice truck." That comment made her laugh a little, so I continued. "Plus, you're helping me get out of here. Soaking wet or not, I can't complain. It's been kind of an adventure."

She relaxed in her seat as we drove slowly back toward town. The rain was so heavy it looked like we were going through a car wash.

"Who knew Texas got this kind of storms?" I said, breaking the pause in conversation.

"It doesn't happen often, but when it does, they're big."

"No kidding." I was thinking of things to say now since the rain didn't give us any hope of letting up. I imagined for a moment the way the camera would set up the scene, pulling in from the rain on the windshield and panning around the cab of the truck, revealing Annie, soaking wet, her hair dripping down her face and onto the shirt clinging to her. I chuckled to myself, not realizing I did so out loud. Annie looked at me.

"What's so funny?"

"Oh," I hesitated, embarrassed to tell her what I was thinking. "I was thinking that this is such the perfect cliché movie moment, two attractive strangers, wet, stuck in a truck together for who knows how long."

"Who says you're attractive?" she sassed back and then laughed through her nose.

"*Not you, apparently.*" *I laughed, finding her momentary flirtation enticing. As I studied her across the cab, I waited for her to fidget with the steering wheel or touch her collarbone or nervously flip of the hair...but she did nothing. She had gone back to being stoic and steady, though soaking wet, yet I realized that she had let go of her cautious defense in that moment of joking.*

"*So, in this movie moment, what cliché thing would happen next?*" *she asked hesitantly without looking at me.*

"*I'm sure there would be a montage of them laughing and talking until all hours of the night,*" *I paused long enough for her to look over at me,* "*and they would grow closer and closer until the male stranger would finally lean in for a kiss and the female stranger would let him. Then they fall passionately onto the seat together as the camera pulls back out to the rain on the window most likely.*"

She was watching me intently until I finished, and though she turned away slightly, I could see the corners of her mouth turn up.

"*I could see how that would be steamy...in a movie. Do you think like that often?*"

I stared at her with an embarrassed smirk overtaking my mouth. Was she really asking if I thought about love scenes? We drove in silence for a moment with only the rhythmic swish of the windshield wipers to be heard.

"*Um...*" *I started to answer.*

"*Oh! No! I meant...directions. Do you think like a director a lot?*"

"*I hear director's notes in my head all the time.*" *It may have been the first time I realized how often I did think that way.* "*Do you ever do that? Do you think in terms of something?*"

She sat for a moment before she answered. "*I guess so. I probably hear stage directions in my head sometimes, and I know that I feel a certain dessert for a certain day. It's kind of dumb, but certain days I just feel like creating certain flavors.*"

"*Like what?*" *I asked, silently thankful I had been able to get the conversation going again.*

"*Like right now feels like hot cocoa and fudge brownies.*"

"*Wow, you're right, it does,*" *I mocked.*

"*I told you it was kind of dumb.*"

"*Nah, it's not. I was just kidding,*" *I said sincerely.* "*Have you ever written any plays?*"

"I've dabbled in writing stuff for the kids, but nothing really worth anything."

"I bet the kids thought it was cool that you wrote it."

"Yeah, they have fun with it. Sometimes I let them write a couple lines here and there. They get a real kick out of that."

"I'll bet." I kicked myself for the way that I sounded plastic when I talked to her.

"Have you thought about directing? Have you done it before?" she asked.

"I've thought about it, but I just haven't found anything that I wanted to put my name on yet. JJ thinks I should wait until I'm sort of the 'veteran,' and then people will be like 'Oh, look—it's a Mace Harlen film! You know that is going to be good.'"

She smiled at me because I imitated JJ in a very feminine whiny voice, even though he didn't sound like that at all in real life. Then she said something that really surprised me.

"Well, maybe you'll find out what's in your DNA, and then it won't matter what JJ says." She smiled sincerely.

"DNA, huh?"

She turned a little and stared out the window. "I think God makes people a certain way, so fundamentally, they're built for certain things, you know."

"Hmm," I said. "I guess I'd have to believe in God to think that way."

"Maybe..." she replied, looking down at the floor.

I could feel that the conversation was fizzling out, but thankfully, we had pulled up at the roadhouse.

Mace was jerked out of his reverie by Chuck saying, "Are you going to sleep the whole way?"

"I'm not asleep. I was thinking," Mace snapped.

"Could have fooled me. Are you going to tell me or not?"

Mace looked out the window and began to recount the story to Chuck. When Mace reached the part when Annie mentioned God, Chuck held up his hands in protest.

"Wait just a second. You're both wet, she's letting her guard down, and then...God? What's that about?"

"I know, right? It was bizarre."

"Okay, but I really like this scene with the rain and everything. I didn't really see this interlude coming." Chuck paused and scratched his face. "So, tell me, the roadhouse—was there dancing? Drinking? Were you still wet? Where's all this going?"

"Trust me, it's not what you're thinking."

"How do you know what I'm thinking?" Chuck joked as he shifted in his seat. They had been sitting on the tarmac for ten minutes, waiting.

"I just know. She even brought up how, in theory, this could be a movie moment, but, in reality, it was just an awkward goodbye between strangers."

"She has a point, but I'm thinking that we can really play that up on screen. The music swells, and we get tight shots of her in the rain…"

"Stop. It can't even be like that," Mace said, shaking his head, "It wasn't like that then, and it wouldn't be that way …with us."

"I can't see why. You're clearly messed up over her, and she sounds smoking hot."

"I don't think I'd say smoking hot, and I'm not messed up!" Mace said harshly.

Chuck smirked at him, seeing right through his defense, but he let it go. "All right, you're really crushing my vision here, but go on. What happened next?"

"We were at the roadhouse for a while, and then I flew back to L.A."

"Stop skipping things!" Chuck motioned with his hands to Mace to keep going. "Material. We've got to have material. Details. Descriptions. Something. Please!"

"Fine." Mace complied as the plane began to rumble down the runway.

10: A CHOPPER AND SWEET TEA

"Seriously, Chuck. Could you have picked out a more noticeable rental?" Mace said, standing next to a black SUV with limo tint, as Chuck walked around it acting like a girl from a game show.

"What? You don't like arriving in style? Don't fool yourself, Harlen. You haven't changed that much."

"Chuck—"

"Yep...shut up, Chuck." He imitated Mace, only in a slightly higher tone. "So, where are we?" Chuck asked, looking up.

The two stood on the sidewalk beneath The Arrow's marquee. Chuck pretended to fall down and clutched his chest, catching himself on the hood of the SUV. Mace pushed him, jokingly.

"What did I tell you?"

"Mace, I think you left out a couple of things." Chuck pushed Mace back.

"I did? Like what?" Mace said shocked.

"Like this amazing marquee!"

"No, I'm pretty sure I mentioned that. It's kind of a big detail."

"And this booth! It's practically historical."

"No, remember that scene we talked about where it's raining, and Annie and I sat under it and talked for a while? Yeah, all of this, in that story." Mace rolled his eyes. "I gave you really good detail."

Chuck was walking around inspecting things, holding up his hands, framing things. He stopped. His hands were framing the glass doors.

"What about this bombshell of a woman? I definitely think you misrepresented her."

"What? Where?" They both peered through the window like teenage boys. The doors were open to the auditorium, and a woman was sitting halfway up the aisle, on the floor with her feet kicked up on the chair across the aisle from her. She had long dark hair that she was twisting around her finger. She was staring at something in her lap with a pen in her mouth. Her flannel shirt that was unbuttoned with a fitted white tank top underneath displayed her thin but shapely figure. Her tight charcoal jeans showed off her boots that were snakeskin at the toe.

"Who is that?" Chuck clutched his chest again. "Dude, she is fantastic. I think I'm in love."

Mace's gaze found the woman, and though he couldn't take his eyes off her, he didn't think he knew her.

Suddenly she looked up as if she had heard something in the distance and followed the aisle with her eyes up to the doors where she found him staring at her. They held eye contact for a few seconds before she scrambled to her feet and disappeared.

Mace's mouth dropped a little. "Chuck. That's *her*," he whispered, not believing that he hadn't recognized her.

"Who it is?" Chuck gripped Mace's shoulders about the time Annie busted through the door.

"You guys are here! I wasn't expecting you for another hour. How did you know I was here?"

"Mace doesn't like rest stops, so we didn't make any," Chuck said, throwing him a malicious look.

Mace knew his face wasn't responding the way he wanted it to. Annie looked completely different. *Has she lost weight or something? Or her hair is longer or a different color, or is it straighter?* He couldn't remember, but he didn't have time to think about that, he needed to say something, anything.

"Actually, we didn't know," he finally managed. "I was just giving Chuck here the tour. Chuck, this is Annie Flynn. Annie, this is Chuck Archer."

Chuck grabbed her extended hand with both of his and held it. "Mace, you didn't do her justice. You, Annie dear, are exquisite!"

Annie raised her eyebrows at Mace playfully and took a bow. "Mace and I had mutually low admiration for one another from the beginning."

"What?" Mace was surprised.

"Oh, come on! She's right. I've heard the way you talked about her," Chuck said, squeezing between Mace and Annie.

"Now you're just making stuff up." Mace impulsively wanted to hug her, but Chuck was now standing between them. "Annie, it's good to see you."

"I am sure that he's told the story all wrong, so I'm glad you are here when I can go on record about the way that things really happened," she said to Chuck, flashing Mace a curious look.

"Marvelous!" Chuck said in an evil villain voice, rubbing his hands together. "Let's get started—unless we interrupted something?"

"Oh, no. Sometimes I just come here to write."

Mace studied her face. He didn't know her very well, and they hadn't had deep philosophical conversations that connected them on some dramatic spiritual level. Now, he felt he didn't know her any more than Chuck did.

"You're a writer? Mace, you left out every good detail. You're terrible at this. It's a good thing we have her!"

"Yeah, it's a good thing," Annie piped in sarcastically.

"Come, Annie, let's discuss how perfect we are for each other," Chuck said melodramatically as he escorted Annie into the theater.

Mace rolled his eyes and intended to follow but took a deep breath as he looked around, remembering the last time he stood here and thinking that he would never see this small town again.

The air was slightly cooler now and held a crispness. Yellow leaves were sweeping down the street in a breeze. They must have blown off a tree from the square. He stepped out to the curb to look down the street. The street was as vacant as he remembered.

Just then, there was distant and vague feeling in him as if he was looking down the street for the first time. He brushed it aside.

"Aren't you coming?" Annie's voice came from behind him, and his right arm got goosebumps. He turned around to find her standing a few feet away.

"Yes, sorry. I got distracted. Where's Chuck?"

"Bathroom." She smiled at him, remembering what Chuck had said about the rest stops.

Mace nodded and rubbed his head. Annie stepped toward him, smiling cautiously.

"It's good to see you..." she didn't finish as Chuck busted through the door.

"Whoa! What is this I am walking into?" Chuck said, pretending to be offended. Embarrassed, Annie released Mace's arm, feeling that she had been too familiar with him.

"Nothing, man." Mace scowled at Chuck. "Just waiting on you, Chuck, like always."

"Oh, I see." Chuck slapped his hands together. "There are so many places we could start, and I have so many details I can't wait to get to...but seeing as Mace just left off at a great place, let's start there with Annie."

"Okay," Annie said, turning toward Chuck and the door. "Do you guys want to hang out here for a while?"

"Yes, this would be a good place to start," Mace said.

Annie caught his eyes before she opened the door and follow Chuck inside, and she gave him a slight frown. She knew that there was an elephant in the room, but apparently, it was changing colors and speaking different languages because she couldn't figure out why Mace was acting so stilted. She seemed more able to be herself around Chuck, who was a complete stranger.

Once inside, Chuck asked whether they should sit down front, and Mace said he liked to sit under the balcony and get a full view of the room. Chuck agreed, saying that it was a marvelous room.

Annie was already propping up her boots on the chair in front of her when the boys both sat down. Mace slouched two chairs over from Annie and crossed his arms. Chuck sat in the row in front of Annie and draped his arms over the chair back, turning toward her. He had the recorder in one hand, pointed in her direction.

"Anytime you are ready," Chuck said.

Annie turned her head and looked at stoic Mace. "Tell me where you left off."

"I've told him some, but I'm sure he would want you to start at the beginning." Mace shrugged.

His sudden aloofness was off-putting, and Annie began to wonder why she had agreed to this at all. She met Chuck's nodding head with a look of anxiety that she couldn't swallow down.

"Mace is right. I'd love that. Let's go back to the beginning of Annie," Chuck agreed with Mace.

The thought of it made Annie shift uncomfortably in her seat. "That's an awfully heavy way to start. Why don't you tell me where you left off? Maybe we'll get to the truth about Annie another day," she said.

Mace felt the phrase *the truth about Annie* weigh heavily in his ears. She was, in fact, a mystery to him.

"Hey," Chuck said, shrugging big in a way that showed off his toned arms. He flashed a wide, bright smile. "No rush. Whenever you are ready." His eyes lingered on hers, bringing a blush from deep within Annie.

Annie felt the blush fade as she thought about where to start. Mace leaned deeply on the left armrest and sighed as he closed his eyes. Annie looked at him and then looked to Chuck with both confusion and amusement.

Chuck shrugged, saying, "He does this."

The blue neon sign cast inviting shadows across Annie's hair even though it was wet and stringing across her profile. Her eyes were closed as she listened to the band on stage. In her seat, she swayed slightly with the beat. Her right hand lightly gripped her sweet tea, her fingers occasionally tapping, not necessarily matching the particular rhythm in the song, which was annoying but funny. Condensation was sliding down the side of her glass and pooling on the table, but it didn't seem to bother either of us because we were still soaking wet.

Until now, I hadn't noticed the narrowness of her nose or the scattered freckles high on her cheeks. I hadn't really been paying attention to her all day, not the real her anyway. I'd been cataloging all of her flaws, but something had changed. With the thought that she might catch me looking at her, I dropped my gaze and followed the floor back up to the stage.

The bass player wore a worn-out floppy cowboy hat and a wallet chain. I had always secretly wanted to be a musician. I had picked up a guitar for a while for a movie role. I could jam a little, but that was about it. In my life, I'd played many characters who could do things that I only wished I could do, and I now found myself wishing I was on stage creating the music she was swaying to, which startled me.

The song ended, and the lead singer took a moment to switch guitars. I was watching the guitars when I saw a cowboy walking toward us out of the corner of my eye. He had a definite swagger that came from slightly bowed legs. He wore a white shirt and starched jeans. I never understood starched jeans, but several people in the room wore them. He tipped his hat to me, and I nodded hesitantly back at him.

"Pardon," he said.

His voice startled Annie. She opened her eyes to look at me and then found him leaned over toward her.

"Annie, can I ask you to dance?"

"Hey, Jonathan." She looked at me I supposed just to be polite. It wasn't like I cared whom she danced with. I wondered whether I was supposed to object, saving her from dancing with him. She turned back to the cowboy.

"Just one, okay?"

The cowboy shrugged, saying, "I'll take what I can get." He winked at her.

I took a swig of my beer and tried not to watch them, but watching her was like watching a flame.

The cowboy took her hand and led her to the dance floor. He spun her and brought her in close. She put one hand on his shoulder and one in his other hand. They began to slow dance. He had picked a slow romantic song to come ask her to dance. Maybe that meant he couldn't dance well. Probably, *I thought as I finally dropped my eyes, and then wanted to laugh out loud.* Mace, you idiot, why else does a guy ask a girl to dance, and why do you care?

I retrieved my phone from my pocket, relieved that it was ringing. She looked over at me. I pointed toward the door. It was JJ. She nodded and smiled. She's probably the nicest woman I've met this far in my life. *My own thoughts continued to startle me as I answered the phone and headed toward the door.*

"Hey JJ!" I walked through the door and out into the rain.

"Mace, we're thirty-two minutes out!" He was yelling over the sounds of the chopper and the storm. I didn't hear anything else he tried to say, but I didn't need to. He was almost here.

I'd be back in L.A. by sundown.

Thirty-two minutes was all the time I had left in this town.

I wondered if Annie was still dancing with that cowboy. I hoped they were done. I stood under the tin-roofed porch and tried to make out what surrounded the roadhouse, but all I saw was rain.

Everything felt clearer here. Even the rain, the air, the night sky, and the people were simple and clear. I hadn't thought much about my meeting the next day or Lithgow since arriving in Penumbra, but I thought about it at that moment and wondered if it would backfire. I shook my head. No, it would go well. It was just that here, I didn't really have my game on or have my front up. I didn't even have to think a lot—I could just be. There was something about tonight that I didn't want to let go of, and it was sticking to me like my wet shirt. I felt the clock ticking on my wrist, and a feeling crept up my legs that compelled me back inside to her.

As I pushed through the door, my eyes readjusted through the neon glow and the smoke. She had a fresh glass of tea, and I wondered if she drank anything else. The cowboy was in my seat. I stopped by the bar and picked up something for myself. Undoubtedly, the cowboy had bought her a round. They sat making small talk, and I watched her face and realized, just like she had been all day, she was being polite. The cowboy was telling a story. She laughed when it was appropriate and nodded occasionally.

From across the room, I could see another cowboy walking their way. He pulled up a chair, spun it around backward, and straddled it. He seemed to know the first cowboy; they had a laugh together and shook hands. The first introduced the second to Annie.

She seemed sincere as she said, "Nice to meet you." She looked down at her drink, but it was empty. The second cowboy motioned toward the bar for another. Annie followed his motion and found my eyes on her, watching the scene. She smiled at me and shrugged her shoulders. I shrugged back. She motioned for me to come back and sit down. My elbows propped me up with my back on the bar. I sarcastically mimed a yawn.

I didn't want to look like the third wheel. She laughed, nodding, and I think she knew. She lay her hand on the table softly, stopping the cowboys from talking. As she politely said something, they looked my way, tipped their hats, and stood. One touched her shoulder as he walked by, and the other handed her a piece of paper.

She looked back over at me and pointed at the now-empty chairs. I nodded and kicked off the bar and found my way back to the table, and once again, we were face to face. Somehow, with 32 minutes ticking down in my ears, I couldn't resist cataloging her smooth skin, her tan from working with horses, and her large green eyes. She smiled at me shyly, noticing that I was studying her face. She looked away, her smile soft and a bit crooked on the left side. She probably didn't even know it. As her hair dried, it was even more of a mess and seemed to glow in the neon. I remembered earlier when, in the sunlight, the red of her hair danced and flickered. It was beautiful.

"You seem to have some...attention," I said, breaking my gaze and looking around the room to find several men looking at her. She was watching the band onstage, but she laughed and shook her head slightly and turned to meet my eyes.

"It's partly the booze and partly that I'm sitting with you. It's a small town. Everyone knows I'm single."

"I suppose that is by choice, gauging how they are all in line for a date or a dance."

She laughed. "I'm not really looking to be some farmer's wife. I've made my own way. Plus, Sammy needs me, and I'm happy out there." She started picking at a chip on the rim of her glass.

77

"And what do you mean, it's partly because you're sitting with me?" I said playfully.

"You are famous, and this is a small town." She was playing along.

It felt like we were flirting. *"Give them something to talk about, eh?"*

"Oh, trust me, I'm sure they've concocted all sorts of rumors already." She took a swig of her tea.

"Moving on...another question for you—is every place here named after the person who owns it? Antoinette's, Max's, Randy's and now Billy's?"

"Mostly, yes. It's easier that way. This is a small town, and we try not to be too clever. Besides, people just end up calling it whatever they want to. And to be fair, mine is not named after me."

"If your full name is not Antoinette, then what's with the name?"

"I just always wanted to name a bakery after Antoinette. You know...Let them eat cake?"

"Ah, now I see. You were trying to be clever."

"Yeah, I guess so." She smirked.

"I like it. You're kind of odd. You know that, right? I mean you're this super generous lady who does these amazing things for others, and you seem to have great relationships with everyone around you. You're so unassuming yet overly cautious. You're mysterious and sometimes not very truthful. And you freak out anytime I bring up Chicago. Beautiful, but odd."

She stared at me blankly for what seemed like a whole minute before she excused herself. She headed toward the bathroom and disappeared. I cussed myself under my breath and then realized I was out of beer. As soon as I reached the bar, I remembered my ticking clock, and I wondered where I thought I was going to get in the next few minutes. The bartender handed me a new bottle.

"Annie's the best thing around here. Keep that in mind, scout."

"The name's Mace."

"Yeah, I know who you are." He wasn't barking at me, but I could tell he was standing his ground.

"Thanks, man." I grabbed the bottle and started to turn around.

"You should ask her to dance."

I tried to ignore him and walked back to the table, but the bartender was right. I needed to dance with her. I wasn't even sure why, but I knew that I would regret it if I didn't.

Annie was making her way back toward the table. Several people waved at her and tried to get her to sit down, but she declined. She looked as though she was dodging a gauntlet of people. I realized I was tapping my foot in anticipation, watching her. I took my eagerness by the reins and tried to slow my heart rate. She smiled at me just before another cowboy cut her off by stepping in front of her. He was tall and broad. I couldn't see Annie on the other side of him.

A twinge hit my stomach as I wondered who he was. I guessed that was my cue, so I pushed off the table, took a sip of my beer, and walked toward Annie. The cowboy had touched her hair and tried to slip his hand onto her waist. Annie backed up slightly.

"Annie?" I touched her arm.

They both looked at me, his face surprised, hers relieved.

"Yes, Mace?" she put her hand in my hand. She smiled, knowing what was happening. Her face was calm and relaxed.

"Can I tear you away from this gentleman? I'd like to dance with you."

Annie met the cowboy's eyes and shrugged. "Sorry, Matt. You don't mind, do you?"

The cowboy shrugged and shook his head no. He backed away and tipped his hat toward us. I grabbed Annie's hand and led her to the dance floor. Knowing she wasn't aware I could dance, I spun her out and back in. Our feet moved in unison, and we began to two-step. She let her mouth slip into a wide smile, and she laughed.

"Knight in shining armor, aren't you?" She was definitely flirting now.

"Nope, I just really wanted to dance." I winked at her.

She giggled again and kept her eyes on me. My hand was on her waist. I tried not to squeeze too tight, but it thrilled me to be that close to her. I had no idea what was coming over me.

I whispered in her ear, "I'm sorry for my analysis earlier. I wasn't trying to be critical. I'm an idiot." I spun her out. She looked puzzled. I spun her back in.

She looked up at me. "No harm done." She released one of my hands and patted my chest. "You're a fine dancer, you know that?"

I couldn't tell if she hadn't thought a thing about what I had said earlier or if she was side-stepping it. At that moment, I decided it didn't matter, so I held her close. We continued to dance until the last note melted out of the speakers.

The lead singer slung his guitar to one side and said, "You guys have one last song to figure out who you want to take home. Y'all have been great tonight. Be good, and be safe. Thanks for coming out."

The final song began. Some of the other couples filtered off the dance floor, heading back to their seats, and Annie broke our embrace softly. My head knew that it was time to meet JJ, but my arms didn't want to let her go. I wanted to continue holding her and maybe even kiss her. What was wrong with me? I'd spent the entire day annoyed with her and this place. Now I was thinking about wanting to kiss her?

Before I could act, we both heard chopper blades slicing through the rain with a forceful thwack, thwack, thwack.

She gave me a soft smile. "Guess your ride is finally here." She nodded toward the door and began moving that direction.

I followed her toward the door, knowing on the other side was a goodbye I didn't even know how to start or finish. I had no idea how to thank her. I wanted to tell her that things had shifted inside me and that maybe I could become something else, but I knew that sounded strange. I wanted to tell her that she was the singular most interesting person I had ever met, but I knew that just sounded lame. I wanted to tell her that I wasn't ready to leave, but I knew that sounded creepy. My mouth felt dry and brittle, and my tongue felt fat and heavy.

Before I could say a word, she pulled at the handles to the door, and it swung open, leaving my chance to say anything behind. She grabbed my hand and pulled me out into the rain. We stomped through the grass, sloshing and splashing as we ran around the side of Billy's and spotted the chopper 200 yards back in the field.

"We'll just have to run, okay?" she yelled above the rain in my ear. I nodded at her, and we took off running as she dropped my hand. Nearing the chopper, I willed myself to say something, anything. Nothing came out. She backed away, and I ran to the chopper. JJ grabbed my hand and pulled me up. As the chopper lifted off the ground, I stopped myself from jumping back out to her.

I looked down as we lifted off. Even from a distance in the rain, I could see her eyes. They held the same disappointment and fear that I felt. As the distance between us grew, she lifted her arm in the air and waved for a moment before pausing, her hand simply outstretched to me. My breath caught at the sight of her. As she wiped the rain from her face, the moment was gone.

Soon, I'd be back in L.A., and I'd never see her again.

11. FREEDOM AND ROADHOUSE FRIES

While Mace lost himself in his memory, Annie's phone interrupted her conversation with Chuck. Sliding it out of her pocket, she studied the number. She tried to control her eyebrows although they naturally wanted to fly to the top of her forehead in surprise. She didn't want questions from Chuck about the phone call, so she casually excused herself. She hurried into the lobby and answered, anxiousness filling her thoughts like a cloud of smoke.

"Hello, this is Annie."

"Annie, it's Malcolm. It's over, Annie," the voice on the other end said slowly and controlled.

Annie hadn't realized she'd been holding her breath, but as she exhaled heavily, she thought to assure herself further. "He's truly passed then?"

"He died this morning."

Annie's hand flew to her mouth, and she let the tears escape that she had bottled up for years. *Freedom.* The word formed in her mouth, and it felt warm and sweet to her lips. She was finally free.

"Thank you for letting me know," she said, taking a deep breath to get the words out.

"You're safe now, Annie."

As she hung up the phone, she ducked into a storage closet and let her tears flow. It felt wild yet sweet to let them out. When they slowed and she had regained normal breaths, she called Sam.

After she told him the news, they sat astonished for some time, not knowing how to express anything. It had been too long. She wasn't even sure what it meant to be free of the past or what would change, but just knowing that the final thread to her past had been severed did something to her soul that she couldn't explain even if she wanted to. At the moment, she didn't want to, feeling too overwhelmed by the news to share it with anyone except Sam. They hung up, and the only thing she knew to do was pray.

She fell to her knees in the closet and spoke softly. "Father, freedom is only found in You, and You have given me freedom today. Thank You."

She rose from her knees changed. Her spirit felt released and light, no longer carrying the burden of secrets. She practically glided back into the auditorium. Mace had left sometime during her time out, and she dropped into the seat beside Chuck.

It was almost an hour later when Mace wandered back into the theater. Chuck and Annie were relaxed in the seats, side by side, quietly talking. Mace felt himself harden at the sight of them, but he forced himself to brush it away. *You can't care. This is business,* he told himself. He coolly slipped into the row behind them.

"Let's go back to the roadhouse and the goodbye, if we can." Chuck, hearing Mace come in, pointed back toward him. "At this point in this story, how would you say your character feels about the Annie character?"

Mace uncrossed his arms and sat up a little straighter, one leg crossed over the other.

He looked at Annie's back and sort of squinted his eyes. "If my character analyzed things at this point, I don't think that he would find much. He is still very much only in tune with himself. He doesn't fully see her yet, and nothing pivotal has happened to allow change yet."

Annie's mouth opened slightly in surprise while he was talking, but as soon as he was done, she realized it and regained control of her expression. *Mace Harlen is changing his story. Does he think he's fooling anyone with that rendition?*

"And Miss Annie, what do you think the Annie character was thinking about the Mace character?" Chuck asked, watching her face, which Mace couldn't see.

"I didn't know him very well, and he was leaving. It's not like I needed to put forth a lot of effort to get to know him on a deep level or anything. Still, I think we had reached a point of feeling comfortable around each other. I still had strong reasons for my cautiousness."

"Yeah, I'd agree with that," Mace added flatly.

"I love that part about the flavor of the day," Chuck said, referring back to part of the story Mace had told him. "So help me understand this; what would be the ultimate flavor of the day. The perfect day would feel like...blank," Chuck asked, excitedly anticipating her answer.

Annie breathed in slowly through her nose as if she smelled something.

"Tiramisu."

"Really? Why? Walk me through this." Chuck's eyes were filled with inquisitive delight.

"Tiramisu is a sophisticated, layered delicacy. It's made with rich mascarpone cheese, fluffy ladyfingers, just enough coffee liqueur to give it a kick, and dark, decadent chocolate. It's rich but also light and fluffy; it's fun and adventurous; it's dark and somewhat exotic. All in all, it's exciting. It's like the perfect man or the perfect day. Tiramisu."

"Okay, Okay...I really like where this is going. I love that bit about how it's like the perfect day and or the perfect man. Tell me how."

"Let me see if I can explain this well." She paused, thinking. "The perfect day or the perfect man has many layers. One adjective couldn't describe all that they are. The perfect day would have exciting moments, funny moments, deep philosophical moments, and light casual moments. I suppose the perfect man would be quite the same. He'd be slightly mysterious and exciting. He'd be rich in ways of character and conversation. He'd be funny, and he'd be inviting and friendly."

Mace felt himself warm back up to her. He had leaned way over to be able to see her face. He and Chuck both started to smile while watching her describe the dessert. They watched her mouth as she talked and her closed eyes under her expressive eyebrows. When she was done, she opened her eyes and found them looking at her. They all laughed and looked away from each other.

"There's enough vision for a movie inside this room alone. I mean look around, it's almost *Phantom of the Opera* in here," Chuck said, changing the subject and looking around the stage.

"Are you kidding? It's just a small town theater. It's nothing spectacular." Annie shrugged, being modest.

"But it is! May I have the grand tour?" Chuck stood, offering her a hand. "And then I propose that we go to this Billy's and continue storyboarding. What do you say?"

"I'd be happy to give you a tour, and we can go anywhere you guys want to. I'm your Penumbra tour guide slash guru." Annie laughed. Mace stood up and let her pass in the aisle. Chuck was already bounding out into the lobby. She turned back to look at Mace, asking, "You don't want to come?"

"Nah, I think I will stay here and write a bit. Is that all right? It won't offend you if I don't get the backstage pass?"

She couldn't tell if he was being extremely sarcastic or very considerate, though there seemed to be a fine line between the two. "No, not at all. I suppose you have seen it all anyway."

Mace gave her a half smile and sat back down. Annie walked into the lobby and found Chuck staring into her office, which was off the lobby in a hallway to the left. She usually kept the door closed but had forgotten to close it when they arrived.

Chuck was staring at a portrait on her wall above her desk. It was a black and white portrait of a woman in a gorgeous white gown, statuesque and poised, her mouth open as though she were singing a long note in a big finale. Chuck lifted one hand and braced himself on the doorframe. He looked over his shoulder at Annie.

Annie was waiting for his response, with a knowing smile.

"Who is she? And how can I meet her?"

Annie rolled her eyes. "You're looking at her."

"THAT IS YOU?" Chuck yelled and then took a long gasp. Mace came running into the lobby, looking disoriented. Chuck looked at Mace and then pointed at the picture.

"Did you know that was her? Have you seen this? That is *her*!"

Mace shook his head and joined them in the doorway. They were all three touching the doorway and each other. Annie didn't know why they didn't just go inside. She also didn't know what the big deal was; it was just a picture.

"Okay, okay. Enough of that. This isn't on the tour, Chuck," Annie said, pulling at his arms. "Come on. Let's move along."

"No, I want to stay and stare."

"What? Do I look that bad now?" Annie teased.

"Please. Don't get me started. You do not want to go there." Chuck was mocking a valley girl voice and waving his arms around as he followed Annie down the hall.

Mace, who hadn't said a single word since he stood in the doorway, continued to stand there and stare at the portrait. He again was aware that he didn't know her very well at all. He didn't know when this was taken, what show it was, or where she had done stage theater. He knew that she loved it and that she loved directing the kids, but he never stopped to think how she came into the genre itself.

He felt that there was a spotlight on his face, making it hot. He felt ashamed, ridiculous, and exposed even though no one was watching. He was only exposed to himself, but that almost made it worse because he had been trying to ignore it for so long.

He didn't feel like writing anymore, and he could feel beads of sweat forming over his eyebrows and in between his shoulder blades. He turned away from the portrait and walked slowly back into the auditorium. He sat back down in the same seat and closed his eyes. He could hear Chuck laughing somewhere backstage.

He took a deep breath, and the theater smelled the same. The wood smelled of polish with a slight lemon scent. The air was cool, and the carpets were crisp and clean. When all the smells mingled, it somehow smelled of vanilla.

Mace fell asleep to the distant sound of Chuck and Annie laughing.

They were backstage trying on pirate hats, and Chuck was practicing his "scallywag jargon" as he called it.

"Arg, me sees me Annie. Me wants her for me own. Arrggg. She can't resist me swarthy self in me tall boots and puffy shirt."

"And feather in your hats, good pirate sir. I do swoon for thee." Annie placed a large plume in his hat and then pretended to faint, fanning herself.

Chuck spotted the makeup mirrors, rushed Annie over to them, and pretended to be her hairdresser. He fluffed her hair while pursing his lips and mumbling a series of dramatic "uh-huhs."

"Let's just keep this simple, Chuck-ista," Annie played along, laughing.

"No, honey, we have got to get this mess up and out of your face. The show goes up in five, and I haven't got a bobby pin to save my life."

Annie was laughing so hard that she had started to cry. She pulled Chuck down into the chair next to her. "You've got to stop. You're giving me a stitch!"

Chuck was laughing now as well. "I don't know what a stitch is, but I don't hate making you laugh, Annie."

Annie kept trying to take gulping breaths in between the laughter. "I can't stop laughing."

"Okay, then for real, girl, we knew you were stunning, but we did not know you had all that. Let's discuss that portrait in your office. Mace never mentioned that you were an actress, only a director."

Annie pushed her hair away from her face and propped her elbow on the makeup table. She was still wiping tears away from her face and smiling as she said, "That's because Mace didn't know. There's a lot that Mace doesn't know about me."

"Okay, but let Chuck know." Chuck went back to his normal voice and rolled closer beside her in the next makeup chair.

"I'm originally from Chicago. I grew up there. My father owned a theater company. I acted for several years, through college and then for two years after that. When my father got cancer, my mother and I took over. I acted as house and stage manager."

Chuck was lounging on the makeup table, listening intently.

"Then I lost both of my parents within six months of each other, and shortly after...I sold the company and moved down here."

"Amazing," Chucked breathed, "And tragic, too."

"I don't really think that it's amazing, Chuck. More like pathetic." Annie shook her head.

"Why do you say that?"

"That in and of itself is a long story. We'll get there eventually. Also, I'd say that I haven't always made stellar choices. "

Chuck leaned in slightly and pretended to put on her lipstick. "Well, my dear, I'm completely entranced with you already. You have so much mystery and history. Now, you look fabulous. Look at yourself," he said, spinning her back toward the mirror.

"Gorgeous!" Annie said, acting like a prima donna.

"That's what I'm saying. Now let's go get that other guy and go have us some fun at Billy's." He grabbed her hand and pulled her to the curtain. He raised their arms together and came out of the curtain triumphantly, ready for applause.

Mace was nowhere to be seen. Chuck dropped her hand reluctantly as they walked to the stairs and headed up the aisle.

"Where did he go?" Annie asked.

Chuck shrugged and cupped his mouth and yelled, "Mace Harlen, are you in the building?"

There was no answer. Chuck yelled again. Still nothing. Annie continued up the aisle and walked into the lobby. Hearing water running in the bathroom, she opened the door slightly and said Mace's name in a normal tone.

She could see his reflection in the mirror, leaning over the sink with the water running. She opened the door and slipped in. Mace looked up in the mirror to see her. His eyes were intense though his arms seemed shaky.

"Are you okay?" she said, stepping toward him and wondering if he were on drugs. No, there was something bothering him; she could tell in his eyes.

"Just tired. I'm fine," he said brusquely.

She let it go, not trying to push him further. Even Mace Harlen's moods couldn't bring her spirits down tonight, not after the phone call she'd received earlier.

"Come on, Harlen. Let's get you a beer. You look like death."

They met Chuck in the lobby, and he seemed oblivious to Mace's demeanor or the fact that they both had come out of the men's room together. Annie assumed that Chuck tended to be this way all the time. He kept giving Mace a hard time, saying that they looked all over for him and they had been waiting and waiting. Mace told him to shut up and get in the car. Chuck acted offended and sat in the back seat with Annie.

As they pulled into the parking lot at Billy's, the neon sign was visible on top of the metal roof. Mace caught Annie's eye in the mirror, and they both smiled before Annie slid out of the back seat.

Annie led the way inside and over to a corner booth.

"This place is great," Chuck said, looking around the room. "Mace, do you think that we can re-create it in-studio or should we just shoot on location?" Chuck was pulling out the laptops, cellphones, cameras, pens and legal pads. He spread it all out on the table.

Annie looked at Mace, quizzically. "Wait...you want to make the movie here?"

"Sorry, Annie, didn't mean to jump the gun. Just throwing around ideas, right?"

"It's okay. It's not like you need to apologize, Chuck. I was just surprised. If you guys wanted to, it would be perfectly okay. It's not like it's up to me."

"It sort of is. We would be invading your space," Mace pointed out.

"Why don't we keep brainstorming, and you guys can work out those details later? I'll go get us a round, and then we'll get started. You guys want some food?"

They both nodded, and she smiled as she disappeared to the bar. Chuck began to doodle on one of the legal pads. Mace seemed to brighten up just being there with the grease, beer, and neon.

"Do you know how this ends?" Chuck said in a hushed way.

Mace played with the salt and pepper shakers. "No."

"Do you know how you want it to end?"

Mace shook his head.

"I seriously do not understand you, Mace."

"Chuck, just drop it."

Chuck raised his hands in surrender as Annie reappeared, hands full of baskets and glasses.

"We've got fries, we've got nachos, we've got chili cheese fry nachos, we've got burgers, and we've got more fries."

Chuck and Mace laughed, taking the baskets from her.

They all settled in, drinking and munching on fries. Chuck accidently spilled ketchup all over one of the baskets because he thought it was a squeeze top instead of an open top. After the commotion was over and the ketchup was contained, Mace settled back into the booth and leaned his head against the cushioned back.

They let the ideas flow as casually as the conversation did. They talked of locations and sets, they argued about budgets and crews, and they talked about vision
and bottom lines.

12. COMPETITION AND BEER

Annie was looking at the table and playing with her mug. Both men studied her as she sat there unaware.

"We are boring our friend Annie here with our brainstorm session," Chuck said, slapping the table.

Annie whipped her head up, obviously jerked out of her thoughts. She smiled and laughed slightly.

"I think we need a little healthy competition. I will wager I am a better dancer than my friend, Harlen. Will you take this wager?" Chuck asked. "The wager is…"

Chuck stopped to pull his phone out of his pocket. He looked at the screen and then excused himself saying that "the money" was on the phone. He told them the call may take a bit and to carry on without him.

"Do you want to dance anyway?" Mace asked.

Annie had been looking out toward the rest of the room. "Sure." She shrugged at him and smiled as she slid out of the booth.

Mace followed her out to the dance floor.

Their embrace was static, Annie thought. They both looked at the floor or let their eyes wander around the room, avoiding looking straight at each other. The song was unfamiliar to Mace, though most country or bluegrass was. It was a female singer with a smooth, deeply Southern voice. Mace tried to listen to the words to take his mind off of the awkwardness he felt, but he decided he couldn't stand the sappy song and decided to break the silence.

"So…what have you been up to?"

Annie looked up from the floor. She could tell he was just making conversation, and she knew it wasn't the right time to tell him more about her life, even though she was free to, so she chose her words carefully.

"I've been pretty swamped with some new projects at the theater. That has taken pretty much all of my time."

The song ended on a long, slightly pitchy note. Mace made a funny face.

"Yeah, she's not as good as the band that was here last time." Annie smiled.

"They were so good! That was a party. What happened to them?"

"Oh, they are friends of Billy's. They were just here that weekend. They've made it big since then. Record deals and what not."

"Really? Wow."

They were still standing facing each other and waiting on the next song when Chuck reentered the room. He made a beeline over to them and practically stood in between them.

"Guys, you are not going to believe this. We have potential backers for the movie!"

"It's not even written yet," Mace said.

"I know! It's crazy. Lithgow wants to meet again to hear more. We may have to interrupt this trip to go back and meet with him and then come back to finish writing."

Annie watched the two men react to each other. Mace seemed skeptical while Chuck was trying to overcome his skepticism by being over-the-top enthusiastic, using his expressive face and hands to re-enact the conversation.

"Isn't this what you want, Mace?" she asked.

"Yes, I just thought it would be harder, that's all. Usually, the movie-making process feels like pitching ideas to a panel of judges or something. Now, Chuck makes one phone call, and we're in? I'm just shocked."

"Just because JJ was terrible at pitching doesn't mean that everyone is," Chuck retorted with mocking laughter.

"Was? Is JJ...no more?" Annie asked.

"Yeah. Harlen here kicked him to the curb."

"Really? What happened?" Annie questioned.

"It happened after Harlen got back from his first visit here."

"Dude, let me tell my own stories," Mace said jokingly, shoving Chuck aside.

"Sorry. You've been like a trapdoor since we got here, so I thought you forgot how to talk. I'm going to get another round, but when I get back, it's my turn to whirl the fair maiden around the floor."

Annie laughed at Chuck and pretended to curtsey toward him. He bowed in return.

"He's an idiot," Mace said.

Annie caught a slight jealous flash in Mace's eye. She lifted her nose and said, "I think he's fun—maybe that's something you've forgotten how to be."

"What are you saying?"

"You have been sort of aloof since you got here," she confessed softly.

Can she blame me? After the way I left the last time? Mace thought to himself. He shoved his hands in his pockets.

Annie could tell he wasn't going to admit why he was acting the way that he was, so she shifted gears.

"Tell me about JJ. What happened there?"

"Remember how we were supposed to have some pretty big meeting with a director when I got back to L.A.? JJ was pitching several ideas to him and pitching me to do them as well. JJ bombed all of it. Then, when it all fell through, he blamed me. We ended up fighting because I didn't want to do those parts anyway. I couldn't get directing out of my head, so I mentioned to Lithgow I was interested in directing. Lithgow was listening, and JJ hated that he was listening to me and not him. So JJ stormed out. After that, I no longer wanted him to be my agent. We don't speak anymore."

"Seriously? That's totally *Days of Our Lives* drama," Annie said.

"Seriously. After that, I didn't really want to do any films for a while, and that's when Chuck came to me one day and said he wanted to do this."

"This probably will sound cheesy, but for what it's worth, I'm really proud of you."

Mace felt his face flush, but he hoped it was just the beer. Right then, Chuck walked back up with a bottle in hand and tapped Mace on the shoulder like someone is cutting in.

"My good Harlen, if you would be so kind as to hold this beer and step aside, I shall now dance with the fair maiden."

Mace rolled his eyes but relinquished Annie's hand. He walked back to the booth and slid in. He leaned his head against the tall back of his booth, closed his eyes, and listened to the music.

Out on the dancefloor, Chuck spun Annie in and out and twirled her in a full circle around him. She was laughing and getting dizzy. He dipped her and brought her back up.

"Okay, enough whirly twirly, I've got questions for you, Annie."

"Give me a second. I'm dizzy."

"Okay, deep breaths. You breathe while I sing for you." He sang along with the song in a bad Southern accent and swayed all around her.

"Okay, I'm okay now."

"Oh, all right." Chuck stood up straight in front of her and pretended to fix his imaginary tie. They began to sway slowly together.

"You really got to Mace. You know that, right?"

Annie snickered and looked away. "I didn't know that, really."

"What? Are you kidding me?

She shook her head.

"Oh please, that is so boring. I can't do anything with that. I need a transition, and you're killing it."

"Okay! Good grief, drama queen! Let me think." Annie pretended to be in deep thought. She furrowed her brow and smoked an imaginary cigar. Chuck loved her attempt to play along. In a raspy voice that resembled a *Godfather* impression, she said, "Sorry, Chuck. There's no more to say."

Chuck grunted and spun her out and in again. She craned her neck to the left to look over Chuck's shoulder to see Mace. Mace's eyes were closed as his head rested on the back of the booth.

"I think Mace is tired."

Chuck stopped dancing but didn't release Annie; he just turned to look over his shoulder.

"Nah, he's thinking."

"No, I know that face. He did that the entire time he was here. I'm fairly certain that means he's tired and bored out of his mind."

"I promise you—he's deep in it now."

"I don't believe you. He was so bored when he was stuck here, and I got used to that face."

"How do you know he wasn't thinking?"

"Oh...I guess I don't know."

"Well, let's go see, shall we?"

Chuck finally released his grip on Annie's waist but grabbed her hand and pulled her in Mace's direction. It surprised Annie that she didn't pull her hand away as they walked over the booth and stood over Mace.

"Mace, whatcha doing?"

Mace opened his eyes and lifted his head. He looked at Chuck and Annie and panned the room quickly, gaining his bearings.

"I was thinking about some stuff, and then I guess I fell asleep."

Chuck and Annie erupted in laughter and elbowed each other in the side.

"What?"

"Nothing, we were just taking bets on whether you were tired or thinking. Guess we were both right!"

"I have coffee at the house," Annie said. "You boys want to move this party there? We can brainstorm around the kitchen table over espresso."

"Yeah, let's go. This band is terrible anyway."

They left and got back into the rental. The limo tint on the SUV reminded her of the detective's tinted, unmarked car and the night she was carefully put in the back seat and placed under protection. That night had changed her life forever. Now the tinted darkness filled her with dread as they rode back to her house, even with her newfound freedom.

She was now free to speak, free to live, and free to love...but she dreaded the questions that would surely come.

Am I ready to share this story? Do they even need to know?
They came here for another story; they didn't come here for this.

Though it was amusing to watch Mace and Chuck argue over how to start the coffee pot, Annie slipped out of the kitchen, leaving them to work it out. The heaviness of her silence constricted around her heart, as she searched for Sam down the hall. She had grown so accustomed to how suffocating silence was that she wasn't even sure how to speak the truth.

Sam was propped comfortably in his favorite recliner reading the newspaper.

"There's nothing worth talking about, but still, they somehow manage to fill these pages," he said as she eased up beside his chair. As he looked at her, he saw the tension pulling at her eyes and mouth and the color flowing away from her face each time she took a strained breath. He gently set the paper aside and took her hands in his.

"What is it, my Annie?"

Just the warmth from Sam's wrinkled hands was enough to push the color back up to her face and relax her eyes. She breathed deeply and imagined her breath breaking through the ropes on her heart. Her shoulders fell, and she welcomed the safety she felt with Sam.

"It's time," she said softly.

"You're going to tell your story now?"

"Yes. It's time."

Sam dropped her hands and took her face with both hands, kissing her forehead.

"Annie, *God* has made you brave. *He* has given you strength. *He* will give you a voice."

Annie wiped away a small tear as she nodded. She felt something new rise up and begin to fill her whole body. She didn't have anything rehearsed, she didn't have a timeline to show them, but she knew that she was ready to tell her story now.

As she rose to her feet, she kissed Sam on his cheek and promised to feed the horses later.

When she returned to the kitchen, she found Mace and Chuck lounging at the kitchen table, arms draped over the back of the chairs, legs propped on the seats, coffee mugs filled, and notes scribbled furiously on notepads and laptops.

She seemed to slip back into their midst unnoticed, which she liked. She poured herself a cup of fresh coffee. Inhaling the aroma, she hoped to draw courage from the lavish scent rising from the cup in her hands.

Sliding down into a chair across the round oak table from them, she gently cleared her throat, which caused them finally to notice she had come back. Wide smiles burst across both the men's faces, and she felt herself relax into the chair. As she sipped from her cup, it came to her how to tell these two men how she came to Penumbra.

She began slowly and evenly, making sure her voice was under control and they were both listening.

"I haven't been completely honest with you." As their eyes widened, she continued solemnly, "But it's been out of necessity." She knew she was being cryptic, but all would be exposed shortly. *Lord, help me.*

"His name was Simon Grady."

13. SIMON AND A CINNAMON LATTE
CHICAGO, SEVEN YEARS AGO

Simon Grady's charm was deceptive, and his beauty was fleeting. Since he was a kid, he'd been climbing every ladder put in front of him. Even though he was a middle child, he quickly imprinted himself as the golden child. In high school, he climbed ladders of status, popularity, and influence. In college, it quickly became a game of danger and pleasure. He rose to power in his class, his dorm, and his campus. Everyone did his bidding, and his bidding always including drugs, alcohol, and women who were also asserting their ambitions in dangerous ways. Even his grades could be negotiated. He followed well in his father's footsteps, received a Master's in business, and learned even more ways to attain the things he felt entitled to. Simon's *Vogue*-worthy good looks further assured him that he would get everything in life that he wanted.

The first time he saw Annie, he had licked his lips and smoothed the front spike of his short, sandy blonde hair. Across the Starbucks, he had set his sights on her, set the ladder in front of himself, and challenged himself to climb.

"Excuse me. I think I may have gotten your coffee by mistake." Simon spread innocence over his voice with a knife of lies. Annie looked up from gazing at the bags of coffee on markdown. He whipped the cup around and revealed her name on the side.

Annie realized she must have missed the barista calling her name. *Am I that tired?* She wondered. *Why did he pick up my coffee?*

"Oh thanks," she muttered, hoping he wouldn't try to chat. She retrieved her cup from his hand and realized there was something else written below her name: *I'm Simon. Call me.* As she read his number, she rolled her eyes.

"Are you kidding me?" she said, too tired for civility, but when she looked up, he had already left.

The barista looked at her quizzically over the counter. "Is everything okay with your coffee?"

Annie nodded, tired and cranky that some handsome stranger had just ruined her cup of coffee.

"Yes, the coffee is fine. Thanks."

She pushed through the line out into the cutting cold of Chicago's streets. It was early, the streets still hidden in icy shadows underneath the wings of the skyscrapers. She darted through the busy sidewalks and cut across the street to the Regal Theater. The long frozen fingers of the wind reached her even through her thick green pea coat, and she couldn't wait to be in the warm lobby.

From a block away, Simon watched her fumble for her keys while juggling her purse, three notebooks, and her coffee. He gazed at her movements as she shifted her weight back and forth in an effort to keep moving in the cold. Finally, she disappeared into the lobby of the theater, but he lingered on his corner just a bit longer, listening to his dad's voice in his head. *"Son, people love you. You're magnetic, they can't say no to you. Go after what you want. Be aggressive."*

He felt the cold air whip around him, and he welcomed the warm aggression that was pumping through him. *She can't say no to me.*

Annie tucked her coat away along with her notebooks and purse in her office. She slipped into the theater with her coffee and didn't even need to count the rows to find 33. She plopped down in the seventh chair and sighed. "Daddy, it's opening night, and I wish you were here."

It had been almost a year since Annie's father had lost his battle with cancer. They had worked side by side for so long that to be running Regal Theater Productions alone now felt incomplete. Although she had always dreamed of stepping in for her father, she just always assumed it would be because he was ready to retire and simply sit down in row 33, seat 7 and happily watch shows. Now, she felt like a three-year- old walking around an apartment in her daddy's shoes. She didn't quite feel ready even though this was her seventh opening night as owner/manager.

She sipped on her coffee and thanked the cup for warming her chilled hands. In just a few hours, the backstage would be bustling like the streets she had just escaped, the ticket booths would have lines forming, the popcorn would be popping, and the atmosphere would be intoxicating and unmistakable. For now, though, she savored a moment alone in the quiet darkness of her father's theater.

"There's just nothing like opening night, is there Annie?" Leo asked, his voice bursting with wonder. Annie stared down from the balcony, ignoring her stage manager.

"Annie?"

"Huh?"

"Boy, are you distracted. What's up with you?"

"Oh! Sorry, Leo. What did you say?"

"Only something about how great opening night always is, but I guess you didn't love the show tonight? What's eating at you?" Leo asked, grabbing her hand and yanking her down the stairs. "Let's go eat the leftover popcorn, and you can tell your brother Leo all about it."

"Brother Leo?"

"Well, let's face it, I gave up on being your boyfriend when I was twelve, so I'll settle for acting like we're as close as siblings," he joked.

"Leo, it's creepy that you just said that, and you were twelve only six years ago."

"Exactly. I've put it in the past." He winked at her and flashed her a cheeky grin.

Annie remembered that summer when Leo, a scrawny twelve-year-old, started hanging around the theater when his mom had the lead role in *Kiss Me Kate*. And almost every summer since then, he'd been back. It wasn't until a year before Annie's father had passed away that Leo became an actual employee of the Regal. He'd dropped out of high school and only wanted to work at the theater. His mom had left him on his own, and he begged for a full-time job. As it turned out, he was adept at all the jobs Annie assigned him, and he finally worked his way up to stage manager.

"I'm sorry I'm distracted, Leo. Just thinking about Dad."

His face fell as he said, "I know. I always miss him the most on opening night."

"The show was great. *You* did great tonight," she said, mustering up all the excitement in her voice that she could, but then she admitted, "The theater doesn't feel the same without him here."

As they sat on the concession stand in the grand Persian lobby, Leo lay his head on Annie's shoulder, and she held his hand. They sat on the counter in silence for almost an hour, munching on popcorn.

Leo suddenly jumped off the counter. "I almost forgot! This will totally make you feel better." He started to run off but then stopped and came back, motioning her to join him. "I forgot to tell you about the massively gigantic flower arrangement that came for you before the show started!"

"Flowers? For me?" she said, running after him, shocked. "From who?"

"I wish I could say me so that you'd be so surprised you might feel like kissing me…"

"In the past?" she mimicked him.

"Oh, right. Sorry. Old habits and what not. A massive card came with flowers, but I didn't open it because that would just be crossing a line," Leo stated, drawing an imaginary line and slowly backing away from it.

Annie laughed and shoved him playfully as they reached her office. There, on her desk, sat hundreds of dollars' worth of flowers. Brightly colored daisies and tulips, big bushy hydrangeas and bluebells mixed perfectly. The artistically arranged bright vase of cheeriness brought the biggest, goofiest smile to Annie's face, and she didn't even care Leo was watching.

"I can't imagine who they are from. Only my dad ever sent me flowers." She paused remembering, and then her mouth fell open. "He always sent them on opening night. Do you think? What if he planned to have them delivered?"

"Only one way to find out." Leo handed her card. It was the largest yellow envelope she'd seen. She tore it open and pulled out a bright green single card.

"So much color! I love it."

Her eyes traced the neat handwriting before she read the words.

> *You in your green pea coat were a stark, fresh contrast against cold Chicago this morning. Can I swipe your coffee again in the morning?*
> *Happy opening night,*
> *Simon Grady*

Her heart skipped slightly.

"It's not from Dad." Then she re-read it.

Leo paced at the suspense and asked, "Well, who *is* it from?"

Annie looked up from the card, her eyebrows perplexed and her mouth opened in confusion. "Some guy I bumped into in the Starbucks this morning. This is sort of crazy."

"You made quite the impression, though," he said, circling the flowers. "This is a *lot* of flowers."

"Here," Annie said, thrusting the card at Leo. "Read this, and tell me if I should go."

Leo read the card, and a sneaky smile crept at the corners of his mouth. "Simon Grady? You have the attention of *Simon Grady*?"

Annie shrugged. "Should I know him? Who's Simon Grady?"

"Only the heir to the Grady Empire. His grandfather is the founder and still holds the office as CEO, supposedly. They have quite the powerful reputation, but I couldn't really tell you what they do. Rumors of organized crime have gone around for years, but who knows if that's true? It is Chicago after all."

"Does that mean I should go?"

"Uh, yeah. Otherwise, he might just buy up your theater out of spite because you wouldn't date him," Leo joked but then realized that probably wasn't funny. He shook his head as if that would null the comment that he just made. "I just mean that you should say yeah. Forget the rest. I made that up."

"Hmm, we'll see," Annie said. Soon, they turned out the lights as they locked the theater doors, and Leo helped Annie carry her flowers home.

Annie decided to go to Starbucks again in the morning.

The next morning, Annie stepped to the counter and ordered her usual tall skinny cinnamon dolce latte. She slid out of her pea coat, showing off a fitted purple sweater and pinstriped vest. The young barista who had served her the day before informed her she didn't owe anything for the coffee.

"What do you mean?"

"It's already been paid for by the gentlemen in the corner."

He's already here? Annie turned to Simon lounging in the corner with a computer in his lap. She smoothed her hair and wished she hadn't cut it after her dad died. It felt too short now even though it brushed at her shoulders. Simon leaned forward, placed the laptop on the table in front of him, then unwrapped a gray wool scarf, and draped it over the arm of the chair. He finally looked up to see her walking his way.

She's beautiful, he thought as she reached out a stiff hand for him to shake.

"You must be Simon?"

He laughed, taking her hand but pulling downward, bringing her closer so that, as he kissed her cheek, it seemed like a natural gesture. Her cheeks flamed.

As he pulled away, he said smoothly, "Yes, I am Simon. And you are?"

Annie slid down onto the couch adjacent to his. "I thought since you knew all my favorite flowers and that yesterday was opening night, you already knew my name as well," she said with obvious sarcasm, hoping that she didn't appear already taken with his charm and solid good looks.

He laughed again, this time nodding in a way that suggested surrender to her comment. "Guilty. I will admit that I called to find out what night was opening night, and it worked to my advantage that it was yesterday. The flowers, though, I will say I guessed, based on the green of your coat, that you loved the color. Still, I do not know your name."

Annie smiled, satisfied with herself and with his answer, and she relaxed into her seat, holding her coffee in both hands. "I can't stay long, I have to get to the theater soon."

"Then I will soak up every second," he said so smoothly that she didn't even notice his deception melt into her whipped cream and slide down into her cinnamon latte. She drank up every ounce of his good looks and enjoyed the overt attraction he displayed to her.

They talked about Chicago, favorite restaurants, loyalty to the Cubs, and work. He was climbing the ladder of success in his father's footsteps with goals exceeding any other men his age. She tried to keep the conversation light and somewhat distant, but even as they talked about things any stranger might talk about with another, she found herself wanting to talk about more. Then, as she checked her phone and saw that it was after ten, she began to gather her coat.

"Already? I haven't learned nearly enough about you, and you still haven't told me your name."

She smiled, glad he wanted to talk about more than just Chicago. "I'm sorry, but I really do have to get to the theater."

"Why? The show is not until tonight. Do you all rehearse all day?"

She let out a laugh, realizing what he must have thought. "Sometimes they do, but I go in this early because I own the theater. My name is Annie Flynn."

Simon fell back against his couch, shaking his head. "I'm a fool. I don't know how I missed that. You're beautiful and brilliant and a businesswoman. Amazing."

Annie blushed as she slipped into her coat and slung her bag over her shoulder. "Back to business, then? Thanks for the flowers and now the coffee." She extended a less stiff hand this time to say goodbye.

Simon rushed to gather up his coat, scarf, and laptop, not wanting her to get away from him. "Can I take you to dinner soon?" he asked, taking her hand and holding it.

Surprised by his eagerness, she smiled, considering if she had anything going on later in the week. As usual, she had no social life. "Sure, we don't have a show Sunday night."

"Great. I'll see you Sunday then."

She said goodbye and slipped out into the cold. Her smile warmed her all the way to the theater.

"I don't care if you stayed out too late, Virginia. You're on in five, and you'd better be in full makeup in two," Leo shouted and slammed the dressing room door, whirling around right into Annie.

"That woman!" he said, making Annie laugh.

"Are you ok, Leo? You're hardly ever tense like this. What's up with Virginia?"

"She's in rare diva form tonight, but it's nothing I can't handle. I just haven't been sleeping the past couple of nights. I'm fine."

"Okay. Someone said you were looking for me?"

He furrowed his brow as he thought, and then after a moment seemed to remember what he needed. "Someone was here for you. I told them they could wait in your office, but that was a while ago. We go on in five, so I'm not sure they are still there. They may have found their seat and can talk to you later. Sorry. I meant to tell you earlier—I just got distracted by all this Virginia drama."

Annie patted him on the shoulder sympathetically. "It's okay, Leo. If they need to see me for something important, they will have waited. If not, even better." She winked at him, bringing a faint smile to Leo's young face.

Annie thought to leave but paused. "Why aren't you sleeping? Anything I can do to help?"

"Nightmares," Leo shuddered just thinking about them, "if you can believe it."

Something about the way he said it made Annie feel anxious. She didn't think she dared to ask what the nightmares were about. She just said she was sorry and slipped through a series of curtains to the back door. Before she left through the heavy stage door, Leo was beside her, grabbing her hand.

"Be careful," was the only thing he whispered, but it sent a shiver up Annie's arm and across her shoulders. *What a weird thing to say. Does he know about the date?* She forced a smile and whispered back, "Have a great show tonight, Leo." She shook the bad feeling from her as she took the stairs and passed through a series of hallways under the stage and emerged by the lobby. Passing the concession counter, she stopped to talk to Paulie, who had worked the popcorn machine since her father owned the theater.

Paulie told her a man had been waiting in her office, but as the show started, he had gone into the auditorium. Annie thanked him for noticing and decided to slip in the back and see if she recognized anyone close by.

As she inched through the doors, the welcomed sound of laughter in the audience danced in her ears. With her hands behind her on the wall, she leaned against it and took a moment to enjoy the show. As "So in love" finished, she tried to scan the back rows, but it was too dark. Then, as she turned to duck back out into the lobby, she saw Simon, leaning against the back wall.

Her footsteps quickened as she felt the smile spreading on her face. He hadn't noticed her come in, she didn't think, so she slid up beside him. She breathed in his strong and intoxicating smell that was both musky and expensive.

"Are you the one hanging around in my office?" She could see a smirk hook at the corners of his mouth, even in the dark.

"I couldn't wait. I had to see you again."

Be careful. Leo's words circled around in her mind again. She pushed them aside.

"I'm kinda working here," she said, slightly teasing.

"C'mon—you own the place. Can't you take a break and show me around?" he said, leaning closer to her and whispering low.

"Not really, there's a show going on…right now." She pointed jokingly toward the stage. "We can talk for a bit in my office."

"You don't seem to have a lot of time for me," he joked once they were in the open air of the grand lobby.

Without even looking back at him, she continued on to her office and retorted, "For someone climbing his family's corporate ladder, you seem to have a lot of free time."

A deep chuckle followed her into her office. Leaving the door open, she saw Paulie giving her a concerned expression. No one was used to seeing her with a man around. She lifted her palm out to Paulie as if to say, "I'm fine," and retreated to her desk, thankful to have at least an old man and a young boy concerned about her.

Simon wandered around the spacious office that looked exactly as her father had left it. It was manly, full of leather, iron, and oak. It was filled with pictures of the two of them and smelled like vanilla.

"When did you buy out your dad?" Simon asked, pointing to a picture of the two of them in row 33 just a few years ago.

"I didn't. He passed away a year ago."

Simon's face dropped, and she knew that look of "I just stuck my foot in my mouth" kind of horror. "I'm sorry, Annie. That was stupid of me."

Annie looked at him more with confusion than sorrow. "Why was that stupid of you? You didn't know my father. There's no reason you should have known he died last year. It's fine, Simon."

Sitting in one of the leather chairs that faced the desk, he apologized further, "Still, it was an awkward start to our conversation, and I'm sorry about that."

"It's fine—really."

She's as good at seeming fine as I am, Simon mused, feeling ever-present aggression swirling beneath his skin. He flawlessly held that aggression at bay, smiling at her from behind his mask of calmness.

"Tell me about running a theater. Do you love it?" he asked, settling into his chair, looking prepared to listen intently.

"I do. Theater is what I love. It's what Dad and I loved. I've acted, and I've directed but just keeping this place flowing as it does is amazing. I'm happy to keep it going for Dad," she said, allowing the smile that built as she talked about her dad to spread wide across her lips. "I can't imagine doing anything else."

Simon smiled as he watched her smile. "I can tell you and your Dad were close."

"We were."

"I bet you miss him."

"I do, but I don't really want to talk about it if you don't mind. Let's talk about you. Do you love climbing the corporate ladder?"

Simon studied her and rubbed his mouth and chin with his hand. "I do. I'm unabashedly ambitious and equally confident. My father has raised me to follow him, and someday I'll surprise the old man and surpass his wildest dreams. If you want something in life, I believe you can have it." He was bold and cocky, yet his eyes held a steadiness that left Annie wondering what she thought of this handsome man who was so interested in her.

"That's a very aggressive take on life if you don't mind my saying so."

"As I said, I like to think of it as ambition and confidence. It's working for me so far. I get what I want," he said, flashing her a flirtatious smile that made Annie blush all the way back to her ears.

"I suppose everybody has to find what works for them. My life hasn't been like that. People still die and such. I don't always get what I want, but I try to love life just like it is." Annie shrugged, trying to suppress the blush and regain herself.

He shifted his gaze from her to a painting of the Chicago pier, and in a distant voice, she repeated, "Everybody has to find what works for them."

Annie's eyes followed his to the painting. *What's he intrigued by?* She wondered. *Maybe it's time to excuse myself.* Annie felt a pinprick of uneasiness as she thought about their dinner date on Sunday night. "I should get some paperwork done before Leo gets done with the show."

"Leo?" he sounded surprised and confused.

"Leo's my stage manager and apparently my little brother." She snickered to herself, remembering Leo's adopted title.

"You didn't know you were related?" He seemed even more confused.

"Sorry. It's a long story."

Simon stood and walked over to her side of the desk, then stooping down, kissed her on the cheek.

"I'd love to hear that long story over dinner on Sunday."

As he pulled away, Annie saw Leo standing in the doorway frozen, and Annie suspected Simon had said that for his benefit, not hers. Annie quickly stood and moved to Leo in the doorway; he looked anxious.

"Small fire backstage."

That was all he had to say for Annie to follow him, running and yelling, "Literal fire or figurative fire?" and before he could answer, she stopped for a nanosecond and turned back to see Simon craning out of her office doorway.

"Bye, Simon. Sorry!" He waved her on as if to say that it was fine. Without another thought, she raced under the stage after Leo.

Simon stood for a moment after they'd gone and looked around her office. Like examining a mountain he had yet to conquer, he planned his ascent and the tools he'd use to get there. *I will have her. Go after what you want, Simon. Be aggressive.*

"That was a close one!" Annie said, flopping down beside an exhausted Leo. They were tucked away in a corner of the backstage behind the series of curtains. The finale song raged on, unaware of the near-disaster backstage. "What happened?"

"Virginia was smoking a cigar. She refused to put it out and started to try and burn me with it when she was up, and before I knew it, she threw it down in the trash barrel over there and went on stage!"

Sighing deeply, they leaned against each other and the back wall, listening as the audience gave a standing ovation. Annie had to admit to herself that Leo did feel like her little brother, and she didn't know what she would do without him.

"Who was that smug in your office?" Leo whispered.

"Smug?"

"Yeah, smug."

"That was Simon Grady."

Leo's mouth made a small "o" in understanding, and Annie nudged him in his ribs with her elbow.

"You're seeing him again?"

Annie raised her eyebrows at him and teased, "Not that it's any of your business, but we are going out on Sunday."

"All right, all right! Backing off now. Just wanted to make sure he's on the up and up. Taking care of my girl Annie, you know."

Annie was once again thankful for this young man next her in the dark who cared for her and would do anything to keep her happy and safe.

She kissed his temple and tucked her arm through his. Their ritual had always been to sit in the upper balcony after each show and wind down, talking about the show or life or just sitting in silence high above the stage. Now Annie admitted to Leo that this might just be their new ritual, minus the fire part.

"Leo, I'm stopping by the theater to grab those scripts you left. I'll run them by your apartment later. I know you don't like me to be there alone, but I'll just be a minute. Then I'm headed to dinner with Simon. Call me when you get this, and let me know if you'll be home later." Annie left the voicemail as she walked along the sidewalk.

As she tucked her phone back in her clutch, she felt anticipation crawling up her back, and she could have sworn that there was something different in the air. She loved the city at night and took in the lights far above her head. Her heels clicked along the pavement, and she hurried herself to get to the office and finish up her invoices before Simon got there.

As she reached the theater door and pulled her keys out, voices from around the building caught her attention. She walked to the corner, thinking, *Who is cavorting back here? I am going to kill Leo if he has a girl back there. Maybe that's why he—*

A hushed, growling voice stopped her thoughts. It was far enough away that she couldn't hear what was said. Then there was a second voice. They were in the alley beside the theater. She slowly inched toward the corner, hoping to see who it was without being seen. She took a quick look and then whipped back around to the front of the building and forced her hand to her mouth to stifle a scream. Her eyes widened with recognition. *Simon.* And someone else.

She stood as still as she could and strained to listen.

One voice was mumbled, facing away from her, but Simon's voice was harsh and clear as he said, "Don't worry. I know the owner. She's not going to know, and even if she did, I *own* her. She'll be one of mine soon. Trust me."

Annie's eyes couldn't grow any wider, but they wanted to in shock. *Simon! What are you doing?*

The other voice talked for a moment, and she couldn't make anything out at first.

Then Simon laughed and argued, "Who do you think you're talking to? I'm not some trash dealer off the street. Don't even try to rip me off."

"I'll tell the world about those girls I saw in the warehouse," the other voice threatened.

Girls? In a warehouse? What could he possibly mean? Annie thought.

"I know what you do," the other man threatened. "I'll tell the whole world how you drug those girls and keep them locked up. I'll tell everyone how you make your money!"

"You don't know anything. You don't even know the tip of it, you coward, and don't act like you haven't partaken in my underworld, you dog. The world thanks me on a daily basis for my contributions. They don't need to know how I do it." Simon sneered, half defending himself and half incriminating himself.

They continued to argue fiercely and roughly, and Annie thought if she squatted down she might be able to watch them without being seen. They were fighting over money, blackmailing and threatening each other with torture, death, and curse words Annie had never heard. Annie heard Simon growl and push the other man.

Staggering, he lunged back at Simon just as Annie saw the glint of the streetlight on the knife Simon raised over his head. He pushed it deep into the man's flesh, slicing through coat and shirt straight to the heart. The man crumpled over the knife and Simon. Simon shoved him off, and Annie heard the man's skull crack against the pavement with a sickening sound. Simon dragged him over behind the dumpster and bent over to search the man.

Annie fell back off of her haunches onto the sidewalk, and she scrambled back against the wall. *Get inside!* Her head screamed, but she couldn't seem to get her body to cooperate. She didn't know how long his back would be turned, and finally, she gathered herself up and ran for the door. Her heels sounded like a typewriter on the sidewalk, and she knew the sound would give her away. As she turned the key in the lock and ducked inside, she heard Simon yell, "Who's there?"

Locking the door, she felt her phone vibrating. *Was it Simon? Was he checking? Could she play it off as if she hadn't seen anything and she had just arrived?*

It was Leo.

"Leo, don't talk. Call 911."

"What? Annie, are you...what is happen—"

"Leo. 911 NOW! Theater. Simon. Help me. 911," was all she could stammer out before Simon was pounding on the door with a deranged look in his eyes while sweat soaked his thick hair and made it curl at the ends. His hands were stained with blood, and they shook with fury.

Annie jumped at his fists pounding on the glass. Her heart was crashing in her chest, and she felt her body start to shake. *This is not real. This is not happening,* she tried to tell herself, but Simon barking at her through the glass told her it was a lie.

"Annie, you've got to let me in," he growled through gritted teeth and a wicked snarl. His breath was labored. Annie shook her head in fear.

I'm in here. He's out there. We should keep it that way. Right?

He growled deeper at her, "Annie, let me in. That wasn't what you thought it was. Let me in. I can explain everything."

Annie shook her head again.

"I saw you," she said, her voice shaking and full of fear.

Her phone rang, and it made her jump. She dropped it but saw that it was Leo. She reached for it, but as she did, Simon tapped on the glass and shook his head. Annie reached a little farther, and Simon placed his knife against the glass as a silent threat and began pounding ruthlessly on the door again. Annie held her hand on the phone long enough to slide her finger along the "accept" button as she released the phone in surrender.

"Leo. I love you," she whispered, hoping he could hear it. As Simon came crashing through the glass, lunging at her, she knew that Leo would hear that too.

Annie tried to scramble away from Simon, but he caught her.

"You're not going anywhere!" Simon yelled as he pinned her beneath him.

"Simon," Annie said in a raspy voice as she struggled against him on the carpet, feeling the glass scraping against and embedding in her skin. The rising dread in her stomach turned to a pure fear the farther it crept up her throat. "I saw you..."

"You don't know what you saw. If you quit fighting me, we could work this out."

She shook her head and felt the full force of his palm on her cheek. It pushed her head into the glass, sending shockwaves of hot pain rippling through her left eye and temple.

"Quit fighting me!"

"I saw you kill a man," Annie whispered as she kicked his knee as hard as she could manage.

He cursed her and fell a few steps away, long enough for her to get to her office, but he grabbed her by her hair and threw her against the desk, knocking photographs off and gashing her forehead, blood running down over her right eye. The pain swelled and throbbed, causing Annie to struggle to sit up. She knew she needed to try to get away from him. The blood was warm on her cheek and smelled metallic, which made her gag. Her head was swimming, and her body felt limp.

"Don't make me the bad guy. I never wanted you to get hurt. Didn't I tell you that I get what I want?"

That's when she saw the glint in his eye and his fist tighten and then quickly hide from her sight behind his back. He pretended to soften his face, but she knew it was just a diversion.

Annie tried to stand, propping herself against the desk, hoping to find something to protect herself with. She slowly tried to move away from him as he talked. *Are there scissors in the top drawer?*

"Annie, listen. Beautiful Annie. You just need to understand. I can make you understand." He firmly grabbed her wrist, seeing that she was trying to move away from him. She couldn't reach the top drawer, and there was nothing on her desk to use, at least, nothing he couldn't get to first and use against her.

"I do understand, Simon. You're a drug dealer, a bully, and a murderer," Annie managed to say in a steady tone, masking the horror clawing at her. "I heard what that guy has on you! Where are the girls? Are you going to kill me too?"

Simon slammed his fist down against the wall next to her, cracking the drywall. Then a wicked smiled rippled across his face, and his eyes sneered at her.

"I always get what I want—by any means necessary, Annie. If I want something, I get it. I want money, I want power, and I want you."

"Simon, stop pretending that you didn't do this. They are coming for you. They will find you," she said, out of breath.

He took a swift step toward her, grabbing her right shoulder. Annie tried to rip it away from him, but she wasn't strong enough.

"Babe," he said in a forced tone. His grip tightened, and his body tensed as he moved inches closer.

"I'm not your babe. We just met a few days ago!" Knowing her courage was foolish but also knowing she was probably about to die anyway, she continued, "And I just saw you..."

"You are the only one who saw anything. Maybe we can come to an understanding about what you saw."

"I know what I saw."

His eyes filled with soft lies, and his face became a smooth watery grave. *Or maybe I'm about to black out,* Annie thought. As her head began to swarm with what felt like bees, she watched as the smoothness on his face shattered as he screamed in anger. He began to burn a fiery red behind his cheeks and neck. Annie felt sickening horror swallow her and could almost see evil swirling above their heads.

"If you can't cooperate, Annie, maybe they won't find you. You can still save yourself. You can give me what I want and save yourself."

Annie's simple "No" in reply launched his palm of iron against her chest, landing her against the wall. He pinned her there, her feet barely touching the ground. Her head hit the wall with such force she couldn't open her eyes, and she thought for sure the back of her head was now bleeding. He had a hand at her throat and one at her waist. His grip was sickening and squeezing the breathing out of her. If she could have breathed, she would have vomited. She felt him rip her shirt, but she didn't look.

His voice sounded like a shotgun as it blasted in her face, "I ALWAYS GET WHAT I WANT!"

If she opened her eyes, she thought for sure she'd see his face transformed into a wild animal or a demon. His breath sounded snarly, and his hands felt more like giant paws that were clumsy yet brutishly strong. His screams of wicked passion were evil and hellish as he tore at the rest of her clothes. Annie struggled and clawed at him, screaming for help, wishing she could die.

He took from her what he wanted.

After he was done, she felt the tip of death slice across her wrists, leaving her ice cold with pain. Dizziness and nausea overtook her. *Good, death is near.*

Annie fell onto the floor as he let her drop. He released her, and her shoulder cracked as her body crumpled down onto it.

She could hear distant trickling, maybe from the lobby. She could smell gasoline, and the fumes made her stomach heave, but her body didn't move. She heard footsteps and crackling. She thought she called out, but no one was there. She couldn't hear her own voice. Her eyes didn't open to see if he was still there. Then it seemed that she was lifted off the ground, floating away on the fumes.

Death felt strange.

14. A RESCUE AND A REFILL
PENUMBRA, PRESENT DAY

Annie took a breath and released it through pursed lips. The weight she had carried for so long still sat heavy on her shoulders, though it felt a bit lighter now.

She slowly found Mace's gaze, which seemed made of stone, and then she looked to Chuck, whose eyes were filled with an all too familiar horror.

Give them time. Let them feel it, she felt prompted by an inner voice. She welcomed the instruction and stood to refill her coffee. She brought the carafe back to the table and refilled theirs as well. Their bodies hadn't moved, they hadn't watched her refill their coffee, and their eyes hadn't strayed from where she had been sitting.

Wiping the counter and rinsing a few dishes, she watched them from the sink, wondering what she should do next and how she should tell the next part. The story wasn't over, and the burden wasn't completely lifted.

By the time she finally sat back down at the table, Chuck seemed to swallow his horror, but she saw his brokenness and smiled at him sympathetically.

"I have so many questions, but it seems insensitive to ask you anything at all," he said, letting the conflict he felt seep into his voice.

Annie nodded. "I know it's heavy," she said while glancing at Mace, who was just emerging from his stony expression, though he did not look at her. "If you need some time, we can finish later, but I can handle questions if you want to ask."

"I don't even know where to start. Did Leo hear your goodbye? How did you escape the fire? Did they catch Simon?"

Part of the burden belongs to Leo. Let him help lift it. She felt the prompting again.

"Wait here. I can answer those questions better another way." She headed out the side door to the barn.

Both Chuck and Mace looked at each other bewildered and then jumped up to watch her out the window above the sink. The porch light revealed her walking across the gravel drive to the barn. They could barely hear her slide the big heavy door to the left. As they stared, another figure emerged, taller than Annie. They talked, Annie hugged the figure, and they began to walk slowly back toward the house.

Mace and Chuck quickly returned to their seats at the table and silently sipped on their coffee. Their heads turned as the kitchen door swung open, revealing a young cowboy standing over six feet tall. He had shaggy blonde hair, and he wore a red buffalo plaid shirt with jeans. His face was tanned and dirty like the work gloves that jutted from his back pocket.

Chuck shot Mace a quizzical look before he said, "This can't be..." but before he could finish, Annie entered right behind the cowboy.

She put a hand on the cowboy's shoulder and said, "Leo can tell this part of the story better than I can. Guys, meet Leo."

"He's here? I'm so confused." Mace's mind raced in circles. *Was he here before when I was first here? Does he live here?*

Annie walked Leo to the table, sat him down, and then slid into the chair next to him. She patted his arm for reassurance though his face showed no comfort from her touch. His stoic expression matched his hesitant eyes.

Annie saw the hardened, untrusting lines on his forehead, and she leaned in close and whispered to him, "You don't have to trust them; just trust me. I'm right here."

He bit the inside of his mouth and then nodded without looking at her.

"What do you want to know first?" he asked Chuck solemnly, not even acknowledging Mace was sitting at the table.

"I just asked Annie whether you heard her goodbye to you on the phone. Also, how did she escape the fire?"

Leo gave Annie a glance, and she nodded, saying, "It's okay, I've already told them up to the point where I passed out. They know. We can tell them everything."

Leo took a deep breath and began to tell his side of the story from seven years ago.

CHICAGO, SEVEN YEARS AGO

Leo screamed into the phone as Annie whispered her love and goodbye. He had cursed God as he heard the glass crashing and the struggle. He cursed himself for not meeting her at the theater earlier like he wanted to.

He hated himself for not answering her call and telling her about his nightmares. They had all been about her. Now they were reality, and he couldn't get to her fast enough. The moment she had said, "Help me," he had jumped in his car and run six red lights trying to get to her. He called 911 but knew help might be too late.

Annie was strong, but would she be strong enough? He hit the wheel with his fist. *Why did I leave? I was there this afternoon. I should have just stayed.* He ran another red light, and his tires squealed as he turned left. He was so close. His heart was pounded through his chest, and his whole body was sweating.

As he turned the second corner, his heart stopped at the sight of the theater on fire, and he felt his blood go cold. All his thoughts drained from his head. He saw himself open the car door and pull the emergency brake, but couldn't feel anything. He jumped out and began to run, leaving the car in the road. His legs felt like lead.

The front left side of the theater was engulfed in flames. Through the broken glass door, he could see the smoky layer that covered the whole room. Then he spotted Annie beneath half of a bookshelf that had fallen over on her. *She's not moving.* He yelled, cursed, kicked more of the glass off the door, and stepped through. He pulled off his t-shirt and covered his mouth with it. At first, he couldn't see, but as his eyes adjusted to the smoke, he ran over to the fallen bookshelf.

"Annie!"

There was no response.

"Annie, it's Leo! Can you hear me?"

There was nothing.

"Oh, God, help us!"

He dropped the t-shirt and tried to push the shelf. The books and the shelf had wedged her between the floor and the wall. He couldn't lift it. The flames were crawling the walls and throbbing with sweltering heat.

Panic ripped through his joints. He felt stiff and cold even though his eyes were stinging from the sweat flowing from his forehead. The blaze was growing quickly. He probably couldn't move the shelf; he would just have to try to drag her out from under them. He reached under the shelf and found her arms.

He pulled her toward himself, and he heard her shoulder crack. As he lifted her arms, he saw blood all over her, covering the floor and the books.

Where is all the blood from?

Then he saw her wrists, dripping and now running down his arms. He felt sick horror rising in his throat, and he knew he had to get her out faster. There was no time to vomit and no time for fear. He ripped his t-shirt in two and used each half to bind the cuts on her wrists. Then he gripped each of her arms and pulled. Her torso slid easily along the wood floor her father had insisted on. He got her torso free and then reached back under the shelves and tucked his forearm under her legs. He pulled. Something was stuck. He grabbed at her knee-high boots and shoved the shelf haphazardly, hoping to jar her feet free.

Just then, a ceiling tile broke and crashed to the floor, sending up a flare and sparks. Leo was out of time. He yanked at her legs. He ripped at the shelf. Finally, her boot came loose, and he pulled her whole body free. With every ounce of his eighteen-year-old body's strength, he knelt down and picked her up, one arm beneath her legs, the other around her torso.

Her head and arms fell lifelessly to the side. Almost the whole room was on fire, and he couldn't breathe or see. He stumbled along the wall to the door. He tried to get through the door again, carrying her. He carefully stepped through, trying not to let shards of glass from the door snag on her, but he felt one tear through his back and another rip at his forearm. His body didn't even react to the pain. There was no time.

The cool night air sent sharp pains through his lungs. He gasped for air as they both tumbled to the ground outside the door. Leo crawled a few yards away from the door and dragged her closer to him. He held her limp body. She wasn't breathing.

"Annie, wake up. Annie, can you hear me?"

He brushed her hair from her ash-covered face. He gently set her head down on the pavement, opened her mouth, and put his mouth over hers. He blew as forcefully as he could three times and then pressed her chest as he coughed and sucked air to try to do it again.

"Annie! Come on, Annie. Don't go."

He blew again and pounded on her chest. He did it again. And again. Lightheaded, he felt his head sway. He blew in her mouth once and hit her chest.

"Annie! Come on. Don't do this!"

He hit her chest once more with his fist and fell to the pavement beside her. She coughed. Her chest convulsed, her back arched, and she rolled to the side and coughed again. She fell back to the ground, and he saw her chest rise and fall harshly. She was gasping. He couldn't see anymore, but he reached out for her; he grabbed her bloody, bandaged wrist and pulled her toward him as he passed out. Blackness engulfed him as he heard sirens coming from somewhere.

God, help us, was his last thought.

15. A TRAIL RIDE AND BLUEBERRY PANCAKES
PENUMBRA, PRESENT DAY

Annie's hand was in his, and Leo brushed tears off his cheeks with the back of his other hand. She whispered a "thank you" to him, and he squeezed her hand before pushing off the table and disappearing down the hall.

Annie turned her attention to the men still sitting at her table. It was well after 3 a.m., and she was mentally and physically exhausted.

Chuck started, "I don't know what to say, Annie. I'm in clinical shock, I think."

"He's bigger than I thought he'd be," Mace muttered.

All that, and that's what he has to say? Annie thought. She said dryly, "Yeah, I guess he grew some since this all happened."

Chuck scowled at Mace, and Mace just shrugged. Chuck asked, "How did you recover? Why is Leo here with you guys? Where is Simon? Were you in witness protection? If so, why are you able to tell us this now?"

Annie sighed heavily. "There's much more to the story. All the questions will be answered in due time, I promise, but for tonight, we all need to rest. We can revisit this tomorrow with fresh eyes," she said, glancing at Mace.

She showed Mace and Chuck to the guest room and made sure they had pillows and towels. After bidding them goodnight, she trudged back down to the kitchen. She had a hard time going to bed with dirty dishes in the sink. She found Leo leaning on the counter, arms crossed on his chest.

"I thought you would already be asleep by now," she said in a hushed voice.

"I checked on Sammy and then wanted to check on you."

"For me, it's the dishes. For you, it's us. We can't sleep until we're sure everything's safe and tidy." She smiled at him through her heavy lashes. "Thank you, Leo. It wasn't easy, not for you or me."

"Are you okay?" He stood over her protectively.

"I'm okay," she said, wiping the cup, placing it in the cupboard, then turning to him, and opening her arms for a hug. He was still

121

young and hard as a rock, but Annie hugged him like a pillow. "Are *you* okay, Leo?" She pulled away enough to look up at him.

"Sure," he said roughly.

"Really? This is Annie you're talking to."

"I don't trust that Mace guy."

Annie let go of him, put her right palm upon his heart, and said, "The heart is wicked. You are right. Until it has the love of the Father in it."

"Is that why they are here?"

"I think so. They just don't know it yet."

Once all the cups were hanging in the cupboard and the kitchen lights were out, Annie climbed the stairs listening closely at the top. Smiling at the sound of several harmonized octaves of snoring, she slipped quietly into her room and collapsed on her bed, not bothering to change clothes. Closing her eyes, she welcomed the thick darkness, but before she completely surrendered to sleep, she whispered to the ceiling, "Father, I have a house full of men." As she voiced that sentence, she planted a palm on her forehead. "They all need You in different ways. One is young, one is old, and several are just lost. Would You help me show them who You are?" Annie laughed as she added, "Also, help them all sleep in."

She smiled as she fell into peaceful sleep for the first time in years. No fire threatened her dreams. Instead, she dreamed of golden pastures waving in the wind, people singing, and pink fluffy cupcakes.

Down the hall in the guest room, Mace wrestled in his sleep and dreamed his sheets crawled on him and tried to strangle him, but he clawed at them and threw them off the bed. His mind felt foggy, and no matter how he tossed, he couldn't shake the dreams of broken glass melting in the blaze all around him. Books fell on his head, and he shielded himself and someone else on the floor. An army of disfigured, costumed zombies came after him chanting lies and whispering venomous ideas. As he fell to the ground, they disappeared, and he screamed to the void in his dream, "*I could have saved her.*"

A different voice, maybe in the dream, maybe in his room, spoke deeply to him: *It is not about you.*

The voice was warm and comforting even though it reprimanded him. As it spoke, he relaxed and slipped into a dreamless sleep.

Chuck lay on the floor, listening to Mace wrestle. Then he heard the voice too. He froze. He listened to Mace muttering things in his sleep that he couldn't understand, but he swore he had heard another voice.

Though he didn't move, he looked around the dark room. There was no one there. The voice had authority and a slight danger in its tone of warning, though something about it made Chuck feel safe and at home. He relaxed.

"If it isn't about us, then what's it about?" he whispered aloud. Any other day, Chuck would have laughed at himself for talking out loud to no one, but here in the dark, he felt something in the air, something in the room. Remaining motionless in fear of the presence, he waited, hoping for an answer. Then as if someone had leaned down to his ear, he felt more than heard a whisper.

Look for Me, and you will find Me.

Startled that the voice was so close, maybe even inside his head, Chuck sat up, not caring if he shattered the magical heaviness in the air. No one was there. The air returned to normal, cool and crisp coming through the vent near him on the floor. Mace was snoring and still. Chuck lay back down, weary from the long day and the unexplained voice he had heard, and he drifted away to sleep.

Annie's eyes fluttered open at the sound of Leo's truck grumbling down the driveway. *He must be taking Sammy into town.* Stretching underneath her fluffy down comforter, she rolled over to see the alarm clock on her bedside table. It read 8:32 a.m. She had slept so well she could have sworn someone was gently holding her.

Like wings rather than arms, she thought, which made her smile.

Standing and stretching once more, she slipped out of yesterday's clothes and tossed them in a basket by the door before going to turn on the shower. Steam rose from the shower and billowed over the curtain. A knock at the door brought a stitch of panic in her stomach; she wasn't used to having extra people in the house. She should have locked her door. She grabbed her robe and walked to the door.

"Who is it?"

"Just me, Annie." Relaxing at the sound of Sam's voice, Annie poked her head through, clutching tightly to the top of her robe, just in case someone else walked by.

"I thought you went into town with Leo."

He shook his head. "The game is not until after lunch. I thought you might need me."

"I'd love to have you with us this morning, and I'd love some coffee." She smiled at his sweet wrinkled face.

He poked her on the nose. "Anything for my Annie. Pancakes?"

"Now you're just showing off."

When Annie got out of the shower, she smelled coffee wafting up the stairs and mixing with the aroma of blueberries and batter. *He really is showing off,* she thought. She heard mixed voices and wondered who was up. Slipping into jeans and a thermal shirt, she quickly made the bed and swept up socks and boots before hopping down the stairs.

Sam was busy at the griddle when she set her boots down by the door and padded across the kitchen to kiss him on the cheek, saying, "I didn't give you a proper morning kiss."

"You've never been proper, dear."

Annie knew he was teasing her, and it made her laugh. Sam woke up sunny and spicy, she always said.

"It's true, but I'll kiss you still," she said, giving him another peck on the cheek while grabbing a coffee mug. As she poured the bold black deliciousness, she wished for an IV rather than a cup, and then she noticed the men at the table staring at her.

"You two look terrible. Did you sleep at all?" she asked sadly.

They both exchanged glances. Mace spoke first. "I eventually slept, but I feel like I wrestled a bear all night."

Chuck glared at him. "You did, dude. I got no peace from your snoring and tossing and talking."

"Ugh," Mace grunted and put his head on the table.

Annie moved to collect more coffee cups and plates. Sam tossed her pancakes, and she plated them. Soon both Mace and Chuck were shoveling pancakes into their mouths and guzzling coffee. After the first round, the color was brightening in their faces, and the deep purple bags under their eyes were softening and retreating.

Sam turned to Annie with a spatula in his hand and a towel over his shoulder and asked, "How far did you get last night?"

"Leo saving me."

"Ah," he said in understanding. "The story has taken its toll, but it's not found its hope yet."

Annie smiled at an idea she had. "Men of L.A.? Are you ready for fresh air?"

Both, with forks full and headed to their mouths, smiled. Chuck nodded, and Mace shrugged.

"When will Leo be back?" Annie asked.

"Should be anytime," Sam answered.

"While they finish up, I'm going out to the barn," Annie said, yanking on her boots, "to saddle up."

Chuck's head popped up, his mouth full of pancake. "Saddle up what?"

Annie laughed and walked out the door. Leo was driving back up to the house as she walked across to the barn.

Chuck and Mace scrambled to finish their plates and swallow their coffee. Sam threw several pairs of boots on the floor, saying, "See what fits ya."

Chuck laughed trying on a pair of black snakeskin boot that were worn soft. "This is not what my usual creative process looks like, but I like it."

He looked over at Mace, who was staring at the boots. He slapped him on the shoulder. "Harlen, what's going on with you, man?"

"I don't know. It just seems like too much. I don't want to tell this story. How can we? How is she okay? I'm not really thinking right."

Thinking back to last night, Chuck said, "I hear you, Harlen, but I get the feeling that it's not about us."

Mace stared at him with wide eyes, wondering how Chuck could know he'd heard those exact words in his dream.

"Maybe we need to think less about our project and just listen," Chuck continued, "I have the feeling it will make sense soon."

"I thought we were writing one story," Mace said, "and now...now it's just so much bigger than my accidental arrival in a small town."

"The best stuff, Harlen, is always bigger than ourselves," Chuck said, not knowing where his wisdom was coming from. "Come on, you heard her. Saddle up," he joked, slapping Mace's shoulder again. He exited the kitchen, leaving Mace slouched in the chair, pulling on a pair of brown boots with multicolored stitching all over.

Outside, Leo had all the horses standing in a row, saddled and ready. Sam stood close to Annie talking quietly, and they looked as if they were making plans. Leo was showing Chuck the proper way to mount a horse when Mace joined them. Mace watched Chuck sit awkwardly atop the horse, and at the very least, that sight provided a laugh.

Annie darted her eyes to him; she hadn't heard him laugh since they'd been here, had she? Leo was instructing Chuck to relax and telling him how to control the animal. Annie watched Mace for a moment. Mace was watching Chuck but listening to Leo. She grabbed her reins and stepped into the stirrup, swinging her right leg over. Sam did the same, only needing a steady hand from Leo at the last second.

Soon enough, they were all on horseback and following Leo's lead across the pasture behind the house. They followed Leo single file down a well-worn path. It was early fall, and Annie breathed in the slight hint of crispness that could disappear if you breathed in too hastily. The trees in the distance were bursting into flames of color, which Leo noted casually to Annie.

"I know—it's surprising considering the heat we had this summer," she replied. "I thought for sure all the color dried up, and we wouldn't see any. It's rare here in Texas." Annie turned slightly in her saddle to look back toward Mace and Chuck, pointed, and said, "See that range over there? That's what we call 'The Window.' We live right on the border between two different types of country. We live in Texas hill country, and over there, that's call Big Bend country. When we get to the top, you'll see why they call it that."

"Leo," Chuck shouted from the back of the line. Leo grunted in acknowledgment. "How in the world did you go from theater to horses? I mean that seems like a huge jump."

Mace jumped in. "First, I want to know how he got here."

"On a bus," Leo said.

Sam heard Annie sigh deeply, so he halted his horse and turned him sideways to block off the trail to Mace and Chuck. They pull their horses up short.

"God and Annie have a reason for everything. Now shut it and enjoy the ride."

They nodded with stunned faces. Leo let out a belly laugh from the front that made Mace cringe. Chuck took Sam's words and let them soak in like the sweat ring on his collar. As a breeze came swirling through from the south, Chuck felt something shift inside. He began to catalog everything he saw in his mind—every spiny lizard perched on a red rock, every cactus, and every single tumbleweed.

Mace looked around for something to take his mind off the fact that he couldn't seem to get in rhythm with the horse. He found himself watching Annie in front of him. Her hair flapped wildly as she rode. His eyes wandered from her hair down her back, and he watched the rhythm of her hips in the saddle. He shifted in the saddle, uncomfortable with his own thoughts. Still, he took in the sight of her and enjoyed his vantage point until Chuck's voice behind him broke his stare. He cursed his thoughts and himself. He wondered if he were any different than any other scumbag. He doubted he was. He cursed himself again and accidently dug his heel into the horse.

The horse that Annie had called Cadillac responded to his ill-placed kick fluidly. Mace felt its muscles shift into high gear, and before he knew what he'd done wrong, the horse was galloping wildly off the path, away from the others. Mace grasped at the reins but instead dropped them down in front of the horse's nose. He was out of control.

"Harlen!" Chuck yelled, causing everyone to turn just in time to see the horse carry Mace away. Leo gave Annie a look that Chuck couldn't read, and he took off after Mace, riding furiously.

"That boy had it coming, I'm afraid," Sam said, gruffly shaking his head.

Chuck wiped his forehead with the back of his head. "I don't know what's gotten into him."

Annie said nothing but simply dismounted and walked a little off the path over to a clump of trees with a small creek that ran alongside it. She let the reins fall and allowed her horse to drink. Sam nodded and followed, suggesting Chuck do the same.

"Can Leo catch him?" Chuck seemed, looking back in the direction Mace had run.

"Yeah, Leo will catch him. He might let the horse scare him a bit before he does, though." Sam laughed.

Chuck waited for a minute before asking what Sam meant, and he watched Annie. She seemed lost in thought and holding back her words. She stood near the creek, but her eyes looked out toward the hills. A breeze broke through the trees, and she closed her eyes as if the breeze spoke to her and she was listening.

"Leo will get through to him. It's providence. Sam, if you'll help me with this next part, I'll tell it." Her voice was sure and sweet. Chuck straightened up.

"I'm all yours. No more questions. I'm listening."

16. SEDATIVES AND ROASTED MARSHMALLOWS
CHICAGO, SEVEN YEARS AGO

Voices faded in and out like shadows in the night, creating doubt in her mind whether she was awake or asleep. Lights dimmed and flickered, passing over her in rows. She smelled smoke like dwindling campfire. She tried to smile at the thought of the smell, but her face wouldn't react.

Once when she was ten years old, she had visited Sam at the ranch. They hiked to the back forty and camped for two days. They slept under the stars and roasted everything over a great fire. Annie loved visiting her uncle. He always made her feel like they were having big adventures even though they never went more than forty acres from the house.

In her current foggy state, Annie thought she heard Sam's voice. She wondered if it was part of the memory, but then it blended with a woman's voice that she didn't recognize. She didn't know what they were talking about. She tried to ask, but they didn't hear her. Maybe she didn't speak loud enough or in the right direction; she couldn't even tell where they were. She couldn't lift her head to look around; it was too heavy. She heard their voices again. They said her name and Leo's name.

Where's Leo? He left hours ago—she needed to tell them that. She shouted at Sam, trying to get his attention.

The lights passed over her faster and faster until they blurred together into one long bright streak that changed from fluorescent white to gold. Somehow, she felt she was falling into the gold light, even though it was above her. She wanted to tell Sam where she was going, but then she wasn't sure if Sam was there. Hadn't she heard his voice?

She didn't resist the warm light as it flowed all over her body and made her feel diluted and thin inside. The gold grew darker and turned to purple, such a dark purple that it became black. It was black for a very long time.

Even though everything was a deep, soothing black, spots of fiery red inside her throbbed and burned. She couldn't tell where they were, just that they stayed in one place and grew hotter and hotter.

Then the darkness grew more relaxing, so she forgot about the spots. She sank into the blackness and determined she should stay here for a while. It felt like taking a hot bath in the dark.

She waited there in the dark for days or maybe years—she didn't know. She kept waiting for her eyes to adjust to the darkness so she could see an oasis or something besides the dark, but it was just darkness until she heard Sam's voice again. *He is here!*

"How's the boy?" he asked.

She wanted to tell him she didn't know what he was talking about. *What boy?*

"Tell him he can come sit with me if he likes. I can help him get around a bit," he said soberly.

Annie wanted to ask him why she had to tell the boy that. She didn't even know which boy he meant.

She heard feet shuffling and something being scooted across a floor. There were people in the room. *What room am I in?* She heard other voices now. Male.

"How is she?"

It was Leo! Leo was here! What was he doing? She wanted to ask, but her mouth weighed a hundred pounds. She couldn't even make noise. Her throat felt like it was made of heavy, shattered glass.

"She is doing well. She's all stitched up, and the sedatives should wear off soon. Everything went well. We ran all the tests we could, so we should know a few more things soon. Be careful when she wakes up; she may not remember what happened. We need to let her come to that on her own terms."

The words echoed through the chamber of her mind. *What had happened? I don't know.*

"How you feeling, kiddo?" Sam asked.

"I've been better, but they got me all sewn up. I should be good in a couple of weeks. They gave me some good stuff for the pain." It was Leo talking.

What did he have sewn up? What happened to him? How come they can't hear me? The blackness lifted to the same purple as before and then the gold, but instead of making her feel fluid, the colors were just moving away from her. She felt the fiery darts again, and then she felt her body return to its normal weight. She could finally turn her head. She turned it toward the voices.

She heard an "Oh!" as she slowly opened her eyes. There were two blurry forms sitting in front of her and a blue wall behind them. Annie rolled her head back up. Above her was a white ceiling with shadows on it. She rolled her head the other way; there was a window with blue curtains. Outside the window was a tree and brilliant blue sky. She rolled her head back to the blobs as they came into focus. It was Sam and Leo. Annie smiled. They stood up quickly and came to the edge of the bed. She realized she was lying down. She looked at the walls again.

"Hospital?" she managed to croak through the broken glass in her throat. They both smiled softly at her.

"Yes," Sam whispered.

"Oh." She looked at Leo.

Annie studied his face. It was tired and broken. He was bandaged all along his right forearm and around his waist. She pointed at his bandages and looked confused. He grabbed her finger. His hand was cold.

"I'm fine."

She looked at Sam. He had deep circles under his eyes. He smiled at her.

"How do you feel, Annie-girl?" He patted her head and brushed her face with his hand.

She felt one of the fiery spots flame up. It must be in her head, she decided. Leo was still holding her finger, and he squeezed it gently. Sam touched her face again.

"Does your head hurt?"

Annie nodded.

"Okay, I'll get the nurse. Anything else hurt?"

She shifted in the bed to find the other spots. There was one on each wrist, which was heavily bandaged, and one on her leg. She pointed to each one, and then she remembered the shattered glass and pointed to her throat.

Leo and Sam looked at each other. Sam nodded and left the room. Leo handed her a plastic glass of water. He helped her lift her head to take a drink. The shattered glass softened a bit, and everything faded back into blackness.

She dreamed that she was on stage, wearing a Wonder Woman suit, and some people grabbed her from behind. They gagged her so she can't scream, and she had no super powers. She tried and tried, but her powers were gone, and her attackers were too strong. Nearby were women in chains, and she couldn't get to them. Then suddenly the room was on fire, she was on fire, and she smelled blood.

Annie woke up screaming. *What happened? Does Sam know? We have to help those girls.* She thought nonsensical and frantic thoughts.

Sam came running in the room, and suddenly, she remembered everything. She cried hysterically for three hours until Sam had them sedate her again so she could rest.

She didn't dream that time. She was glad. She didn't want to relive it again and didn't want to see Simon's face or hear the foul things he had yelled at her.

She woke up slowly, but she couldn't open her eyes much because they were too swollen from crying. She blinked heavily, trying to adjust to the light coming from the window. There was someone by the window. It was Leo.

She rolled her head toward him, feeling tears slide from her eyes at the sight of him. His sweet young face was stained with tears, and his eyes were filled with devastation. He turned to her but kept his distance, leaning on the window, clutching his bandaged arm across his chest.

"You were there, weren't you?"

He nodded as the tears fell involuntarily.

"You saved me, didn't you?"

He nodded again.

Annie reached out for him, and he closed the distance between them, grabbing her hand hungrily. Annie closed her eyes and let the tears fall.

"Thank you," she whispered.

Leo sobbed and shook his head. "I didn't get there in time. I'm so sorry, Annie. I tried to get to you..."

Annie forced herself to keep her eyes open and look at his sweet face. She knew if she closed her eyes, Simon would be there, screaming at her.

She took Leo's face in her hands. "You did get to me. You did. You saved me."

"I know, but he..."

Annie put her hand up to his mouth. "Let's not speak of it."

Annie asked for more pain medicine, and soon the nurse returned and ushered out Leo to let her rest. Annie sobbed into her pillow as she felt the medicine drag her under once more. She mourned wildly in her dreams.

Hours later, Leo was at her bedside again, his head resting on the bed near her feet. When he heard her stirring, he sat up and scooted to sit beside her because he didn't have much time.

"Annie," he whispered in an effort not to startle her. Her eyes fluttered.

"I have to go soon. So do you."

"Where are you going?"

"We're in some sort of protection program. Simon is in custody, but they want to keep us safe from his father's reach. It turns out the Gradys are involved in a lot of seedy, underground activities." He instantly regretted sharing so much. She probably wasn't ready for any of that.

"Where will you go?" she questioned with fear in her eyes.

"They won't tell me, but I promise you, when this is all over, I will find you. I will keep you safe."

"Leo, I don't understand. Don't say that."

"It's what best friends do."

Annie leaned her head back against the pillow in surrender. Her tears began again. She needed him, and she didn't know if she could get through this without Leo, her savior. "Leo, I love you—"

"Don't. You tried to say goodbye to me once, and it almost killed me. Don't do it again. This is not goodbye. I will find you." He leaned down and kissed her on the cheek, letting his tears fall on hers.

Within minutes, he was ushered away, and he was gone. Within an hour, she was
loaded into a helicopter and flown elsewhere.

17. A LASSO AND MOUTHFUL OF DIRT
PENUMBRA, PRESENT DAY

Leo's back throbbed as he fought to catch up to Mace and the runaway horse. He brought his rope out and looped his lasso. He would try to ride up alongside and grab Mace off, but in case he couldn't, he'd have to throw a rope over the horse's neck. His hat had flown off as he spurred his horse into a gallop, and his long hair whipped wildly against his ears and neck. He pressed the horse beneath him as hard as he could, and finally, he galloped fiercely next to the runaways.

Mace's biceps burned as he held to the saddle horn and struggled to stay on the horse. He saw Leo pull up beside him. Mace knew he had no idea how to stop the horse on his own, but the sight of Leo still tore his stomach in anger. *I don't need this kid's help*, he thought.

"Get away!" he shouted above the pounding.

"Grab my hand. Jump!" Leo shouted back, offering his hand close enough for Mace to reach it.

"No." Mace glared at Leo, and Leo brought his lasso off of his saddle horn.

"If you don't, I'll have to stop the horse myself, and you're going to get yourself hurt. Just give me your hand!" *What does this city idiot think is going to happen?*

"No!" Mace insisted.

"I either stop the horse, or you have to ride it out," Leo barked. "I doubt you'll last that long."

Leo let his horse fall back a few paces and began lassoing his rope above his head. Mace's face went wild as Leo roped the neck of Mace's horse. Leo let the rope catch and pull tight, instantly pulling the horse to the left. Leo sat strong in his saddle and tugged against the rope. The horse lurched against the lasso and jerked in an effort to slow. Mace bucked off to the right, rolled, and thudded on his back, gasping and heaving. Leo pulled tight on his reins and slowed his own horse while pulling the rope taut, bringing Cadillac near enough that he could reach down to grasp the fallen reins. He walked both horses over to stand above Mace, who was writhing in pain on the ground.

"I ought to latch you on and *drag* you back," Leo barked down at him. Then he jumped down in one swift motion. Leo rubbed the neck of Cadillac and watched Mace roll to his side, still gasping but sneering up at Leo, who was winding up his lasso. Mace mumbled something under his breath and went to stand up. Leo threw the lasso over one shoulder and across his chest, freeing his hands. Then he pushed Mace back down into the dirt.

"What?" Leo yelled. "What do you think you need to say to me? Say it." Leo clenched his fists, ready and willing for the confrontation Mace was bent on starting.

"You didn't save her," Mace said coolly. "You couldn't."

Mace didn't even feel the punch Leo blasted him with, not really. His whole body was already screaming at him from the ride and fall, so the knock to his jaw was just another place that was throbbing.

"You pompous, arrogant son of a—" Leo stopped himself.

Mace went to block another punch, but Leo withdrew and stepped back, taking a deep breath to regain control.

"You all talk about God. Why didn't God save her?" Mace said, kicking the dirt. "I can't write this story because I can't think about her helplessly bleeding in the fire. I can't think about it without somehow hating myself for it. We came here to write something else. I thought the story was about us and our relationship. It was going to be fluff romantic comedy. That stuff sells."

Leo dropped in the sand and dirt beside him. He was exhausted but finally felt some sympathy for this idiot next to him.

"I don't suppose we're all that different," he said, shaking his head. "I hate that, trust me. But we're not. We both, apparently, can't bear for life to be anything but perfect for that woman."

Mace gave him a sideways glance and wiped his face with the sleeve of his shirt. He felt compelled to ask again what Leo and Annie were to each other. *It sounds like Leo loves her,* he thought. *Does she love him? Surely not, he is so young. Why do I care?*

"You don't know how many nights I've lain awake, arguing with God about all the 'I could haves' and the 'if onlys.' In the end, He's got His reasons. Annie knows that better than I do. I just know He turned our tragedy into something surprisingly beautiful, and it'll grow into something greater than we could've ever been." Leo paused and looked back toward where he knew Annie was. "Not that He's surprised—God, I mean. Just me."

There he goes again, Mace thought. *"Our tragedy," he said. Are they together?* Leo interrupted his thoughts, and Mace was glad since he couldn't seem to control them.

"I suppose that won't make much sense to you if you don't believe in God."

"What makes you think I don't?" Mace fired back defensively.

Leo shook his head. "I can just tell, Harlen. You're a self-made man. You're arrogant, and you think you can control everything. The truth is…you can't even control a horse." He stood and dusted himself off and offered a hand to Mace.

Mace refused.

Leo shrugged and stepped up in the stirrup. "That's the trouble with pride, Harlen. It'll run off with you and leave you in the desert to find your way home."

Chuck was speechless, trying to take in the emotions flowing through Annie's story like the creek they sat beside.

Sam touched Annie on the shoulder and said, "Annie, I'll wait here for the others. Why don't you take him up to the ridge?"

Annie asked Chuck, "Want to?"

"You bet. What's up there?"

Annie smiled and shot Sam a look. "You'll see." They both saddled up again, and Chuck tried his best to ride next to her on the path.

Annie's shoulders were relaxed, and she smiled easily at Chuck whenever he would glance at her. He knew he wanted to remember how her hair bounced in the wind and brushed against her shoulders as she rode and the way she patted the neck of her horse reassuringly.

"Sam is the reason I'm alive," she started. "He helped me feel safe again. I couldn't get out of bed for days, and then the days turned into weeks. Daily, he would sit by my bed and read me poetry and songs. He would whisper to me in my sleep about God. Then when I finally felt up to it, we started riding." Annie paused as they climbed up a trail that ended on a cliff jutting out from the hillside like a shelf. "One day he brought me up here," she explained as she swung her leg off her horse and motioned for Chuck to do the same.

The ledge was wide and flat, allowing them to stand side by side with the horses behind them. Annie looped their reins around a tree leaning out of the side of the hill. From the ledge, they overlooked the entire valley and the town. There were rolling plains and plateaus in the distances. The winding rivers with spindly tributaries cut through the landscape without reservation.

At the base of the hillside and the plateaus that surrounded it was thick foliage and tall lush grass, overcast by long shadows of the ranges thrown across the open plain. The further away from the mountain that the landscape traveled, the drier it became until rose up into the center of the town of Penumbra.

"Legend goes that when the settlers came here, they couldn't decide whether to settle in the hills with the shade, thinking they would be hidden, or settle out in the open where they could see their attackers coming."

"Why didn't they choose the shade?"

"They came up to this hillside on a summer day when the shadows were thrown a long way, and right in the center of the valley was where the shade ended. They knew they could always run for the hills and take refuge in the shade but thought it was better to be exposed and ready out in the open than to be always cowering in fear in the hills."

"Hmm," Chuck said as he studied the valley and the shadows that played across the plains. "Penumbra, huh?"

"It's where the shade ends."

"Where the shade ends. I like that."

"Sam brought me up here that day and told me this story just like I'm telling you. He said there was nothing wrong with shade. Every now and then, everyone needs to hide in the shade for a while. The sun can be direct and harsh sometimes, but a person can't hide in the shade forever. He told me there would come a day when everything could be laid bare, and we could stand together in the sun and face the world," Annie said.

Chuck barely breathed, listening to her words as they seemed to float in circles around him. He saw them before him, piecing together.

"How long did you hide in the shade?" he asked.

"About a year," she answered softly, turning to him and wondering what he was thinking.

"What helped you step into the sun?"

"God."

"God?"

"Sam kept whispering to me about God. He never gave up even though I was angry for a long time and blamed this God I said I didn't believe in. When I finally accepted the things Sam was teaching me and praying over me at night, I realized that the thing about hiding is that you feel you are protecting yourself. You are hunkered down with cautious movements and weathered eyes, but you leave no room for someone to save you. The thing about stepping out from the shadows is that you expose yourself for who you are and where you've been. Then you have the chance to be utterly transparent and ask for a savior and a protector."

At her words, Chuck felt the earth shift beneath him, and he braced himself on Annie, who looked stable and sure on her feet.

"Didn't you feel that?"

She smiled. "It happened to me that day too. God will move heaven and earth to help, you see."

Chuck looked around, bewildered at the sensation rising from the earth after it had shaken apparently just for him. The feeling soaked into his boots and warmed them, climbing his legs and circling his waist. He didn't dare move, and the warmth traveled through his arms, across his chest, and up his neck, flushing his cheeks.

Annie watched compassionately and took his hand in hers. His eyes were wide with fascination.

"God helped me step into the world and start living again years ago, but we haven't been able to let everything be exposed until now, until you guys came. God gave you to us so we could step into the sun and face the world with our story."

After a long pause, Chuck asked, "What now?" He shivered down his spine, unsure whether he was asking about God or the story.

"Well," she said, "I think it's time for some baseball."

18. BASEBALL AND CONCESSIONS

The roar from the stands made the earth feel as if it moved. As Mace sat on the metal bleachers beside Chuck, he knew it was just the vibrations from the stands, but after being on a runaway horse, he wished for something steady and unmoving.

The crowd stood, jumped, and stomped in competitive excitement.

"Who knew Little League baseball was so engaging?" Chuck elbowed Mace in the ribs just as Annie stood and yelled something at the umpire, who sneered at her. Sam pulled her back down to the bleachers.

A sandy-haired boy stepped to the plate. He looked like all the others, but he was tall compared to his teammates. He paused above the plate, checking his stance and grip. Then he looked their way. Annie lifted her arm, giving the boy a slight wave and pointed one finger at the sky. The boy did the same.

"Do you teach young kids, too?" Mace looked at Annie quizzically.

"No," Annie said without looking at him.

The sandy-haired boy found his footing at the plate and adjusted his helmet. Taking a practice swing, he nodded to the coach that he understood the signs. Annie sucked in her breath. Mace watched her from the side, realizing she was nervous.

"People around here sure do take sports seriously," Chuck joked while he scarfed down a bag of chips. Sam shook his head as if Chuck had missed something. Mace's body began to feel heavy, and he felt as if he was watching everyone from far away. He thought maybe he was missing something too. What could it be? He started to feel like he didn't understand what they were doing here.

Then, seconds before the stands erupted again, Mace saw it. He noticed the sandy-haired boy's eyes, his nose, and his strong, determined stance.

As his bat connected with the ball, the simple 'clink' regurgitated all the conversations. *Sammy.* All Annie's sidesteps. *Sammy.* All the questions. *Sammy.* All the backpedals.

The boy ran the bases with confidence, and Annie stood on her seat, yelling at the top of her voice. Sam was clapping furiously beside her.

As the boy slid into home plate just for show, it hit Mace like a line drive to the temple. Annie's *son* had just hit a home run. Then as Sam sat back down with a tired *thud* on the bench, Mace realized who Sammy's father must've been, and he ran to the ballpark bathroom and hurled up the nachos he had just eaten.

The rest of the game, he hovered by the bathroom, leaning against the wall watching them. Leo and Annie were so casual with each other, affectionate even. Chuck too. There was something between them. Sam was fatherly with her. As the game ended, Annie ran to Sammy, and they hugged, Annie tousling his sweaty hair.

Is this how she planned for us to find out? Is this why she brought us to the game? Mace found himself wondering. *When would she have told us that part of the story? Would we have met Sammy, or would he still be part of her secrecy? Where has he been all this time? Why do I care? I came here to write a story. I need to be more professional. Just write the movie, Mace, and don't get involved,* Mace chastised himself.

Annie was kissing the top of the boy's head, but her eyes found Mace's, and his dark expression betrayed his thoughts. Her expression fell, and she waved him over. Chuck and Leo had circled around the boy as Mace reluctantly joined them. Annie hugged Sammy to her and spoke slowly but confidently. Her eyes went to Chuck first as she spoke, sensing that he would understand what would follow. She had seen in Mace's eyes that he already knew, but she saw the anger too and knew he wouldn't like what she had to tell them next.

"The final chapter to this story is Sammy." She paused, finding strength in Leo's smile. "Sammy is my son. He just turned seven this year."

Chuck's face was still searching for a way to get his eyebrows to come down when he shook Sammy's hand. "It's a real honor to meet such a baseball star like you, Sammy."

Sammy looked up at Annie with a shining grin. "Mom, I'm a baseball star."

Annie laughed and smiled widely at Chuck. Patting Sammy's back, she sent him after Sam, who was heading for more popcorn at the concession stand.

"I'll, uh, leave you guys to fill in the details. I'll see if I can get some nachos out of Sam," Leo said, winking at Annie.

"You guys feel like sitting or walking or what?"

"Walking," Chuck said, rubbing his backside and pointing to the metal bleachers.

"There's a little walking trail that goes around this whole park," she said, pointing to the trail and waiting to see if Mace would follow. He stared at her blankly with dark, vacant eyes and still hadn't said a word.

"I'm sorry," Chuck whispered as he walked toward her so that Mace wouldn't hear. "He's not responding well."

"It's okay. Give me a second." She patted his arm and moving back toward Mace, who stood planted in the center of the walkway through the center of the ballpark. She walked up to him, boot heels clicking on the pavement. She stood close enough to be able to talk quietly but far enough away that there was no risk of touching him.

"I can tell you're upset." Her words seem to break the vacant trance he was in, and he hung his head, shaking it slowly. He shoved a hand in one pocket and rubbed his chin stubble with the other. "I know this is not the story that you thought you'd be exploring, but 'I don't think it warrants this silent treatment I'm getting from you."

"Have you been hiding him? Where was he the last time I was here? How come you didn't tell me?" Mace finally spoke, as darkness returned to his eyes and anger flared in his nostrils.

Seeing his anger for what it really was—hurt—Annie said his name calmly, "Mace." She watched his shoulders relax and then continued. "The last time you were here, he was at church camp for a whole week, and even if he had been here, in town, I might have kept him from you anyway because I didn't know anything about you, save that you were famous. I couldn't trust you. I didn't know you yet."

"You didn't know me? I'm the one who doesn't feel like I know you now!"

Feeling his anger was unfair and misplaced, Annie reached for his hand and took a step toward him, but he recoiled and stepped further away from her.

"Mace, we spent one day together," she said, trying to sweeten her voice to soften the truth. "What does it even matter that you didn't know everything about my life? We spent only one day together—and quite begrudgingly if I remember, but to hear you tell it…"

A small growl formed on his breath as he pushed passed her and blazed an angry trail for the SUV. Chuck was staring at him wide eyed and opened his mouth to say something, but Mace cussed him. As the engine revved and the tires squealed, Leo came running over to Annie, who was quickly joined by Chuck.

"What was that about?" Leo fired at Annie, concerned.

"He's mad at me for not telling him about Sammy." Annie shrugged, looking defeated. *Or is he mad he wasn't the first to know?*

Leo flared and tensed up. "How can he be mad at you for that? Doesn't he get it?"

Annie stopped him with a hand on his forearm. "No, Leo. He doesn't understand. He can't. It's okay. He just needs to work through all this. It's a lot to process."

Leo relaxed under Annie's touch and calmed his voice. "Are you okay? What did he say to you?"

"I'm fine, Leo. I think I'm going to go to the theater for a while. Do you mind taking Sammy home?"

Leo's eyes narrowed, and he took a step closer to her even though Chuck was watching. "I once let you go to the theater alone against my better judgment. I won't ever make that mistake again. I'll go with you."

"I'll be fine, Leo. You don't need to come." Leo stood a breath away, and Annie's heart raced, either at the thought of being alone in a theater or having Leo stand this close to her possessively...she didn't know which. She felt Chuck's eyes on her and silently willed him to say something.

"I have a lot of questions that we didn't get to talk through because Mace stormed off. Do you mind if I tag along?"

"See, Leo, Chuck will come with me. Is that okay, bodyguard?" Annie teased Leo. He didn't laugh.

"I'll take Sammy home. Call me later," he said as he stalked off.

Annie huffed as she and Chuck turned to walk toward the truck. "Great, now I have two men angry at me. It feels like a storm brewing."

At the theater, Chuck offered, "I've got calls to make and writing to do if you want to be alone."

Annie nodded and said, "Okay, I'll just be in here. If you need me, just text, and I'll come running."

He smiled at her and patted her shoulder. She could tell that he didn't really want to leave her alone, but she was glad that he was willing to. She watched him shut the door to her office, and she turned toward the auditorium.

Annie walked down the aisle, slowly. She took in every inch, even in the dark. She could hear the train outside clanking through town rhythmically. The air conditioner kicked on, and she felt the cool force of air push on her neck and hair. It felt good knowing Chuck was in the building and that she wasn't alone. She'd have to admit that to Leo later.

She'd clicked on the spotlight as she'd entered the theater. It was now glowing brightly on the dark stage. Annie walked to the stage and stepped into the spotlight, closing her eyes and feeling the warmth. She stood there for a long time in silence until a nearby voice threw her off kilter.

"We may have only spent one day together, but I'll be honest, I felt like that one day changed my life. As ridiculous as that sounds now, I thought it back then too. I was even considering this whole concept of God that you talked about. But now...?" Mace's voice bellowed out from the darkness beyond her light. She stood still in the spotlight but allowed her arms to float down to her side, easing the alarm that ate at her heart at the sound of his voice.

"Don't you see why I couldn't tell you?"

"Yes. But no...I mean. Annie? Is your name even Annie?"

Annie didn't say anything. She was frozen in her shoes, and her legs felt like they were sliding down into the floor. Her mind flashed back to Simon's angry face several times, and she felt flushed as if she might pass out. She wished she could blink or twitch her nose and disappear.

"What, Annie? Do you think I'm not supposed to feel betrayed? Or lied to? Do you think I can just forgive you and run to you and sweep you up."

Annie felt like she had to catch her breath after being crushed by his hammering voice. He shouted bitterly from the balcony, but Annie felt like he was standing right in front of her, sneering at her. She desperately tried not to cry.

"No, I guess that only happens in the movies, huh?" she said, feeling like a child.

"You, probably more than anyone, should know that this is real life, no scripts, no cues, and especially no re-shoots. Life can be cruel." He was talking in metaphors, but he was so angry that they weren't very clear.

Annie assumed he was referring to the fire and Simon and Sammy. Just the thought of Simon made Annie's skin crawl. Her heart raced, and she grew defensive. *Life isn't cruel. People are, Mace,* she thought. *You're the one being cruel now.* But she didn't tell him that. Instead, she said, "I'm so tired of that. You know, Mace, you talk about life all the time in terms of scenes and movies, but I don't see you actually living your life. You're too scared to."

"What!?" he bellowed.

Annie couldn't believe they were actually fighting from the stage and the balcony.

"Are you kidding me, Annie? Do you hear yourself right now? You've been hiding here ever since Simon's execution."

Annie couldn't breathe. Her chest felt heavy, and her stomach hurt as if he had just shoved a knife through her. Tears were involuntarily escaping from her eyes. She slipped behind the curtain and ran up the fly stairs. She curled up against the wall and hugged her knees. She felt like she was twelve. She was starting to hyperventilate, and she couldn't believe that he could make her feel this way. He obviously didn't care about her.

Up in the balcony, Mace threw up his hands, kicked the panel of the chair in front of him, and stormed out. He knew he'd feel guilty for saying what he did even as his stomping strides carried him outside to the SUV. He pulled out of the parking lot and drove away. He was leaving town.

He'd driven for 23.7 miles when he passed an abandoned football field. He reversed the truck, pulled off the road, and parked, leaving it running. He slammed his hand down on the wheel, cursing the God she believed in.

How can she believe in God? He practically left her to die, and then when she didn't, He gave her a daily reminder of the horror He's allowed. What kind of God does that?

It was dark now as he sat staring out at the headlights.

Am I angry with her? Am I angry with myself? Why was I so cold to her? Even as he asked himself those questions, all he could see was what was right in front of him—himself. He should have been trying to process all that she had been through, but all he could think about was himself. He grabbed some paper from the backseat and started writing.

He sat in the truck for a long time.

Suddenly, he realized that he couldn't deliver the line that cued the music and faded up the lights. Mace realized he couldn't reshoot the last scene. Up until now, he might have just been acting. This was real, and he couldn't take it back.

She deserved better; she and Sammy both deserved better than that.

Mace climbed back into the SUV and stared at the key in the ignition. *Am I going to leave without saying goodbye?*

"Yeah, I am, and I'm going to leave with a whole slew of other things that I need to get off my chest," he said aloud to no one.

He put the SUV in drive and crept back out onto the highway, back toward town. As he passed the bakery and the theater and turned toward the interstate, he tried not to catalog any details of the town on the way out. He was angry, and he didn't want any of it to matter.

19. THE FLY AND A BAG OF CHIPS

"Annie?" Chuck called out her name in the auditorium. She didn't answer, but he could hear crying from the stage. He ran up the steps.

"Annie," he called again.

She still didn't answer.

Chuck pushed back the curtain. "Annie, where are you? I heard yelling, and I came looking for you. Now I can hear you crying."

A faint "I'm up here" floated down from the fly. Chuck looked up and saw the spiral stairs that led to the walkway around the fly. He went upstairs and saw Annie leaning against the wall as if she were hugging it, her face drenched in tears. Chuck hesitated but then gathered her up in his arms and held her head against his shoulder.

"Annie, what happened?"

Annie just sobbed into his shirt.

"Annie, I need you to breathe. Take a deep breath."

She clutched Chuck's shirt and took a breath slowly, allowing her body to relax.

"Good. Another."

Annie breathed again. She was calming down and had almost stopped crying.

"Mace and I had a huge fight."

"Mace was here?"

"I came in and found him on the balcony—only I was on the stage."

Chuck pulled away and looked at her. He wiped her face and brushed her hair back.

"What did you fight about?"

Annie shook her head. She looked wounded, and Chuck knew that Mace's mouth was unleashed when he was angry. He pulled Annie back into his side and leaned against the wall. She relaxed against him, still trying to catch her breath.

"Listen. Whatever he said was out of line. He didn't mean it, I'm sure."

"You don't have to apologize for him. He did mean it. He was upset that I didn't tell him before, he's angry at God, and he thinks I'm a coward and that I've been hiding."

"Wait what?" Chuck leaned away from her a little so he could look at her. She looked up at him over her shoulder.

"We were in legitimate protective custody only until Simon's execution. After that, we just built our own until all of the Gradys were gone."

"I understand."

"I know you do, and I'm glad you do. But Mace is resisting God, I think, and if he's resisting God, he's going to keep resisting this story. If he's resisting that, then there's not really much of a project."

"I think he just needs to hear all of this. He needs to understand. You need to make him understand. You're very persuasive, you know."

"How can I when he keeps running away?" Annie muttered harshly under her breath.

"I thought you were the ultimate comeback kid. What happened to her? You're just going to let him go?"

"That only applies to things that are worth fighting for."

Chuck moved over in front of her. "What are you saying, Annie?"

"You should have heard the things that he said to me, Chuck. They were heartless and cold. He thinks I'm the coward, but he's the one who's always running away from things. That's even how he got to this town in the first place! He was running away."

"That's not true, Annie."

"It's not, Chuck? Then where is he now? Huh? We trusted him enough to let him into our circle and tell him the story that we've protected all this time, and what does he do? He walks out on it because he wasn't the first to know. It's childish."

"He may have walked out, but I'm still here, Annie. I will write it. All of this will not be in vain." Chuck looked into her hurting eyes and felt a desperate need to fix everything and show her that she was worth fighting for, but the words wouldn't form. The more he thought about words, the more he just wanted to kiss her instead. She stared at him as if she were waiting for an answer, and Chuck bent low and kissed her mouth but didn't bring her close. Annie pulled away quickly.

She stammered, "I'm sorry." She looked away embarrassed.

"No, I'm sorry. I shouldn't have."

"No, it's not that. It's just that caught me off guard. It felt a little..."

"Stolen?" Chuck admitted as he tucked her hair behind her ear, hoping she wouldn't retreat from his touch. Annie shook her head.

"No, maybe foreign?"

Chuck fell back against the wall, realizing why a gentle kiss would feel foreign. "Annie..." he sighed heavily and buried his head in his hands briefly, feeling the mixed heaviness of the moment between them and all that wasn't being said. He opened up his arm and motioned her to scoot over. "Come here." Annie scooted over, tucked herself against his side, and relaxed against his shoulder. They sat in silence for a while before Annie looked up toward Chuck and with a soft hand turned his face toward hers.

"Chuck, everything is okay."

"That's heavy, Annie. I'm just glad you didn't punch me in the throat for kissing you."

Annie laughed a little. "Punch you in the throat," she said, shaking her head, "No, but what if I said it was okay to try it again—only without the element of surprise?"

Chuck smiled and cocked his head to the side, asking himself, *Is this a test? Am I passing or about to fail? It sounds like she wants me to kiss her.* Chuck traced her cheek with his thumb and tilted her chin up to meet his. Her breath caught, and he kissed her gently and slowly until she kissed him back. Her hands were on her lap, and although she didn't lean toward him, her kiss suggested she wanted this subtle electrifying moment between them.

Annie's heart was slamming against her chest, and her thoughts felt blank. She pulled away slightly to breathe and find her thoughts again but stayed very near. When her pulse slowed and her thoughts emerged from the void, she found herself reaching up to touch his face.

As she did, he kissed her again, this time pulling her in with one hand on her back and one hand on her neck, and she let him. Chuck felt himself on the verge of crashing into a place mentally that he knew he couldn't return from and he could only guess she wasn't ready for. He didn't want to stop, but he knew that he had to. He released her and pushed away from her.

"Chuck?"

Chuck scooted back near her and sat beside her against the wall. He took her hand, and they let their hands fall together down on the floor of the walkway. Chuck rolled his head and looked down at her.

Annie looked up at him and met his eyes. Their eyes spoke volumes to each other. They looked out at the ceiling and the lights that hung in the fly. They sat side by side in a comfortable silence for a long time. The only sound was the quiet purring of the air conditioner.

"This is one of my favorite places."

"It's quickly becoming mine," he said, and Annie elbowed him in his side. He chuckled and then asked, "Why is it your favorite?"

"When I was a kid, my father would sometimes make me so mad I would run away up into the fly. He was always so busy he never knew I was up there until after the show was over. I watched a lot of shows from the fly. I called it the bell tower."

"That was another of my questions. I wanted to hear more about the theater in Chicago before your dad died."

Annie closed her eyes. She tried to see it in her mind. The memories were becoming hazy after so many years.

"My father used a cleaning service that used some sort of peppermint and lavender carpet cleaner. I remember the carpet and upholstery always smelled so strong when no one else was in there. Then, by the time a show started, all the people and their perfumes and colognes masked the smell."

"That's funny."

"My favorite night was opening night when an intoxicating energy filled the air. I would arrive five hours early on opening night and just walk around. Then, I loved being backstage on opening night when they call, 'Curtain, five minutes!' It gives me chills right now even talking about it. It was great, even as a manager. I mean, I loved opening night as an actress—stomach in knots from not having eaten all day, feet with blisters from dancing, and voice about to go out at any point from all the rehearsals—but there was such thrilling anticipation that I felt like royalty."

"Go on," he said quietly.

"In old theaters, the folding seats squeak, and the murmurs of the audience sound like crickets in the summer by the pond. The audience is excited about the show, and they're flipping through the programs and wishing they had better seats. It's the greatest thing

I've ever been a part of so far. I loved that theater in Chicago." She trailed off for a moment, not wanting to go on about her father's theater. "As much as I loved that theater, though, I love this place more. I love these kids more. It's not all about me anymore. It's about giving them a place to go and a safe place to grow up."

"What you're doing is amazing. You, yourself are amazing."

Annie gave him a sweet smile but didn't respond to his compliment. Then, changing the subject, she asked, "How are you feeling about the story so far?"

"It's hard to say. It's definitely not what I came here expecting to write. Your story changes everything. I want to spend some time writing out timelines and plot points because I'm not even sure what we're writing anymore. I wasn't expecting to do it alone. I was hoping my business partner was going to help."

"Yeah, I'm sorry."

"Don't do that. You know that it is not even close to being your fault. We'll roll with it. Mace is obviously wrestling with some stuff. As I said, you really got to him. I'm going to give him some time to cool off, and then I'm going to head back to L.A. We'll meet with Lithgow, and then hopefully, we'll both be back."

Mace drove to the nearest airport and caught the first flight back to L.A. He pulled into his driveway as the sun was coming up. He left his bag in the car and went inside. He kicked off his shoes, dropped the keys next to them, and pulled off his shirt, letting it fall on the floor. He stripped all the way down the hall, leaving everything on the floor.

He felt like he'd passed out before he'd even gotten to the room, but somehow he made in onto the bed. Fumbling for the remote, he closed his window shades and turned on the fan.

Mace twitched awake. He'd heard something.

"Annie?"

He rolled over and tried to look around. *How long have I been asleep?* His body ached all over. He relaxed back onto the bed.

His eyes closed again as he repeated, "Annie?"

There was no answer.

Time passed, though he was unaware how much. He heard the noise again. His heart raced, and his mind spun in the pitch black. He sat up.

Have I even been asleep? Where am I? Am I at my house or the ranch? I heard music, and I was at the bar. I can hear the band and smell the beer on tap.

Mace heard the noise again and realized it was his phone. He felt around on the floor until he found it, and without even opening his eyes, he answered groggily.

"Hello?"

"Harlen! Where are you, dude? We've been worried all night about you."

"At home."

"Home? What do you mean? Please do not tell me you left town!"

Mace opened his eyes but didn't answer Chuck's question. He was lying halfway on the bed and halfway off.

"I can't do this with you right now, Chuck," he said and then hung up the phone.

Mace had slept for an entire day by the time he wandered down to his kitchen and scrounged something to eat. He stared at the coffee pot as he ate his way through a bag of Doritos. He flipped through the cascading stack of mail on his counter as he drank from a two-liter of Dr. Pepper. He stood at the fridge with the door hanging open, staring vacantly at the shelves freshly stocked by his housekeeper. None of it was what he wanted. He decided to go for a run to clear his head.

He threw on some shorts, laced up his shoes, and headed outside. As he jogged, he felt adrenaline pump through his body as he picked up the pace. He extended his long strides toward the beach, away from the confusion that circled him at his house.

His heart was beating fast, his muscles were pumping, and his feet were pounding against the sidewalk, but even his rhythmic breathing couldn't drown out his thoughts. He felt his fists tighten as he ran.

As he breathed in through his nose and pushed the breath out of his mouth, it began to come out as words.

You.

The thought formation startled him.

Almost.

Who was he talking to?

Killed.

He couldn't control his breathing, much less these involuntary words that were coming out of his mouth.

Her.

What was he saying? As he reached the sand, he bent over in exhaustion and pushed the last of his breath out.

You almost killed her. As he tried to catch his breath, he kept repeating it. *You almost killed her, you almost killed her, you almost killed her.*

A cool breeze swept off the waves and blew right through him, and as the wind swirled around him, a voice spoke back to him.

I allowed it. I didn't cause it.

Mace whirled around, thinking someone was behind him. No one was there. The beach was suddenly strangely empty. Still trying to catch his breath and let his heart slow, he put his hands on his head and forced his lungs to expand.

"What kind of a person would just sit back and allow such evil?"

I am not a person. I am God.

"Right...I'm sitting here talking to God."

I am God whether you believe in Me or not, Mace Harlen.

The sound of his own name made a shiver run up his spine. The voice was clear and deep. He couldn't tell if it was outside his ears or inside his head. Mace wondered if it would follow him to the water's edge. He kicked off his shoes and put his feet in, letting the tide wash over his burning soles and toes.

"I just don't see why You let such horrible things happen to people—especially someone like Annie."

But it didn't end horribly. Did it? What man intends for evil, I intend for good.

The voice seemed to take over his mind, and the last words and images of Annie flashed through Mace's mind that he didn't want

155

to conjure. He didn't want to remember...but the voice wanted him to see. Images of her at the bakery, her directing the kids at the theater, her and Sammy, images of Annie with him, walking down the middle of the street and dancing at Billy's.

"Okay. I get it."

No. You don't. You just want to make it go away so you can keep running.

Another breeze swept over him, only blowing out toward the ocean as the waves rolled back out. The voice was gone, but Mace knew it had spoken truth. He had run.

He'd run away from Annie, the project, and even his own thoughts in his house. Then, despite his running, God had found him, and Mace knew he wouldn't be able to run away anymore.

I don't want to tell this story, but I have to.

20. STOLEN MOMENTS AND MASHED
POTATOES

"When did you arrive on the ranch, Leo?" Chuck asked before shoving a fork full of mashed potatoes in his mouth. Sammy sat between Sam and Leo, who were across from Chuck and Annie on the booth seat. Annie noted that Leo seemed more relaxed without Mace around and was talking casually to Chuck about anything he asked.

"In order to answer, I'll have to back it up for you."

"By all means, my friend." Chuck gestured for him to keep going, but Annie piped in before Leo could continue.

"Sammy, here's a few dollars. Why don't you go play in the arcade?"

Sammy scooted off the bench seat and ran toward the arcade yelling, "Awesome!" As soon as he was occupied, Annie nodded at Leo to continue.

"They caught Simon within hours. His trial went fast. It caused a huge scandal, but like all organized crime, these things can be taken care of. His father wanted it out of the public as much as possible even though there was no way to get him acquitted. He was on death row for murder, attempted murder, rape, drug counts, as well as arson and breaking and entering. However, there were things they couldn't get him on even though a ton of stories surfaced about sex trafficking, racketeering, and extortion. He was executed before the year was out. After that, it took me another year to track Annie down."

"And what? You just showed up at her door?"

"Yep. There she was, standing on the front porch with little Sammy in her arms. I will never forget that sight for as long as I live." Leo studied his plate for a moment and then continued. "At that moment, seeing her with a baby, I felt a hope that redeemed all the angst I had gone through for those two years."

Sam was quiet, pushing green beans around his plate. He let out a sigh, and Annie noticed a tear escape his eye. She reached across the table and squeezed his hand.

Chuck saw this interaction and turned to Annie to ask, "How did you feel when you saw Leo from the porch?"

"I was surprised, obviously, but during my time in Chicago, Leo had become the closest thing I had to a brother or a best friend." Leo caught her eye in surprise when she said this. "It just felt like home, then. I had all my boys there with me, surrounding me and protecting me."

"That is so good," Chuck said, still savoring his mashed potatoes.

Annie laughed. "The potatoes or the baring of our souls?"

"The souls and the story," he said, putting his fork down. "However, the potatoes are also pretty amazing."

This made everyone laugh, which caught Sammy's attention, and he turned from the arcade and ran back to the table. "Mom, I don't really want to tell you this, but I still have homework."

"Thank you for being honest. I'm glad you got a little arcade in, and now we can get you home where you can focus on that science."

"Are you guys done?" Sammy asked.

"Yes, let me get a to-go box, and then we'll head home."

"Why don't you let me take him and Sam home? I'll help him with his science," Leo offered.

"Thank you, but I need to take him home. I haven't put him to bed all week."

"It's fine. Besides, don't you have that pie order for tomorrow anyway?"

"Oh!" Annie exclaimed, slapping the table. "Yes, I do. Are you sure you don't mind?"

"I don't mind, although maybe you could take this yahoo with you to the shop," Leo suggested, shoving Chuck's shoulder as he scooted past him.

Annie shot her eyebrows up at Chuck and asked, "Want to hang out in the bakery while I make some pies?"

"Love to. Do you mind if I write while you bake?"

"Sounds perfect."

Annie worked quietly, pressing crusts into pans and whipping chocolate cream to fill the crusts. She had music playing softly enough not to bother Chuck, who sat in one of the green barbershop chairs, facing her but engrossed in his laptop as he typed furiously. Occasionally, he'd look up and catch her casual glance; they'd smile and go back to working.

Annie made fifteen pies and placed three trays in the oven. She clapped her hands softly together to dust off the flour.

Chuck looked up from his computer.

"You done?"

"Need to wait for them to bake. How's the writing coming?"

He closed the laptop and stood up, stretching. "It's easy. The story is incredible and inspiring, so it's just flowing out of me. Maybe I should come here to write all my scripts." He winked at her and wandered over to her worktable.

Annie felt like she'd left the oven door open as he walked over closer to her.

"I have spoons," she blurted nervously.

"Spoons?"

"You know," Annie sputtered, feeling nervous, "lick the spoons. Didn't you ever lick the spoons after someone made brownies or cookies?"

"Ah, yes. Licking spoons. Give me that big spatula over there. That one is mine," he said, laughing. They sat at the worktable side by side, cleaning up the bowls, in delicious silence. Chuck finally set his spoon down and tapped the table.

"Aww. I'm done. It's so good I don't want to be done, but if I don't stop, I'm going to be sick."

Annie laughed and gathered up the bowls and spatulas, taking them to the sink. Chuck turned his stool to the side and leaned on the table.

"I need to head back tomorrow. Do you think Leo would mind driving me to the airport?"

"I can take you," Annie offered as she sat back down on her stool, facing him.

"I figured you needed to be here, but I'd love to steal more time with you."

Steal. There was that word. Annie looked down at the table, feeling his gaze on her. Her fingers tapped lightly on the worktable to distract from the shaking she felt in her arms. When she could finally still her nerves, she met his deep blue eyes with small flecks of yellow. She was surprised to see the usual wide smile gone from his face.

His thick honey hair was pulled back in a low ponytail, and he scratched at his trimmed beard. He reached out and tucked a rebellious strand of Annie's auburn curls behind her ear. Annie caught his hand on the way down.

If Mace hadn't left and we hadn't fought, would I still be feeling this way? She wondered.

"Why is everything stolen, Chuck?" Her stomach twisted at his closeness, and she second guessed asking that question. He stared at their hands together and stroked the back of her hand, seemingly tenderly. Still, his smile remained hidden, and suddenly he stood up, dropping her hand, and huffed to the opposite side of the table.

"Ahh." He let out a loud sound in frustration. "Everything in my whole body is fighting me right now."

"Fighting about what?" Annie asked softly, wondering where her defenses were with Chuck. They didn't seem to be there.

Chuck walked back around the table and stood over her. "The other night in the theater," he said, leaning down inches away from her face, "You know what."

A small "Oh" left Annie's lips as Chuck slumped down on his stool again in defeat and said, "Annie, here's the thing."

Embarrassed to look at him now with his "breakup" tone, Annie stood and turned toward the sink to wash the bowls, hoping to delay whatever he was going to say. She had started to consider her feelings in the past few days for Chuck. She was even willing, though surprised at her attraction for him. Though her usual preference was less hair in general, she found Chuck ideal in most ways.

She let the water run until it was hot, and she scrubbed away at the bowls. With her back to him, Chuck threw his head back and let it hang for a moment in pure frustration with himself.

I think You're there, God. I don't know that much about You yet. I know this is childish, but it's really not fair. Just for the record. Chuck prayed before sighing and lifting his head back up.

He began again, "The thing is, Annie." Annie stopped mid-bowl and turned off the water but stayed facing away from him. "I know deep down that you're not mine. It's been a heavy truth in my stomach since I first saw you. It's been my gravity, per se. Our paths are crossing for one blinding, whirlwind moment, but I think that it's just that...crossing. I feel like you're someone else's destiny. You've shown me your God—and I know this sounds insane—but I feel like He's told me all of this.

"This," he paused as he leaned over and briefly touched his lips to hers, "is just selfishness on my part. This blinding, fleeting moment in our timeline will be something that is burned into my brain. You will forever be my muse, and I am thankful for this stolen moment with you."

Annie watched him with curiosity and wonder, and she suddenly could see where his beauty came from. He was physically beautiful, it was true, with his perfectly shaded hair and eyebrows and his strong cheeks and wide full smile. But his bold honesty and emotional awareness were the true magnets. She knew, in that moment, that he was right. Maybe just like he had said, these moments were stolen, but why did he have to be perfect and right?

Annie touched her lips where he had kissed her and then smiled sweetly at him as she shrugged. "I think I might agree with you."

Chuck stood up and paced around the room for a moment, shoving his hands deep in his pockets. Annie took the moment to slip over to the oven, lift the pies out, and turn the oven off. The room seemed quiet now, without the roar of the convection oven.

As she walked to the door to the back storeroom, she untied her apron and threw it on the washer in the back. *So, if these moments are stolen, is there someone else that they belong to? If they really aren't Chuck's, then why do I like him so much?* Annie wondered to herself. She paused in the doorway to find Chuck, hands in his pockets, just gazing at her. Her face flushed, and she felt something familiar and somewhat dangerous rising in her chest. He stepped up to face her.

"I'm going to have to leave tomorrow because I don't think I know if I can trust myself to be alone with you anymore," he said, putting his hands on her shoulders.

"Could you steal just one moment more?" Annie whispered, wondering what in the world was coming over her. Though she expected a mischievous grin, Chuck's expression was full of pain and passion at the same time as he crushed her against the doorframe. Annie indulged in his kiss one last time.

"Harlen, it's Chuck. Annie's driving me to the airport. I'll be back in L.A. tonight. I hope you're ready to do some explaining."

"I'm sorry, man. I want to, but I can't."

Irritated, Chuck turned away from Annie as she drove and looked out the window, saying, "What do you mean? What in the heck is going on with you, Harlen?"

"I seriously do have stories to tell you, but I'm actually on a plane myself right now. I'll be back tomorrow, and we'll have a full day to get ready for the meeting with Lithgow."

"Wait—you're on a plane going where?" Chuck was confused.

"I'm going to Chicago. Chuck, I have to go now. The plane's taking off, and this lovely stewardess is giving me the death-ray stare. I'll call you when I get there." The phone clicked off before Chuck could say another word. He turned back to Annie and then stared blankly out the front windshield as they pulled up to the airport.

"Everything okay?" Annie asked.

Chuck shook his head. "For some reason, he's on a plane to Chicago. He says the meeting with Lithgow is still on. I seriously don't know what is going on with Harlen."

Annie's mouth fell open. She quickly recovered but couldn't completely mask the surprise in her voice as she asked, "Why would he go to Chicago? What's he going to do?"

"I don't know," he said. Suddenly aware of the time, he started to get out of the car. Annie followed him, wondering how this had become such a mess. "Listen, Annie. I don't know where this project is going. I don't know if I'll see you again. Don't get me wrong, I want to. I just have no idea what's going on with Mace right now."

Annie turned him to face her in front of the security checkpoint. "Chuck, it's fine. You don't have to do all that right now. We don't have to know the future, right? And you'll call me after the meeting with Lithgow. You can say goodbye then if you have to," she said, trying to be perky while simultaneously pushing down the knot in her stomach.

Chuck laughed through his nose and shook his head. "You're amazing, Annie. Truly." They hugged quickly. "I'll talk to you soon, then?"

She smiled. "I'll talk to you soon," she confirmed as she waved him on through the checkpoint.

Just as he was about to head down the terminal to his gate, he looked back at her, his expression unreadable. Chuck heard the voice again, and it said, *"You're not the man she needs."*

In Chicago, Mace hailed a cab from the sidewalk at the airport and recited the address to the cabbie. He counted the blocks as they wove through traffic. It was dusk, and the sun's fading orange light crept between the buildings and then hid from his view as they turned a corner. The driver pulled over, and Mace leaned out the window to see where they were, certain that they hadn't arrived.

"Are you sure?" he questioned.

"This is it, pal. You getting out?"

"How long has it been like this?" Mace asked, bewildered by what he saw.

"The theater? About two years."

Mace stepped out of the cab, not believing what his eyes were seeing. As the cab pulled away, Mace stood motionless in front of the vacant lot that once was Annie's theater.

He remained speechless for moments until his cell phone rang in his pocket. As he dug it out, he saw that it was Chuck calling.

"Chuck, it's gone."

"What's gone? Where are you?"

"The theater—Annie's old theater. It's completely gone."

"What do you mean?"

"They must have bulldozed it."

"Do you think Annie knows?"

"I have no idea. Hang on. I think there's a placard or something. Let me see what it says." Mace stepped to the left, and on a small stone pillar was a bronze plaque. It was a plain sign with simple lettering. Mace ran his hand over it and looked back toward the barren lot next to the historic buildings that rose up all around it. Chuck's voice reminded him that he was on the phone.

"Well? What does it say?"

"You won't believe it. It reads, 'Dedicated to the souls who escaped the tragedy of the Royal Theater.'"

"Wow," was all Mace heard Chuck say through the phone.

"Guess who funded the plaque?"

"I got nothing, so just tell me."

"The Martha Grady Foundation. And get this, Chuck, it was funded this year."

The next morning, Mace tapped his fingers on the counter at the Martha Grady Foundation, waiting for the receptionist to return. The brunette with long lashes and bright red lips scurried away nervously. Mace had asked to see the chairperson of the Foundation since Martha had reportedly passed away two years before.

Mace had sat up all night researching the Grady family, their businesses, and the Martha Grady Foundation. Nothing seemed to make sense as to why the grandmother of Simon Grady would fund a memorial at the site where her grandson had failed the family and ruined lives, including his own. *Was it to atone somehow, or was it shame or, even worse, just some PR stunt?* Mace wondered.

The receptionist returned but was following a tall, lanky man whose hair was in a perfect horseshoe around his head, thin-rimmed glasses perched perfectly on his angular nose.

"Hello, Mr. Harlen. It's a pleasure to have you here. I'm Nigel Otto. I hear you are inquiring about the Foundation?"

"Nice to meet you, Nigel," Mace said, shaking his hand. "Yes, I have some questions about the Foundation and its funding of memorials."

Nigel stiffened and cut a glance to the receptionist, who looked down at the ground. She clearly had not gotten enough information from Mace before she retrieved Mr. Otto. Nigel smeared his expression with false graciousness and asked Mace to follow him.

The Foundation was in one of the historic buildings on the east side of Chicago. Large marble pillars were swirled with gray slate, and the ivory-colored floors echoed under Mace's feet as he followed Nigel down hallways and corridor until they reached a large open room. Nigel ushered Mace to sit on the right-hand side of a long mahogany table that had ornate grapes dangling off the corners just above the legs. Nigel sat adjacent to him at the head of the table. The two studied each other.

"All right, Mr. Harlen, I'm cutting to the chase. What's this about?"

"I'm doing some research on the Royal Theater, and I have a few questions about the memorial plaque."

"I see." Nigel folded his hands and lay them on the table strategically. "May I ask the nature of your research on the Royal Theater?"

"May I ask you the nature of your secrecy? The Foundation did put the plaque out there in the public eye, did they not?"

Nigel nodded in understanding. "Mr. Harlen, I can see that we both have assets to protect here. The memorial plaque that you have obviously seen is only the first stage in a project that Mrs. Martha Grady designed just before her death. The rest will come to fruition in due time. For now, that is all I am at liberty to say for both our sake and yours."

Mace pondered his words and studied his face. "I can't really accept that. I need you to answer one question for me."

"It depends on the question. I'm sure you know that, Mr. Harlen," Nigel said, narrowing his eyes.

"Why would the wife of the Grady Empire start a foundation that protects the futures of women who are victims of rape and human trafficking? Isn't it a slight conflict of interest to memorialize the site of the tragic undoing of her grandson?"

Nigel licked his lips and sighed, standing to his feet and pressing his hands into the table. "That was two questions, Mr. Harlen, but seemingly the answer to both is that you need to do some more research on the late Martha Grady and how she came to be the wife of Mr. Grady. As I said before, the rest of the project will unveil itself in due time. I think that will be all, Mr. Harlen."

Mace rose to his feet and nodded. "I guess it has to be. Thank you for your time, Mr. Otto."

"Thank you for coming."

Nigel escorted Mace back to the lobby and then quickly disappeared through an ornate door at the other end of the lobby. Mace apologized to the receptionist for possibly getting her in trouble and then left.

Nigel slipped inside the room quietly and closed the heavy door carefully. The hunched figure in the red winged-back chair tried to straighten up as he came in. Nigel held up his hand as if to say, "No." The figure sunk back down in the chair and then in a raspy whisper said, "Does he know?"

"In part. I believe he knows her location and possibly the boy's."

"Good." The figure coughed into a napkin and placed in on the table. Nigel looked away from the napkin. "Is he the one? Is he the storyteller?"

"Yes."

"Well, then, Nigel. Ready the cannons. We have our megaphone in place. It's time for the reign of Grady to end."

Mace opened the door to his hotel room and stepped on what he thought was a bill, but as he picked it up, he realized it was a note card. The slant of the handwriting was harsh and mysterious.

The blank white card and the red letters intrigued Mace but caused him to pause. They read, *We're watching you.*

Six hours after stumbling over the note, Mace looked at the clock on the bedside table. *3 a.m.? Have I really been reading that long?* For the past six hours, Mace had been scouring the internet for anything he could find about Simon Grady the first and how he and Martha got married. He'd contacted his buddies who worked at large newspapers and asked them for anything they could get their hands on about the Gradys.

The more he looked, the more convoluted it got. All the news reports and articles seemed to link Martha to a teenage rape case, though the case went cold and the offender was never caught or brought to justice. Connected to the beginning of the rise of the Grady empire were accusations of organized crime, drug rings, and prostitution. All of those rumors died down in the late 1990s when

Simon the second took over as acting CEO when Simon the first was diagnosed with lymphoma. Though the rumors died down, success did not. The Gradys purchased several professional football and basketball teams as well as over twenty major corporations.

As Mace continued to research and follow every link, he began to see Simon the third emerge mostly as a major playboy who was speculated to have started the most successful and most viewed pornography site in the world. As Simon the third rose through the ranks following his father, rumors began to swell again. Crimes began to be linked to the Gradys from the present all the way back to the 1920s. Suddenly, new faces were coming forward, only then to be suppressed or disappear. Mace began to notice the trend of Simon the third's reign of terror with women. Adding to that was the rise of the popularity and accessibility of porn, which Simon clearly propagated by flagrantly dating porn stars among other social media stunts that gained him a lot of attention.

How did Annie miss all of this? Was she seriously so busy with the theater that she had no idea who he was? Maybe I am only connecting all of this because I'm digging. Maybe the average person who follows the news wouldn't know it was all linked to the Gradys, especially because the Gradys would have ensured that the link wasn't easy to find, Mace thought. He began to think back over Annie and Leo's account of the night of the rape. He focused in on the detail of the girls in the warehouse. It made more sense now. *What if the girls in the warehouse were prostitutes? Or perhaps the warehouse was where Simon made porn? Were those girls forced to be there, in the warehouse, for whatever purpose Simon wanted them for? Who were they? Where had they come from? Had Simon intended for Annie to become one of them?* Mace shuddered at the thought. *What on earth did all of this have to do with Martha? Okay, so she was a victim of rape herself. But what had Nigel meant, it's only the first phase? What did phase one accomplish? What were the other phases? Why would she have gone to such great length before she died to set something in motion against her own name?* The more he thought, the more questions he had and the greater his speculations grew. He knew he had to go to sleep since he had that meeting with Lithgow in the morning. Chuck would be there, which he dreaded. Mace had screwed up and been a jerk to Annie, and Chuck would surely ream him for it.

Shortly before 4 a.m., Mace quit worrying and fell asleep. He had just a couple hours before he needed to catch a flight back to L.A.

21. STORYBOARDS AND PISTACHIOS

The conference room was all clean lines with an urban appeal. The ergonomic gray chairs swiveled smoothly as Mace studied the storyboard on the smooth, clear conference table. He ran his hand along the curved edge of the table and wondered what was taking Chuck so long. They had five minutes until Lithgow would walk in, and Mace felt the pressure to perform rising from the thick nervousness in his stomach and starting to squeeze at his lungs.

He felt short of breath just as Chuck and Lithgow walked in shaking hands and laughing. Mace looked at Chuck, puzzled, and his head began to swirl. Everyone's voices were muffled, and Mace wondered if he was going to pass out. Lithgow said something, and Chuck responded and jumped up from his seat, talking rapidly, pitching the story synopsis. Chuck talked with his hands and gestured toward Mace several times, but Mace couldn't focus on what he was saying.

He looked down at the table in front of him. It seemed to be the only thing in the room that wasn't spinning. *What is happening to me?* He stared at the storyboard spread out on the table before him. He focused on it hard and tried to forget the nausea in his stomach and the pin-wheeling that the room was doing.

Then he saw it.

The storyboard looked alive, pulsing and threading itself together with a slivery, glowing rope he was sure he was the only one seeing. As he watched the thread weave through the storyboard, tying one board to the next, Mace felt childish that he actually needed a storyboard to see it, but there, spread out on the table, he saw it clearly for the very first time.

The room stopped spinning, a breeze settled his nausea, and like a sip of hot tea, Mace felt the warmth of the same voice from his dream travel into every corner of his body. Mace closed his eyes and relaxed.

If you are going to tell the story, you need to see it the way I wrote it. It spoke to him, from within, like a salve on his mind and body.

Mace sighed, welcoming whatever was happening because he saw the truth, and that was all that mattered. He heard Lithgow mutter, "Everyone these days loves spirituality. They'll eat that up."

"No," Mace said, feeling taken over. He stood to his feet, shaken but somehow confident. All heads turned. "No, it's not spirituality."

Chuck stared at Mace as if he'd gone mad. Then a slow conspiring grin hooked the corner of his mouth. He nodded.

"I see it now, Chuck. Right here," Mace said, spreading his hands over the storyboard. "I've been so blind. Here, where she saves the theater after her dad died, it begins. Then Leo saves her from the fiery death. Then she saves the child, even though it was conceived through horrific circumstances.

"She gave new life to the theater. She is given new life after tragedy. She births new life. Leo joins her in new life. Don't you see, Lithgow, it's not generic spirituality. It's… a sort of re-birth."

Lithgow had his chin cupped in his hand, staring Mace down, analyzing both the man and the story. He motioned for them to pass him the storyboards, and he studied them in silence until the phone in the center of the conference table rang. Lithgow reached for it and listened cryptically.

"Yes, thank you for your call," was all he said, and he hung up.

"Well, Mr. Harlen, it seems you have a movie to make," he said as he presented Mace with an envelope. "And though I don't particularly buy into your passionate vision, I'm willing to back the project as well."

Chuck and Mace both jumped up and raced to shake his hands, their eagerness making Lithgow laugh.

"It's surreal," Mace said, throwing pistachio shells off the dock. He and Chuck sat on the edge of the dock as the sun went down.

"No kidding! I'm still having a hard time wrapping my mind around it all. I mean two days ago, I thought the whole thing was off."

"I know. I am the world's biggest jerk. I would say that I don't know what came over me, but I do."

Chuck caught his eye and wondered if he meant Annie. He felt a quick pang in his stomach but pushed it down and out to sea.

Mace continued, "I just was seriously, by nature, a jerk. Wasn't I?"

Chuck laughed, "Yeah."

"I'm sorry about that. I'm sorry about the way I acted in Texas and for just running off and doing my own thing."

"Harlen, we're best friends. You don't have to apologize to me...but Annie... you've smashed some delicate trust there."

"I know," Mace said simply, not revealing that she was all he had thought about since he left Penumbra.

"So what happened to you? What's changed?"

Mace cracked another pistachio and ate the nut slowly. "It's weird to explain, and it's going to sound crazy. I've been running from stuff my whole life, and I think I've come face to face with God. I can't run from Him."

Chuck didn't look at him. He just continued staring out at the deep purple waves as they frothed a lavender foam against the sand as the sun set. "It's a strange thing when God gets hold of you."

"Strange is right," Mace said, thinking back to the experience of hearing the voice on the beach. "Ever feel like He talks to you?"

Chuck laughed. "Yeah, a couple of times."

"Why are you laughing?"

"Sorry, I know it's not a funny thing. It's just that the times that I've felt like He's told me something, we haven't really seen eye to eye."

Mace let out a hearty laugh and started to stand up. He drew up his knees and push off the dock, as he stood he cocked his head to the side and laughed again.

Chuck gave him a quizzical look. "What?"

"I don't know. This whole thing is just ironic."

"What do you mean?" Chuck asked, following suit to get up and start walking down the pier toward his car.

"I just get thoughts in my head that I know aren't mine. I just thought, 'Yeah, that's because He's God and He has better thoughts than us.' I know that's not me. It's crazy."

"I know, man, but it's really cool. Like today, with Lithgow?"

Mace threw his head back and pretended that his knees buckled out from underneath him. "Exactly. That was crazy. I keep having these moments where I feel overtaken or something."

"I know. I've felt the same way. It gets me stoked about this project and the movie. I can't wait to see how it is all going to come together."

They walked back toward the parking lot as the fog began to descend and pool around the lampposts and blanket their cars. Mace shoved his hands down in his dark jeans. Feeling his keys pressed against his leg, he found himself thinking about the word "key." He followed his thoughts and then looked at Chuck as they reached the car and mumbled, "Annie is the key."

"What did you say?"

"Annie. She is the key, isn't she? We can't do this without her, can we?"

"Like, she needs to be in the movie, or something else?"

"I just realized that it's not only her story. Somehow, she is the key to pulling this off. Maybe she plays herself, or maybe she just agrees to be a part of it...I don't know. But she's the key." *She's also the key to the plan Nigel mentioned*, Mace thought though he kept that to himself.

Chuck shrugged his broad shoulders and pointed east. "Sounds like you need to get yourself back to Texas."

Mace turned to look in the direction Chuck pointed as if he could see Annie all the way from where he stood.

22. A COOKOUT AND RUINED SOUFFLÉS

"How can you call my bluff when you can't even tell you have a good hand or not, you old coot?" Dale blurted from the back room.

Annie watched as the orange soufflé caved in the center and collapsed all the way to the bottom of the dish. She let out an exasperated growl and banged her palms on the worktable, angry she had ruined three soufflés this morning.

Sam popped his head through the screen door from the back. "Annie girl, are you all right?"

She pointed toward the three concave soufflés and then huffed again.

Sam walked to them and took a fork to the edge of one, sampling it. "It still tastes good," he observed, trying to conjure a small smile from Annie to no avail.

Her shoulders were hunched, and her brow was heavy with lines of frustration. Sam put down the fork and took her hands in his.

"Annie, what is it?"

"I'm so off lately. I make perfect soufflés, yet I've ruined three today. Yesterday, I burned the cheesecakes."

"It's not the desserts that are really bothering you, is it?"

She shook her head without offering any explanation.

He patted her shoulder and said, "Well, listen. We'll dispose of these for you." He grabbed several forks. "You go do something else. Relax and take your mind off whatever or whoever is bothering you. We'll lock up and see you for dinner. The boys are grilling over at the house. I'll call Leo and have him pick up Sammy. Okay?"

"No, I can pick up Sammy. Leo has been doing too much Sammy chauffeuring lately, but yes to the rest of your suggestions," she said, patting his hand that rested on her slim shoulder. She helped take the soufflé dishes into the back room, causing an immediate pause in the poker game and broad smiles from Dale, Gus, and Tom. Then Sam shooed her away sweetly, and she complied, leaving the bakery with a fuzzy mind and soggy heart. She knew where she wanted to go.

She crossed the tracks and walked along the sidewalk past BeBe's Salon, waving to BeBe in the window where she was working late on Sally Cotton's silver-blue hair that reminded Annie of Marge Simpson. She passed Mr. Jenkins standing on a ladder hanging Christmas wreaths from the lampposts.

"Surely it's not time for that already, Mr. Jenkins?"

"They go up earlier every year," he said, shaking his head and smiling at her. "I keep hoping if I put them up earlier, it will cool off earlier." Annie laughed, and she waved goodbye to him as she crossed the street to the Arrow.

The brass on the doors needed polishing, but she hadn't come here to work. With forty-five minutes until school let out, she decided just to sit. She needed to be alone with the red velvet and the cool air.

She locked the door behind her, slipped into the dark theater, and sank down into the aisle seat on the last row. Even as she let the cool silence envelop her, her thoughts bumped and raged in her head until she took a breath and whispered, "Lord."

Her thoughts stilled as she clarified what had bothered her for days. "I haven't heard from Chuck or Mace—not that I really expected to hear from Mace. I know my heart is filled with fear of my own making, but even so, I'm afraid I have loosed something that I have held so tightly and controlled for so long. I've put my story in the hands of someone I can't fully trust now, and I am scared. It sounds childish, but when it comes down to it, I'm just scared. I don't know what to do."

As she finished whispering her prayer, she relaxed into the seat and closed her eyes, thinking about the stories she'd told Sammy over the years—Bible stories about faith and God's plans for people's lives. In the stillness of the room, she felt a whisper in her soul that said, *Trust Me,* and it sent a fluid warmth flowing through her heart. Without realizing she had been holding her breath, she gave in to the warmth that flowed through her, releasing her breath. Then she remembered the verse she and Sammy had read the night before.

"But when I am afraid, I will trust in you. Psalm 56:3," she repeated aloud. She smiled in the darkness and felt her heaviness lift and dissipate into the cool darkness. The ringing of her phone snapped her away from her thoughts; grabbing it from her purse, she saw that it was Leo.

"Don't get mad, but Sam called and asked me to pick up Sammy. He said you'd be here. We're outside."

Annie laughed as she rose from her seat. She loved that Sam knew where she'd be and that he didn't listen to her. He rebelliously took care of her at every turn. She told Leo she'd be right there to unlock the door. As she picked up her purse and entered the lobby, she silently thanked God for the few moments alone and for what He had spoken to her.

"Hey, Mom," Sammy said, wrapping his small arms around her waist. "Can I play on your computer?"

Annie looked to Leo. "Are we not leaving?"

"Sam said you needed some time, so I told pint size here, if you said it was okay, he could play games until you were ready to go."

Marveling at Sam and Leo's thoughtfulness, Annie smiled at Sammy. "Then yes, by all means, go play." She shooed him toward her office door, which he galloped toward while yelling "Thanks!" behind him.

"So? What were you doing before we got here?"

"Sitting in the dark," she said, motioning toward the auditorium. Leo pretended to usher her toward the door, saying, "Then shall we?"

"I suppose so," Annie said, laughing and following him in. She settled back down into her seat, and Leo did the same beside her.

"Do you want to talk about it?" Leo's voice was non-threatening and lately had a light rasp to it from yelling at the cattle.

Annie leaned her head back on the seat and sighed. "My soufflés fell. Three times."

"Call Dan Rather! That is breaking drama, girl," he joked and nudged her with his arm. She pushed him back but didn't say anything, so he continued, "I know it's not just the soufflés. You need to talk about that?" She leaned into his shoulder and put her head on his flannel shirt that smelled like sweet feed.

"No, I don't suppose. When I was in here earlier, God told me I should trust Him, so I think I should. If I still needed to talk about it, that might mean I didn't trust Him."

Leo chuckled and commented, "I suppose you might be right," as he smoothed the top of her hair with a rough, calloused hand. "You always come here, don't you?"

"What do you mean?" Annie said, looking up at him, her head still resting on his shoulder. She could feel his breath on her nose, and just like at the ballpark, her nervous system overloaded. Her stomach caught up in a knot as he whispered to her, and his lips accidentally grazed her nose as he spoke.

"When you're sad, when you're stressed, when you're confused, or when you need to think…you come here."

In the cool dark air, his whisper was intimate, which made Annie squirm and feel the need to jump the aisle. She turned her face back downward at the thought of his lips being that close. "I'm just like Dad. There's something about being here that is peaceful."

"I know. I miss our balcony—" Leo started.

"Don't," Annie interrupted, grabbing his forearm. "I don't want to talk about that place."

Leo covered her hand with his own. "Annie, it was still your dad's theater. It holds more memories than just that one."

"Isn't that one enough to ruin all the others?" she said with choking, painful regret in her voice.

"No—at least, not for me. The first time I met you was in that lobby. The first show I saw was in that back row. The first job I had was the one you gave me. I could keep going…"

Annie was silent, but she had pulled back into her chair, not touching Leo. He couldn't see her face, but he could sense her anguish just at the thought of speaking about the Royal Theater.

"Annie, the way you feel is valid, and it's real. I'm not trying to say it's not." He found her hand in the dark and covered gently it with his own. "All my good memories of the place are still good because they all involve you. Plus, I still have you…so they are still good to me. Do you know what I mean?"

She turned her hand under his and interlaced her fingers with his. "I do," she said softly and then sat in silence for a moment before saying, "Leo?"

"What?"

"You don't feel like a brother to me."

Her words made Leo's stomach flip, and he squeezed her hand without thinking.

She continued on, "I could swear that you are more like my guardian angel. I don't deserve you and how you watch over me."

Without revealing his disappointment, he relaxed his hand and pulled it away from hers so he could wrap his muscular arm around her shoulders. "You deserve a whole army to keep charge over you," he said.

"Tom, come take this over. It keeps fogging up my glasses," Gus complained and handed Tom the metal spatula he was using for the burgers on the grill.

"Oh no, you don't! Tom burned them last time," Dale shouted across the patio. "Let me do it."

Tom wielded the spatula around and held it in an attack position toward Dale. Dale pushed it aside, saying, "Take your tomahawk somewhere else, Silverstreak. I ain't afraid of you."

Tom offered him the spatula as a peace offering and ushered him to the grill. Sam laughed at the whole exchange and gave Tom a high five as he walked back to the table.

"I saw what you did there."

"I don't grill," Tom shrugged, "but Dale doesn't listen unless it's his idea." A sneaky grin flashed across his dark skin.

Gus pushed his glasses up on his nose and smoothed his mustache as he looked out toward the house just as Annie strode through the kitchen door. "Annie, where ya been?" he asked in a jolly voice.

"Hey, boys," she said, smiling at all of them and walking over to Sam, whom she bent down to hug.

"Feeling more like yourself?" Sam asked quietly. She patted his head and nodded. Sammy and Leo had followed her out of the house, carrying trays of beans, coleslaw, and chips.

"Were you feeling like someone else?" Dale retorted over his shoulder from the grill. Sam scooped up an acorn that had fallen on the patio and threw it at the back of his head. Dale wheeled around, surprised, "What?"

"Dale, you know how, when you forget to take your chill pill, you feel not quite yourself? You feel pretty cranky? Or wait…that's just your personality," Leo poked at him. Tom let out a bellowing laugh, and Gus snickered to himself, like he might get into trouble for laughing.

"Oh, the young one wants to pick fights with the old guy, huh?" Dale puffed up.

"Leo's got a point," Sam added.

"What is this—ganging up on the grill master? Completely unfair," Dale said, turning back to the grill to lift the burgers onto a platter.

"All right, you guys. Settle down, and let's eat." Annie sweetly herded them to the table and poured sweet tea into their glasses. She sat next to Sammy, who was sitting next to Leo.

Sam stood up to offer a blessing over the food. "We are thankful, Lord, to enjoy maybe our last backyard evening meal before You bring the winter on us. We are also thankful for these friends and family, Lord. Bless them, each one. Amen."

A resounding "Amen" echoed from the table as the phone rang inside the kitchen. Annie stood to go answer it.

"Want me to get it? You just got here," Sam asked, bidding her to stay and sit.

"It's fine, Sam. It's probably just a telemarketer. I'll get rid of them and come right back," she said as she disappeared through the door. The phone rang for the fourth time, and she jogged across the kitchen to grab the receiver off the wall, laughing to herself that Sam still insisted on having a landline.

"Hello?"

"Annie?"

Annie sucked in her breath quickly. Mace's voice was eager and pleasant, and the way he said her name made her chew on the inside of her mouth.

"Annie, is that you?"

"Yes," she said flatly.

"It's Mace."

"I know. What do you want, Mace?"

"I know that I left on bad terms. That's why I'm calling. I want to talk. Do you have a minute?"

Annie thought about the way he left, the screeching of tires as he sped away from her as fast as he could. As her angry answer formed in her throat, she also felt the calming reminder float into her mind again. *Trust Me.*

She sighed, surrendering to the notion of trusting God more than she trusted her instincts or her anger.

"I have a minute, but, to be honest, I don't know what you could say that I would want to hear."

"That's the funny thing, isn't it? Sometimes what we need to hear isn't always something we want to hear, especially if God says it." He let the words fall out as light as possible, not sounding forced or practiced. He hoped they would hang themselves on the wall built between them and crumble it.

"God? God is talking to Mace Harlen?" Disbelief snapped from her tongue like a whip.

"I suppose the more important part is that Mace Harlen is finally listening."

Something burned in her nose, making it twitch and causing her to blink. Annie took a deep breath, realizing she was about to cry. She held the phone away from her face and mouthed a silent "*What*!?" up to the ceiling and then shook her head and fanned her eyes to try and gain her composure.

Annie, isn't this what you wanted? For Mace to find Me?

The voice was heavy in her ear, and she felt at odds with His presence, which made her uneasy and restless. She had prayed for both Chuck and Mace to know God, but she hadn't thought it would come with a lesson of trust for her.

Mace said, "I have a lot to explain, Annie, and a lot to ask your forgiveness for. Also, I want to talk to you about the movie, but I don't want to do any of that over the phone. I'm calling to ask if I can come talk to you in person."

Her defensive heart slammed its door shut, and her pride started presenting its case in her mind and building a platform for a speech. God's voice tried speaking truth to her again about trust, but her pride wouldn't hear it.

"Mace, I don't think that's a good idea."

"Annie, I can't undo what I've done, and I can't even repair the trust that I've shattered singlehandedly. All I can do is what God is telling me to do. You might feel like saying no right now, but sleep on it. Pray about it. Call me tomorrow, please?" He wasn't arrogant or even confident. He sounded sincere, a tone that Annie wasn't sure that she had ever heard from him.

She managed to say, "Okay," and they said goodbye.

After hanging up, she slumped down at the kitchen table and lay her head, forehead first, on the cold, hard surface.

23. AN EMPTY ROOM AND ICE CREAM

That night, Annie didn't bother to pull her jeans down over the tops of her boots. With stealthy grace, she slipped past Sam, who had fallen asleep on the couch again. She carefully closed the kitchen door and moved swiftly across the patio on her toes so the heels of her boots wouldn't sound against the boards.

The barn was closed up, and Annie wondered if Leo was already sleeping. She felt a gravitational pull to talk to him, but just before she yanked on the huge barn door, the memory of his face so close to hers in the theater shivered down her back. As it ran all the way down to her tailbone, she lifted her right leg and kicked it to the side as if kicking the memory and the shiver out of the bottom of her boot. Then she used both hands and all her weight to pull at the door. Finally, the momentum set the door rolling on its wheels, and it rumbled open.

She stood in the doorway, waiting to see if the door's noise would rouse him. Twisting her hair back, she threw it over her shoulder and put her hands in her pockets. After a minute, Leo's door opened, and he stumbled out, shirtless.

"Annie?" he said, trying to gain his bearings. He had obviously been asleep even though he had his jeans on. She stared at his broad shoulders.

"Annie, is that you?" he asked, his eyes adjusting to the darkness in front of him and her silhouette backlit by the streetlight outside the barn. "What's wrong?" He stumbled toward her sleepily and put a hand on her waist, thinking something must be wrong for her to come out to the barn this late.

"It's nothing. I'm sorry I woke you, Leo," she said, trying to look away from his muscular chest and arms.

"It's okay. I heard the door open. Are you sure you're okay?"

"I couldn't sleep, and I wanted to talk to you. I need some advice."

Leo rubbed his eyes and said, "I'll grab a shirt. Go up to the moon roof, and I'll meet you up there." He jogged back over to his room. Leo had built a small apartment off the end of the barn's office when he first moved here, insisting that he not live in the house with them.

Annie climbed the ladder to the loft and found the moon roof, a cutout in the roof to let light into the loft. Moonlight shone down through it, highlighting a soft pad of hay below. She sat down on the hay and leaned against the hay bale behind her. She lifted her chin and looked up at the night sky. The stars sat brightly in the sky, hiding from her every now and then as thin clouds wafted over them.

She rested her head on the hay and closed her eyes, imagining being bathed in blue moonlight just as she would do in warm sunlight.

She drifted away for a minute, and she heard the babble of the brook nearby and pictured Sammy when he was three, picking flowers for her.

Leo's voice brought her back. He slid down beside her, now wearing a dark gray t-shirt. Annie rolled her head toward him.

"Hey," he said sweetly. "No trouble sleeping now?"

"Mace called tonight."

Leo leaned back on the bale beside her, looking up through the moon roof. "I wondered who it was. You were so stoic when you came back."

"He wants to come here again and talk. He wants to film the movie here, and I think he's going to ask me to be a part of it."

Leo didn't mask his surprise. "What did you tell him?"

"I said no." Annie sat up a little and leaned over her knees, hugging them.

"Why?" Leo asked.

"Because I trust God, but I just can't trust Mace."

Leo was thoughtful for a moment, extending his legs out in front of him and crossing his arms across his chest. "Annie, I can't believe I'm going to say this, but I think you need to give him a chance to explain, at the very least."

"What happened to not trusting Mace?"

"Something I've learned lately applies here. A stage manager can feel in control of a play, as can a director, right?"

"Right."

"But the playwright might say, 'No, I'm in control of the play. I wrote the story.' The same is true in real life. We've got to quit trying to control the play or the story because we didn't write it. You've got to quit trying to control the story."

Anne let out an aggravated sigh and fell back against the hay again. "You're right," she admitted. Then she was silent for a while, staring out the moon roof. "How did you learn this lesson? What were you trying to control?" Annie asked curiously.

"I was trying to control how you felt about me and who came into your life."

"How I felt? Leo, you know I love you."

"I know you love me, but I'm not talking about that." He shook his head.

"Then I don't understand."

Suddenly, in Leo's mind, her voice faded out even though her mouth continued to move, and Leo drifted off into his imagination.

He leaned toward her, but he imagined that she didn't move although her eyes welled with surprise. She felt his breath on her as he moved closer and kissed her.

For a moment, he stopped, only releasing her about an inch. He imagined that Annie let out a breath and struggled to get another. With his face still almost touching hers, he closed his eyes and said, "That's what I'm talking about... if you returned those feelings."

Annie's eyes held both wonder and fear. She touched her lips with her fingertips and then his.

"I didn't want Mace around because I thought there was something between you two, and I couldn't stand it. But I can't control who God allows into your life, and I can't control how you feel about me."

"Leo," she whispered, brushing her thumb across his bottom lips. He put his hand on her waist and pulled her toward him. His lips met hers again, and this time, she responded to his kiss with the same sincerity that he did. When she couldn't breathe again, she pushed against him, and he released her. This time, he scooted away from her. Annie tried to catch her breath.

"I've wanted to kiss you for years, Annie."

"Leo...Leo?"

Leo's head popped back in horror as if Annie might see on his face what he was just imagining. "What?"

"Where were you just then? You weren't even here with me were you?"

"No, I was. Trust me." He slumped down farther into the hay. "I was here—just distracted. Sorry."

"It's okay."

"Okay."

She relaxed against him, and soon they both drifted off to sleep.

Annie didn't attempt to bake the next day. She called Mandy in early to do the morning baking so she could focus on cleaning, organizing, and tackling a small pile of neglected paperwork.

She waited almost the entire day before calling Mace, constantly pushing down any thoughts about him. Every once in a while, when they started to creep up the back of her leg, she would stomp her right foot, causing Mandy to wonder what she was so agitated about. Annie would only shrug her shoulders and go on about her chores.

Finally, she sent Mandy home, thanking her for being there the whole day. Then she sighed at the task ahead. She hadn't formulated words or planned paragraphs to explain herself.

She knew Leo had been right last night when he had told her to quit trying to control things. She decided not to plan the upcoming conversation but rather just say that she was sorry for her hasty "no" and let the rest flow from there.

She dialed Mace's number and waited for him to answer. She listened to it ring in her ear only twice before a voice interrupted it.

"Hello." It was not Mace, and the hint of charm in the voice made Annie smile and relax.

"Chuck?"

"Annie?"

"Yeah. Did I call the right phone?"

"Depends on who you were aiming for," he said, and Annie could hear the smile in his voice.

"Harlen," she admitted.

"Then, yes. I saw it ringing here on the table and grabbed it. He just stepped outside, but he'll be right back."

"Okay. How are you?" Annie said, not disappointed in the least to have caught Chuck instead of Mace.

"Insanely busy but good. I guess you know that the project is underway, so things are crazy. How are you?"

"I'd probably call myself a mess," she said.

"You, a mess? Never!"

"It seems to me that ever since Mace Harlen wandered into my life, everything has gotten a lot more complicated."

As if he held the phone closer to his mouth so no one near him could hear, Chuck halfway whispered, "I'd like to talk to you about that, but speaking of the devil—here he is." At that, Annie heard Chuck hand the phone off and Mace asking Chuck who it was.

"Annie!" Mace's enthusiasm caught Annie by surprise so much so that she barely uttered a greeting back, but Mace began to fill the awkward silence by rattling on about his excitement about the project.

Finally, Annie took a deep breath and interrupted him, "Mace…"

He paused.

"I called to apologize for my hasty rejection yesterday." Annie felt no relief in her apology and felt as though it were just hanging in the air, like flour that got dusted still floating around in the air waiting to fall to the ground.

"Why do I feel like there's still a 'no' hanging between us?"

"It's not so much a 'no' as a hesitant and leery 'yes.'"

In L.A., Mace jumped up and pumped his fist in the air while yelling, "Yes!"

After he settled back down, Annie could hear Mace retell Chuck what Annie had said, though she couldn't hear Chuck's reaction because Mace started talking into the phone again.

"What changed your mind?"

"Leo, I think," Annie said, stomping her foot again at the sound of his name from her mouth.

"You're not sure?" Mace said, sounding confused.

"You'd be surprised at all the things I'm not sure of these days."

"That doesn't sound like the Annie I know," he said sympathetically.

Annie shook her head, feeling bewildered. "Mace, I don't know what's come over you."

"What do you mean?"

"Just a few weeks ago, you stormed out of Penumbra because you didn't feel like you knew me. Now, you're talking as if we've known each other our whole lives."

Mace took a deep breath, and Annie could hear the smile in his voice as he said, "Like I told you yesterday, I have a lot of explaining to do. I'd like some time with you once I get there to properly apologize and share some really important stories."

Something in his voice was uncharted, a gentleness and a confidence that Annie had never heard before, and the way he requested time with her made her stomach flutter.

Somehow, she managed to mutter, "Sure," which made her feel idiotic.

"Chuck and I have meetings tomorrow, but I can be there by Friday. Does that work for you?"

Annie wondered whether Chuck had listened to the whole conversation. Her thoughts led her back to their last kiss, near where she was standing now. *Why am I still lingering in that moment?*

"Annie? Are you there?"

"I'm so sorry!" Annie's face burned with embarrassment at her thoughts. "What did you ask?"

"Can I see you on Friday?"

"Yes," she agreed and then told him goodbye, feeling more bombarded by her feelings than ever before as a rush of emotion flowed through her. Leo's mixed signals, Chuck's passion, and Mace's newfound chivalry…she'd never been more confused.

"You need to clean your room before you hop in the shower, okay, bud?" Annie called up the stairs after Sammy.

A distant and begrudging "okay" was called back to her. She smiled and shook her head.

"Boys," she said to Sam, who was standing at the sink. She patted him on the back and hopped up to sit on the counter. Sam looked at her, turned the water off, and crossed his arms.

She threw her hands up in playful defense. "What? What did I do?"

"Leo told me," Sam huffed.

Annie felt like a child, guilty and caught red handed, but she couldn't be sure what exactly Leo had told him. *Would Leo really tell Sam that we fell asleep together in the barn?* Even the words in her head sounded childish. She should not have gone into the barn last night. She knew her face was red, and she was starting to fidget.

"After all this, you're not going to see this through with him?"

"What do you mean?" She had no idea what Leo had told him, but she flamed with embarrassment; she'd never meant to fall asleep with him.

"I mean Mace. Famous or not, he needs somebody strong enough to see this project through with him. Just the story itself is going to put a bullseye on him, and he's going to need all the help he can get. He swallowed his pride to call you, and what do you do?"

Annie felt a wave of relief sweep over her.

"I called him today," she interjected.

Sam looked at her skeptically and drew up his hand armed with a soapy sponge, ready to throw it at her. "You did?"

"Yes, Sam. Don't you dare throw that at me!" Annie laughed before she continued. "I called him, apologized, and told him that I was willing to hear him out. He's coming to town Friday."

Sam withdrew the sponge and smiled at her. "Leo didn't tell me that. What say you tell me all about it over ice cream? Leo also told me about you two falling asleep in the barn. Cat's out of the bag."

Annie laughed and shook her head.

Over two scoops of rocky road, Annie told Sam about Chuck and their unexpected moments. Then she told him about her recent confusion with Leo and about the changes she saw in Mace.

"Sam, I'm just so confused by all of them," she said.

As he pushed his bowl to the center of the table and leaned back in his chair, he eyed her for a moment before postulating, "Isn't possible, Annie, that God brought you all three of those men?"

"But, Sam, you know that for the longest time I never thought this—this trusting men, much less feeling romantic about them—would ever be an option again. Also, it's not okay for me to feel this way about all three of them, right?"

Sam crossed his arms. "Annie, God wants to save these men. Men need to be saved from themselves. Sometimes the best way to save a man from himself is for him to recognize who he could be and who he needs to be. No one teaches a man that better than a strong woman."

Annie spooned the last of her ice cream into her mouth and contemplated Sam's words as if they were in the bottom of her bowl. "So you're saying it's entirely possible that I'm not supposed to be with any of them and that I shouldn't have these feelings?"

Sam shook his head and reached for a toothpick, which sat in a small red glass jar on the lazy susan in the center of the table. He began to chew on the pick. "I've never pretended to know anything about a woman's feelings. I'm just talking to you about God. His plans, Annie, are always bigger than how you feel."

"You'd think I would know that better than anyone," she said in a solemn voice.

"Now don't go beating yourself up about things. Go tuck in your boy, and then saddle up. Be alone with your Maker and ask Him about all this. I don't know everything, but He does. Go ask Him." Sam leaned across the table and tousled her hair.

"You might not know everything, but you always know what to say to me."

"Go on now," he said, shooing her up the stairs.

"Thanks, Sam."

"Get up those stairs," he said, pretending to scold her.

She turned and bounded up the stairs two at a time. Halfway up she heard "You're welcome" float up from the kitchen, which made her smile. Opening the door to Sammy's room, she found him asleep half on and half off the bed. His feet were propped up on the bed, while his head and most of his body were on the floor, a comic book open near his nose.

"I don't know how he does this," she said out loud, shaking her head. Tidying up the clothes that were on the floor and hanging up his baseball gear on the wall, she made a path to where he was. She lifted his limp body onto the bed and scooted him into the center. She pulled the covers up over his body but left his arms out on top, just the way he liked it.

She kissed his forehead and sat next to him. Closing her eyes and placing one hand over his heart, she prayed the prayer over him that she did every night.

"God, this boy is Yours. Make his heart like Your heart. Make him strong, and keep him safe. Amen."

She kissed Sammy again and silently slipped out of his room. She closed the door behind her and quickly changed in her room. She briefly looked out the window as she pulled her old boots on. It was getting dark, and it had been a long time since she had a night ride up to the bluff.

Downstairs, Sam was already settled in his lazy-boy recliner with the remote and decaf cup of coffee. "Take your phone with you. You hear me?" he scolded as she breezed past him and into the kitchen.

"Yes, Sam. I'm going up to the bluff just so you know where I'm headed."

"Okay. Goodnight."

"Love you."

"You too."

Then she was out the side door, heading toward the barn, which was quiet tonight. Leo had been gone all evening, and now that she thought about it, she hadn't seen his truck most of the day. She wondered where he was but was also glad that he wasn't around so she could saddle her horse and slip away into the cool dusk of the evening without having to encounter him.

She lifted the saddle on to the gray and white painted back of her horse. "Let's get out of here, girl." She patted the mare's neck and tightened the straps underneath her girth. The horse whinnied as Annie stepped into the stirrup and swung her leg over.

Annie settled into the saddle as she guided the horse out of the barn into the evening air. The sky had blushed into a dusty shade of purple, and the sun was slipping away through the trees as if it was melting. She took her time riding the trail up the ledge on the plateau. The cicadas sang loudly over the babble of the creek that ran away from her through the rocks and the tall grasses. She heard a woodpecker working on a nearby tree, and she heard the wind whip around small brush. She smiled, enjoying being in God's creation.

The trail grew dark as the sun disappeared, but she trusted her horse. Besides, she knew the path as well as she knew her own truffle recipe. Reaching the top of the plateau, she looked down over the town that would soon bustle with movie sets and actors. She tried to imagine it—the sets, the lights, the cameras, and the people. The more she thought about the movie, the more her thoughts bounced from Mace to Chuck and then to Leo. She felt the wind stir up, and she remembered Sam's words from earlier. *God's plan is bigger than the way I feel.*

As the wind danced, she breathed each man's name softly, letting the wind carry each one away. Then she sat atop her horse, calm and alone. She wanted to go back to normal. *Whatever "normal" is*, she thought. *No, I do know what that is. It's baking, it's theater, and it's Sammy.*

Then, deep in some hidden resonating cavern in her heart, she hoped and even ached that God would not leave her to bear the past alone. As she allowed that cavern to echo in her mind, she spoke her heart out loud to the Lord.

"The only arms I've ever known were angry ones. Please don't let that always be true." She paused, shocked that she had spoken the words out loud. Closing her eyes and feeling the pressure of her unspoken aches lift, she continued, "Also, please let Sammy know a real father."

When she opened her eyes, she saw it. Like the layout of the streets below, she saw her life and how it intersected with each person who came along.

God had brought her Leo, who had witnessed her past, and He had brought Sam. Both men helped her bear the weight of her past all these years. Annie thought of all the times that Leo had held her and let her cry. His arms had been strong, firm, and full of love and safety.

God had surrounded Sammy with men like Sam and Leo, who loved him as a father would. God had already answered her prayers, just not in the way she expected. She remembered something that Sam always used to tell her: "God not only saves us from the past, but He redeems the past."

He is redeeming my past, she thought, and though she had avoided thinking about Leo most of the day, she saw him differently now as she watched the streets below intersect and converge but then later fork. Leo had been part of her redemption story, but what if he needed his own? What if he was staying because he couldn't let go of what happened? What if he felt responsible and therefore felt trapped? Maybe she needed to let him find his own story, a fresh story, one that wasn't tainted by hers.

Annie gave her horse a kick, and they raced back down the path, never slipping a shoe or stumbling over a rock. She knew if it were light enough to see it, there would be a cloud of red dust behind them. She slowed the mare just before they reached the barn so that her heart had a chance to slow as well. She couldn't be sure how this conversation would go, but she knew what she had to do for Leo's sake.

Leo came to stand in the doorway and shoved his work gloves in a back pocket. He leaned a shoulder against the doorframe and watched her dismount and lead her horse inside.

"You're out riding late," he observed casually. "Something on your mind?"

Annie scooped some sweet feed into the horse's bucket and let the reins fall. Annie turned back toward Leo, who was still facing out of the barn.

"Leo, you didn't have to come to Texas, and you didn't have to stay with us and take such good care of us all. I know you wouldn't have done any of those things if you didn't love us or me, right? Do you love me, Leo?"

He spun on his heel so fast she was surprised he didn't fall. The barn cast shadows across him, but she could still see that he looked almost pained as he found her eyes. In two long strides, he had his arms around her waist.

"What are you asking me, Annie?"

She felt his breath on her face and began to panic about the way the conversation was already going. "I guess *how* is a better way to ask it. *How* do you love me?"

"How?" he asked, confused but unwavering in his hold on her.

"Do you love me like a sister, a best friend, or what?"

He tilted her chin with one finger, and then lightly brushed his lips over hers.

"Does that answer your question?"

"Leo!" she said, pulling away from him in shock. "Leo, please don't." She sighed and cursed out loud this time. "Please don't do that again. I have something I need to talk about, and that will only make it harder." She led him to the hay bale by the door where there was fresh air. She needed to clear her head.

"What I need to know is if you love me like that because of what we've been through."

"I thought you knew back then that I was crazy about you...before."

"I know. I mean, I knew back then that you had a crush on me, but it changed...after. You were strong, loyal, and protective—all of those things could be said of a brother. Then, when other men came into my life, suddenly that brother was...is...Leo, you are *in* love with me, aren't you?"

Leo looked away and retrieved a toothpick from his pocket, placing it between his teeth to chew on and avoiding looking at Annie.

"I know this is going to sound weird, but I feel like I need to release you. Let you go live your life."

"Release me?" Leo barked in confusion, and Annie could see his defenses flare.

"Maybe our past had some hold on us."

"I don't necessarily see that as a bad thing, Annie," Leo commented.

"I know, but I don't want you to miss out on life and love because of some unspoken obligation to protect me," Annie pleaded.

"I don't understand."

"I've seen the way you flirt with that waitress over at Max's and the bartender who gives you free drinks. While it might surprise my jealous side, I don't want you to feel like you can't explore…"

"Just stop."

"Leo, don't be mad."

"Stop it, Annie!" Leo growled, and Annie backed away from him.

Tears threatened her eyes, but she swallowed them down and tried to stand her ground.

"Please don't get mad. I'm not saying any of this right."

"Then what are you trying to say?"

Annie closed her eyes and took a deep breath. She remembered the wind dancing around her on the ledge earlier, and she so badly wanted to make him understand.

"Tonight, I was on the mountain, and I prayed for you and about you. God showed me how He had brought you to me not only for salvation but for redemption too. You've shown me what it is to be safe, to be held by pure arms, and to be loved, and you've taken care of Sammy. You've helped redeem what was broken, damaged, and lost. But what if God has bigger plans for you, but you refuse to see them or be open to them because of what happened in the past?" She heard her own truth hidden in the words she spoke to him.

Leo's face had softened, and he relaxed back against the bale, crossing his arms. His voice was adamant yet soft. "What if your past is part of the bigger plan for *me*? What if *you* are refusing to see it because you're always running away from it?"

Annie couldn't believe the line he had just crossed, and she got angry.

"Have I ever run? When have I ever run? Having Sammy? Do you call that running?" she yelled and turned away from him. She couldn't dam up the tears any longer, and they tumbled down her cheeks in hot salty pairs. She didn't know if she should just walk away or try to make sense of their fighting words.

Finally, Leo spoke. "Why can't you admit you have feelings for me?"

Annie shook her head but didn't turn to look at him.

"I don't know how I feel, Leo. I'm not sure of a whole lot right now except for what God told me up on that ridge tonight."

Leo tried to reach for her arm, but she pulled back and continued.

"I came here tonight to give you a reason to figure out what God's plans for you are. If it ends up including Sammy and me somehow, then so be it. But I don't want you to never ask Him just because we live on the same ranch and share a tragic past."

"Yeah, right," Leo sneered. "Are you sure this isn't about those other two men and your feelings for them?"

"Leo, when the woman you've confessed love to says she's confused, don't respond with hateful words." She angrily wiped at her tears.

"Annie, I'm sorry. I stepped on all kinds of lines, I know."

"I am honest-to-goodness confused, Leo."

"Well, I am not. You're right about one thing. I am in love with you, Annie. I've never been confused about that. Maybe you need some time to sort this all out," he said, his hurt-filled eyes boring into her. "Maybe you need some space."

This is going terribly, Annie thought to herself. *This is not how I saw this going. Now he's talking about space. What is that even mean?*

"Leo? What are you talking about?"

Leo pushed off the hay bale and towered over her. "I'm talking about maybe I should find my own place." He stomped off into the darkness of the barn.

Annie winced as his door slammed.

His own place? He has his own place out here. Maybe he'll cool off and not really act on that. Yes, those were just impulsive words, she thought as she slowly made her way back to the house.

This time, it was evening instead of early morning when Mace showed up at Annie's bakery.

Annie had been working hard all day, and she knew Mace would eventually be knocking on her door. This time, he was seeking her out instead of finding her on accident.

The Corner Baptist Church was having a fundraiser on Sunday, and she'd been baking pies and pastries all day to donate. She'd sent Mandy home around 4 o'clock and made sure the boys had dinner before taking some time to clear her head.

As she scrubbed bowls and soaped spatulas, she prayed.

"Lord, I've not known what You wanted to do in my life since Mace Harlen entered stage left. It seems that I'm making a mess of things even when I think I'm acting on what You've told me. Please show me what to do. I've got all these girl emotions, and I wish I could gather them all up and just bake them out. Help me, Lord."

She heard a knock on the door as she whispered, "Amen." Drying her hands, she wished her anxiety would absorb into the green and white polka dotted towel just as much as the water from her hands was. She took a deep breath and opened the door for Mace. It had been so long since she had first seen him standing there in her doorframe. It was somehow ironic that he even was, considering both of them thought they'd never see each other after that first day.

"Annie," he said affectionately. He smiled and offered her a hand to shake, which she thought was funny and somehow more business-like than their history called for.

She shook it anyway, saying, "Hi, Mace. Good to see you again. Come in. I'm just finishing up the dishes."

"Somehow I knew that. You know my grandmother used to say Jesus sat at the right hand of the sink."

Annie squinted at him and cocked her head, "First of all, you call your grandma Grandmother? Secondly, you never told me you had a believing grandmother!"

Mace laughed and followed her inside. "Actually, no. We called her Cece, but sometimes that can be too much information. So I introduce her as Grandmother. She was very formal. Secondly, yes, she was a believer, though I never thought about how much she prepared me to know Jesus until lately. A lot of memories are coming back to me."

Annie didn't try to hold back the smile she felt inside. She let him see it just before she turned toward the dishes. There was one bowl left, so she unplugged the sink as she washed it. Rinsing it thoroughly, she talked over her shoulder without fully turning to look at him. "How was your flight?"

Mace surveyed the room, both remembering sleeping in the barber chair and seeing the room in a new visionary light. "It was good. I slept. We've been going non-stop for weeks now, and I have not slowed down enough to sleep. Once I sat down on the plane, I was out."

"That's good," was all she could think to say. She untied her apron and dried her hands again. Looking over everything she had already tidied up, she made sure there wasn't anything that needed to be done that couldn't be left until the next morning. Finding nothing, she shrugged and smiled. "Guess I'm ready. Are you?"

"Yes, where should we go?"

"There's the usual—Max's or Billy's—but both are loud. There's a new place over across from the theater, sort of a sit-down place. And if we want, we could always get take out and eat in my office at the theater."

"What would you prefer?" he asked simply.

Annie was thrown by his thoughtfulness, so different from his typical opinionated way. She tried to think about what she would actually prefer.

"I'd like to try the new place if it's okay with you."

"My theme lately is trying new things," he said, flashing her a smile.

"Randy?" Annie questioned the tall waiter that walked toward them. He had his ponytail pulled back and wore a black vest and white button-down shirt with a tie. "What are you doing? Do you work here?"

Randy briefly hid behind the menu. He finally lowered it to reveal a blushing embarrassed face. "Business has been slow, so I've been picking up shifts here on the weekends. Since this is

Ethel's place, she let me have the job, though I'm a better fit for the crowd over at Billy's."

Annie smiled. "You look quite dashing in that vest." She shot at glare at Mace, who was trying desperately not to laugh.

Randy smoothed his vest and cleared his throat. "Well, ma'am, what can I get you to drink?"

"Just sweet tea, thank you, and he'll have..." she trailed off and pointed to Mace to finish the sentence.

"Water."

"Hello, Mr. Harlen. Good to see you again."

"You too, Randy." Randy nodded and then disappeared into the kitchen.

Mace lifted his eyebrows. "I see it's a season for trying new things for more than just me."

Annie looked up from the menu and gave him a quizzical look. "What do you mean?"

"He was not my biggest fan before. Now he is trying really hard to be nice."

Annie thought back to Randy apologizing to her about the way he had acted when Mace was in town before. After the apology, Randy had nothing but high remarks to say about him since, but she didn't tell Mace that, thinking it might feed his pride. Both of them studied the menu in comfortable silence until Randy returned with the drinks.

After Randy had taken both of their orders, he left for the kitchen again, and Mace sat up a little straighter and lay his hands on the table.

"Annie," he started softly.

Annie felt prickly at the way he said her name. He seemed so different she couldn't anticipate what was coming next.

"I have a lot I want to talk to you about, but I don't want to overload you. So where would you like to start?"

He was sweet and attentive, and she couldn't ignore how handsome he was. If she weren't careful, Annie knew that she could misunderstand what was between them. Maybe she had from the beginning, she thought. Had she secretly been hoping to fall for the famous actor? Though his countenance was softer and his attitude less selfish, she knew that this dinner was solid business.

"I want you to feel comfortable, but I have something I want to say no matter what," he continued.

She felt secure in her expectations of the evening with Mace, took a reassuring breath, and then smiled at him.

"I am comfortable, Mace. I will let you know if you overload me, but you came here to get things off your chest. I want you to be able to do that."

Relieved at her response, Mace leaned back in his chair, relaxed enough now to talk freely. He was about to launch into his apology when she stopped him.

"Can I just ask one thing?"

"Sure. Anything."

"What exactly has changed? Where is the Mace who first showed up at my door?"

"That's part of my apology. I want to apologize for the man I was although he didn't know any better. All he knew was how to be selfish, protect himself, love himself, pursue himself, and promote himself...the list keeps going."

"What changed that?"

"I'm not saying I know *how* to change completely now, but at least I know I need to. I had just been running away from everything for so long, but God had been chasing me as much as I'd been running. Finally one day, He just stopped me in my tracks and spoke to me, and I couldn't run anymore. I met God while I was literally running."

"Wow. That's ironic."

"I know, right? Then during Lithgow's pitch meeting, God opened my eyes to see what this whole project is about and what your story is actually about."

"What did you see?"

"New life. After all, that's really what every story is supposed to be about."

Annie shook her head, and her eyes grew wide. "I am amazed."

"I knew you would think so, but more than being amazed, I want you to forgive me. Please forgive me for the way I treated you, for the things I said to you, for running away from you, and for just being me."

Annie reached across the table and squeezed his hand.

"I forgive you, Mace Harlen." For a moment, the room slowed, not stopping entirely but pausing as if something in time was shifting and things would never be the same again.

Annie looked into Mace's eyes and realized that she had indeed wished for a romantic connection between them at one time, but what had just passed between them was much greater. Just as Sam had said, God's plans for her and His plans for Mace Harlen were bigger than how she felt.

Over breadsticks, Mace recounted every meeting he had been to and all the progress they had made on the movie. Finally, he paused and let her chew her food before he continued.

"Annie, this is your story. So many lives have already changed because of you. You are the key, and I want you to be a part of this project."

Her sweet tea helped her swallow the last bite, and she set her napkin on the table, folding it as she thought about her answer.

"I've had my share of complications the past few weeks. I have been so confused and frazzled. What I want is to go on with life as I knew it."

"What if God wants you to try new things?"

Annie laughed and then smiled a surrendering smile.

"Then I need to ask Him about it."

Mace nodded. "I can understand that. You ask Him, and let me know what He says."

"Okay," she agreed, unsure what God might say when she asked.

Over dessert, Mace questioned her about the complications she had spoken of, and Annie confided in him about Leo and her fear that when she got home tonight, his apartment would be empty. Mace snickered when she had told him about the kiss, but he intently listened as she told him about her encounter with God on the ledge and about releasing Leo. He even wrote down the line she told him from Sam about God's plans being bigger than people's feelings, saying Chuck would love that line. Chuck's name gave Annie a warm feeling, but she kept the stories about the two of them to herself. Distracted by her own withholding, she didn't notice Mace swipe a sealed envelope lying under the bill and stuff it his pocket coolly.

After they left the restaurant and walked along on the streetlamp-lit sidewalk, Annie asked casually, "When will shooting begin?"

"Well, not to harp, but I really do feel like you are key. I will wait for you to feel comfortable, and then we start up as soon as possible. I'd like to use some of the local people and even some of your theater kids...with your permission, of course."

"Of course," she agreed, realizing she already was acting as if she was a part of this whole project. As she acknowledged that to herself, a swirling breeze swept some bronze foliage across the street toward them. Something about the way the leaves danced in and out of the breeze made Annie stop and watch. As she watched, she found herself straining to see the spindly arms of the wind that carried them even though she knew it wasn't there.

Unaware that Mace had stopped a few feet in front of her and turned to look at her, she watched in amazement as the leaves came to rest on her boots. Then the breeze swept upward around her, blowing her hair all around. She laughed and tried to wrap her hair up, but she struggled against her own curls. Then she heard the voice speak in the breeze just to her, saying, *You don't have to look so hard for Me. You can see what I am doing.*

Annie's eyes flew wide, and she caught Mace's gaze. A smile spread like sweet jam across her face as he closed the gap between them. What a sight she must have been just then, but he wasn't laughing at her though his eyes held a glint of mischief.

"I know that look. God just spoke to you, didn't He?" Mace asked.

Annie laughed, thinking that she never would have thought Mace would understand a conversation like this. "He did. It's the craziest thing."

"I bet it's not. Tell me."

Mace had her by the elbows, and though they were standing close, all she felt was the wonder of hearing the voice in the wind. It was new and engulfing every time she heard Him, and she knew that she'd never mistake His voice.

"He said that I need to quit looking so hard for Him because I can already see what He's doing. I think He's telling me that this project isn't your project. It's His, and I am already involved." Annie's smile hadn't faded, but she shrugged in surrender.

Mace laughed and couldn't help but hug her as he said, "So you'll do it?"

Annie pulled away and let her arms fall away from him to let the moment settle a little. "I'll need to talk to the boys because this involves them too, but I think that my answer is yes. Although, I think that yes depends on what you're asking me to do."

Mace's brow furrowed an inch, and he cocked his head to the side in confusion. "With your theater background, I figured you would know what I was asking?"

"I don't."

"I want you to play…you." Mace's momentary elation dropped to apprehension, waiting for her answer now. His voice hung in the air between them.

Annie's hand flew to cover her mouth, and her eyes grew wide again. She shook her head, grabbed his hands in hers, and pulled him down to a bench on the sidewalk. She closed her eyes and took two quick deep breaths. Holding his hands, she spoke calmly and sweetly.

"Mace, we haven't known each other very long, so I don't know much about your childhood. Maybe it's been a fairytale or maybe you have your own horror stories to tell. I don't know. For me, telling you and Chuck was one hard thing entirely, but re-enacting it is something I can't fathom. It would just be…I can't…" She closed her eyes again as a small tear escaped from the corner of her almond-shaped lids. "I know there's a place for me in your project, but I can't act in it. I'm sorry."

Mace could see the pain she held at bay as he wiped the tear from her cheek, and suddenly, as if a new lens had been placed over his eyes, he saw the magnitude of what he'd just proposed. *Harlen! How could you be so moronic and heartless? What is wrong with you?* He berated himself silently, then said aloud, "Annie, please forgive this visionary boy who didn't think about the emotional ramifications of what I was asking. I am such an idiot. Please forgive me."

"Thank you, Mace. I do want to be a part of your whole vision, just maybe more behind the scenes?"

"Like I said, you're the key. We'll find a place where you'll fit perfectly and feel comfortable."

All the way back to the ranch, Annie retraced their conversation. She was so excited to tell Leo how it had all gone. She was still smiling, thinking back over the leaves and the breeze, but as she pulled up to the barn, her heart sunk a little as she saw his truck was gone.

Maybe he's just out late, she reassured herself as she hopped out of the cab and walked into the barn. It was black and vacant. She didn't need the light because she knew the way to his door like the back of her hand. She opened it, and even in the darkness, she could feel the emptiness. When she slowly flipped the light switch on, it took the breath from her chest to see the empty room. The sheets were folded on the end of the bed, and the shelves were bare. Everything was blank and harsh, which brought fresh tears to Annie's eyes as she looked around the room.

Leo was gone.

She touched the counter where she wished he'd left a note. Silently, she walked to the house, where she searched the kitchen for a note, for anything, but it seemed that he had simply walked out.

Annie trudged upstairs and flopped onto her bed. There, in the dark, she questioned why God had asked her to release Leo. She felt scared knowing he wasn't in the barn, and she felt empty knowing he was angry with her. She stared up at the ceiling, thinking through all the years they had spent together and the history they shared.

24. AN APPENDIX AND COFFEE

The creamer swirled into the coffee, blended into the rich darkness, and mixed with the sugar Annie poured from her spoon. It landed lightly and danced together, creating the perfect shade in her cup. Sam watched her from the sink and smiled at how intently she was on focusing on anything but the fact that Leo was gone. He glanced out at the barn where he usually saw Leo feeding the horses or working on the tractor. He shook his head at the empty space where Leo had always parked his truck.

"It just doesn't seem real, Annie."

Annie slumped, knowing what Sam was bringing up. She took a long draw from her coffee cup and pressed her cold palms to her puffy, weary eyes.

"I know, Sam. I can't make sense of it. But I did what I thought—"

Sam interrupted her. "No, dearie. Don't you do that. Don't doubt in the dark what you knew in the light. God spoke, and you obeyed. Let it fall where it may." He had come to stand beside her. Despite his age, he still had the power to gather her wits up with his arms around her and lift her out of the pit. "God never promised that if you released Leo, everything would be hunky dory."

Annie smiled with tired eyes and nodded. "You're right, Sam. It's hard not to back away from what I thought was right when it seems to backfire."

"Stick to your guns, Annie. It'll be hard without him, but God knows what He's doing."

She abandoned her coffee and embraced him back, thanking him for loving her and always knowing what to say.

"I certainly know what to say now…get out there to that barn and feed the horses!" He pushed her jokingly toward the door. She laughed and reached back for her coffee, willing to pick up the work Leo usually did, but she'd need more coffee to do it.

Just as she was almost out the door, Sammy's blonde head peeked around the corner, his eyes curious and concerned.

"Mom, is Leo gone?"

Annie froze and immediately looked to Sam for help. He shrugged his shoulders and smiled as if to say that he wasn't interfering. Annie shot him a glare, quickly sat down at the table, and beckoned Sammy to come sit down beside her.

"Sammy, you know how sometimes your dog Bags runs off?" His floppy blonde curls bounced as he nodded, so she continued, "Where does Bags go?"

"I don't always know. Sometimes he goes out into the hills, but he always comes back."

Annie smiled at his sweet blue eyes, filled with hope. "That's right, sweetie. Sometimes he just needs to get out for a while. He needs some space to run, but he always comes home. What do we do for Bags while he's out in the hills alone?"

"We pray for him to come home," he said.

Even though he was much too big for her lap, Annie scooped him up and hugged him tight.

"That's right, Sammy. We pray for him."

They sat, hugging for a long moment with Sam watching from across the kitchen.

Suddenly Sammy sat straight up, looked at Annie with brow furrowed hard, and said, "You mean Leo has run away?"

Annie fought back a laugh and then said, "Well, sweetheart, not exactly. Leo just needed some space."

Sammy shook his head. "I don't know what that means, but I'll pray that Leo comes home." He bounded off Annie's lap and back up the stairs. Annie let out a laugh and a tear at the same time. Sam nodded and pretended to tip his hat to her.

"Well done, Annie girl."

"Thanks. Can we pray Leo comes home? What if that isn't what God wants?" she asked as she stood up to refill her coffee cup.

"You can always tell God what you want to happen, but He'll always do what is best."

Annie nodded and kissed him on the cheek. She pulled on boots, grabbed her coffee in one hand and her gloves off the coat rack in the other, and slipped out the door. Cool air brushed her hair off her shoulders and greeted her sweetly on the cheeks, but before she reached the edge of the porch, she stopped in her tracks at what she saw.

In the driveway, Leo stood, bathed in gold morning light, adjusting his hat over his shaggy blonde hair. He wore a flannel shirt under his canvas vest, and Annie thought he had never looked better.

He's come home! If there are country cowboy angels, they must look like that. I hope he never leaves again, Lord.

As if he sensed her plea, he looked up to find her gaze fixed on him. Annie wondered if he could see surprise and delight on her face despite her swollen eyelids. She knew she must look a mess from the long, tear-filled night before. As his eyes dropped back down to his boots, she felt as though she had just looked in his empty room again for the first time.

Wait, she thought. *What if he's not really coming home? What if he's not here to stay? Do I dare ask?*

Something other than hurt welled up in her chest, and she almost felt anger. She stuffed her gloves in a back pocket and stomped down the stairs. She *did* dare to ask.

She wanted to get face to face with him. If she were honest, she felt like pushing him, but she kept her distance. She stepped off the last stair and stood facing him, still a good distance away. She wanted to bring her six-shooter words out blazing, but she shoved her hands in her pockets and tried to relax.

"Thought you were gone," she said flatly.

Although he must have heard her step off the porch, he hadn't looked up until she spoke.

"I am," he said harshly.

Annie stared at him for a moment. *He hasn't come home.* She tried to let it sink in, but it wouldn't. *Maybe this is not his home.* She looked around and slapped her legs as if to say they were wasting time. "And yet you're here."

He scowled at her from under his straw hat. "Annie, I may have moved out like I told you I would, but I won't shirk my duties on this ranch."

Before Annie had time to react, Sammy exploded out of the side door.

"Leo! You came home!" he screamed as he tore past Annie. She tried to stop him, but he evaded her arms and reached for Leo, who grabbed him up and swung him around while shooting a glare at Annie.

"Momma said you needed space to run and that you'd come home, just like Bags," Sammy said, hugging Leo's neck. Leo's glare softened. It was obvious he hadn't thought about Annie having to explain to Sammy where he'd gone or why he'd left the ranch.

"Is that what Mom said?" he asked.

Annie shrugged at him as if to ask, *What else was I supposed to say?*

Leo squatted and set Sammy down. "Well, buddy, I found my own place. I'm not going to live here anymore, but I'll still see you when I come do all my work here on the ranch. Okay?"

"Why don't you want to live in the barn anymore? I like having you here," Sammy pouted.

"I know, buddy. I did too. This is just something I need to do."

Sammy cocked his head, wrinkled up his nose, and asked, "Grown up stuff, huh?" Leo laughed and said, "Yeah, something like that."

Sammy slapped Leo's back. "I never understand any of that, but I'm glad you'll be around." With that, he ran off toward the creek.

"Just a little while, Sammy. We're going to town, okay?" Annie called after him.

"Okay!" he called without looking back, leaving Leo and Annie standing in the driveway.

Leo moved a little closer without overstepping the invisible boundary that they both knew stood between them.

"I'm sorry. I didn't think about needing to explain things to Sammy. Maybe I should have left him a note."

Annie looked toward Sammy running through the pasture toward the creek, his curls bouncing in the wind, and then she looked back at Leo. She said, "I thought the same thing last night. I was angry that you'd left without leaving so much as a note. You weren't thinking about anyone but yourself."

"How can you even say that?" Leo asked angrily. "You did this. I left because of you. Besides, who were *you* thinking of when you 'released' me?"

Annie stomped closer to him, ready to stand her ground, Sam's words in her ears. "I was thinking of you, Leo. I was willing to forego the comfort of having you here so you weren't entrapped in my confusion of feelings. I may have presented this chance to you, but make no mistake, Leo, you chose to leave."

Leo's silent scowl proved that he was cut by her words, but his pride had billowed up inside, suffocating any humility he needed to show. He pushed past her and stormed off to the barn.

Annie felt the familiar hurt of a man walking away from her, but as she watched his long stomping strides, she was reminded of

Mace last night. *Leo may storm off, but he may also return a better man later, just like Mace did.* Though he couldn't hear, Annie whispered after him, "You can come home anytime."

The theater auditorium buzzed with voices. Excitement wafted down the aisles and pulsated in the seats. A whole section of teenagers huddled together and expectantly waited for Annie to direct them. She stood before them and bid them to quiet down. She said a few encouraging words and explained how auditions would work.

After talking to the teens near the front of the auditorium, she climbed the stairs and went to the center of the stage. From there, she projected her voice to the back of the auditorium where, under the shadow of the balcony, sat a cluster of adults. She explained that the adults' auditions would begin after the teens were done.

Then Annie took a seat in the middle row of the middle section, between Mace and Chuck, who had arrived just before auditions began. As all the teenagers took to the stage, they insecurely searched Annie for a nod or a smile to help get them started. Some had to start over because of nervous stuttering and jitters.

Throughout the auditions, Mace and Chuck scribbled madly on their legal pad and typed notes on their laptops.

At one point, Chuck leaned over and whispered in Annie's ear, "Aren't you going to write any notes? He's going to want them…"

Annie turned her face toward his just enough so Mace wouldn't hear their exchange. "Don't boss me tonight, Chuck. I'm not feeling well. Plus, I know them all so well I don't need to write their names down to remember later."

"Do you want to go home? We can manage," he said, though she thought he did not seem enthused by the prospect. She shook her head and turned away at Mace's nudge in her side.

Mace commented, "Closed auditions can begin. Do you mind calling out the names?"

"Not at all. Let me usher the kids out." She again took the stage and thanked the teenagers for coming and being courageous in their auditions. The girls giggled and huddled together as they walked slowly up the aisle, trying to stare as long as they could at Mace. The boys whooped and hollered as they raced toward the door.

Annie again directed her words back toward the shadows where the adults sat, explaining that when their name was called, they could pick the gender-appropriate script and take the stage.

As she headed back to her seat, she overheard Chuck whisper to Mace, "She's so natural when she's on stage, even when she's explaining rules. It's a shame she doesn't want to act." Annie pretended she hadn't heard anything.

Twenty-five nondescript actors later, Annie called out, "Sarah Lee Makin." A rush of red-haired waves blew past them and whisked up the stairs. As the woman turned to face the audience, Chuck, Annie, and Mace let out a collective gasp. She had fiery hair that was a much bolder shade than Annie's auburn, but aside from that, she could have been Annie's sister. She read her part well, her voice having a clear strength but also a sweetness that captivated both Chuck and Mace. Annie noticed their eyes and their smiles were wide as they watched the woman, but when she was done, they gave her a simple and professional, "Thank you," as she left the stage.

Annie looked down at the page to read off the next name. Her eyes traced the letters, but she couldn't believe them. Was she seeing them right?

Mace whispered, setting his pen down, "You can read the next name. I'm ready."

She traced and retraced the letters, but they weren't going away. She couldn't get her mouth to work.

"Annie, is everything okay?" Mace asked, noticing her frozen posture. Annie flashed him a look, gripped his forearm, and pointed to the name.

With the slight surge of courage she felt from gripping Mace's arm, she heard her voice project while her eyes stayed on Mace.

"Leo Chase?"

Why is he auditioning? To spite me? To hurt me? To prove something? Why didn't he tell me this morning he was going to audition? Annie turned to see Leo rise from his seat underneath the shadows and walk down the aisle toward them. He caught her shocked expression for a moment but looked to the floor. All three heads followed him as he strode up the stage, boots echoing in the silence of the theater. Annie scooted back in her chair and tried to relax down into it.

Leo began the hospital scene, but he didn't even use the script. Annie felt like every one of her muscles was rigid, and although she willed her stomach to unclench, it refused.

When the audition was over, Leo casually stood facing the three shock-filled sets of eyes. Annie felt tears threatening, but she scolded herself silently not to cry in front of any of these men.

Finally, Mace cleared his throat and said, "Leo, tell us. What makes you want this part?"

Leo shoved his hands deep into his pockets and rocked back on his boots slightly. While his legs were planted wide apart and his face was casual, Annie felt that his eyes glinted with arrogance, which sent a wave of nausea over her.

"This is partly my story, so I want to help tell it."

A sharp pain in Annie's side sent her doubling over in pain, grasping at her stomach and shirt.

"Annie?" Chuck reached for her. She let out a quiet, high-pitched moan and grabbed her side harder in agony.

"Call 911," Mace said as he lifted her from the chair.

Chuck's face dropped to a pale concern as he said, "I don't think they have that here." He followed Mace toward the aisle.

Mace and Chuck simultaneously looked up at Leo, who stood stunned on the stage. He looked helpless.

Mace shook his head and said to Chuck, "Let's get her in the truck. I'll drive her there. You call Sam."

As Annie clutched his shirt in pain, she whispered, "Sorry about auditions."

"Annie, don't be sorry. Just be okay."

They reached her truck and tried to position her in the seat, but every way they tried to lay her down, she howled in pain. Finally, as Mace fired up the truck, Chuck scooped her and got in, holding her close.

"I'll just hold her. You drive."

Mace sped through the street, leaving a group of bewildered actors standing on the sidewalk. Leo stood in the middle of the street, staring after them.

Annie hid her face in Chuck's shoulder so they couldn't see her crying. She clawed at his arm as each wave of pain hit her, leaving a plaid of red lines on his arm.

Chuck stroked the back of her hair and reassured her. Though her face was mostly hidden in his shirt, he saw her forehead was pale and beaded with sweat.

"Mace, we've got to hurry," he said. "She's going into shock."

"I've already got it to the floor. We're almost there. Just keep talking to her. Don't let her pass out."

Moments later, they pulled up to the emergency door of the hospital. A stretcher and several nurses were waiting to greet them.

"News travels fast in a small town." Chuck managed to laugh.

Annie gripped his neck and didn't want to release him when the nurses tried to take her out of his arms to get her on a stretcher. Chuck knew it was a fleeting moment he would never forget, her cool hands grasping tightly to him in panic.

Then, in a sterile moment filled with blurring scrubs, she was whisked away, and the two men were left standing alone in the waiting room.

They both sat down, several chairs apart and, as if on cue, leaned forward with their elbows on their knees. Muffled sounds of the baseball game on the TV tempered the silence of the waiting room, and the second hand on the red clock hung on the wall in front of them ticked softly. Mace's leg bounced in anticipation while Chuck chewed on his thumbnail. Soon, sliding glass doors rattled on their tracks as Sam rushed in with Sammy on his heels.

"Mace, Chuck—what's happened?"

Both men flew to their feet at the sound of Sam's shaken voice.

"We were hosting auditions, and she just doubled over in pain," Mace said.

"What's going on?" Sammy asked.

"We haven't been here long. The doctor hasn't even come out yet." Chuck patted Sammy on the head.

"Where's Leo?"

Mace shrugged and began to explain but was interrupted by the doctor barging through the wide double surgery doors. He took off his mask and directed his handshake to Sam but his words to Mace.

"It's a miracle she's alive. You got her here just in time. Her appendix ruptured as we got it out. She's going to be fine, though."

Everyone sighed heavily in relief.

The doctor continued, "We're getting her to a room, and you can see her shortly."

"Thank you, doctor," Mace said.

The lanky doctor nodded at Mace and led Sam away, asking, "Sam, can I talk to you in private?"

"What's an appendix?" Sammy asked as the doctor and Sam moved away.

"C'mon, Sammy, let's go see what the cafeteria has," Mace said, trying to distract him despite wanting to keep a watchful eye on the exchange between the doctor and Sam.

Chuck slapped Mace's shoulder. "I'll come too. Sam will handle whatever the doctor didn't want us to hear. It's not really our business anyway. Plus, I love me some pudding."

As they walked away, the doctor and Sam stepped into a side hallway just around the corner from the registration desk.

"I'll cut to the chase, Sam," the doctor began. "We've known each other a long time. While we were extracting the appendix, we found something on her uterus."

"You found what exactly?" Sam prodded, slightly irritated because the doctor wasn't exactly cutting to the chase.

"We found a tumor. We went ahead and biopsied it, but it's possible, once we get lab results back on it, Annie will need to choose to have a complete hysterectomy."

Sam sighed, feeling the weight of the doctor's clinical words settle on his heart. *She's already faced so much, and I think she wants more children. What could You possibly be doing, Lord?* Sam wondered in the honesty of his heart.

"I see," he said softly.

"I'll let you know when she's awake."

Sam, lost in his muddled thoughts, managed a nod but said nothing as he walked back to the waiting room, which now seemed bleak and dismal with its pale, aqua green trim and bench seats. The fluorescent lights were harsh, and he longed to take Annie home and let her lie on her own couch when she heard the news, comfortable under her favorite down blanket and cozy in the dim living room, lit only by the fading firelight.

He was reminded of when she was younger and they had gone camping near the creek and the crease of the ridge where it rose up out of the plains. The night had grown cold after the sun went down, and Annie was wrapped up in her sleeping bag, trying to be brave and not wanting to complain. Eventually, after she had fallen asleep, Sam carried her back to the house, set her down on the floor in the living room, and lit a fire in the fireplace.

I know she'll be brave enough to face this, Lord, but I fear I am too old. This old man's faith wavers as much as my knees do...though I never want her to know that. Help me see her through this, Sam prayed as he waited.

Annie felt the dense medicinal fog lift as if an elephant had been sitting on her and was getting up slowly, waking her with pain as it stood. As her eyes fluttered, she looked around the room. The pain in her side was gone, but her whole body felt sore and heavy.

A voice startled her.

"Oh, good, Annie! You're awake." It was the doctor walking through her door, chart in hand and stethoscope stuffed in his coat pocket.

"What happened?" Annie managed to say through a coarse throat and heavy tongue.

"We removed your appendix. You're going to be fine. It's a miracle those two men got you here in time."

"Then why do I feel like there's a shadow lurking in the corner? I don't feel fine."

The doctor pulled up a chair beside her bed. He explained the tumor they had found and biopsied while removing the appendix. Awareness filled her eyes, and before he had even explained the ramifications, she jumped in.

"I won't have any more children, will I?"

"No, I'm afraid not. Not if you choose to have the preventative hysterectomy."

Annie's eyes filled with tears. She looked away and tried to look for God out the second-floor hospital window.

Sammy lay on the bed with Annie and cried, unsure what the words meant that she said to him, but he cried because his mommy cried. Sam held her hand and patted it. Annie slowed her breathing and tried to control the tears.

"Dearie, you don't have to say anything more."

"I do. I have to get this out," she said through sniffs. "Fairness has never really been in my vocabulary, but I can't really see where *He* is going with this." Sam nodded silently, letting her go on. "Not that I really had the option to have more kids, but it was possible at least. Now it's just impossible. Knowing that breaks my heart."

Sammy looked up at his mom. "But, Mom, you said the Bible says nothing is impossible with God."

Annie couldn't fight the small smile that spread across her face at her son's sweet honesty. She cupped his face and kissed his cheek. "I'm so proud you know that, Sammy. The Bible also says God gives us things and takes things away. Either way, we are supposed to say, 'Blessed be the name of the Lord.'"

As the words left her lips, a peace settled into the room, and the shadow of despair left the corner. Annie sighed in relief, deciding not to speak of the shadow while Sammy was around, but she silently thanked God. She felt a resolve solidify within her to trust God. She asked for a cool cloth to wipe her face, which felt like peace itself as it wiped away the clamminess of sleep and the sweat crystals that caked her forehead and neck. Feeling refreshed and less emotional, she asked if Chuck and Mace were still waiting.

"Yes, real troopers, those two," Sam said, handing her a second cloth.

"I believe they both know God now. Maybe they need to see that belief leads to trust. Somehow He keeps wanting me to show them."

"So...it's unrelated to your appendix?" Chuck probed, seemingly perplexed by her recounting of the surgery and tumor.

Annie struggled to scoot farther back against the bed in order to sit up more. "Yes, unrelated. But truly, nothing is unrelated when it comes to God. He allowed my appendix to rupture, possibly so that the doctor would find the tumor."

Chuck mouthed a silent "Wow."

Mace leaned forward and set one arm on her bed near her legs, without touching. He asked, "And...how do you feel about the hysterectomy?"

Annie looked out the window again as if the words she needed were beyond the glass somewhere out among the stars. "It doesn't seem like I have much choice, but it does mean I won't have anymore—" She paused, unable to voice the finality of it.

Sammy, who was still snuggled up close to Annie, chimed in, "Momma can't have any more babies in her tummy."

Leave it to a child to be able to speak the hard stuff, Annie thought, kissing the top of Sammy's blonde head.

"No more kids," Chuck said flatly, feeling the weight of Sammy's words.

Mace rubbed his chin now rough with stubble and leaned back in his chair. He tried fiercely to focus on what he should say to her or how he should feel about it, but his mind kept fighting with him and overwhelming his senses with the odd serenity of the moment.

It was an exquisite scene of strength and beauty lit with a glowing grace. He remembered just moments ago walking from the harshly lit waiting room, down the dim hallway, and into her room, which was filled with an ethereal glow he couldn't explain. The whole room smelled of lavender and vanilla, just like the theater. Annie looked like an angel lying against the stark white pillows and hospital sheets. While earlier her hair had been matted by sweat and her face pale, now she had swept her hair up into a loose, curly bun.

She hadn't spoken with strong resolve, but he saw it in her eyes. *That's the resolve she must have felt when she learned she was pregnant with Sammy*, Mace thought. *She must have been terrified but resolved.*

Chuck's low and almost intimate voice drew Mace out of his own thoughts. "You are so strong, Annie. I don't understand why God is asking you to handle all of this."

Mace silently scolded himself for not saying anything as he watched Annie touch Chuck's arm lightly, their eyes meeting as if Mace was no longer in the room.

"I don't feel strong. I just feel tired," she said as she mustered a weary smile. "I don't know why God would ask me to go through this either, but my heart still wants to believe He is good."

25. MOVIE SETS AND CRANBERRIES

All of the southwestern Texas plains seemed to resist winter that year. Every third day a biting wind swept across, causing people in town to wonder if they would actually see winter for the holidays this year. Then the cold would quickly dissipate, and a balminess would return to infuriate them.

One day, Sammy bounded down the stairs with his boots and favorite straw hat. "Hey, Momma!" he exclaimed in excitement.

Annie stole her eyes away from her grocery list to smile at her son.

"What, Sammy?" she asked, matching his excited tone.

"Know what I'm thankful for?"

They played this game every year, and it thrilled Annie's heart every time. She knew his answer because it was always the same.

"What?" she said, playing along.

"You!"

She squeezed him and kissed his cheek, realizing that he was taller than she expected. He was growing again.

"And I am the most thankful for you."

"Love you, Mom."

"Love you, sweetie. Be careful in the barn, okay?"

"Okay!" he yelled as he bolted through the side door toward the barn. Annie laughed and turned her attention back toward the list.

"Cranberries, that's where I was," she said, but before she could consider her mother's cranberry sauce recipe, her thoughts found their way back to her barren abdomen and her aching heart. She placed a light hand on her scar and closed her eyes before any tears had the chance to fall. It had been weeks since she sat alone in her room, staring out the window toward a horizon that seemed unsympathetic and bleak. She surrendered her desires to carry a child conceived in love and holy union, and she relinquished her hold on her dreams, silencing any bitterness that grew in her heart. She also grieved that Leo had never called.

"Lord," she whispered out loud, leaning over her grocery list. "I have grieved. I am resolved. Please take this pain away."

"What you need is to be thankful," Sam announced from the porch. "You need to be thankful for this turkey I bought!"

Did he hear me, or is his timing just that impeccable? After all, I do need to be thankful, she thought.

Her eyes widened as he walked through the door, struggling to hold up the turkey. "Sam, that is huge! Why do we need a twenty-pound turkey?"

"Well," he said, heaving it up onto the counter, "I ran into Chuck and Mace over at Billy's and invited them for Thanksgiving."

"Oh!" Annie said, realizing she needed to rethink her whole list. "Maybe I'll stop by and see them on set and work out some details."

"Are you sure you're ready to get out?"

"I think so. I do need to be grateful, but I also need to just get on," she said, trashing her list and grabbing her purse. "You know?"

"Yes, dearie, I do. Call me if you need me."

"I will. Sammy is out in the barn. I'll be back later."

Sam waved her off, proud she was venturing beyond the ranch sooner than he expected. He silently hoped she wouldn't run into Leo.

Annie wove between light stands and scissor lifts, stepping over rivers of cords and ducking under reflectors and green screens dangling from a giant crane, sitting unused for the moment. A young woman checked her badge and allowed her on set, giving her an obvious gesture to be extremely quiet. The set was cluttered with carts filled with wardrobes and props and a herd of cameras moving all at once in every direction. Annie spotted Mace behind one of the cameras, surrounded by a team of men and women. They were filming a scene with Leo. Annie's thoughts growled, but she walked toward Mace anyway, careful to stay out of the cameras' line of sight.

Once he called cut on the scene, he turned to her.

"Are you sure you feel up to being here?" he asked softly.

She leaned over and replied, "I feel great, Mace. Other than wanting to throw a boot at Leo Chase, I'm fine. Thank you, though, for caring. I just dropped by to talk about Thanksgiving, but I don't want to interrupt."

In a fleeting, momentary squeeze, Annie touched his hand, but it was enough to send what felt like a lightning bolt through his arm and made his back tense.

He smiled, nodded, and then yelled, "Again. Scene 1, take 7. Quiet on set."

Mace thought about the new notes that had arrived stealthily over the past few months that he kept close in his jeans pocket, but he decided not to tell her. He thought of all the things he'd wanted to tell her since the hospital, but the movie needed to come first right now. She looked at him from the side, but he resisted looking back, choosing to remain focused and intense.

Mace walked over to Leo and the actress playing Annie, and Annie watched Leo with a bitterness biting at her every nerve. She looked away to keep it from spreading and spotted Chuck grazing at the food table, which made her laugh. She walked softly over behind him, careful not to let her heels click on the pavement.

Feeling like she'd snuck up on him, she was just about to kick out his right knee when he said, "You know I smell you, right?"

"What?" Annie exclaimed a little too loudly. Chuck whirled around with a mischievous grin.

"Yeah. Smell."

"Is my perfume that strong?"

"No. It's just like an animal attraction thing." He winked playfully. "I can smell you a mile away."

Annie laughed and then pushed him playfully. "That's flattering…and creepy, Chuck."

"I creep myself out," he said, laughing with her.

Annie surveyed the food and made a mental note that she needed to tell Mandy to bring by some more muffins and tarts.

"How are you?" Chuck half whispered.

"I'm good. Thanks for asking. How are you?"

"Good. What do you think of Leo and the new girl?"

Annie pretended not to have noticed though she knew her pretense was thinly veiled. "Uh. Yeah, they look like they're doing good, right?" she asked it like a question.

"They have great chemistry."

"Chemistry?" Now she knew her voice betrayed her. "That's good," she over- corrected.

"It helps compensate for how distracted he was when you walked on set."

Annie flashed Chuck a look of surprise.

Chuck looked toward Leo and leaned over to whisper in her ear, "We all are."

"Chuck!" Annie breathed. *Coming here today was a bad idea*, she thought. *It's too hard.*

From the other side of the set, Leo's watchful eyes furrowed on Chuck, and he finally looked away.

"Sorry. I'm being selfish again," Chuck admitted.

"It's okay. Maybe I should go. Tell Mace I'll be at the shop. He can come by later," she said, pulling away from him, anxious to leave.

"Annie, I'm sorry," Chuck pleaded.

"It's okay, Chuck. It's not you. I just don't think I should have come here."

Chuck, Leo, and Mace all watched her hurry off the set.

Whether it was the tart cranberries that matched her mood or the plans of Thanksgiving that bounced around in her mind, she was sure Sam would love the cranberry-orange muffins with a sweet cinnamon crème glaze.

As she filled each muffin cup a quarter full, she watched the batter spread to every corner of the foil linings, and feeling as empty as those silver accordion cups, something in her heart begged God to fill her up to every corner. She put the spoon down and hovered over the muffin pans as sudden tears threatened to spill out of her eyes into the batter.

"Don't do this, Annie," she scolded herself, wiping her eyes and whisking the trays away toward the oven. As she tucked the muffins away in the oven and closed the doors on them to bake, a brisk knock came at the door. Brushing off her hands, she remembered Mace was planning to stop by. Wiping her eyes and hoping it wasn't completely obvious she'd been crying, she walked toward the door. The knock sounded again.

"Hold on. I'm coming," she called as she reached for the knob. The door swung open, and Chuck shrugged in response to the look of surprise on her face.

"I thought Mace was coming," Annie said, stepping out of his way to let him in.

"He sent me," Chuck said as he casually walked by her, breathing in deeply the sweet air. "What are you making?"

"Muffins," she said, still holding the disappointment in her voice.

Chuck took a dramatic breath in through his nose. "Let me guess…" he paused, pretending to waft the air up toward his nose. "I detect a hint of orange…and wait! Cranberry. You are in fact conjuring the Thanksgiving baking spirits, are you not? I hereby command you to share all that you have made with me."

Annie laughed. Chuck, of course, was the one who could make her laugh and lift her mood. She was glad he was here.

"Well, good sir," she said, playing along, "Whence the timer goes off, I shall make my penance to you."

"Very well, my lady. I shall sit here forthright on this stool. I await thy timer's ding."

"I love that you just shifted from some sort of Sherlockish style right into some sort of Austentonian man."

"Well, you know. I am shifty," he joked pompously.

"You know that's not a compliment, right?"

He laughed. The timer rang out from opposite side of the table. Chuck pointed to the oven and then pointed at her. She laughed again and retrieved the muffins, which were red and orange speckled perfections. She pulled one out of the pan and left the trays on the cooling racks but walked his steaming muffin over to him.

"My good sir," she said, curtsying to him and holding out the muffins with her oven mitts.

"I'm dropping all charges. Sit. I will eat." Chuck bowed slightly from his stool.

Annie pulled up a stool next to his and plopped down beside him. He took a large bite, not caring that it was much too hot to eat. He even tried to blow on it from the inside of his mouth while the muffin sat burning on his tongue.

"Oh my gosh, Chuck, stop. You're making my face hurt I'm laughing so much."

"At least I can make you laugh."

"Yes, you do always make me laugh, Chuck. I'm glad you stopped by. In truth, I needed some cheering up."

"You're not disappointed it wasn't Mace outside the door anymore?"

Annie sighed and said, "I'm sorry it was that obvious." It was funny how comfortable it was to be laughing one minute with Chuck and then talking honestly with him the next.

Chuck put the muffin down and crossed his arms on the worktable. "He's got a lot on his mind right now. He's really busy, and he's under a lot of pressure. Most of it is self-imposed, which can sometimes be the worst kind. Nonetheless, I feel I should warn you—he's sort of 'all business' lately."

"I don't have any sort of expectations or ulterior motives if that's what you are thinking. I just thought he could swing by and talk about plans for Thanksgiving since he was too busy earlier," she said, defensive about how embarrassed she felt.

Chuck reached for her hand. "No, now Annie, I don't think any of that. I just meant that he is all business and that this is sometimes how business works. When he's working late on a scene or whatever, he sends me. I'm just the writer."

Annie relaxed and said, "Oh."

"That's all I meant," Chuck said, patting her hand.

Annie ducked her head and sighed loudly. "Sorry. I'm sensitive these days."

"It's understandable. You've been through a lot."

"Ugh. I don't want to talk about this. I hate that my life is such a *Lifetime* movie sometimes. All I wanted to do was keep my head down, teach theater, and bake."

Chuck shook his head. "But, Annie, people who just keep their heads down don't change the world."

Annie let her head fall and land face down on the table. From underneath her hair, she murmured, "I didn't want any of this. I never set out to change the world."

"What was it you told me about God's plans for us being bigger that what we want?"

"How we feel."

"What?"

"God's plans for us are bigger than how we feel. Sam said that."

"Close enough. It applies. I still don't know that much about God, but from what I'm learning He knows what he's doing."

Annie groaned, resisting admitting that Chuck was right.

"Let's change the subject, what do you say?"

"Please."

"Thanksgiving. Go."

Annie lifted her head and smiled at Chuck. He slid her notebook over toward her. She knew that she needed to be thankful, and tonight she was thankful for Chuck.

"Everything looks and smells amazing, Annie," Chuck said, reaching for a roll with one hand, which Annie blocked and pretended to swat away.

"Quit it! Now get out of here. Go watch football or something until dinner is ready. Quit sampling."

"All right, all right...but come on, who wouldn't rather be in here with you and all this food?" Chuck joked, not knowing that Leo's name immediately rang in Annie's mind before she could stop it.

Where is Leo? Annie wondered. *Does he wish he were here in this kitchen with me? Does he miss arguing about the right way to baste the turkey or how tall the perfect roll needs to be?*

"I can see that you're deep in thought over those sweet potatoes, so I'll leave you to your culinary magic."

Annie looked up, embarrassed to have forgotten that Chuck was standing there. "I'm sorry. I got sidetracked. I promise it will be ready soon."

"No, no, I am the one getting sidetracked. I'll leave you to it."

Later, around the table and before a full Texan Thanksgiving spread, each person sitting said what they were thankful for. Sammy decided they should go counter-clockwise, at which point he announced he was thankful for the mini marshmallows that were perfectly puffed and golden.

Everyone laughed heartily at his simple young enthusiasm until Sam stood and lifted his wineglass.

"Several years ago," he began and then cleared his aging throat and started again. "Several years ago, my brother called me with the news that he'd had a baby girl. I gave him the hardest time, ragging him that he wouldn't know what to do with a girl. You know what he said to me? He said, 'Sam, she's already changed me, and she'll change you too. Just you wait and see.' Today, I'm reminded of the baby girl who changed my life and the woman who continues to change the world. I love you, Annie, and I'm thankful for your brilliant life."

Annie teared up a bit only to smile a moment later at the thought of her father. She saw so much of her father in Sam. They had the same wide, warm smile and bright, jolly eyes. Her smile widened as she saw a flicker of a wink from Chuck, and she was reminded of their conversation the other night at the bakery. *Almost the exact same words. Change the world.*

Annie raised her glass to Sam, noticing the others were waiting for her, gauging the moment by her as if she were their thermometer. She smiled and lifted her glass slightly higher.

"I'm thankful for…" As she began to speak, though, she noticed Leo's empty chair, and her heart sagged a little. She pushed his name aside and continued, recovering with a laugh, "I'm thankful for a table full of men, men who make me laugh, make me think, make me step out in faith, and make me a better person."

"Here, here!" Chuck chimed in. "To follow her comments, I'm thankful for all you guys. If you'll allow me to say so, you all feel more like home than I have felt in years."

Annie smiled and longed to hug him. He did feel like family, and she was thankful for the comfort she felt around Chuck. After a quick drink, all eyes seemed to travel to Mace, who hadn't spoken yet. His forefinger traveled in circles around the rim of his glass, but his eyes were intensely trained on Annie. His other hand was securely in his pocket on the envelope that he'd received that day. Annie looked away from him, feeling self-conscious.

Chuck commented, "Mace is obviously distracted but thankful. Shall we pray and carve?"

Mace snapped away from his distant thoughts and realized how rude he had been; he stood and raised his glass, shaking his head.

"Forgive me," he said. "I'm afraid I am distracted. I am also thankful because I met God this year, and that is the biggest reason to be thankful. Though I don't understand His methods, I know He's got a plan." He finished with a less intense glance toward Annie. Everyone raised their glasses and toasted except for Sammy, whose fingers were already covered in sticky marshmallow residue.

Annie wove through trunks of props, lights, and fans and climbed under a camera crane to get to her office.

"Mace, what in the world? I said you could store some stuff here, not completely take over the theater. I could barely get into my office!" she complained lightly to Mace, who had relegated her office materials to the corners and replaced them with computers and laptops and other electronics Annie didn't recognize.

"It's only for a little while. Then I'll clear out. I promise."

Annie let out a loud sigh and climbed back under the crane. She heard Mace half-heartedly apologizing as she walked away. She missed her quiet theater, her sanctuary. Now it was always bustling with crew and extras, makeup and wardrobe, and Mace. She also missed the way he had just begun to be before the filming started. Now he was distracted, edgy, and absorbed in shoptalk. She missed her schedule, her privacy, and her kids. Now she was always running to meet Mace's needs, and she felt invaded all the time. In addition, she had to suspend theater until after the movie. However, she had called all the kids to the theater for the afternoon to talk.

"Lord, I miss my life."

Let it go.

"Why?"

Let it go, and let Me.

She wasn't sure she knew what that meant, and she wasn't sure she was ready to say, "Okay," so she just kept walking. She approached the auditorium and smiled as she heard the kids' chatter. She found them already sitting in a circle on the stage, and she jogged up the stairs, happy to be back with them. For a few moments, she could forget all of her frustration and confusion.

"Miss Annie!" Several of them shouted in unison.

"Hey, guys. It's so good to see all of you," she said, sitting down beside Miles and Kristin.

The black-haired girl playing the lead role in the play strode in the auditorium, tossed her backpack aside, and walked briskly toward the stage, talking loudly. "Guys, I've just come from the set, and you are not going to believe what I just heard. Leo is dating his costar!"

Biannca stood and tried to cut her off before she finished, but she wasn't fast enough. The diva scowled at her for stealing her thunder and waving her down until her eyes followed Biannca's eyes and pointed finger to Annie.

"I'm sorry, Miss Annie. I didn't know you were in here already. I—"

"Never mind. Sit down," Annie said coldly, pushing all of her feelings down into her boots and trying to pretend they would stay there.

Biannca couldn't let it go and tried to apologize again. "I'm so sorry, Miss Annie. It was thoughtless to bring up Leo. We heard he moved—"

"Biannca!" Annie snapped. "Enough." She closed her eyes and took a deep breath before she said anything else. What she wouldn't give for Chuck to pop in right now and help her. He had such a way of lightening everyone's moods, including hers. "We are going to talk about your experiences so far. I want to hear all about them. But we will not, I repeat, NOT be talking about the romantic involvements of any of the cast, crew, or director. Is that clear?"

"The director is involved with someone?" the diva asked shocked, revealing her hope was shattered.

Annie glared at her. "We are not discussing it. Period."

The freckled redhead chose this perfect opportunity to chime in, "I had a really great time yesterday working with the lighting director. He showed me a lot about ambient and accent light. He showed me a lot of new things that can work for the stage as well as the screen."

Annie breathed relief. "Thank you. It's so gracious of the studio to allow some of you not only to act in the movie but also to shadow the crew. Tell me how your experiences have opened your eyes to something new."

The diva looked around the circle and then raised her hand; Annie nodded at her reluctantly. The girl said, "I really have learned a lot about acting. It's been interesting acting for a movie director and not a theater director. I really like acting, but I think I prefer the stage."

Annie was surprised by her admission. "Why do you think you've come to that conclusion?"

"There's just something about having the audience there for you. You sort of get…I don't know, that immediate satisfaction. If a line is supposed to get a laugh, the audience laughs. If you're invoking shock or sadness, they gasp or cry right then. But on the movie, although you know it probably will get a laugh, you don't get to experience the audience experiencing it."

"Wow, that's deep," another boy joked.

"No, don't joke. She has an excellent point. I can tell you've been thinking about this a lot. What she has described is one of the greatest things about theater. But don't think of it as theater vs. the movies. The two are simply different formats of the art form of acting. What else has opened your eyes?"

Another girl raised her hand and commented, "I realized I don't want to be famous."

Annie cocked her head. "What do you mean?"

"Well, without naming names, like you said, I have been watching all the famous or even almost famous people. I just don't think they always act right. I'm not talking about acting, though; I'm talking about their attitude or their life. Do you know what I mean? It's not all of them, of course, but just some of them," she rambled on, trying to clarify.

Annie leaned across the girl next to her and patted her knee. "You make perfect sense. I'm proud of you for expressing that to everyone. This isn't a therapy circle, but I'm so glad you all are being honest with each other. Fame is something most people secretly want. Every person wants to be known. But fame—the kind she is referring to—sometimes can cost you other things in return."

Several of the kids nodded at her as if they understood exactly what she was talking about. She knew that they didn't, but she hoped the things they were learning through these experiences would stick with them. She hadn't started this program for the kids they were now but for the people they would turn out to be.

"Anybody else? It doesn't have to be deep. It can be anything, really."

"I'm not deep. Y'all probably know that," the lead boy said while the girls erupted in laughter. He scowled at them, but then a smirk crept at the corners of his mouth. "I've learned some cool stuff about cameras. My grandpa has some old movie cameras that I've always liked, but it was cool learning to operate a modern one. I think it might be something I'd like to look into in college, or whatever."

"That's very cool, Jacob. I didn't know you were interested in cameras. That's great."

"Miss Annie?" Colby spoke up, hesitantly. Annie noted his nervous eyes. He had been cast as "young Leo," and she had to admit he looked a lot like Leo when he was younger. Colby had been busy with filming and had even broken up with Maggie during production, which made Annie assume that was why he looked nervous to talk in front of the others. She smiled at him and nodded.

"Colby, you've been working very hard. How's it impacted you?" Annie prompted encouragingly.

Colby brought his knees down and crossed his legs, and then leaning over on his elbows, he spoke directly to her, not to the group, which the others had seemed to do.

"Being a part of this movie, it has…" he paused, rubbing his buzzed head. "Well, I realized how much I take you and this theater for granted."

Annie felt her eyes grow wide. "What makes you say that, Colby?"

Colby looked down at the floor and rubbed his head again. "I have seen how much work goes into all this kind of stuff, and you do pretty much the same thing for us even when it's not about making a movie that is going to change the world or blow away the box office. It's all for us. You, this theater…you do so much for us. And I have been pretty ungrateful up until now."

Annie knew, though it was in seventeen-year-old jargon, he had spoken to her heart. She was not only impressed but also touched that he has realized such a personal lesson.

Pray for them, she heard.

No. Now? she replied.

Right now. Pray for them now.

"Guys, I know I don't do this, and all of you don't have to join in. I'm going to close this meeting with a word of prayer. Okay?"

There were looks of confusion and several sheepish "okays," but after an awkward moment, they all bowed their heads.

Tell me what to say, Annie pleaded.

"Father," she began, hoping the words would just start tumbling out of her mouth. "I believe You created the world, and I believe You created each of us. We are each uniquely made, and You have given each one of these students different gifts, and You have different plans for each of them. Thank You for each of them and for what they are learning. Amen," she closed slowly and opened her eyes to see several pairs of eyes staring at her, several bewildered looks, and Colby with his head still down. Without drawing attention to him, she dismissed the others.

"Thank you all for coming. We'll start back up after movie production ends, which should be after the New Year. I'll be calling all of you. Bye!"

After everyone had left and their voices had trailed off out of the lobby, Annie scooted over in front of Colby, who still had his head down.

"Colby," she said softly.

He didn't answer, and Annie once again silently begged God for words to say.

"Sometimes I just want to be alone, Colby. If you want to be alone, you can have this whole stage, but if you want to talk about what is bothering you, I'm right here."

She waited for a response. He held his head in his hands and bent low to his legs. She heard him sniff and wondered if he was crying. She thought maybe she should leave him alone, knowing that most teenage boys wouldn't want anyone to see them cry.

As she pushed up on her legs to stand, he lifted his head and said, "Wait."

His eyes were red from trying not to cry, and his nose was running. He said, "All this God stuff has me so messed up."

Whoa, Annie thought. *He's the reason You wanted me to pray.*

Yes.

"What do you mean, Colby?"

"I live with my grandpa, you know. He never taught me any of this stuff, and he'd get mad if he knew about it. Anyways, I've been talking to Mace a lot, and it's making a lot of sense to me, you know. Blowing my mind too," he said, pausing and wiping his nose. "Then the past couple of days I've been around Leo a lot because of the shooting schedule, learning his mannerisms and such. He's got me thinking the opposite. It's all making me confused, and I feel like I'm going crazy. Plus, everything everyone said tonight got me thinking about all of it. I'm sorry I got so weird. And then you prayed…and something in me just lost it."

"Colby, can I tell you something?"

"Please do."

"I don't know what Leo said, and please don't tell me because I might spit. But no matter what he said, it doesn't matter. Also, it doesn't matter what Mace says or what I say. It only matters what God says."

"I don't know what you mean."

"Have you ever read any of the Bible?"

"Mace has been talking a lot about it, but I don't have one. So, no."

"Come with me," she said, pulling him up to his feet. They walked out of the auditorium toward her office. Mace had thankfully had the crane moved, so they could just walk in. Mace was still at work on her desk but paused to watch her walk to the bookcase and lift a Bible.

"Here. This one is mine. Go home and find John. Read it and then come talk to me. Remember, it only matters what God says, and He wrote this whole book." She placed the Bible in Colby's open hands. She smiled as he smiled.

"Thanks, Miss Annie, for everything."

"You're welcome, Colby. Now, get home before it gets dark. We'll talk soon, okay?"

Annie slumped her shoulders once he was out of sight and buried her head in her hands.

"Why so down?" Mace interrupted her thoughts. "I was just about to give you two thumbs way up for that."

"I am just so angry about Leo."

"Oh, you heard they were dating?"

"That too. But right now I'm more upset that he's been talking Colby out of faith in God. I could just walk over there and punch him in the face for that."

Mace smiled, thinking that would be comical to see, but said, "I hope you won't because I don't need him having a black eye for the final scene tomorrow."

"Fine, I'll just figuratively punch him with rhetoric and maybe some yelling," Annie said as she marched out only to turn around. "You'll lock up?"

"Yep. I'll be here a while," he said, already staring at his monitors again.

Annie marched out of the building with heavy determined boots that clicked against the pavement. She knew just where Leo was because she had seen his truck in the parking lot as she headed to the theater earlier.

What should I say? I know what I want to say, but I doubt that would be beneficial. He's probably with her, and I don't want to make a scene. Or do I? I really want to punch him, but I told Mace I wouldn't. She argued with herself as she stormed down the sidewalk all the way over Max's. She pulled up short and got out her phone. *I'll just call him, and then he can excuse himself and come throw down in the parking lot.* She dialed his number and waited for him to answer.

His voice was sincerely surprised. "Hello? This is Leo?"

"I know, Leo. I meant to call you. I'm outside. Can you excuse yourself and come out for a minute, please. We need to talk."

"Um…sure. Just a second," he said and then hung up. She knew that he must be with his co-star. She wondered if he would lie to her in order to excuse himself or if he would tell her the truth. Within seconds, he came through the front door and down the steps.

Annie gasped silently at his short hair and his clean-shaven face. She hadn't seen him that way since Chicago. She reminded herself why she was here and told herself to breathe. As he sauntered over, she felt the bitterness rise, and it felt easier to tell him what she came here for.

"What do you need, Annie?" he said with a forced flatness.

"You may have second guessed the grace that God showed you. You may have lost the faith you thought was so firm. You may have even forgotten where you came from." She could see the façade fade a little in his eyes, and his walls became penetrable for a moment. "That's between you and Him. He'll deal with you on that someday. But don't you dare muddy the waters for Colby and the others. You keep your baggage away from him. Don't you dare, Leo."

"You think I've lost my faith?" The shock in his eyes filtered into his voice, and he rubbed his face with his hands and looked around the parking lot.

"That's what it sure sounded like from what Colby said."

"He's a kid, Annie. He's confused." Leo's voice rose as he defended himself.

"Yes, Leo, and you're the one who confused him."

Leo staggered back a step or two and leaned on his truck. "Annie! Everything about this movie has made me question everything, from going back to Chicago and the mysterious letters Mace keeps getting. Reenacting our lives and falling for someone who plays you—all of it is crazy. I don't know what to think. But you're probably right; I shouldn't talk about all that with Colby."

Annie's heart was skipping every third beat and hammering the fourth with a force she'd never felt before. She couldn't tell which statement made her head spin more or which statement stung worse. *Going back to Chicago? When? Mysterious letters? From who? Falling for her?*

She shook her head involuntarily and fought back tears. She needed to get away from here and from Leo.

"I should go," she whispered and started to back up, feeling weakness in her knees.

"Your golden boy hasn't told you about the letters, has he? You don't know, do you? I guess I'm not the only one you'll be storming tonight, huh, Annie?" he hissed at her.

As she turned to the sidewalk, her tears responded to his cruelty, and she let them fall as she jogged away from him. She didn't look back to see him kick the dirt and curse himself. She ran all the way back to the theater. Under the marquee, she bent over half sobbing, half trying to catch her breath. As she let the tears roll off her eyelashes and fall to the pavement, she wondered, *How did it come to this, Lord? What has happened to him? I thought I obeyed You. What am I supposed to do? How is this my life? What is all this pain for?*

There was no answer.

Her back muscles screamed as she relaxed and stood up. She used her flannel sleeves to dry her eyes off. Looking at her reflection in the glass, she shrugged at her swollen eyes and red nose. She tried the door, but Mace must have already locked it. She knocked anyway. He was going to hear all about it, so he might as well see her tear-stained face. She couldn't even be sure she was done crying for the evening.

Mace jogged toward the door, and the state of her face registered as he unlocked it for her. "I thought for sure you'd come back with a broken hand, but your tears are more heartbreaking. Come inside. What happened?"

Mace hugged her from the side and ushered her into the auditorium. He sat her in a chair, sat down in the row in front of her, and turned back toward her. Annie's breath was still catching and labored from crying. She tried to take several deep breaths to regain control but failed and ended up hiccupping.

"It's okay, Annie. You don't have to tell me now," Mace said, placing a hand on her knee.

She shook her head and said, "No, it's okay." She finally caught her breath and filled her lungs. "I let him have it, and that felt really good. But then he said something that caught me off guard, and I cowered away. He was cruel as I left."

"Annie, I'm so sorry," Mace said, not truly understanding what was between Leo and Annie, knowing their history but also seeing that he didn't fully understand the depth of their relationship. "What did he say?"

"Something about how you've received mysterious letters and are going back to Chicago. And then that he had fallen for the actress."

"I was going to tell you about the letters and Chicago myself. I just haven't had the chance. As for the last thing he said, I'm so sorry, Annie."

Annie gathered control and shook her head, "It's fine. I don't really want to talk about Leo. Can you just tell me what the letters are about?"

"They started arriving about a week after we did. Even before we'd started filming, they started showing up. At first, they unnerved me, but because they weren't quite threatening, I didn't tell you. Especially after your appendix, I didn't want to add stress to your life."

"What did they say?" Annie's face was full of fear and curiosity.

Mace told her that he'd go get them, and he disappeared for several moments. She slipped her eyes closed, and her lids felt like solace for her burning, salty eyes. She felt empty from the tears and calloused from the pain that brewed in her heart. She wasn't sure what to pray even though her heart longed to cry out to God. She heard Mace's footfalls behind her as she opened her eyes and turned to look at him.

"This first one just says, 'We're watching.' This one," he said, handing a folded heavy cardstock, "says, 'Remember this is war,' the next one says, 'Never shrink back.' It goes on. There's at least twenty. Some even felt like encouragement. Others felt like warnings—statements like, 'Opposition will come.' But each note just added to my…"

"Resolve," Annie added, feeling empathetic as she handled each note. "Do you know who sent them? Has it just been notes? Nothing else weird happening?"

"No, nothing else. I don't want you to worry. We've got lots of security, and we've been really cautious this whole time. Honestly, I don't think it's as sketchy as it seems. I have a feeling it has something to do the Martha Grady Foundation."

Annie's face went slack and white, her eyes wide in confusion. "Wha-wha-what do you mean, Mace?"

Mace looked away, toward the west wall. "I can't explain everything just yet. I was approached by the Foundation when I went to Chicago earlier, and I think they may have a hand in our funding."

"Is that why you're going to Chicago?"

"Not really. We need actual Chicago B-roll. I really need you to go with us, Annie."

"Mace," she said breathlessly. "Do you know what you're asking me?"

"I know it will be hard."

"I haven't been back since that day, Mace. I don't know if I can revisit it."

"Chuck and I would be there, every step of the way," Mace said, grabbing her hand in reassurance.

"I just don't know, Mace." She pulled her hand away, withdrawing into her insecurities and fears at the thought of Chicago.

"Annie, will you just think about it and pray about it?"

Annie sighed heavily. "I'll think about it. When do you want to leave?"

"Well..." he said in a way that made Annie think she should expect more unpopular news. "The other thing I needed to talk to you about is tomorrow. It's the final shoot here. I want you to stay home."

"Home?"

"Yes. I really don't want you in town at all. It's the fire scene, and I just don't want anything to upset you."

Annie stared at Mace, surprised by his thoughtfulness. She hadn't even thought through the fact that they would film the scene where Leo saved her from the fire. She coughed down a quiver that tickled her throat and angrily blinked her eyes to stifle tears. "I will have no problem staying home. Thank you, Mace, for thinking of that."

"You're welcome. You've already had enough upset for one evening. I don't want to be the cause of more upset tomorrow," he said with a sweet smile. For a moment, Annie felt like smiling back at him, but she was too tired for that.

"Thanks, Mace. I'm exhausted. I think I'm going to go on home."

"Okay, and to answer your question, after we wrap up shooting here, I've given everyone time off for Christmas. Then we'll meet up in Chicago after the New Year."

"Okay," she said, dragging herself up out of the chair and trudging up the aisle toward the door. "I'll let you know by Christmas."

"Goodnight, Annie," Mace called after her.

26: CONFRONTATION AND HOT COCOA

"Why do you want to wait until tomorrow to decorate?" Sam prodded from the living room where he had already rearranged the coffee table and loveseat to accommodate the Christmas tree.

"It will be a good distraction and something to do tomorrow," Annie chimed in a hopeful voice from the kitchen. She stirred her hot chocolate and made a silent wish that its frothy top would cheer her up.

"Don't you have enough to do at the shop?" Sam asked.

"Mace asked me to stay out of town."

"Why'd he do that?"

Annie tilted her head to the side and remembered the expression on Mace's face when he'd asked her to stay home. The thought of it made her smile.

"It's possible my wellbeing is important to him," she said with slight sassiness playing in her tone.

"Maybe he just didn't want you around," Sam retorted back from the other room.

"Very funny." She walked around the corner into the living room holding two cups of steaming hot chocolate. "Now, which movie do you want to watch?"

"The one with Jimmy Stewart."

"Again?" Annie joked setting her mug down and handing the other to him.

"I like what I like. What can I say?"

Annie put in the DVD and settled into the couch as Sam set himself up in the recliner.

"Hey, where's Sammy tonight?" he asked.

Annie finished her sip of hot chocolate before answering, "He went home with Braedon. He should be home soon, though."

Sam nodded and turned back toward the TV just as the black and white title came across the screen. Annie heard the front door open.

"There he is now," she said, setting her mug down and getting up to greet Sammy. She was surprised to see his head hung low and shoulders slumped with his backpack hanging heavily down his back. His feet dragged across the wood floors with a scraping sound.

"Sammy, are you okay?" Annie asked as he trudged through the door and closed it. He shot her a look that made Annie know he wasn't okay. He threw his bag down by the coat rack. "Did you eat with Braedon? Can I fix you something?"

He shook his head and said, "I think I'm just going to go to bed."

"Sammy, are you sure? What's wrong?" She put a hand on his shoulder.

As soon as she touched his shoulder, tears welled up in his large blue eyes, and he pushed past her.

"I just don't feel good. I'm fine." He huffed as he started up the stairs. Annie started to follow and passed Sam, who went to stand, but Annie lifted a hand to tell him to stay put. "I'll go talk to him. I think something happened at Braedon's."

"Do you want me to talk to him?" Sam asked from his recliner.

"Let me try. If he won't talk to me, then you can try." She started up the stairs.

Annie walked the stairs slowly, hoping to give Sammy a few moments to himself before she went in. When she reached the top, she realized all the lights were off. She softly knocked on his door, the first door at the top of the stairs. There was no answer.

She opened the door an inch and whispered, "Sammy, it's Mom. Can I come in?"

There was still no answer.

"Sammy? Can I come in?" she said a little louder, opening the door wider.

"I'm in here," his little voice said softly. Annie realized it was coming from her room down the hall. She padded to her dark room and found him beneath her covers in a heap. She heard faint sniffles, and she crawled in the bed and found him under the covers. She pulled him into her arms. He didn't protest, and she held him close and talked softly to him.

"You may not want to talk about whatever has upset you, but you can tell me anything. Mom is a safe place. You can talk to me, but if you don't want to right now, that's okay too."

Annie held Sammy and silently prayed over him, begging God not to have let anything bad happen to him. She asked God to help him talk to her and to give her the right words to say if he did. After a long silence, Annie heard the rain start softly splashing on the windows and the roof above.

"Mom?" Sammy whispered as he snuggled closer.

"Yes?"

"I did something that I shouldn't have today."

Annie felt her emotions swell at the fact that he wanted to admit to her what was so heavy on his heart. She also felt fear for what he would tell her next.

"Braedon and I didn't walk directly over to his mom's salon after school. We went to the set to hang out with Chuck."

Annie's heart shuddered, remembering the scene Mace was shooting that day.

"Everything was fine. I even got to see Leo for a minute, but then they started filming. We sat in the back by the snack table so no one would notice us. We thought it would be cool to watch them film the movie. I wanted to hang out with Chuck. But they were filming something really scary."

Annie shuddered again and silently cursed all three men for not seeing her son crouched in the back, watching her worst memories and fears acted out. She wondered if that was the real reason Mace had wanted her to stay home the next day because Sammy had been there that day. *Why didn't Mace tell me?* She pushed that aside to be dealt with later, kissed Sammy's hair, and held him tight. She didn't say anything just in case he wanted to say more. She heard him choke back tears and then ask, "Why was my dad so mean to you?"

As the rain fell, Annie felt her heart fall to her stomach. "Oh, sweetheart. No, no. Simon might have been the reason Mom got pregnant with you, but he is not your dad."

"He's not?"

"No, Sammy. A dad is someone who protects you, watches out for you, and takes care of you. A dad hugs you, loves you, and helps you grow up to be an honest, strong man. Simon was none of those things."

Annie could feel his little head turn upward and look at her even in the darkness. She leaned down and kissed his forehead.

"Is Leo my dad?"

Annie's heart clenched, and her chest tightened. "No, sweetie," she said as she closed her eyes and allowed herself to remember Leo. "But he does all those things, doesn't he?"

"Yeah."

As they snuggled down further into the blankets, rain swept across the leaves outside, creating a soft hushing sound. As it lulled them to surrender the evening to sleep, Sammy whispered into the dark solace in Annie's room, "I hope someday I can have a dad."

"I think we'll have to use her office. I don't see a way around it," Mace said.

Chuck looked around the room, realizing the meaning of filming the "office scene" in her office. "Did you talk to her about it?" he asked.

Mace's silence as he continued to work told Chuck the answer.

"Mace! Seriously, man, you have to talk to her. You can't just do this and hope she'll forgive you later. This may be your movie, but this is her life." He began to pace. "I thought she was here tonight; why didn't you talk to her?"

"She was here, and we did talk about Chicago and the letters and Leo. Then I asked her to stay home tomorrow."

"Hoping she wouldn't find out?" Chuck asked, raising his voice more than he intended.

"After what happened with Sammy today, I…I just couldn't do it." Mace felt defensive but also guilty beyond expression. "And Leo was horrible to her tonight; I just didn't want to upset her further."

"What did Leo do?" Chuck asked, ready to protect her, but then he changed his course. "Never mind, that can wait. Or maybe it doesn't even matter, I don't know. Here's my point, Mace. This is Annie we're talking about. Tell me she's not the strongest woman you know."

"You're right. She is. I know she can handle it. It's just that I'm under a lot of pressure—"

Chuck interrupted him. "So this is about you then?" he asked with a snarky, agitated tone.

"No, it's just that a lot of that pressure, I know, is self-inflicted, but—and I can't believe I'm about to admit this to you—it's about Annie. I feel this enormous pressure to do this right for her. I care what she thinks."

Chuck shook his head and laughed. "If that's true, Mace, then you should care about what she thinks about her office."

Mace looked stunned, and he thought through what Chuck had said for a moment before he nodded. "I'll talk to her first thing tomorrow."

"Good. If you don't, I will. Lock up. I'm done here." He turned to leave.

Mace grabbed the keys. "I'll walk out with you," he said, ignoring Chuck's irritation with him.

Outside, Mace was locking the doors when Chuck said, "I think I'm going to head over to the hotel. I'm burnt out. I'll talk to you in the morning."

Mace felt awkward asking, but he knew he had to. "Chuck, are you all right, man?"

"I don't want to talk about it. I'll see you tomorrow," Chuck said flatly, turning to leave. He turned the corner toward the hotel so quickly that he didn't see the figure that had been sitting on the bench across the street stand and move out into the street with cautious steps.

Mace just finished locking the doors when he turned to see a man walking toward him. Mace reassuringly felt the knife in his pocket and his phone in his hand.

"Can I help you, sir?" he began firmly but politely.

The man who had been staying in the shadows finally stepped into the light under the marquee and held up his hands. Mace exhaled slightly when he saw who it was.

"It's just me. Randy."

"This will come as a surprise to us both, but I'm glad it was you, Randy."

"Don't be so glad yet." Randy opened his coat and reached inside. Mace stiffened with paranoia, but Randy just retrieved an envelope. It looked exactly like the other ones that the mysterious letters had come in. Mace looked at it both in surprise and with wariness. Then he looked at Randy quizzically.

"Randy? You've been bringing these?"

Randy gathered himself up and stood a little straighter. His deep widow's peak made his brow line look harsher than it probably was. His thin, distinct nose cast a strong shadow on his serious mouth, which Mace felt like he recognized. Randy shoved the note at him and stepped back away, folding his hands.

"Mr. Harlen," he said in a voice that was not his typical Southern drawl. His voice now was refined and almost Northern, reminiscent of someone else's voice, but Mace just couldn't think who. Even the way he said, "Mr. Harlen" sounded just like...Nigel from the Foundation.

Randy continued, "I'm not at liberty to explain everything. Though it will all be explained in Chicago. I'll be with you the whole way."

"You and that Nigel guy from the Foundation. You guys are twins, aren't you?" Mace said reeling from his discovery. Randy nodded but didn't offer any other information. "What are you doing here? I thought you had been here for years. All the mechanic stuff is an act?"

Randy huffed with impatience. "Let's just say I'm security. And yes, I only arrived in Penumbra a day before Annie did."

"Does she know?"

"No, but I plan to discuss it on the way to Chicago."

Mace felt uneasy about that conversation as well as the one he would have with Annie in the morning. Neither would actually encourage her to want to go to Chicago. He wondered why Randy insisted that he was coming with them to Chicago. He wondered what the Martha Grady Foundation was up to.

"Mr. Harlen, know that we are on your side. All will be explained in due time. We'll be in touch soon." Randy disappeared into the shadows of the small town street again.

Bewildered, Mace stood with the note in hand. He had the urge to call Annie, probably wake her up, and tell her everything, but he refrained, slid his phone down in his pocket, and opened up the note. It simply read, "Fight the good fight."

Mace threw his head back in exhaustion and closed his eyes. "I wanted to make movies, God. Not fight fights."

Yes, but did you ask Me what I want?

Mace tried to call Chuck for a third time, but when he still wouldn't answer, Mace fell back against the headboard and closed his eyes for the first time in forty-eight hours. Sighing, he let himself relax into the sleep that his body craved. His mind faded into a dream.

He shouted at Annie. "Let me finish it. You'll see." Annie faded to an illuminated, translucent figure, shimmering in moonlight. She whispered, "No, you can't change the ending, Mace. It's already been written." Then she was gone as he reached for her.

He felt eyes on him. They bore into him, and someone shouted at him and began to chase him.

He ran through the desert, constantly looking over his shoulder. His heart pounding and legs aching, he ran until the sun was coming up just beyond the horizon. His pursuers were hot on his trail, but the sun was ever before him. As it rose, it uncovered everything the night had hidden. Mace stopped and turned around. He stood alone, on the line of demarcation between the shadows of night and the morning light. Within minutes, the sunlight had illuminated every inch of the desert and engulfed him in warmth.

The dream dissipating, his eyes felt like garage doors, heavy and robotic as they tried to open at the sound of his phone ringing. He pulled himself up to sit and fumbled for his phone in the sheets. He reached it too late, and the call was missed. It was Chuck. He decided to return the call later. Right now, he needed some paper. Finding some on the desk under several stacks, he settled back on the bed, hunched over the pad of paper, scribbling facts and words all over the page, drawing arrows and underlining important details. Then he threw the pen down and sighed.

Am I trying to change the ending?

He went back to scribbling and connecting bullet points with other points. He wrote the words "shadows and light" and retraced them several times, boring into the paper until he quit.

"It's penumbra!" he exclaimed while suddenly standing up on the bed. "It's penumbra—that place where things become clear, everything is laid bare, and the light reveals the truth. You can choose to stay in the shadows or be embraced by the light. The son! It's Jesus. Oh! That's good." He sat back down to write what he'd just said. After a moment, he stood up and began to pace the room.

"It's funny, God. I think You are trying to tell me something, but I don't see it all yet. There's something about the ending. There's something about Annie. There's something about a threat, but the part about You is so clear. It's incredible." Pausing, he closed his eyes and shook his head, remembering that he needed to talk to Annie. *Truth is illuminating; lies are the shadows*, he thought. *Penumbra is the place you get to choose, Mace*, he told himself.

He picked up the phone and dialed Annie's number.

Before he could even say anything, Annie answered with anger in her voice. "Have you started filming yet? We need to talk."

"Not yet, and we do need to talk."

"I'm in the truck," she announced gruffly into the phone. "I'll meet you at your hotel in 10." She abruptly hung up.

While Mace sat in his hotel room looking at his phone, Annie tossed her own phone across the passenger seat. She'd woken from sleep with her tousled-haired boy in her arms to a feeling of anger growing in her chest.

Sam jogged with a slight limp across the gravel driveway to the truck window.

"I thought you were staying home today." Concern filled his words.

Annie gripped the steering wheel with determination. "Sammy told me something last night. I need to confront Mace about it."

Sam knew that if Annie was confronting something, it was better to let her do it. She hadn't confronted things often since she moved in with him.

"Want me to talk to Sammy?"

Annie felt a small swell of guilt against her anger, but she swallowed it down. "Sure, it won't take long. I'll be back soon, and we can decorate the tree."

"Okay. Be careful," Sam said, wanting his words to mean more than "careful." His thoughts wanted to say "wise" or "cautious," but all that filtered out was "careful." They had had many long talks, and he could trust her to handle it wisely.

Annie drove stiffly into town, faster than she should have, rehearsing what she wanted to say to Mace. Once at the hotel, she tried not to storm through the lobby or stalk up the stairs even though she felt like a tornado blowing through. Outside his room, she took a deep breath before harshly knocking several times.

The door swung open, and a concerned Mace stood before her. *He knows why I'm here*, she realized, which stung a little in her throat and caught her off guard. *He said we needed to talk. Maybe he wants to confess*. Feeling her anger back down out of her throat, she decided to let him talk first, give him a chance to apologize.

Still, she crossed her arms and passed him coldly. He closed the door and turned to face her.

Somehow, even in her visible anger, she was still beautiful, he realized. Her brow angled deeply over her large green eyes that glowed furiously, and her full lips pulled into a thin angry line.

He struggled, fumbled even, over whether to tell her about his dream, confess his plans, or apologize for Sammy being on set. He reluctantly decided to begin.

"Annie."

Something in the way he said her name made her feel guilty for her anger, but she remained unchanged as she waited for him to continue.

"I can see that you are already upset. Maybe you've already talked to Chuck, so I'll just be honest with you, and then you can tear me apart if you want."

"I haven't talked to Chuck." She fumbled a bit, wondering what Chuck had to do with anything.

"Oh," he paused and then continued, "We planned to shoot the office scene in your office and lobby today." He pushed the words, spitting them out as fast as he could.

Annie felt the winter in his words, and they made her suck in her breath.

"My office?" she panted with her eyes searching his face for any hint of sarcasm or irony. Then her eyes filled with reality, and she stepped to him with betrayal weaving in her tone. "That's why you wanted me to stay home, isn't it?"

Mace looked away from her, drowning in his shame.

Her voice went cold as she took another step forward, challenging him. "For a fleeting moment, Mace Harlen, I actually thought you cared about my wellbeing, but you're still just out for yourself. Just like Simon, you don't even care who you trample in the process. Look at what happened with Sammy yesterday! You haven't changed at all."

Her words hit the intended mark, and his face twisted in defensive anger and guilt as he said, "Annie, don't say that."

"Too late, Mace. It's too late. You've already made your plans. You've betrayed my trust, and the damage is done with Sammy."

"I'm so sorry."

"I was finally beginning to…" she paused and let her unsaid words crush the air between them. His eyes met hers again, and she

243

felt the words heavy between them. "Trust you," she finally finished.

"I know." Mace softened, stepping out of his defensiveness. They stood toe to toe, and he held her shoulders. Annie almost recoiled, but something in his warm touch held her still.

"Annie, I can't earn your trust and forgiveness because, honestly, I'll probably never deserve it, but I'll still ask for it. I'm not the man I was when I first broke down in front of your shop. I hope one day you'll see that."

Annie couldn't stop the tear that slid down her cheek, and she knew she didn't need to. Mace wiped it away, his finger leaving a blazing trail along her skin. She caught his hand and held it to her cheek, feeling its heat on her skin. Her eyes closed as she spoke softly to him.

"You have no idea what it means to talk to your son through who his biological father is. You can't imagine reliving your worst nightmare every day. I worry, Mace." She opened her eyes to see his face was closer than she thought, and feeling his breath on her lips made her neck quiver.

"I worry," she continued breathlessly, "that this is just a movie to you." She pushed away from him.

He felt his palms pulsing, and he wanted to hold her again. He forced himself not to and crossed to the bed to retrieve his notebook. He turned to face her and sat down.

"Annie, I don't know how I can ask you to come to Chicago with me now, but please read this. Please consider coming with me." He wondered if he had lingered too long on the last word.

Annie studied him pensively and then took the notebook he held outstretched. When she whisked herself through the door, Mace felt as though all the fresh air had been vacuumed from the room and all he was left with stale regret.

"Dude, what are you so sour about? I have been trying to reach you for hours," Chuck fumed.

"I had a strange night and then had a confrontation with Annie this morning. I'm sorry, man. I wasn't ignoring your calls for no reason," Mace said, walking next to him toward the theater.

Chuck's look of surprise prompted Mace to explain, "She's about as happy as a hurricane, but she's not going to stop us."

"That's it?" Chuck asked unsatisfied.

"No, there was much more, but that's the gist of it. It's possible..." he paused, unsure of how much to say, "it's possible we...never mind."

Chuck's controlled face told Mace that he was withholding his emotions. Then the sour frown that had momentarily lifted returned.

Is it possible Chuck is jealous? Mace wondered. He pushed those thoughts away and remembered Randy coming to him last night. He recounted to Chuck the interaction with Randy and the last note. He also told him his dream and his theories of what he thought it might mean.

Before he was finished, they arrived on the set bustling with cameramen and stunt coordinators and special effect gurus.

Chuck lost himself amidst the crowd quickly, thankful to duck the conversation about Annie. *Get yourself together, Chuck. This is going to be the worst day yet. Be objective, and get to work. Quit thinking about her,* Chuck chastised himself.

Mace sat on the front lobby counter with a megaphone and got everyone's attention. At once, he saw Leo across the room, standing alone, his face trying hard not to reveal turmoil.

"Any of you who have any knowledge of this incredible story or personal connection to it know that this is going to be a hard day. I won't downplay that. But because it's the hardest, it's also the most rewarding. Here is where the story steps out from the shadows and lays the graphic truth bare. That's not easy, but the truth is always worth telling."

The crowd that had gathered clapped and produced an energy that Mace felt proud of. He jumped off the counter and got pats on the back all the way over to the wall where Leo leaned with his arms stiffly crossed.

Mace squared off to him and said, "Quit trying to control it, Leo."

Leo shrugged him off and glared down at the floor.

"I see it all over your face. Use your anger to help Colby make it through this day."

Leo's eyes shot up and stared wide at Mace. Mace nodded.

"I've decided to let Colby do this scene. He's literally the age you were at the time, so it will be more realistic. It will be rawer for him, which will evoke more emotion from the audience. I need this scene to be powerful not tainted."

"Tainted? By what?" Leo fired angrily at him.

"This. Your anger. Your regret. Colby will portray you before all this, back when you were just simply in love with Annie." Mace hadn't intended to wound Leo, but he could see that his comment had struck a deep nerve. "I need you to tap into that old love for her and help Colby understand what's happening between you two during this scene aside from what's happening all around Annie."

Leo was again silent and withdrawn, but he nodded his head.

"We're starting with the alleyway scene, so you and Colby have some time to rehearse in the auditorium," Mace directed, motioning to a pensive Colby standing nearby. Leo pushed off the wall and huffed past Mace.

Before long, the lobby had cleared out into the street and alley behind the theater. They worked on the drug deal scene for hours, perfecting the light, the fight blocking, and the camera angles.

After a while, Colby and Leo joined the crew outside and watched from a distance as the actress playing Annie began her scene. The camera followed her shoes along the sidewalk, no noise except her clicking heels. Leo watched hesitantly as she hid behind the corner, crawled out of sight, dialed her phone, and scrambled to get to the front door. It made his skin crawl to watch the scene from this angle, remembering what it felt like to be on the other side of the phone. He could still hear Annie panting as she ran to the door and hear her soft words into the phone.

His palms began to sweat, and he looked away as the actress locked the door behind her.

He flashed back to Annie's voice saying, *"Leo, I love you."* He couldn't force himself to watch any longer. He patted Colby on the shoulder and walked away.

He sat for hours in the darkened hallway that separated Annie's office and the auditorium. His drawn up knees supported his elbows and his hanging head. He didn't even notice Chuck finding him there and sitting down along the wall next to him.

"Hey," Chuck said flatly, wondering why he was even bothering.

"Hey," Leo murmured back from underneath his arms.

Chuck decided to let the silence hang between them and ask God again what in the world He was up to, but before he could even think a prayer, Leo spoke.

"Mace said the truth was always worth telling," he announced with slight accusation behind his voice. "I guess I found myself wondering, 'Yeah, but what is it costing her?'"

The truth is coming out now, Chuck thought before he answered Leo.

"The truth is always costly..." he hesitated, wondering how to formulate what to say. Then the words started flowing from what seemed outside of his brain and off of his tongue. "But it will suck you dry to stay silent. Pretty soon the very truth that you feel is so costly will cost you everything."

Leo looked up from beneath his arms and asked, "Hasn't it already cost her everything?"

Chuck nodded, knowing where Leo was coming from.

"To some, yeah. They may say that, but I'm starting to see how much she has. She has a theater again, she has a bakery, and she has a purpose. She has Sammy and Sam. She has other people who love her. And...and she had us to help her tell her story. The world needs her story."

"Why does the world need to hear it so badly? Look what the world did to her!"

Chuck shook his head in dismay at Leo's attitude, but the more he watched the turmoil in Leo's eyes and the tension just beneath his hairline under his skin, he understood what Leo was fighting with. He'd been there too. In fact, he was still there, if he were honest. He had come to know he needed God, but there was still a lot that Chuck didn't understand about God. For maybe the first time, he understood a small glimpse of Leo Chase.

"Leo, the story needs to be told for the countless souls trapped in their silence, for those who are quick to judge, for those who are lost in their ignorance to the destruction that porn and lust cause, and for all those who don't yet know they need to hear a story of redemption because they haven't admitted that they're in bondage yet." He paused, feeling the words pressed into his mind that he needed to say, but the weight of them sat heavily on his tongue. "And for you too, I think, Leo. For those like you, trapped in past tragedies."

"Me?" Leo flew to his feet, towering over Chuck. "I was there, you idiot!"

"I know, Leo, and you're so consumed in your savior role you won't let yourself see things from her perspective."

"Why do I need to? It won't change anything."

"It's not meant to change the past. We can't change the past, but we can try to understand it. We can change because of what we know. The future is better because we're not stuck in the past."

Leo went to speak again, forming a sort of growl at the corner of his mouth when Mace burst in the front door.

"We did it. We finished the scene. Chuck! Where are you, man?"

Chuck popped up and rounded the corner to show himself, and Leo followed.

"There you guys are! Let's get some pizzas in this place and watch the dailies!"

Annie gave Sammy a sly look. "You ready?"

"Yes!" Sammy squealed from his perch on the back of the couch. Annie plugged in the lights, and the tree shimmered to life.

"Oh, would you look at that," Sam said flatly from his recliner. Annie glared at him playfully.

"Mom, it's the best tree yet," Sammy gushed.

"It is beautiful, isn't it?" Annie admired the tree as she snuggled in close to Sammy.

"How many days until Christmas, Mom?" Sammy asked with childish wonder.

"Only two."

"Okay. Can we watch a movie now?"

"Sure, bud. Go pick one out."

Sammy launched off the couch and started to dig through the drawer when Annie heard the phone ring from the kitchen. She hesitated, and Sam shot her a knowing look.

"I know how to put a movie in. Go talk to whoever that is."

"Okay," Annie said reluctantly. She got to the phone just before the last ring.

"Going to Chicago won't be a mistake. There is much to uncover there."

Recognizing the voice but confused by the words, she asked, "Randy?"

"Yes. There is much I haven't told you—all of which I am happy to explain…but not right now."

Annie felt bewildered, almost as if she were dreaming. "Ok…"

"Go to Chicago. You need to," he urged her with an insistent tone.

"This is all very cryptic, Randy. I'm not sure I know what to say…or do."

"God will make things clear." With that, he hung up the phone.

Annie held out the phone and stared at it as if it were an alien object. *I've never heard Randy talk about God or Chicago. How did he even know I was considering going? What can Randy possibly explain?*

"Mr. Harlen, this has been an incredible experience. Thank you for giving me the chance to work with you," Colby said, extending his hand to Mace.

"Colby," Mace said, shaking his hand, "you've got talent. What you did today was outstanding. It was really courageous and from the heart."

"Thank you, sir."

"Oh no. No 'sirs' here," Mace said, patting him on the shoulder. "Here, sit down, we're just reviewing the dailies from today and attacking some pizza."

Chuck, Leo, and Mace sat in a semi-circle in front of several computer monitors with boxes of pizzas spread out on the floor at their feet.

"Thanks," Colby said excitedly as he grabbed a chair and sat down next to Chuck, who offered him a slice of supreme pizza. After several more clips, Mace paused it, freezing the screen on an image of Colby, as Leo, on the phone.

"I think that's enough for today."

"Agreed," Chuck said, stretching from his seat. "I thought it went well, all things considered."

Mace nodded, his mouth full of pepperoni.

"You did great today, kid," Leo said somewhat expressionlessly, nodding toward Colby.

"Thanks, Leo. That means a lot coming from you. I can't believe you actually rescued her. It blows my mind to think what she's lived through."

"She's pretty incredible," Mace agreed as he looked up to her portrait on the wall.

Chuck watched Leo harden once again against the comments about the past and compliments of Annie. Leo watched Mace carefully as he studied the portrait.

"So," Colby started with youthful ignorance to the inner struggles of the men that surrounded him, "How's it going to end? I never saw the ending of the script."

Mace laughed. "I thought I knew. Didn't I, Chuck?" Chuck nodded, and Mace continued, "When we first wrote it, I was so sure I knew, but more and more, I'm not sure."

"What do you mean?" Colby asked.

Mace was still looking intently at the portrait on the wall as he said very thoughtfully, "It's possible it could end one of three ways."

Mace didn't have to look at Chuck. Chuck knew what Mace meant because Leo's face revealed more that he meant to, and Chuck also knew what he fought in his own heart. He knew that it was entirely possible that all three of them could love her.

"Colby?" Annie asked as she answered the door, wrapping her robe around herself. "Are you okay?"

"Yes, ma'am. I'm sorry to just show up at your door. Can I talk to you?"

"Sure. Come inside. I'll fix you some hot cocoa."

Colby trudged through the door and slid down into the booth side of the kitchen table. Annie studied him out of the corner of her eye as she stirred cocoa into a steaming mug of milk. She was aware that it had been his last day of filming, and he was probably feeling heavy about the scenes. Annie sat down and handed him the cup.

"What's on your mind, Colby?" Annie asked in a hushed tone, remembering that Sam and Sammy were sleeping upstairs.

"You, actually," he said, letting the concern show in his voice. "I just have some questions."

"Well," she hesitated, "I'm not sure I can answer them, but I'll let you ask, and we'll go from there."

"That's fair. I've been thinking a lot about what you said the other day. And then after shooting today, I just wondered—were you ever mad at God?" Colby sat, looking into his cocoa as if he were asking the steaming chocolate the question.

"Yes, but only because I didn't really know Him. I had only heard about Him, so I felt like I knew Him. When you think you know someone that you truly don't, it's easy to assume things about them. Then, when you assume wrongly, it's easy to get offended. I got offended at God because I assumed that if God loved people, He didn't let bad things happen to them. Because something awful happened to me, I was mad at God and assumed that He was a liar or that He didn't love me."

Colby took a sip, considering what Annie had said. The cocoa traveled down his throat, warming everything it touched, but he felt something else at work, starting in his head and trickling down his neck and shoulders. Everything felt alive with a surge that faded but left him with clarity and awareness he'd never had before.

"I felt angry today even after the shoot and everything. I was angry that you had to live through that. I was angry at Leo for the way he's acting lately, knowing what you've been through. I also felt angry at God, but even when I felt angry at Him, I felt desperate to talk to Him." Colby felt dumb for admitting that but continued anyway. "But I don't know how to talk to him or if He would even listen."

Annie thought her lungs and heart were beating through her skin, but she tried to remain composed so he would know she took him seriously.

"It sounds like you *want* to know Him."

Colby smiled. "Yeah, I think so."

"You know what? He is always listening, even if it's just you telling him that you don't understand, and you're angry. He listens. Something I know about God is that He always answers—maybe in an unexpected way—but He always answers."

Colby nodded and scratched his head. "So, why do you think He lets bad things happen?"

Annie felt the weight of his question in the air. She let it fall to the table, and she stared at it for a moment, as if it were really written there on the oak.

"See if you can follow my thoughts, and I'll see if I can explain what I have learned."

"Okay."

"When bad things happen to me, I feel like I'm stuck. I'm desperate because I see that I can't find my own way out, and I can't fix my life on my own. Desperate people, like me, eventually lean hard into someone or something they think can fix their problem. That's where God comes in. He is the only one who can truly mend our lives. If we look hard for Him and find ourselves in need of Him, then He can start to show us who He is. When you find out who God is, it changes who you are and who you want to be."

Annie couldn't remember ever putting that into words before. Although she felt exhausted and her mouth was dry, her soul was sloshing over and extinguishing the fires of confusion that had long been burning in a deep place inside her. She patted Colby's arm and wondered if he understood a word she was saying, but she couldn't help but continue.

"When you find out who God is, you know that you can trust Him. Then, when you trust Him, you begin to trust through the bad things and not just be desperate for Him to get you out of the bad things. All the while, people are watching. People who need to believe are watching. Other hopeless people are watching as you and I respond to God."

As Annie paused and her words slowed, Colby could sense that she was coming to her own realizations as she spoke, just as much as he was.

"Really, the whole world is watching," she said softly. "If we never had anything bad happen, we'd never know we needed anyone but ourselves."

Colby stirred the marshmallows around his mug for a moment before timidly responding, "I think I understand."

"I'm glad, Colby," she said, patting his arm again. "Have you been reading the Bible?"

"I have. I even prayed the other night." His voice sounded unsure and unsteady. "I told God I thought I could believe in Jesus and I know I got sin in my heart and all that, but I was angry about stuff that has happened. Maybe I wasn't ready."

Annie remembered hearing about the car accident that had taken Colby's parents when he was young, leaving him to his elderly grandparents, and her heart softened for him as he confessed his feelings about God, knowing that most teenage boys wouldn't dare talk about their feelings to anyone.

"What do you think now?"

"I feel like I need God, and I need to talk to Him. That must mean I believe in Him."

"It's certainly a good start. What about sin and the cross?"

"What Jesus went through to save people from sin was horrific, but it served a purpose. Just like you said, the tragic things in our lives serve purposes too."

"Yes, Colby, everything has a purpose."

"Then what do I do now?"

"Well, I think we should pray—not that the prayer saves you—it just helps you solidify your decision."

Colby scooted the mug away from him and folded his hands on the table. Annie felt a prompting to hold his hands, and without questioning it, she reached to his hands, holding them between hers. Her touch stilled his fidgeting. Annie prayed a short prayer over him, thanking God for loving Colby and showing Himself to both of them. She was quiet for a moment, and Colby started to pray, without being prompted or led. He spoke like a child in short sentences and sounding very unsure, but then, at the end of his prayer, in a confident voice, he said, "I believe in You, God, and I want to know You. Amen."

Annie was overwhelmed by his childlike faith and his pursuit of the truth. Tears streamed down her cheeks clashing with her joyful smile. Colby finally opened his eyes and let the tears that were trapped behind his lids flow out and down his tan cheeks.

"Now what?" he whispered.

"Well," Annie sighed and sniffed while wiping away her tears, "The Bible says God gives us everything we need for life and Godliness. He gives us His holy spirit in here." She patted his chest. "And this sword and guidebook, the Bible." She patted her worn leather Bible.

"I wish you and Sam could teach me everything you know. I have so much to learn, but Pa would be real angry if he found out. He'd lick me something awful."

"Colby, we would love nothing more than to teach you. You are welcome here anytime," she said, standing to her feet and opening her arms to him. Colby stood and hugged her with hungry, childlike arms, even though he towered over her. He thanked her again for letting him come in and talk. She told him that it had been a great pleasure to be able to talk to him about knowing the Lord.

After Colby left, Annie sat alone at the table, staring at her Bible. She didn't close her eyes or bow her head, but she responded to the little voice that spoke.

Talk to Me.

"I think it's clear to me what You're doing. When this movie is finished, the world will literally be watching. I need to go to Chicago and help Mace make it, don't I?"

Yes.

"Can You promise You'll be with me and protect me?"

I will never leave you nor forsake you.

Annie knew the words were just for her even though they echoed from an ancient time on a page in her Bible. She breathed deep and exhaled before picking up her phone.

"Mace," she said in a hushed tone, realizing she was calling him in the middle of the night.

Groggily, he answered in a whisper, "Annie?"

Her stomach fluttered at the way he whispered her name, and she said, "I'm so sorry. Did I wake you?"

"Yeah, it was a long day. I must've dozed off."

Annie blushed softly at the intimate feel of their whispered conversation.

"I don't know what I was thinking. I didn't mean to wake you. We can talk tomorrow."

"Okay, I can come by in the morning."

"Okay. Bye."

"Goodnight, Annie," he whispered into the phone.

27. CHRISTMAS AND PLANE PEANUTS

"Hold that thought, Sammy. Let me get the phone," Annie said, turning the pancake onto a plate and walking toward the ringing phone on the wall.

"Hello," she said in a chipper voice.

"Hey, it's Chuck."

"Hey, Chuck. How are you?"

"Good. How are you?"

Annie couldn't tell if he was fishing for something, but she replied, "Good, I'm making pancakes for Sammy this morning and loading up on the coffee. What are you up to?"

"I'm calling because I'm on my way back to L.A."

"You are?" Annie let out more disappointment than she intended.

"Yeah, I'm in the taxi. I wanted to say goodbye in person, but my flight got bumped up. I had to kick it to get to the airport on time."

"I'm glad you called. Why are you headed back? Did you guys finish shooting here?" Annie asked, returning to the griddle to turn another pancake.

"We did. Mace gave everyone a few days off for Christmas. Then we're meeting in Chicago."

"Oh, I'm glad everyone gets to be home for Christmas," she said, trying not to wonder what Leo was going to be doing on Christmas since he usually spent it with them.

"Yeah, makes you want to bust out in 'I'll be home for Christmas,'" he said sarcastically.

Annie laughed and then cut it short with a smile. Somehow it was fitting, at this moment, to tell Chuck first. "I'll see you in a few days, though…"

"What? You're coming?"

She smiled at his excitement. "I haven't told Mace yet, so don't tell him. But yes, I decided, or rather, the Lord told me to go."

"Excellent! When will you tell Mace?"

"Actually, I think he just arrived." Annie looked out the front kitchen window to see Mace's car pull up. "I'd better let you go. I'll see you in a few days, though, okay?"

"Okay. See you at the airport. Merry Christmas, Annie."

"Merry Christmas, Chuck." Annie hung up the phone right as she saw Mace walk up the porch steps. He knocked on the door, and an excited Sammy ran to open it.

"Hey there, bud." Mace gave him a high five.

"Hey, Mace!" Sammy exclaimed, stepping back to let him in. "We're having pancakes."

"Yum," Mace said, walking into the kitchen and taking in the sight of Annie at the stove, wearing an apron. He smiled, remembering their whispered conversation on the phone last night.

"Good morning," he said quietly in her direction, unsure if he should hug her, kiss her on the cheek, or refrain from touching her altogether.

"Good morning. I was just on the phone with Chuck. Glad you could stop by on your way out of town," she said as she flipped pancakes.

"Oh, Chuck called?" Mace asked casually.

"Yeah, he wanted to say goodbye," Annie said quickly, trying to nip a potentially unraveling conversation in the bud. "I have something for you." She lay down the spatula and grabbed a sheet of paper off the counter.

Taking the paper from her, he asked, "What's this?"

"My flight itinerary," she said with expectation in her voice. "So you know when to pick me up at the airport."

Mace's eyes went wide with surprise. "You'll come?"

Annie nodded in confirmation. Mace rushed her with a hug, trapping her arms down by her side.

"Annie, I'm so glad," he said softly just for her to hear, which sent a certain fire to her cheeks. "I have something for you too. It's for Christmas, which seems fitting." He released her and reached for a bakery box.

She raised an eyebrow and a suspicious smile crept across her mouth as she asked, "What did you make me?"

Mace laughed and replied, "I didn't make it, but I had tiramisu flown in from Chicago. I want you to have one of those perfect days you talked about."

A look of surprise ran over Annie's face.

"Tiramisu from Chicago?" Annie smiled hugely, and at that, Mace felt certain he had done well and possibly made up for some of her frustration with him the past several days.

"Thank you, Mace. This is so thoughtful. I can't believe you remembered!"

Mace gave her a playful wink and moved away from her toward Sammy, who wasn't paying them any attention, too concerned with his pancakes. Annie smiled, wondering at the warm feeling in her heart.

"That is what I call a stack!" Mace said, sliding down next to Sammy.

"Yeah, I must have at least ten pancakes. That's a lot. Can you eat that many?"

"Ten! Wow! I only see four, but that's more than I can eat anyway."

Sammy shrugged and stated, "You have to be a champ like me to eat like me."

Mace laughed heartily and agreed, "Yep, you are a champ, Sammy."

"Are you staying for Christmas?"

"No, sorry, bud. I have to leave today to go home for Christmas."

"Aw, man!" Sammy said in a high-pitched drawn out voice.

"I know, but I'll see you again soon. In the meantime, I have a Christmas present for you—if it's okay with Mom to open it early?"

Annie smiled and nodded, bringing the last of the pancakes to the table. Mace disappeared to the porch and then returned with a large box. Sammy tore into it immediately.

"Whoa! My very own camera?" Sammy squealed with delight.

"I thought you might like to start telling your own stories."

"Awesome! Mom, did you see? How cool is this?"

"Unbelievably cool, Sammy," Annie said.

"Thank you, Mr. Harlen! Can I go show Sam?"

Before she was even done saying he could, he was out of the room and halfway up the stairs, leaving Annie alone with Mace and a plate of pancakes between them.

"Mace, I don't know what to say. It's an amazing gift."

"He's an amazing kid. Someday, the world will need to see things his way."

"Well, thank you for both our gifts."

"Thank you for mine," he said, flashing her the piece of paper. "What made you change your mind?"

Hearing Sammy coming back down the hall with Sam in tow, Annie shrugged in their direction and then said, "It's a long story."

"Well, maybe you can tell me later—maybe over dinner in Chicago."

Annie blushed slightly and whispered a "maybe" back to him just as Sammy and Sam came back into the room. Sam was barking about why he hadn't been made aware that there were pancakes. Sammy was already getting everything on film. Eventually, Mace said goodbye and slipped out the front door. Annie knew she wouldn't get an intimate goodbye, but she was suddenly feeling unsure about the possibility of something new transpiring between her and Mace. She peeked out the front door and waved quickly as he backed down the driveway, and he waved out the window and then drove away.

That evening, Sam sat in his recliner, watching Annie finish the last of the wrapping in the middle of the floor.

"You're sure it's okay if I go?" she asked.

Sam stamped his cane into the carpet and gave her a stern look. "Don't go soft on me, Annie. When God tells you to go, don't make it about anybody else. Just go."

"Okay. You'll be all right with Sammy?"

"Sure, he'll take good care of me," he said with a facetious grin.

The next morning, Sammy bounded into Annie's room, full of Christmas excitement. Annie felt exhausted from staying up late but also felt the joy that came from Christmas with her boys. She let Sammy pull her out of bed and pretended to beg for more sleep while fumbling for her robe and slippers.

Soon the morning was filled with coffee, cinnamon rolls, wrapping paper strewn every direction, awe and wonder, and glowing festive faces as they enjoyed every moment by the tree.

Sam caught Annie looking at an ornament Leo had made last year and smiled knowingly at her. She silently wondered what Leo was doing and prayed for him, while Sam prayed that she'd be able to let him go if she needed to.

By noon, Dale, Tom, and Gus were in the house, helping make Christmas dinner, which had become a tradition. Annie was glad since she needed to get ready for her trip the next day.

She slipped upstairs to start packing. Her cell phone rang just as she was picking out shoes.

"Hello?"

"Annie, it's Randy. Did you decide to go?"

"I did. I'm flying out tomorrow."

"Good. What time?"

"8:15 a.m."

"Do you mind if I escort you? I can pick you up at the ranch at 6:00."

Annie paused momentarily, feeling uneasy and confused, and then said, "Randy, I don't understand."

"Just think of me, Annie, as your security."

"I'd like to talk to Sam about this first, Randy. Can I call you back?'

"Sam already knows, but you're welcome to call me back whenever you feel comfortable with it."

"When did you talk to Sam about this?" Annie fired off, feeling defensive.

"What I meant was, he's always known, Annie."

Annie fell silent, and a cord of fear grew taut in her heart with sickening vibrations that traveled all through her body. "Always? As in you've always been my security?"

"Yes," Randy said. "Annie, please don't worry. I will fully explain everything on the plane."

The thin veil of delicate safety that Annie had created around her life threatened to tear and unravel, but she remembered asking the Lord to be with her in Chicago, and His answer reverberated in her mind: *I will never leave you or forsake you.*

"Okay, Randy. I'll see you at 6:00 then."

Sam knows? Who else knows? I feel embarrassed that I was so ignorant. Why have I needed security? Simon isn't even alive. What other threat is there? Why hasn't Sam ever told me?

Annie's thoughts circled above her like taunting vultures. She sat on the edge of the bed, not bothering to defend herself from the questions.

Have I ignored reality for too long? Was I really ever safe? Have I really been living, or has this all been a careful façade? Am I still in the shadows? Before her questions completely overtook her, Sam's voice interrupted softly from the door.

"Dinner's ready," he announced just as she turned to look at him with solemn confusion in her eyes. "What is it, Annie girl?"

"I just spoke with Randy on the phone." The words felt like rocks, simply falling from her mouth, emotionless.

A weariness mixed with a certain transparent guilt spread from Sam's brow down to his soft smile that was fading. He came and sat on the bed next to her.

"You're angry at me," he stated.

Annie sat in silence, contemplating what she was feeling.

"Confused, mostly, which I hate to say because I have felt confused so much lately," she admitted.

"I can explain, but I don't know that I should."

"Why not?"

"It wasn't my plan. I sort of had to agree to it."

"Discovering that people you love have known something and kept it from you is like thinking your life is real only to find out you're actually in a play."

"I know Randy will explain everything, but that knowledge won't help you forgive me. I pray that, in time, you'll understand."

Annie's heart clenched at the tension she felt between her and Sam. She had never had any reason to fight with him or resent him.

They went down to dinner, and Annie did her best to let her confusion get swallowed down with a glass of wine and sweet potatoes. Later that night, though, as she lay in her bed, feelings of bitter confusion rose in her chest, burning as they bubbled, like acid in her throat.

She wasn't sure why God would bring her to a place of questioning everything just as He was taking her back to the place where everything changed. She felt consumed with questions and thoughts of what she might find out and what Randy said she would uncover. She didn't sleep that night.

The next morning on the plane, Annie settled into her seat, and Randy slid down next to her, looking completely out of place in his three-piece suit and his long hair pulled back in a ponytail. She began her barrage as soon as he clicked his seatbelt.

"All right, Randy—if that's even your name. What should I call you?"

"Randall, officially."

"Randall. I guess it goes with the outfit today."

"I know you're used to my being greased up like an oil pan—not to mention my constantly hitting on you, but believe it or not I come from a very refined background."

"Very well. What's this all about? Who sent you? Who else knows? Spill it."

Randy paused, letting the attendant speak over the intercom before he turned toward Annie and began, "You're familiar with the Martha Grady Foundation?" Annie nodded, and he continued. "The Foundation set up the security detail during the case. You didn't know me back then, and when they sent you to your uncle's, they thought it best to post me in town as a permanent resident so that after the year of witness protection was over, you'd still be protected and surveyed."

"I can't even tell you how creepy and betrayed I feel right now. I mean, you weren't even serious about all those proposals?"

Randy could sense the last question was sarcastic, and he felt safe enough to laugh. "No, I'm afraid it was just a tactic to build a relationship with you, however creepy it may have been."

"What if I had said yes?" Annie was not able to keep herself from smiling.

"I guess I would've had to marry you and keep the charade going for the sake of everyone's safety." He winked at her.

"In all seriousness, have I been in danger this whole time and just unaware?"

"Not like you're thinking." The plane took off from the runway, and Annie sucked in a small breath when she felt the plane lift off the ground. Randy continued, "It's not like there are schools of people lurking around every corner, waiting for the chance to hurt you. We just wanted to protect you and Sammy from the press and others who would try to persuade you to never speak out or would try to twist your story into something else. We needed to protect you until it was time to wage war."

"Wage war?" Annie looked up at the stewardess and shook her head no to the in-flight snacks. "War on what or whom?"

"The Gradys."

"The Gradys? As in the family, the corporation, or the alleged crime ring?"

"Essentially the corporation, which in turn takes out the crime ring."

"What's that got to do with me? Isn't corporate espionage highly illegal?"

"I know the Foundation would like a chance to explain things themselves, so let's save some of that strategy talk for later. Anything else you want to know?"

"Is it just you, or are there other fake citizens in Penumbra?"

"Just me."

"Who else knows?"

"Sam knows. He wasn't keen on the idea, but he went along with it because I wasn't going to be following you around and stalking your every move. I was more of a protective observer. Leo knew, and Mace knows now, as well."

No wonder Leo never minded that Randy was always so forward with his feelings; he knew they were false. What an idiot I must've looked like to him.

"How long has Mace known, and why does he know?"

"Just two days ago. The Foundation has been supporting the movie project from day one. I only introduced myself as myself the other day. He doesn't know anything more than that, but all will be clear soon."

"I hope so because nothing is clear at the moment," Annie said, leaning her head back against the seat, the effects of her sleepless night pushing down on her eyelids.

"Why don't you get some rest? There's plenty of time for questions later." Randy reached up to turn off their reading lights. Annie nodded, relaxed her shoulders, and let weariness pull her down against the seat. Although she wanted to process all Randy had said, her tiredness and the drone of the plane engine clouded her mind and dragged her into her dreams.

She searched through a sand castle for his plaid shirt, yelling, "Leo!" No matter where she looked, she couldn't see him. She ran through the fragile halls as the castle began to crash down around her. She scrambled to find him. Was he still in here? Was he trapped in this elaborate sand maze? "Leo," she screamed again, but her screams made the walls, pillars, and sconces topple and avalanche toward her even faster. She saw light up ahead through a large window, and she realized she had to save herself from the sand that was rushing in on her. She had to leave Leo. She hoped he was already out safely. She jumped through the open window and slid down the avalanche of sand as it rushed over grass and shells on the beach. She finally stopped near the water and looked up to see Leo, standing on a rock, out in the middle of the ocean. She was calling out to him as a hand gently grabbed her arm and shook it.

"Annie?" Randy said as he shook her arm slightly. She opened her eyes slowly. "We're here, Annie. Wake up." She felt the plane touch down and felt the pull of the brakes as the plane slowed down the runway. "Are you okay?"

"Yeah." She blinked her eyes several times to try to get them to open all the way. "Strange dream, but I guess that means good sleep."

"Guess so. I assume that someone is picking you up at the airport?"

"I believe Mace is," she said, gathering her coat and carry-on. "Will you be following me around Chicago as security, or will you go elsewhere?"

"I won't follow, per se, but we'll be around. And we'll be in touch."

"Then, Randall, thank you for escorting me to Chicago."

"You're very welcome. Thank you for not fighting it, and for not freaking out."

"Oh, I'm freaking out all right, just on the inside," Annie said, laughing as they exited the plane together and headed up the tarmac. Soon they reached the waiting area and beyond that the luggage claim.

"I'll talk to you soon."

"Yes, Annie, you will. Be careful. Call if you need me. Have a good day." He shook her hand and bid her goodbye with a cautious seriousness. Annie watched him disappear into the crowd, and a sudden slight ping of panic bounced around her heart.

She scanned the crowd as she stood alone, searching for Mace's dark hair and broad shoulders. Then across several heads, she spotted Chuck, staring at her and holding a small sign with her name on it. Her stomach both sank and swelled at the sight of his blonde hair, now long enough to be pulled back away from his chiseled face in a low swept ponytail. He smiled as their eyes found each other, and she walked briskly toward him, feeling the desire to get out of the thick of the crowd. As she got closer, she dropped her bag and pretended to jog in slow motion toward him. He laughed, threw the sign to the floor, and pretended to run in slow motion toward her too, clumsily. They reached for each other in slow motion only to be too far apart to grasp each other.

Annie bent over laughing, and Chuck grabbed her around the waist, breathing hard from laughing.

"What are you doing here? I was expecting Mace."

"He sent me. You don't seem too disappointed, in light of your Bo Derek-esque arrival, just now."

Annie's cheeks hurt from all the laughter, but it felt good to laugh with Chuck. "No, not disappointed. Just surprised is all. Where to now?"

"We're off to meet everyone for lunch once we grab your bags."

"So Mace was too busy to meet me, but we're meeting him for lunch?"

"He got caught up in something at the Foundation and asked me to fetch you, but he said that lunch was still on."

Annie crossed her arms and stopped cold in her stride, raising one eyebrow. She flashed him a wickedly sassy smile and said, "He sent you to FETCH me?"

"Well, you are quite fetching, if I do say so myself."

"Those two things don't mean the same thing, Chuck!"

"Come on. Don't be angry. I'm here, we're funny, so get over it," he said, nudging her along. "Am I right, or am I right?"

"Fine. I am hungry."

"Well, let's fetch Miss Derek some lunch, shall we?" Chuck said, pretending to escort her over to baggage claim. Annie slapped his elbow away and stomped playfully in front of him.

"I don't need any more fetching today, thank you very much."

While they waited around the conveyor belt for the bags to arrive through the hatch, Chuck pulled something out of his coat pocket.

"It's a little late, but Merry Christmas," he said, handing her a small wrapped package. "I had it in Penumbra, but I had to leave before I could give it to you. Then I decided it was better to give it to you here."

His thoughtfulness warmed Annie, and she took the package from him, slid her finger through the tape, and pulled out a slender leather journal, the color of cognac and trimmed with white stitching.

"I figure you might need to write new memories down while you're here."

Chuck grabbed her bag and pulled it down between them. Annie stood motionless, looking at the journal, studying its color and texture and the thought Chuck had put into this gift.

"It is perfect, Chuck. Thank you."

His smile twitched, and she thought she sensed sadness in his eyes as she stepped away from him and grabbed the handle of her suitcase from him, their hands touching in the exchange.

"Shall we go?"

Annie nodded and rolled the suitcase behind her as they stepped out into the gray afternoon of Chicago. The light blinded her after being inside the airport, and she shielded her eyes for a moment, feeling the wind bite at her fingers and cheeks. Chuck took her hand to steady her, feeling her sway next to him.

"I guess maybe I wasn't ready for Chicago again."

"Maybe not. Some things you can't prepare for, especially matters of the heart, but we can take it one sidewalk at a time."

One sidewalk at a time. I like that. She took her hand from her eyes and nudged Chuck with her shoulder. "Let's make some new memories, so I have new things to write about."

28. CHICAGO AND DEEP DISH PIZZA

If I were speaking to Leo at all, I would have told him that my footsteps felt heavy as I walked through the terminal and baggage claim. I would have told him that the wind stole my breath, just like it used to as we wove through the high rises. The streets smelled of old memories. I might have mentioned to him that I thought I recognized the cabbie and the toy pistol that hung from the rearview mirror, dancing with each bump.

But, as it turns out, we're not speaking now, so I'm just writing it here.

Chuck watched her close the journal with the pen in it and gaze out the window. They sat shoulder to shoulder in the cab as they darted through traffic heading uptown. Annie felt his eyes and glanced at him quickly, giving him a forced smile. He could feel the tension in her shoulders that sat stiffly touching his and the silent but heavy sighs that made her back slump a little more with each one.

He leaned over to her. "Cheer up, Annie," he said sweetly in her ear. "You're not doing this alone."

Annie took in a deep breath and mustered up a real smile for him, nudged him with her shoulder, and grabbed his hand resting on his leg. "Thanks, Chuck," she said as the cab pulled over to a curb and stopped. "Could you order for me? I think I'll duck into the bathroom and throw up first."

Chuck laughed through his nose, thinking she was joking, but she hopped from the cab like a rabbit and jogged away before he could say anything more. Mace and Leo got out of a car in front of them, and Mace walked briskly over to Chuck, pointing in the direction Annie went and asking, "Is she okay?"

"I'd say," Chuck gauged, "not at the moment."

Mace cocked his head and gave him a curious look. Chuck shrugged and didn't feel like explaining everything to Mace. If he hadn't anticipated how difficult being in Chicago would be for Annie, that was his shortcoming.

"She told me to order for her. We can go inside."

"Okay, great. Our table is ready, and I'm ready to get started," Mace rattled off as if it were an order.

Within a few minutes, Annie joined the table, apologized for not being there sooner, refused to look Leo in the eyes, and thanked Chuck for ordering soup for her. For the next two hours, she sat between Mace and Chuck, listening to Mace jabber about cameras, angles, and wind speeds. She pretended to be interested in cranes, dollies, shot sheets, and permits for filming. Eventually, she found herself staring out the window. The traffic provided a busy pattern for her eyes to follow, and some cars with squeaking brakes afforded some music to the stop and go. But the more she watched the streets of her heartache, the more her heart jumped with each honk. It began to race, and her legs squirmed under the table until, at last, she stood, bringing all three men standing up with her.

"Please excuse me. I think I need some air or some rest."

"Annie," Mace leaned over closer to her so as to not appear to be scolding her, "We have a full day. I really need you."

She nodded, trying to still her legs and slow her breathing. "I'll just step outside then for some air. I'm very sorry." She ducked her head and quickly exited the restaurant. Leo stiffly sat back down, watching with wary eyes as she walked through the front door out onto the street.

Chuck couldn't seem to wipe the shock off his face as he stood and said, "Mace. I think that was a little insensitive. Don't you?"

Mace had already sat back down and looked up at Chuck, who towered above him still holding his napkin in his hand. Mace looked around slightly confused. "I thought I handled that well. I didn't want to tell her what to do, but if she's going to be here, I need her to be all here. And we do, literally, have to hit the ground running today. We have no time to waste time."

"Don't you see that you can't be all business with Annie?"

"I do see that, and I'm doing my best to balance."

"None of us can really imagine how hard it is for her to be back here."

Leo leaned back in his chair and said coolly, "I can."

Chuck dropped his napkin on the table. "Yes, Leo, I'm sure you do, but you're not exactly doing anything to make this easier for her, are you?" He didn't wait for Leo's answer; he turned and left.

Outside, Chuck walked over to Annie, who was hugging her waist, bent over on a park bench. He said, "Not a great foot to be starting out on, is it?"

Annie laughed, but it sounded more like a huff.

"I'm sorry Mace can be—" Chuck started to apologize for the way Mace acted, but Annie interrupted him.

"You don't have to apologize for him, Chuck."

Chuck nodded. Annie stood and stretched herself out, smoothing her coat down and wrapping her scarf around her neck and stuffing it down her coat.

"What's next?" she asked, desperately trying to sound chipper.

Chuck glared at her and commented, "You don't have to be this strong, you know."

"Don't I, though? You heard Mace. We have a lot to do today, and I didn't come here to have an emotional breakdown. I came here to help. And I'm not helping if I'm falling apart."

"That doesn't sound healthy, all that stuffing."

"I'm not stuffing, Chuck."

"Yes, you are."

"Maybe I just want to stuff it in front of certain people, and then I can let it out when I'm alone in my hotel room. Is that so unhealthy?"

Chuck looked back through the window, following her quick eyes as they landed on Leo and bounced back to him. "You don't want Leo to know that it's painful for you to be here? Don't you think he knows that?"

Annie turned away from him in frustration only to spin back around to say, "I can't explain everything to you. I appreciate your caring. Remember what you said earlier…one sidewalk at a time? I can't deal with this place one sidewalk at a time if you are jumping in all the time trying to get me to spill my entire guts to everyone in the hope that they'll understand."

Chuck looked at her pleading eyes, and for a selfish moment, he wished they were pleading with him in a different way. He swallowed those thoughts down and nodded to her. "You're right, Annie. I'm sorry. I won't push anymore."

"Thank you. And seriously, what's next?"

"I think we are walking from here, doing some sightseeing and land-marking. We might drive by the theater site later. You up for that?"

Annie took a deep breath, and Chuck could see the breath pool out of her mouth in the cold air.

"One sidewalk at a time," she said with a sincere smile, which faded as Sarah, the girl who played her in the movie, stepped out of a cab in heels and a short skirt. Leo and Mace poured out of the restaurant and quickly embraced the girl.

Who wears heels when you're going sightseeing? Could that skirt be any shorter? How can I possibly compete with that? Wait...why do I need to compete? I'm being so ridiculous right now. Note to self: Wear jeans and boots tomorrow, and be yourself.

"Hi, Annie!" Sarah squealed, hugging her quickly without warning.

Annie's arms hung stiffly at her side, and her eyes widened, looking over her shoulder at Leo and Mace, who matched her expression of shock.

"Did you just arrive? I'm so glad you are here," Sarah chirped.

"Thanks," Annie managed as the girl released her. Leo's eyes were dark, and he tracked her as she stepped aside from Sarah, closer to Chuck.

Mace stepped forward, intervening in the awkward moment. "Shall we start the tour? Leo has agreed to be our guide of sorts. Annie, feel free to chime in at any point. Ready?"

Everyone agreed. They started walking, and all along their route, Leo shared the history of landmarks, buildings, street names, and noteworthy people whose stories intertwined with Chicago. Annie listened to every word as if he were talking directly to her, but it was not lost on her that, while he talked, he directed everything toward the actress who looked so much like Annie it was unnerving. The sun had begun to play peek-a-boo between the skyscrapers, and its glow turned a brilliant shade of orange and sagged in the sky opposite the pier. Everyone split up and explored the pier, but Annie leaned on the rail and decided to enjoy a moment alone outside the busyness of the pier. She leaned out over the water and saw a shadow of her reflection on the water along with the flickers of the Ferris wheel lights, shimmering around on the surface. Soon another shadow appeared beside her, and an arm slipped around her shoulder and briefly squeezed it.

"I'm sorry if I was insensitive earlier," Mace said.

Annie continued looking out at the dark, slippery surface but smiled softly.

"It's okay, Mace. I don't expect you to understand."

"Ouch."

"I don't mean that as a dig. I just don't expect it. It would be unfair."

"What if I wanted to understand?"

"What if, Mace? There are many what ifs that I can't afford to entertain," she said laughingly.

"Why?"

"Because they don't change what is or what was."

Suddenly Mace felt the weight of the conversation he had started, and he knew they weren't talking in a slightly flirtatious way anymore. He realized what Chuck said had been true; he couldn't be all business with her, but he also knew that he couldn't be all there for her either. That was something he couldn't afford.

"It's hard to separate what was and what is for you while here, isn't it?"

Annie propped herself up on her elbow and turned to face him. She said, "Maybe there's a way to do that, but I don't know how. You can't rewrite history. It's fact. It can't be unwritten. That doesn't mean I live there, but being here speaks to both the past and present. And no, to some extent, they can't be separated."

"How so? I think I disagree."

"I am here today in the present because I left Chicago in the past. I couldn't meet you or work on this project if I had never left, just the way you wouldn't be here, directing a movie now if you hadn't broken down in a small town and subsequently changed your life's direction."

"You are quite fascinating, Annie. You know that?" he said, a playful smile tugging at his lips.

"But am I right?"

"And boisterous! Yes, you are right. Okay? You are right." He laughed, pretending to be pained by his admission.

Annie smiled with satisfaction.

Mace got serious for a moment. "I want you to know that I'm here for you. Okay?"

She squinted at him and pulled her mouth over to one side. "I know you want to be, but you also have a lot on your plate right now. You don't need to worry about me."

"You sure don't make this easy."

"What's that?"

"Being your friend."

"I don't suppose I do."

271

Annie looked at the DSLR camera in her hands and wondered what to do with it. Mace had given one to each person and explained how he wanted them to explore and document Chicago. He had handed out thirty cameras in all and sent them on their way. Some had headed out on foot, while others had whistled for cabs and dashed away in yellow. Annie stood like a statue on the corner, staring at the camera in her hands.

"You can do this," Chuck said softly, giving her a hug from the side. Annie couldn't help relax and smile, feeling wrapped up underneath his lengthy arm span.

"Thanks for not assuming I couldn't and for not pushing." She pulled her lips to the side with a shy smile.

"Walking or riding or biking?" he said, edging toward the curb and releasing her reluctantly.

"Walking, I think."

"Call me if you need me. I'll come and find you."

She silently nodded. Chuck whistled with two fingers, and the screech of brakes met his pitch as the cab slowed by the curb. The cabbie honked to let Chuck know he had him. Chuck waved to her just before he ducked inside. She smiled and waved back as his window rolled down enough for him to say, "Have fun with it, okay?"

"Okay." She tried to assure herself more than him. "I'll try."

"There is no try, my grasshopper. There is only do or do not," he teased as the cab began to pull away.

What can I show them? Everyone else will probably go for the hot spots, but Chicago is more than that. How can I show them something new? I don't even want to show them the hidden gems of the city either. What can I possibly add to this project?

Annie closed her eyes and listened to the traffic and rumble of the L train. She inhaled and assessed her senses, feeling her head lift. Her eyes opened to see the sky above her pushing through the tops of the buildings, breaking her vision wide open.

I've got to get up above. I've got to get above all this.

She decided to get on the transit and take it down to the John Hancock. Standing shoulder to shoulder with strangers would normally make her nervous, but the excitement she felt as she held her camera up to the window to get "city blur" exhilarated her. She was being creative and visionary. Once at the John Hancock, she traveled up to the 94th floor, where she got 360-degree aerial footage of the city, the pier, and the shoreline. She paused as she stared out over the city and saw how trivial street life looked from up there.

Rise above it, the little voice resonated in her head.

"I'm not sure I know how. Help me," she whispered to the glass.

Then the thought bumped from her left brain to her right brain that she should get this same kind of aerial footage of the old theater plot. She was losing light, but she thought she'd have just enough by the time she rode the L train downtown to the theater district to even get a sunset shot.

"Rising above it while the sun goes down on. Brilliant, Annie." She smiled to herself.

Once she was near the theater, she scanned the opposite side of the street and found the fire escape on the side of an abandoned drug store being renovated into a restaurant on the corner. She climbed up and cautiously looked around the roof to make sure it was still safe to walk around on. Finding it in remarkably good shape, she walked to the front ledge that had large scrolling architecture, which she could use to brace the camera on for a moment. The scrolls covered her about chest high, and she was glad she was almost hidden and wouldn't attract attention. She held up the camera and did several sweeping shots of the city in segments. She braced the camera on the scrollwork to do some final shots of the empty plot across the street. The sun was a fiery red as it dipped below buildings behind her, casting nice bold glows on the street below. As she adjusted the settings on her camera, she checked the framing before recording. Through the viewfinder, she saw two people standing on the street in front of the plot. In one beat, her heart dropped out of her chest and plummeted down to her stomach, which seemed to send it bubbling back up with acid.

With a slight zoom she knew she'd regret, she saw Leo, embracing the actress around the waist, and as Annie's head screamed, "No!" the girl tilted her head toward his and kissed him. Annie turned away, clutching the camera and sinking down below the scrolling wall.

No. No. No. She repeated without control. *He's kissing her. There. In front of the place where I almost died. He's kissing her there. How could he? I knew they were dating, but to watch them kiss? There? Is he that heartless?* Her thoughts were running rampant and turning to furious tears that spilled out her eyelids and raced down her cheeks. Her tears turned to sobs, and her breath became harder to catch. The sun slipped away, leaving her in the twilight on the rooftop with her heart breaking wildly open.

Is this it? I released him, and he ran so far away. I pushed him away...into someone else's arms.

Rise above it, Annie. She heard the voice all around her.

"How can I?" she asked plaintively.

The wind died down as the sun melted away into night, and the voice seemed to drift away from her on the wind. She sobbed into her scarf until her stomach hurt. She felt like she was hyperventilating, and she realized she would have to get down off the roof to meet the street, alone and in the dark. She was too late to meet up with everyone to return her camera and cast her vision, not that she had one left at this point. She wasn't sure which scared her more, the darkness or facing the group. Pulling out her phone from her coat, she searched for his number, knowing he wasn't far away and that he would come rescue her before her next tear fell. She tried to slow her breaths and sniffs, but it helped little.

"Randy?" she said his name desperately into the phone. Before he even responded, she heard him shuffling to his feet, and he was on the move. She felt her shoulders relaxed as his reaction.

"Annie, where are you? Are you okay?"

"I'm on the roof of the drugstore across from the old theater. I'm not okay. I...I...It's dark, and I'm alone. I didn't know who else to call."

"Stay there. Do not try to come down. I will come get you, and, Annie?"

"Yes?"

"You are not alone," he said earnestly.

He reached her within a few minutes and climbed the fire escape with ease, rushing to her against the ornate front wall. He lifted her under the shoulders and knees, cradling her as she cradled the camera.

"I've got you, Annie. You're safe now. I'm going to carry you to the ladder, and then you're going to have to climb down. Okay?"

"Okay," she whispered.

He carried her across the roof to the landing where he set her down and retrieved the camera from her, strapping it across his shoulder and on his back. Annie climbed with shaking arms and legs down the ladder to the next landing where she waited for him to nod to her to go down the next one. When they finally reached the ground, Annie felt light and weightless as the streetlight began to flicker and dance while the length of the street began to shorten and expand at seemingly the same time. As she pointed to it, she was swept up, and her head hung back limply. Before she faded into the hovering blackness, she saw the stars above the buildings, rising to meet the velvet canopy.

Annie touched her forehead with what felt like an amputated hand, responding to her brain yet not feeling like her hand. Her fingers felt cool against her warm forehead, and as they drifted down her cheeks, she felt the warmth grow. Her eyes slid halfway open to see the dancing flames in front of her, and she scrambled back in fear. As her eyes widened, she took in her surroundings, including a large Victorian fireplace with regal lions on either side guarding the flame. She had been propped up on the Persian rug on ornate pillows and covered in a plush purple blanket, though her scramble had disheveled all of that. Her cheeks and forehead were hot from sleeping next to the fire, but from where she had scurried to, she felt the chill of the room touch her. She scooted back toward the fireplace, wrapping herself in the blanket again and sitting cross-legged in front of the crackling blaze. She stared into the mesmerizing dance and shoved her thoughts into the oblivion that used to be her heart, refusing to think anymore. A knock came at the door, and she softly said, "Come in."

Randy appeared with a tray, holding a steaming bowl and mug to match.

"How are you feeling?"

"Okay. Is that for me?"

"Yes. Are you hungry? That's a good sign. You've been asleep for a few hours."

"I have? Goodness," she said, taking the tray from him and immediately lifting the mug to her lips. "Mm, this is good. Thank you, Randy. Thank you for everything."

"You're welcome. I'm glad you called." He sat watching her for several minutes as she slowly sipped spoonfuls of soup and drank from the mug. He sat pensively on the light blue velvet colonial couch, but he didn't rush her in any way.

When she finally set the tray away from her lap, he said, "I have someone who would like to speak with you, someone who's been waiting to speak with you if you feel up to it."

Annie nodded a brave nod. Randy disappeared through the door and closed it behind him. He reappeared a few minutes later, assisting a hunched figure, his twin assisting on the other side. Annie gasped softly under her breath at the sight of the twins. They held the figure under each elbow with strength but delicateness that Annie couldn't help but notice. The room was layered with flickering shadows, and the figure they assisted was shrouded in the layers as they moved, shuffled actually, toward the couch that Randy had just vacated. Annie scooted away from it to give them room to move in front of it. Annie repositioned herself to sit on her knees, her back toward the fire. As they lowered the person onto the couch, the firelight glowed on the figure's face, and Annie's mouth fell so wide open she felt her jaw pop. The woman's face, though aged and folded with soft wrinkles around her eyes and mouth and neck, was a perfect preservation of the many photographs Annie had once seen of her.

But how can this be? Annie wondered. "Mrs. Martha Grady?" her voice cracked as she asked in dumfounded amazement and confusion.

"Annie. May I call you Annie, my dear?" Martha asked in a steady voice as she extended a shaky hand out for Annie.

Annie scrambled closer to shake the petite hand of the supposed dead wife of the patriarch of the Grady family.

"I'll let you in on a little secret," Martha said with a smile, patting the seat beside her.

Annie moved to sit beside her. She looked at Randy, who stood behind the couch, next to his twin.

"You're alive?"

"Yes, indeed I am, dear. I am still alive."

"How? Why? I mean, does anyone else know?"

"The *how* is quite simple. These days with the right allies, dear, anyone can fake their own death. The *why* is a little harder to explain. I needed to be dead to accomplish the things necessary to bring down the Grady family. As for who knows, I'm afraid, dear, you're the only one who knows besides Randy and Nigel here. Oh, I'm so sorry. Please let me introduce you. You know Randy, of course, but let me formally introduce you to Nigel and Randall Grady," she said, fanning her hand toward them as she paused, hanging her entire tone on the final word. "They are my boys."

Annie couldn't seem to control her gaping jaw as it fell open again. Her hand flew to her mouth to cover it up, and she felt her eyes grow wide. Nigel and Randy both silently bowed to her, knowing that the moment needed no words from them.

"I had no idea that you had twin boys, much less that one of them was my bodyguard!"

"People went to great pains to keep my boys protected and secret. It pained me as they grew up, but it has proven to be my saving grace now as we wage this war."

"Ah, yes. The corporate espionage."

The elderly woman chuckled heartily. "That's illegal, dear, and that's not what we're doing. I like to think of it as bringing down the house."

"I guess I don't understand the war. Why go after the Gradys? You are a Grady."

"Boys, leave us. I will tell Annie my story. I won't burden you with listening to it again."

Annie tried to read Randy's expression as he and Nigel backed out of the room silently, closing the ornate door behind them.

"My dear, I will speak frankly with you though I will do my best to be gracious." Martha took Annie's hand, patting it with her own. "You remember that there comes a sense of freedom when a Grady man dies, yes?"

Annie recalled the memory of the day she heard Simon's execution was final and the day the call came that Martha's husband had died. Freedom had flooded her life that day.

"I do."

"I know that feeling too. I was trapped for so long, and now, I have the chance to vindicate my life and my boys' life. In doing so, I can also help so many others, but we must do it under the radar, or it is all for naught."

"How? What does this have to do with me?"

"It's the friend of yours, Mr. Harlen."

"Mace?"

"Yes. He's going to help me bring down the house."

"So he knows? I thought you said I was the only one who knew?"

"He doesn't know this, but he will be a vital player. He will be our storyteller. And you'll tell him when the time is right."

"Why me?"

"If he'd never met you, dear, he never would have gotten to the place he is now. He wouldn't be telling your story. Someday he'll help tell mine, and we'll help bring a stop to all this bondage."

"Bondage? What do you mean? Will you tell me your story?"

"Of course, my dear. That is why you are here."

As the fire fizzled and popped down to a deep glow within the logs, Martha told Annie a tale of heartache, of bondage inside the Grady family's profitable porn industry, of betrayal and crime, and of a deep pain that resonated in Annie's chest. Martha told her of the joy her boys brought her as she lived in such agony of the marital prison she was in. Annie listened with such empathy that by the end of Martha's story, they were hugging.

"Why have you taken such an interest in my life? Is it just the similarity of men, the Grady men?"

"I have followed you from the moment I heard not only because of you but because of that sweet son of yours. I am able to break down the walls that will allow him to walk through the rubble and into a new heritage and a new inheritance."

"I don't want Sammy to have any part of the Grady money."

"That's just the thing, dear. There won't be anything left of the Grady money. It will all be Foundation money. We will redeem it and use it to rescue others. Your boy can go to college and find his own way in this world without being tainted as a son of Grady."

Annie had no idea what to say. They talked well into the evening until there was nothing left of the fire and nothing left of Martha's dwindling energy. Eventually, Martha asked Annie to retrieve her sons to help her to bed. Before long, she stood, assisted once again by Randy and Nigel, and embraced Annie.

"Thank you for entrusting me with your secrets, and thank you for all you have done to protect mine," Annie said.

"God gives deep purpose to our pain. You have been part of my purpose." She touched Annie's face the way a mother would have. "Good night, dear. I will see you again soon."

Her sons whisked her away, leaving Annie alone in the dark colonial parlor. She pulled out her phone, quickly dialing Mace.

"Hello, Mace?"

"Annie! Where are you?" Mace quizzed, frustration evident in his voice.

"I can explain. First, can you come get me? I'm at the Foundation."

"The Foundation? What are you doing there? Why are you there at this hour?" He sounded increasingly irritated. "I'll be there as soon as I can." He hung up the phone.

Randy reappeared several minutes later, asking, "Can I give you a ride back to your hotel?"

"No, I called Mace. He's on his way."

"You sure? It's no trouble. In fact, Martha insisted."

"I'm sure. Mace will be here any minute."

They both heard the knock at the front door moments later, and they laughed.

"He's here, I guess."

"Before you go...whatever or whoever made you so upset tonight, should I be concerned?"

"I can't be certain that I won't ever get upset over it again, but I won't be getting stuck on a rooftop at night over it."

"Very well. All the same, you can call me anytime."

"Thanks, Randall," Annie said, giving him a quick hug and opening the door. She was a bit taken back to see Chuck, not Mace, standing at the door.

"Chuck?" Annie questioned.

"Hey." Chuck shrugged, knowing he wasn't the man she expected to see.

"I thought Mace was coming to pick me up. What are you doing here?"

Chuck's words fought his tongue as he pushed them off. "Mace sent me."

Annie managed a smile and waved to Randall as she followed Chuck out the front door. Once the door was closed and she was tucked away in the cab, she looked at Chuck. "Of course, Mace sent you."

"I also wanted to make sure you were okay."

Annie huffed, feeling tired and irritable.

"So, are you okay? You never showed up after the assignment, and I couldn't reach you. What happened?"

Annie sighed heavily. "I'm okay. I wasn't earlier, but I think I am now."

"Do you want to talk about it?"

"Yes," she said, leaning her head on his shoulder, "Over a Lou Malnatti's pizza and a glass of wine…and after I've had a shower."

"You got it, Annie. Whatever you need."

Annie closed her eyes and felt the city whizzing and dodging by outside her little yellow cab. The rhythm of the seat bouncing and the warmth from Chuck's shoulder carried her into the darkness that she had not wanted to come out of earlier. She didn't even wake until Chuck whispered her name as he set her down on her bed. She opened her eyes to the hotel room and covered her face in embarrassment.

"You carried me in?"

He nodded as he unwrapped her arms from his neck.

"I'm sorry, Chuck. I didn't mean for you to carry me."

"I didn't hate it," he said, giving her a smirk. "You get in the shower, and I'll order us some pizza."

"Deal," Annie said, wiping her eyes and heading off to the bathroom.

Chuck followed her with his eyes, wondering what on earth he was doing in her hotel room. He forced himself as he heard the water turn on, to think about the pizza, find the number, and order the delivery. By the time he was done, so was she. She appeared minutes later in sweatpants and a Rangers t-shirt with her hair wrapped up in a towel.

"Where's that pizza?" She smiled, noticing how he stared. *He likes me even in my sweatpants,* she noted.

Forcing his eyes up to her freshly washed face flushed from the hot shower, he smiled, slightly embarrassed that his wandering eyes maybe had revealed his thoughts.

"It's on the way."

"Okay." She slid onto the bed and folded her knees up to her chest, hugging them with her slender arms. Setting the phonebook down, he joined her on the bed but sat a good distance away.

"Do you want to talk about what you were doing at the Foundation?"

Annie sighed. "First, will you watch my shots from today? It all starts there." She flitted over to the desk where Chuck had put her camera. She turned it on and queued it up from the beginning.

As she handed the camera to Chuck, he wondered what on earth had happened to her since he left her standing on the sidewalk. He watched the clips carefully, the city whizzing by on the train. "I like that, and Mace will like that too," he commented as he watched. Then the scene changed to high above the city, then the shoreline, and then the pier. It changed direction and scene but stayed well above the street view. Then the perspective and the lighting changed to the old theater site. He watched the camera zoom in to see the couple kiss. The camera fell, illuminating Annie in the fading sunlight, crying on a rooftop. Chuck shut the camera off. *It's beautiful, tragic and moving, but I can't tell her that right now.*

"I had this brilliant plan," Annie said. "It was going to be a fresh take on how I viewed my history. *Rise above it*, God said to me. And I did, I was beginning to take off, you know? Then I saw them, and I came crashing down, Chuck, as if my ability to rise above the past hinged on Leo. I felt paralyzed on that roof, and then it got dark. I couldn't be alone in the street crying, so I called Randy. He carried me back to the Foundation."

"Randy is here?" Chuck seemed confused.

"Yes, he…escorted me here. No, that's sounds wrong. He's essentially my security."

"Always has been?"

"Yep, though I didn't know it until earlier today."

"That makes a little more sense now. Okay. So, he took you to the Foundation. Why the Foundation? Wait. Before we go there, let's talk about Leo."

Annie huffed again, but this time, Chuck felt like it was forced. She huffed, pushing out the lump in her throat that might force tears out if it rose any further.

"I don't know what there is to say. Can we just talk about the Foundation?"

Chuck responded, "Sure." As he answered, a knock at the door came with the wafting smell of pepperoni under the door. He jogged to the door and paid the deliveryman for the pizza.

"That smells divine," Annie said, reaching for it. She settled on the bed and opened the box, letting the heat from the box rise up between them. For minutes, they sat in silence, devouring slices of famous deep dish.

"I have missed Chicago's pizza." She laughed, pushing the box more toward Chuck after she had eaten two slices. Chuck threw his crust down into the box and propped himself up on his elbow, lying on his side.

"So, we got some food in you. Now, talk to me."

"I don't know how much of this I'm supposed to tell you, but you're like the only friend I have right now. I'm going to tell you." She was sitting cross-legged, facing him. "The Foundation is in Martha's name, you know," she began, and then she told him every detail as it was so delicately told to her. Chuck's eyes widened, and he shook his head in disbelief. He was quiet for a long time and found himself staring out the high-rise hotel window at the distant black sky.

"Are you going to tell Mace?" he asked, returning to her.

She shrugged. "Martha told me that I would know when the time was right."

"Well, then I'm sure you will." Chuck smiled. "You have great purpose, Annie. You know that, right? Tonight just proves it. You're a part of something big."

Annie bent over her crossed legs and buried her face in the comforter. She growled low in her throat out of frustration or surrender, Chuck couldn't decide.

"I sometimes wonder, Chuck," she said muffled in the champagne colored duvet. Chuck reached across the bed and tousled the towel on her hair, letting it unravel and fall off her head, her auburn waves spilling out, dangerously close to the pizza box. She lifted her head, gathering her wet locks and tucking them over her right shoulder. She put her head in her hands and stared at the bed, not looking at Chuck. He picked up the pizza box and her towel, dropping the towel back in the bathroom and placing the pizza box on the desk. He flopped back on the extravagant and overstuffed feather pillows on the bed. He patted the opposite side of the bed, gesturing her to join him. She reluctantly crawled to the side of the bed and curled along the pillows, facing him but realizing how far away he was on a king-sized bed.

"What do you wonder?"

"I wonder if that's true—about being a part of something big."

"Heresy," he said jokingly, trying to get her to smile, maybe even laugh. A slight smile played at the corner of her mouth but faded as she thought to speak again.

"I know. It does actually sound like that, but there are times, like today, that it seems His purpose for me is just that He takes everything away."

"Come on, Annie. You don't mean that. You have a lot of really great things in your life."

"I know. I sound so ungrateful, don't I? I just…"

Chuck waited for her to finish, watching the way her mouth would open to speak and then close in uncertainty.

"You just what?" he urged softly, watching her eyes fill with unsteady tears even though her voice sounded sure.

"Life isn't perfect. I know that God didn't promise it would be, but I guess I had in my head that everything He took away, He'd restore later, better. Maybe in a different way, but He would still mend it." Chuck nodded, following her thoughts as she continued. "I feel like He's taking everything, and everything is just staying broken." Her tears finally spilled over as she said, "I'm not saying any of this right, and now I'm crying. I'm sorry."

"You think because of what you saw today that you've lost Leo forever, right?"

She stilled at the shift in the conversation and chewed on her lip, tears still rolling off her lashes unmanageably. "I guess, before, when he left the ranch, I thought he was mad, but he'd come around. Today I realized that he's making his choice. And it was a malicious choice against me."

"What makes you say that?"

"He kissed her right in front of where…" she raised her voice and then trailed off at the end. "Sorry, I don't mean to yell."

"It's okay. I know that must've hurt."

"It felt like a shotgun blast to my stomach," she paused, laying her head on the pillow, "and a dagger to my heart."

"You love him?" Chuck asked though not wanting her to answer.

Annie let out a slow sigh and wiped her face from the tears that were soaking the pillow. "Of course, I do, but I'm not even sure in what way. Now he's turned his back on everything he said he believed, and I don't think he loves me in any way anymore."

"You don't think?"

"I think he's proven that much over the last few months, don't you think?"

Chuck shrugged, not wanting to upset her. He propped his head on his hand and stretched out his legs. Annie bit her lip and curled up into a ball with her knees to her chest, looking like a child. Her tears came bitterly this time as she confessed to Chuck, "It just feels like God's taken everything away."

Chuck scooted close enough to reach her, and he wiped the tears off her cheeks and brushed the matted hair back away from her face.

"Not everything, Annie. You have Sam and Sammy. And you have me," he said softly to her. Her red swollen eyes found his, and the amber flecks seemed to plead with him.

"But I don't get to have you, do I? Not really," she whispered as if it was unutterable.

He pulled her by the waist over to him and let her head rest against his shoulder. He smoothed her hair and stroked her shoulder.

"I know," he answered. "But I'm here, aren't I?"

She nodded her head and hiccupped from all the crying. His warmth permeated her, and she stopped shaking and shivering. Her body relaxed into his embrace, and she closed her eyes and rested on his shoulder.

He sighed deeply and closed his eyes, trying to think of something to pray, but he felt blank with her beside him. Against the bed that looked like soft champagne clouds, they drifted off to sleep, side by side.

Mace shifted the coffee cup in his hand to holding it in his other arm, pinning it against his side carefully with his elbow. With two cups in one arm, he rapped lightly on the hotel room door. He noticed the door was propped open with the deadbolt lock folded over, and he cautiously pushed the door open.

"Annie? It's Mace. I—" he stopped short, catching his breath before it escaped in shock, seeing Chuck and Annie lying on the bed, asleep. They were lying on their sides facing opposite walls, with their backs touching each other, not even underneath the covers. *They're both fully clothed*, he reminded himself. He couldn't help but feel bewildered and confused, not to mention the jealousy that almost made him lose his concentration on carrying the cups and drop them. Recovering quickly, he backed himself out of the room without making a sound and was careful to close the door silently.

That was not what I expected. He shook his head to himself as he rode the elevator back down to the lobby. He decided to call her room from the front desk and wake her up. *You should have done that in the first place, Harlen. What were you thinking?*

He set the coffee cups down on the lobby desk and asked the petite Indian woman at the front desk to dial Annie's room. The woman nodded, dialed, and handed Mace the receiver.

It rang four times.

"Hello?" Annie asked out of breath. He had seen her sleeping soundly, and he almost felt bad for startling her with the phone ringing, but his jealousy held empathy at bay.

"Annie, it's Mace. I'm in the lobby. I brought you some coffee. I wanted to apologize for yesterday."

Up in the room, Annie felt her wild hair and covered her eyes with her hands. Falling asleep with it wet was always a bad idea. "Okay. Let me, um…Can you wait like 5?"

"Sure. I'll just grab a table. Come down when you're ready."

Annie hung up the phone and couldn't bring herself to look at Chuck, who was sitting on the opposite side of the bed. *What is it with me? Falling asleep in the barn with Leo, and now this! What is wrong with me? I've got to quit doing this.* She swept her hair up into what Chuck thought looked like an artistic bird's nest on the top of her head, slid a ponytail holder off her wrist, and somehow secured it.

Chuck smiled at what a beautiful mess she was in the morning. She buried her head in her hands, and after a minute, he heard a soft chuckle, but she still wouldn't look at him.

"Mace is downstairs," she finally said, still facing the wall.

"He is?"

"I have to go down there. He wants to apologize."

"Okay. It's fine, Annie. I'll go."

She was silent, and Chuck could feel her tension.

"Come here."

She finally turned around to look at him. He scooted to the middle of the bed. She followed.

"Okay, now lay down."

"What?" she demanded.

"Just humor me," he said motioning her over. "No funny business." She followed. Chuck lay down alongside her but far enough away that they weren't touching. "Now close your eyes and pretend you were sleeping."

She closed her eyes and took a long breath, somehow anticipating where he was headed with this.

"Now, pretend you weren't startled by the phone. Pretend you just woke up on your own. Open your eyes."

Annie's eyes fluttered open to see Chuck next to her on the bed and the sun illuminating the room through the window with the skyline behind him. She smiled at his tousled blonde hair and his scruffy face.

"I would've remembered how you stayed with me and let me cry. I would have remembered that you talked to me about my breaking heart and that you didn't leave me alone." Annie reached for his hand, and Chuck took her slender hand in both of his. "Thank you for being there for me."

Chuck didn't say anything, but he brought her hand to his mouth and kissed it sweetly. "Now go. I'll see you later, okay?"

Annie twitched her mouth and finally rolled away from him and kicked herself off of the bed. "Can I just go down there like this?" she said, grimacing at herself in the mirror over the desk.

"Yeah, you look like weekend bird's nest couture."

"Thank you. That's so reassuring," she said as she walked out of the door.

After she was gone, Chuck flopped back on the bed and growled at the ceiling, "I don't have a clue what you're doing, God," and that was all he felt like saying.

Annie spotted Mace at the far end of the lobby, folding and re-folding a napkin as he stared out the window at the street. She hurried over to him and sat down opposite him before he could stand up. He chuckled at the sight of her hair.

"I know I'm a mess. I fell asleep with it wet, and well…here I am. Sorry."

He pushed the coffee cup toward her with two fingers. "I know coffee doesn't say 'I'm sorry,' but I figured you needed coffee. And I needed to say I was sorry."

Annie took a long draw from the cup and exhaled in satisfaction after. "Oh, that's good. Thank you."

"I don't know what happened to you yesterday, but I wasn't there for you. I apologize."

Annie took another sip and sighed. She wanted to talk about anything but last night.

"I forgive you, Mace. I know that you have a lot on your mind. That last thing you need is an emotional woman."

"Annie, please don't misunderstand...."

Annie interrupted him. "Mace, I haven't. Believe me. I understand completely, and I promise it won't happen again. I'm ready today to be just business. We have a lot to get done while we're here, and I don't really want to talk about yesterday. You can trust that it won't be happening again."

Mace studied the resolve in her eyes even though her eyelids were still pink and swollen from crying. She was right that they needed to get to business in order to get everything done, but fragments of a dream he had the night before flashed in his mind. He knew that the part she misunderstood was that he was only business, but he was starting to think he did want her in his life. His jealousy about whatever had happened between her and Chuck the previous night confirmed that he did, but maybe now was not the time to tell her that.

He nodded his head. "If you ever do want to talk about it, I'm not ALL business, you know."

Annie smiled. He didn't know how much that wasn't true, but she appreciated his trying.

"What's on the docket today?" she said, sipping on her coffee and eyeing him over the lid.

He retrieved his phone and said, "We are reviewing projects from yesterday at 11. Lunch at 1, and I have a meeting at 3, then scouting until sundown, and I thought I'd take you to dinner at 8."

"Wow. That's a full day," Annie said, pleased at the thought of dinner with Mace. Then her face drained of pleasure and filled with concern as she thought of her camera upstairs and the footage she had on it. "Who all will be reviewing the footage from yesterday?"

"I thought just you, me, Chuck, and the director of photography. Why?" He noticed the apprehension in her eyes and the tight thin line her lips made.

"Well, you'll see when you see my footage. I guess I should go take care of this," she said, swirling her hand above her head. "Where should I meet you at 11?"

"This address." He slid a card across the table to her. "We've rented some space for the next few days. I've got all the monitors set up, and we'll be able to…anyways, you don't care about all that. I'll let you go get ready. Are you okay getting yourself there? Should I send someone after you?"

Smiling at the thought of him yet again sending someone to fetch her, she said, "No, I am fine. I'll see you at 11. Mace, thanks for the coffee." Rising from the table, she excused herself and hurried back to her room, wondering if Chuck would still be there. The room was empty, save for the pizza box from last night and a note on the desk that read, *See you at 11*.

Hurrying, she picked out a sensible sweater and jeans, remembering that she had chastised herself yesterday for not wearing her boots, so she pulled those on and sighed at how more like herself she felt in them. With her hair back and wrapped in a butter yellow scarf, she paused to sit on the end of the bed and call Sam and Sammy. Sammy was out in the barn feeding the horse, but she talked to Sam for a few minutes about his usual, the boys, the weather, and her safety. She didn't tell him about the events of the previous day, not wanting him to be upset or concerned for her. She told him she'd call again after dinner and asked him to tell Sammy to take a bath.

Grabbing the camera, she headed down the grand stairs and out onto the sidewalk from the lobby of the hotel. She decided to walk a few blocks and get some breakfast. If she remembered right, there was a bagel place just two blocks up. After that, she could hail a cab to get to the warehouse.

For several hours, she and the three men sat in front of monitors, reviewing countless clips of Chicago. Annie stood to stretch and walked over to the table filled with snacks and coffee. She smiled, remembering that this table was her job back in Penumbra. Chuck joined her at the table, filling his coffee cup or "reviving it," as he said. She smiled; they were closer after last night, and she could feel it.

"Annie," Mace said emphatically. Annie spun around to see Mace facing the monitor, watching her footage. She groaned. "This is yours?"

"Yes," she said timidly.

"I really like it, the motion blur with the train is great, like time flying by or things happening too fast. It's brilliant." Annie watched them view her footage, though she stayed a distance away. The scene changed to the bird's eye, and Mace nodded his head, saying, "Fresh. No one else took that approach, Annie. I like it."

Annie covered her mouth, and Chuck left his coffee on the table and came to stand behind her, placing his comforting hands on her shoulders. The scene changed for the final time, and Annie looked away, unable to watch it, but she heard Mace's breath catch. As the camera fell to reveal Annie crying on the rooftop, both Mace and the director of photography let out audible gasps. Annie turned around and buried her face in Chuck's chest. Forcing herself not to cry, she pushed away from Chuck and told him she'd be outside. Mace turned just in time to see her run out.

He jogged toward the door to follow her; Chuck stopped him, saying, "Just give her a minute."

"That was excruciatingly beautiful," Mace said, feeling out of breath.

"I know," Chuck said solemnly. "But don't tell her that."

"No, of course not," Mace said, pausing and then pushing through the door. Annie had her back against the metal wall, hands tucked behind her and head hung low.

He tried to think of something to say and even opened his mouth twice to speak, but the words died away even before they came out. He finally just leaned against the building with her and waited.

A muskiness drifted their way on the breeze, and Mace wondered where it came from, but before he thought too much about it, Annie pushed off the wall and stood up straight, took a deep breath, and said, "I'm fine."

Mace squinted at her in the afternoon sun. "You sure?"

"Yeah. I just needed to clear my head. We can go." She paused a moment to watch him kick off the wall to follow her. He did, extended his hand for her to lead the way, and they returned inside the warehouse to find Chuck and the director of photography still gathered around the snack table. When they glanced up, they looked as though they'd gotten caught. Chuck smiled and shrugged at Annie; then looking at Mace, he noticed a peculiar expression, and he wondered what had happened outside. When he looked back to Annie, her expression warmed at the sight of his guilty snacking, and she laughed a little through her nose, to herself.

"Are you guys full, or do you need us to pick you something to hold you over before we go sightseeing?" she asked sarcastically, picking up her purse.

Everyone laughed, and as Mace began closing down the warehouse, Annie walked to the door to wait. Chuck watched her as he gathered his laptop and messenger bag. He walked to her before Mace was done, hoping to have a brief private conversation.

"You okay?"

She reached out and touched his arm. He looked down at her hand and then to her.

"I'm not sure I know what okay is, but somehow I think God wants me to be more." She pinched her lips together after she said that to keep from crying, sucked in a deep breath, and shook her head slightly, and from the several times that he'd seen her do that, he knew it was her way of gathering herself up or pushing her feelings further down, one of the two.

"You are much more, Annie. Maybe He just wants YOU to know it."

Before she could answer, the two other men joined them with "ready" written on their faces. They all turned to leave, leaving the paused video on the screen of Annie crying.

The rest of the day was a bouncing blur in a cab, filled with stories, history, and smells of Chicago. Leo and the actress Sarah joined them midafternoon but rode in their own cab, which Annie was grateful for. As the sun was going down, Mace leaned over to Annie, their shoulders colliding, "The last stop is the site of the theater, but I'm going to send you back to the hotel, I don't want you there. Chuck can ride with you. That way you can get dressed for dinner. I'll pick you up at eight, okay?"

Annie was stunned by his thoughtfulness; she looked to Chuck, who sat on the other side of her nodding. "Okay. Thank you, Mace.

That'd be great, though I don't need an escort. I can get myself back to the hotel."

Chuck elbowed her in the ribs. She elbowed him back.

"Are you certain?" Mace asked.

"I'm sure. Chuck probably has work to do." She got a rib full of Chuck's elbow again, not hard enough for Mace to notice but enough to make Annie smile. "And thank you."

Before long, the cab pulled alongside the curb, and Annie briefly stole a glance of the vacant site and the plaque, which Martha had told her about the other night. Her heart slowed to a small thud, and Chuck squeezed her knee before sliding out of the seat. Leo's cab pulled in front of theirs, and she watched him get out, his eyes meeting hers just before her cab pulled away, his expression dark and unreadable.

She exhaled deeply, pushing her breath out from her lungs, thankful to be yanked away from the claws of evil she felt as she sat so near that spot.

In the hotel, hours later, she realized that she hated waiting on Mace because it gave her too much time to stand in front of the full-length, framed mirror in her suite, second guessing her dinner attire, but finally, her room phone rang.

"Annie, I'm downstairs. I'm sorry I'm so late. Shall I come up?"

"No, no—I'll hurry down."

After she hung up, she adjusted her cocktail length navy dress for the last time and scolded herself in the mirror for buying a strapless gown. The wispy curl that kept falling in the back got re-pinned with a subtle gold flower just below the mess of curls on her head. In the elevator, she studied herself in the mirror, checked her teeth for lipstick, and readjusted her dress until she noticed there was an elderly gentleman in the elevator with her. She sheepishly smiled in embarrassment and moved away from the mirror.

The man shifted his cane to the other hand and pointed at her dress and then her hair. "Whoever he is, you'll blow him away."

She smiled at his kind eyes, thinking that he looked an awful lot like Sam.

She exited the elevator and was met with a "wow" from Mace.

"You look gorgeous, Annie."

"Thank you," she said, finding herself trying to be sweeter than she might have otherwise been, even though Mace was making a habit of being late, preoccupied, or absent altogether.

He offered her his arm and escorted her to a limo that sat pristinely next to the curb. Annie raised her brow at Mace. He shrugged and patted her hand that was curled around his arm.

"I figured you deserved a night out in style, and seeing how you dressed for the occasion, I'm glad I did."

Annie bit her lip in excitement and ducked inside the limo. Once they were settled inside and on their way, Annie begged, "Where are we going?"

"I made a reservation at the Signature Room. I liked your idea of rising above the city, so I thought we'd just get above it all for a while tonight."

Annie's heart swelled in response to his thoughtfulness and her anticipation of the restaurant. "I've been there once with my father, but I was young. I've always wanted to go back and actually be able to appreciate it."

Mace had reserved a table right by a window so they could sit and stare out the window, which made Annie giddy. They talked, laughed, and ate through three courses of decadent food. As the night descended thoroughly over the city and the shore, the city lights glowed like low hanging stars within their grasp. When the waiter delivered their dessert, Mace took note that Annie had ordered the orange brulee cheesecake and not the tiramisu. They sipped lattes and ate their desserts in a comfortable simmering silence as they stared out the window at the city below.

Annie finally folded the napkin over her plate. "Mace, thank you so very much for dinner."

"Thanks for agreeing to it. You deserve it." Mace pushed away from the table and folded his arms across his chest. "Tomorrow is our last day. We'll head back to L.A. for a while. What's next for you?"

"This has been such a big adventure, but I'm ready to get back and focus on some things. Sammy for one. The theater kids for another. Did you know Colby met God right before I left?"

"No!" Mace said, clapping his hands together in excitement. "That's amazing, Annie."

"I know. Colby wants Sam and me to mentor and disciple him. I think that it's time to shift all my energy to the kids and move away from baking. Baking was always just for me anyway."

Mace was lost in thought as he shook his head at her, "You truly are a one of a kind, Annie."

As they rode back to the hotel, Annie found her thoughts traveling down winding paths. She wondered what Mace thought of her and if this evening had simply been an elaborate token of appreciation. Or had it been a date? Could anything ever happen between them? They'd had moments where Annie felt like it was possible, but she wasn't sure.

The more she thought about her feelings, the more her mind turned to Chuck. And she wondered where he was and what he was doing. And she wondered why nothing could happen between them. *It seems to be happening anyway,* she admitted to herself.

Chuck found himself at the snack table again, waiting on Mace to show up after his dinner with Annie. He knew what Mace had told him about making things up to her and treating her to a celebration, but Chuck couldn't help the pang of jealousy that he felt when he thought about being the one who was sweeping her through the city on a cloud.

Leo's voice shattered his thoughts of Annie, and they seemed to fall into the bowl of potato chips, which made him realize he wasn't even hungry.

"I thought I'd find you here."

"What can I do for you, Leo?"

"Well…" Leo finger-combed his hair and scratched the stubble on his chin with the back of his knuckles. "I noticed Annie didn't stay tonight."

Chuck knew where this was headed before Leo could ask it, and he had the urge to give him a left hook to the chin. He refrained, backing away from the snacks and pulling over two folding chairs.

"Have a seat, Leo."

"I just wondered…"

"I want you to see something," Chuck said, walking toward the monitors.

Leo heard several clicks, and a video loaded up to the larger monitor.

Chuck felt the adrenaline flow through his arms. He wasn't sure how Annie would feel if she knew he was showing Leo her footage, but something told him that he'd take her wrath if it meant getting through to Leo.

The scene changed from the towering view to the view of the theater. Leo and Sarah kissed, and the camera fell.

Leo stood and kicked his chair in fury while Annie's sobs still echoed in the warehouse. Leo growled and paced. Regret filled his chest.

"That's why she didn't stay?" he barked.

Chuck sat on the desk and kicked his legs out in front of him, crossing them. "Can you blame her, Leo?"

"She can't even be around me? How has it come to this?" Leo's mind was spinning and screaming at him so that he couldn't listen to Chuck. He was filled with his own questions.

"Do you want to know, or are you just asking angry rhetorical questions?" Chuck crossed his arms, and Leo stopped, shoving his hands in his pockets. He nodded once as a sign of concession, and Chuck continued, "Annie asked you to take some time to search yourself. Analyze. Reflect. Pray. Whatever you want to call it. But you didn't; you just moved on. She has been patient with you and tried to understand what you might be going through, but there comes a point...probably she feels the way you're living is her answer." There was silence between them before Chuck continued, "Why haven't you just told her?"

"Told her what?"

"That you don't love her."

"I do love her!" Leo barked, clenching his fists in his pockets. He sighed, and his voice softened. "I do love her. I just don't think I believe in God the way she does." He paused, expecting a reaction. "I know for her the two go together."

Chuck nodded silently and considered what to say. "Well, Leo, that is something that you are going to have to search out yourself. In the meantime, you need to be honest with Annie because what you're doing now is just selfish and hurtful."

"Did she say that?"

"She doesn't have to, Leo. I'm her friend. I know when she's hurting."

Leo knew that he'd come to Chuck asking questions that he should have known the answer to. He used to be the one who knew because he used to be her best friend. Now he was the one who was hurting her, and that thought drove a thousand spikes through his heart. His eyes stung a bit, so he just said, "Thanks," to Chuck and quickly exited the warehouse, trying to get as far away from his guilt as he could.

"Are you ready?" Randy said from behind Annie. Not knowing he'd already arrived, she spun around, happy to see him.

"Yes, are you coming back with me?"

He gave her a sly grin. "Of course."

"Oh, good. I'll be glad to have someone with me," she said cheerfully, while to herself thinking how strange it would be to go back to her small town without Mace and Chuck. She said she craved the quiet and the privacy, but she knew if she were honest that she would miss the hustle and bustle. She knew she would miss Mace's stuff tangling with her in her office and having brainstorming meetings over a table full of food. She wondered if life really could go back to the way she used to like it. She remembered that she told Chuck she thought she was supposed to be more than okay, and somehow she knew that, once she stepped off that plane and stepped back into her normal life, things were going to be different. Had she just been trying to be okay for so long that she'd never tried to be anything else? She knew she was about to find out.

She watched the attendant take her bag, weigh it, and move it onto a belt. She watched it disappear into a tunnel as she heard Randy's voice again behind her.

"Hey, Leo. You headed back with us?"

The question made her heart pause. She felt her body turn, but she didn't remember telling it to. Her head hung slightly, but her eyes met Leo's. They were sad and...were they red? Had he been drinking or crying? Randy had asked the question, but Leo kept his pained eyes on Annie.

"No," Leo said, "I'm not heading back to Texas."

Annie clamped emotional arms around her heart and squeezed so that if it were breaking open, she wouldn't feel it. She took a deep breath, and Leo watched her gather her courage.

"I'm going to go to L.A. for a while."

Annie heard Randy congratulate Leo, and they continued talking. Annie's mind filled with fog, and she floated around, handing the attendant her ticket. She lost all awareness of herself moving or speaking or even hearing. All her energy had been drained by the bravery that circled around her heart, and she felt she was moving and thinking in a cloud.

She didn't speak to Leo; she didn't even nod to him or wave goodbye.

She moved through security and boarded the plane. It began to rain inside her cloud until she sat down in her seat. She closed her eyes.

God, just get me home.

29. A VISITOR AND ROTTEN FOOD
PENUMBRA, ONE MONTH LATER

"Mandy, this is what I want." Annie touched the gray-haired woman's hand across the worktable.

"You're sure? I don't mind to go on like we have with me running it and you owning it."

"I'm sure. I want you to have this place."

"Why, Annie?"

"It's time to focus on the people in my life. Besides, this bakery was just something to help me stay busy and feel fulfilled. It's time to do things differently."

"And you don't want me to buy it?"

"No."

"I really don't understand."

"Mandy, I don't know how you feel about God, but I believe that people can have a personal relationship with Him. He talks to me, and He told me to bless you with it."

Mandy's eyes filled with glassy tears.

Annie couldn't help but choke up as well. She cleared her throat and forced out a laugh. "I can't promise that I won't come over and bake just for fun."

Mandy smiled and wiped her eyes, nodding.

"I'll get the paperwork done and clean up my stuff over the weekend, and she'll be yours by Monday."

Mandy stood and rushed Annie with a hug. "Annie, I don't think I can every say how grateful I am. I am humbled."

"How did it feel?" Sam asked, leaning heavily on his cane in the middle of the kitchen. Turning off the water, Annie wiped her soapy hands and threw the navy checked towel over her shoulders.

She leaned against the counter and smiled at her aging uncle, saying, "You know, it felt freeing. I can't explain it very well, but I just knew it was what God wanted me to do."

Sam nodded and closed his eyes, smiling for a moment, as if he were praying.

Annie went on, "Mandy seemed touched, and that helped me know it was the right thing."

"What will you do now?" Sam asked, shuffling to the kitchen table. Annie joined him.

"I'll focus on Sammy, and I've got the theater kids who might need me for more than just theater. I think I'm ready to..." She trailed off, unsure how to explain it.

Sam nodded again, solemnly this time, "I know, dear one. I know. You're a brave soul. It takes bravery to admit the difference between surviving and living."

Annie shook her head and smiled, which turned into a small laugh. "You know me so well, Sam, and you are so patient with me."

Sam patted her cheek. "I won't be so patient for dinner."

A forceful pounding at the door interrupted Annie's burst of laughter. Wide-eyed, Annie and Sam exchanged a look before she hurried to the door, opening it halfway to see who it might be. Sam heard Annie gasp, and he rose to his feet. Before he even made it to the door, he saw a bruised and bleeding Colby leaning on Annie as she pulled him inside.

"Father in heaven, what has happened to the boy?" Sam prayed aloud in panic.

Annie helped Colby to the table, tears streaming down his face. As she sat him down, she rushed to the freezer for an ice pack and grabbed several washcloths. Sam stepped in front of her with a hand up, asking her to stop. Sam tried to ask the boy what had happened, but he was silent.

Sam whispered to Annie, "Don't clean him up just yet. Someone's done this to him. We need to know who it was, and we'll need evidence. I'll call the police. He'll talk to you."

Annie sunk down onto her knees at Colby's feet and reached for his hand, which startled him. He recoiled for a moment until he realized it was her.

Annie prayed to herself before she softly asked, "Who did this, Colby?"

"My grandpa."

He had a black eye, a gash on his forehead, and a busted lip, which was gushing blood and swelling quickly. He was dirty from head to toe as if he'd been fighting in the pasture. Through his ripped jeans, his knees looked bloody, but Annie couldn't tell how much was open wounds and how much was blood spatter from something else. She gripped his hand firmly and turned his face to look at her. He reluctantly met her eyes. His bright blue eyes had turned a shade of gray, filled with anguish.

"Colby, this is a safe place. Okay?"

He nodded, and she continued, "I need you to tell me what happened."

He dropped his head again, tears threatening to fall on his jeans, but Annie squeezed his hand until he turned his face back and looked at her.

"I finally got up the courage to tell Pa about what we talked about before. I knew if I really believed in God, I shouldn't be afraid to tell him as much." His hand started to quiver, and his voice cracked. "I've never seen him so angry. He chased me..." he started to trail off, and Annie gave him a moment to collect himself.

She patted his knee and firmly held his hand to let him know she wasn't going anywhere.

Colby cleared his throat and tried again. "He chased me out of the house, hitting me, and I ran out to the barn, which was stupid, but I wasn't thinking real straight. I just was trying to get away from him. He was hitting me with everything he could find in the barn. I finally scrambled to my feet. Then..."

"What happened then, Colby?" Annie said, slight fear creeping into her heart.

"I shoved him against the wall as hard as I could. I think I knocked him out, but I'm not sure. I ran. I ran through the pastures. I ran all the way here. I don't know what I did to him."

"Oh, Colby," Annie said, standing up and covering him with a hug. Colby sobbed into her shoulder. "Colby, it's okay. It's going to be okay." She kept reassuring him until Sam entered the kitchen again.

"Police are on their way. They'll take pictures, and then we can get you cleaned up."

"Thank you, sir. I didn't mean any disrespect by not speaking to you."

"No harm done, son. I'd rather talk to Annie than myself any day." Sam patted Colby on the back and then pulled Annie into the hallway quickly. "They sent a separate squad over to his place to look for Merle."

"Thank you," she said, breathing a small sigh of relief before she heard Sammy's voice chime in through the side kitchen door. She wheeled around to the kitchen just in time to see Sammy drop his boots in shock and splatter mud all over the floor.

"What happened to you?" Sammy asked Colby.

Colby simply shook his head. Sammy went over to him and scanned Colby's broad build with his eyes.

"I suspect you'd better stay with us," he announced in his sweet, matter of fact voice. Annie relaxed, thinking he would be upset at the sight of Colby's wounds but his heart was strong and open.

Later that night, after the police had informed Colby that his grandfather had been arrested and was in police custody, Annie cleaned his face and treated his wounds. She showed him the shower and a clean change of clothes. She fed him with Sam and Sammy and put him to bed in the guest room.

Only when everyone else was in bed did Annie collapse on hers. Her mind began to spin in an effort to unwind the day's events, but a quiet voice interrupted her thoughts.

Trust me, Annie. I've got the perfect plan.

Annie felt the anxiety that skimmed the top of her heart float away like a feather on the breeze, far enough away that she didn't feel its weight. She fell asleep with peace.

That night, she dreamed of three eagles flying boldly in the sky. They swooped, dove, and then glided steadily over the wind. They soared above her and seemed to sing to her with their caws. Then she noticed three hawks hobbling around on the ground near the stream. They each limped from a different infirmity. One hawk turned to look at her, and as she reached for it, it fell over, dying and slipping into the bright glittering stream. She knelt beside the other two limping hawks, and she whispered to them as she woke up, "Don't worry, dear ones, we'll make eagles out of you yet."

"Colby, I have some work to do down at the theater. You are welcome to come with me, or you can stay here with the boys. It's up to you," Annie said while clearing the breakfast dishes from the table.

"Yes!" Sammy exclaimed. "I've got some perfect places to play with my camera, and I bet we can catch Uncle Sam snoring on the couch. It's super spy work with the camera. You'll love it, Colby."

Colby gave Sammy a half-hearted smile and looked to Annie. "I think I'll come with you, if that's all right?" Then turning back to Sammy, he said, "Maybe later, okay, Sammy?"

Sammy swept his cup off the table. "No problem. I'll see you for pizza and movie night."

"Huh?"

"Saturday is always pizza and movie night. It's tradition at our house," Sammy chimed before bounding out of the room and skipping up the stairs.

He talks to Colby like he's a brother, Lord. He's so welcoming. Annie thought as she refilled her cup of coffee. *Help me to be as brave about whatever it is You are doing here.*

"Let me tell Sam we're leaving, and then we'll be off," she said, patting his shoulders still sunken with the weight of shame and guilt. She squeezed his shoulder and whispered, "We're okay, Colby. Everything is going to be fine."

"Hang on. I'll have to call you back. There's someone at the door." Annie hung up the phone and rushed across the theater lobby to the police officer at the front door. "Officer, what can you tell us?"

"We came by your house, but Sam told us you were here with the boy. Is Colby here, ma'am?"

"Yes, he is. Is he in trouble?"

"No, ma'am. We just have some news that we need to tell him in person."

Annie nodded and disappeared into the auditorium, returning with Colby. Colby stood nervously before the police officer, and Annie stepped out of earshot but stayed within line of sight.

The officer spoke with him, and Annie watched as Colby's shoulders lifted. She even felt herself relax though she didn't know what the news was. The officer soon waved her back over and said, "Ms. Flynn, are you in the position to allow this boy to stay with you?"

Obeying the small whisper in her mind, she said, "Yes, Colby can stay with us."

The officer nodded. "Then he'll stay with you until further action needs to be taken. We'll let you know."

They both thanked him and stood there staring at the door as the officer left and then at each other.

"He said I didn't hurt Pa."

"Colby, I'm glad he reassured you of that. Are you okay?"

"I'm okay. Are you sure I can live with you?"

"Yes, Colby, I'm sure. You're welcome to stay as long as you want."

"Thanks, Miss Annie."

"You're welcome, Colby. We can stop by your house later if you'd like to gather some clothes."

He nodded, but Annie noticed his eyes looked unsure. She figured she might have to be the one gathering the clothes.

"I'll just be a minute more here. Chuck called right before the officer came. I need to call him back. Then I need to make a short stop at the courthouse."

Colby nodded and headed back to the auditorium. Annie watched him leave, wondering how he might be feeling and what she was supposed to do, but hearing her desk phone ringing, she hurried back to her office.

"Hello?" she said even before the receiver was up to her mouth.

"Everything okay?" Chuck asked on the other end.

"Yes. Why?" she said, trying to mask the anxiety in her voice and slow her breathing from jogging to the office.

"I don't know. I just got the feeling you were panicked when you said that someone was at the door."

Annie took a breath. Chuck had been the one who was there for her ever since they met, and she knew that he cared for her. "We had a surprise visitor last night. We've been dealing with the police ever since."

"What happened? Who was it?"

"It was Colby. His grandpa beat him pretty badly. He is in jail now, and Colby will be staying with me. That's the short version."

Her summary was met with silence. She pictured Chuck shaking his head and rubbing the stubble on his chin.

"Annie, I mean, wow. I don't know what to say."

"I don't really either. I feel completely bewildered, but I just have this strange peace that God is at work in all this. So I'm hanging on, maybe for dear life, but still…hanging on."

"Do you need anything?"

"I think we're okay."

"Okay. I'll call you tomorrow."

"Always looking out for me, Chuck."

"I probably won't ever stop."

Annie filed the paperwork with the courthouse to sign over the bakery to Mandy, and then she picked up dinner at Max's and drove Colby out to Merle's farm. The dirt road leading to the house was littered with cigarette packages, beer cans, and police tape. A hauntingly dirty feeling filled her with despair as they drove up the path. Colby hung his head down so far his chin grazed the flannel shirt he'd borrowed from Sam. The sleeves were far too short, but he'd rolled them up, which Annie thought offered a clue about how Colby made do with what life dealt him.

She parked in front of the house and shifted in her seat to face Colby, who wouldn't look at her or the house.

"Colby, we can go in together, you can go alone, or I can go alone. It's up to you."

Colby didn't answer, move, or look at her.

"I know this is hard. It's okay to say that you can't handle going back in there right now. I'm not going to make you." She leaned across the cab and took his hand. "You have to trust me when I say I know how you feel."

His eyes flew sideways to hers, and though some of the blue sparks returned, they seemed to question her. He knew she might be the only person who could understand him at that moment, but he also feared being understood because of what lay inside that house.

Annie patted his hand and said, "I'll just go in. You tell me where your bedroom is, and I'll grab some clothes and be out in a few seconds."

"Top of the stairs on the right. Miss Annie, there are things I've never…"

"Colby, don't you worry about what's inside that house anymore. All I care about is what's inside this truck. Sit tight." Annie squeezed his hand and then slid out of the truck. She leaned her seat forward and slid a shotgun out from behind the seat. She checked the safety and filled the chamber with a swift pump of her forearm. Colby shot a look of surprise at her, but she just nodded and headed to the house.

Annie opened the front door with a tap of her toe and wondered if the police had just left the place gaping open. A surge of foul odors filled her nose and mouth as she entered. Everywhere she looked was trash and food scraps. Although no one besides Colby and Merle lived there, she didn't know what made her so quiet, but if she hadn't been, she would have missed the faint growls of hungry dogs from a back room somewhere. Something scurried away across the hallway making Annie catch her breath, but she didn't scream at the sight of a rat. She glanced in the kitchen only to gulp down a gag that threatened to bring up vomit at the sight of the molding food piled on the unwashed dishes. Seeing the same things that littered the driveway littering the living room and kitchen, Annie's disgust turned to anger as she carefully climbed the stairs.

Who lives like this and makes a child live like this? Her thoughts snarled. *What else has Colby endured? Why didn't anyone notice the signs before now? Why didn't I?*

Then, as she opened Colby's door, she knew why. It was clean. Everything was tucked away neatly. Though the furniture was crude and falling apart, Colby had created a space that was inhabitable amidst the uninhabitable space that surrounded him. Annie set the shotgun on the bed and started picking through his dresser drawers. When she'd collected all the clothes worth getting, she noticed a Bible on his bedside table. A lump formed in the back of her throat as she heard a whisper.

See, I was here with him.

"Oh, Lord," she groaned aloud knowing that she'd been so blinded to think that he'd gone through this pain alone.

Just as I was there with you.

"Yes, Lord." She resigned prayerfully.

Now I want him to be with you.

She closed her eyes and felt the presence of God sweep over her, raising every hair on her body. Then, hearing something rile the dogs below, Annie tucked the clothes in a bag she spotted under the bed, threw it over her shoulder, grabbed her shotgun, and hurried down the stairs and out the door. The cool fresh air stung her cheeks and burned in her nose, but she sucked in deeply, freeing herself from the pungent heaviness that she'd felt inside that house. She tossed the bag in the bed of the truck, knowing everything needed to be soaked and washed once they got home. She slid the shotgun back in its place and grabbed Colby in a desperate hug. Out of the overflow of her heart, she began to pray aloud over Colby. Colby wept in her embrace like a child.

"God, You ARE our redeemer. You are the God who sees our pain and despair. Come redeem the years that Colby has lived through. Meet him where he is. Thank You for rescuing him from this house. Thank You for giving him to me."

"For now, Colby's sleeping in the guest room, but I may clean out the apartment in the barn."

"Leo's room?" Chuck asked surprised.

"I just think he's a teenager, and he needs some space. I don't know. We'll see," she said, letting a comfortable silence fall between them. She sat on the porch in the dark, talking into the phone while wishing Chuck sat beside her.

"Annie?"

"Yeah?"

"I thought of something last night. I know it's not legal yet, but I was thinking about how you can't have any more kids." Chuck paused, wondering if he should say that he wanted to say. "But God is giving you another kid."

A breathy "Oh" pushed from her lungs. She looked up to the open starry sky in wonder.

"Wow," was all she could say.

"I've really been thinking about this. It's changed my thoughts on some things—sometimes God takes something away in order to give us something new. And sometimes, as we talked about in Chicago, 'no' means 'not right now' or 'not this way,'" Chuck confessed with caution and left his words to float through time and space to her, wondering if she would understand.

Annie felt the velvety silence that followed his words, and she caressed it with hope but merely said, "Hmm."

She followed that by changing the subject. "How's the movie coming along?"

Chuck groaned a little and laughed. "It's good. We're getting close. I think Mace will get with you on some upcoming details in the next month or so."

"You don't sound like you're living the dream," Annie teased.

"I am. It's not that; it's just that someone walked in who wants to talk to you. And I know you'll kill me for this later."

"It's not Leo, is it? We didn't even speak at the airport."

"I know. He overheard our conversation about Colby yesterday. I confess I had you on speaker."

"Chuck!" Annie gasped.

"I know. You have every right to be mad. Will you talk to him?"

Annie sighed heavily but then agreed. She could hear Chuck shuffle the phone and hand it off. The mood changed even though Leo hadn't said anything yet, and it sent a shiver down Annie back.

"I heard about Colby," he started roughly, not even bothering to greet her. Annie cringed at what they'd become. His voice sounded like sandpaper in her ear, and she shivered again.

"I heard that you heard," she replied dryly.

"The press will eat this up, you know."

Annie felt her fists ball up and her back tighten. She closed her eyes and forced herself to breathe. Maybe his intent was good. Maybe he cared about Colby's wellbeing, or maybe he cared about keeping them safe and away from prying, harsh eyes. But she also didn't trust his intentions anymore. She felt a strong invisible hand on her shoulder, and she felt the tension absorbed. She sighed in relief and suddenly knew what to say.

"I know," she said confidently but meekly. "But we're helping Colby lay low for a while, and someday he will step out of the shadows into his bright future."

On the other end of the line, Leo stood, facing Chuck, stunned. He realized what she was saying. It was exactly what she had done;

she'd lain low for years and, just now, was finally stepping out from the shadows. He knew she had a bright future, just as Colby would.

He feared, though, deep in his stomach, that he wasn't part of that bright future. At that moment, he knew it was possible that he was the one deep in the shadows, just as he'd accused Annie of being.

He launched the phone back at Chuck and stormed out of the condo.

"You have a real way with him lately," Chuck said, hoping she'd laugh. She did, but only slightly.

"It's okay, Chuck. You know, he used to be different. He was protective and attentive. He spoke his inner thoughts with his eyes but kept an almost aloof distance. His love came through in the details—fresh wildflowers on the porch, my mail from the road on my doormat, my horse saddled every Sunday, time spent with Sammy, listening to me rattle on about nothing, and opening my door. The list could go on.

"Then things shifted because I wounded the love he felt for me by questioning it. Then, because he felt wounded, he rejected me and rejected the faith he thought he had. Sam always says if you're dipping from someone else's faith, eventually that well will run dry for the both of you. When Leo's well went dry, he ran to the world, and the world embraced him. He found that it offered him something to ease the pain, but it won't for long."

"That's a sobering thought."

"I know. It's hard to watch."

"Hey, hey, hey! What's this, everyone?" Annie said in a loud voice she strode down the aisle, seeing all the students huddle in a circle, talking over one another, looking like a bunch of chickens pecking in a circle. At the sound of her voice, they all straightened up and moved away from a pile of things on stage. Voices hushing and trailing off, they stared at her as if they'd been caught. One girl stepped forward as Annie ascended the stairs and eyed the pile of items.

"We heard what happened to Colby, and we know that you took him in. We all got together and got you guys some things. It's mostly for Colby, but there are some gift cards for you and stuff."

Annie covered her heart. "You guys! This is wonderful."

"We didn't figure that he'd come tonight, but we wondered—how is he doing?"

"Here, everybody sit down," Annie said, motioning for them all to sit on the stage. She took a deep breath and closed her eyes long enough to launch an arrow of a prayer up to heaven. In return, she felt the small voice reassure her.

"I don't know how all of you feel about God, but I believe in a God who loves us, takes care of us, and uses our hard times for a greater purpose." Some kids' eyes had fallen to the floor, some looked at her in surprise, and some were filling with tears. "That same God is taking care of Colby. He loves Colby, and one day Colby will be able to look back and see how this hard time changed his life for good. But right now, Colby could use love and support, just like you've shown here tonight."

"Could we dedicate the show to him and maybe use it as a benefit?" Kristin asked from the outskirts of the group.

"That's a great idea," several of the others chimed in.

"I love that idea," Annie said. "We definitely can think about that and work on it. In the meantime, let's rehearse so we have a really great show to put on."

Excitement exploded in the group as they all shot up and dispersed to their places to wait for her direction. She silently thanked the Lord for what He was doing in her life and in theirs, and she couldn't wait to get home and show her boys what the others had given them.

30. THE RED CARPET AND A ROOFTOP DINNER

"Hey, Mace," she said, picking up her cell phone. She kicked her feet up on the porch swing and watched Colby throw a Frisbee to Sammy in the front yard. In the several months Colby had lived with them, the two boys had grown close.

"Annie! How are you? I hear we have a lot to catch up on."

Annie laughed, trying to count how many months it had been since they'd talked, and then said, "Yes, I suppose we do."

"How'd you like to catch up over dinner in L.A.?"

Annie laughed again, this time in a more definite way. "That'll be the day."

"I kind of thought you'd say that, but the whole team wants you to come out for the premiere. We've got some interviews lined up, and I think it'd be powerful to have you do them with me."

Something roiled in Annie's stomach, and she pursed her lips. "I don't know, Mace. I am not sure that I—"

Mace cut her off, "Annie, I need you by my side on the red carpet. I need you there with me."

"We have our spring production coming up, Mace. I don't think I can leave the kids."

"We're talking a weekend here, Annie. I'll have you back by Sunday night. I'll fly you out, and you don't even have to watch the film. We can slip out before it starts."

"I don't think I could leave Sam and the boys."

Sam coughed overtly from the doorframe; Annie was surprised to see he'd appeared there. He glared at her. She shrugged and smiled. "Okay...let me think about it."

"I can live with that. Call me later."

As she said goodbye and hung up, Sam joined her on the swing. She threaded her arm through his and pulled herself in tight next to him. "You want me to go, don't you?"

Sam nodded in silence.

"You sure you and boys will be okay?"

"I've got an extra one to look out for me now," he said, not even cracking a smile.

Annie giggled and then said, "All right, but I just don't think I should do interviews."

Sam turned to face her and stamped his cane on the porch. "Annie, you've been telling that boy for months now to trust God, but you act like you don't know how sometimes. You've got to know that He'll protect you even in the spotlight."

As soon as her boots hit the tarmac, a whirlwind of flashing cameras, microphones, and questions bombarded her. Then came the wardrobe changes. She was whisked from one studio to another, posing for pictures in between. Mace held her hand through all the interviews, and Chuck was just off camera with a huge smile and a wink whenever she looked unsure, which was most of the time.

Later, she was ushered into a hotel room where her own prep team styled, curled, painted, and pampered her. After they had zipped her into her gown, she quietly and respectfully asked them to leave. She stood in front of a full-length mirror, much like the one she'd had in her room in Chicago. It was cracked bronze with ornate swirls and angel wings in each corner. She studied her flowing gown; the one-shouldered bodice hugged her tightly but not enough to pinch anywhere. The crème brulee colored chiffon fell in folds from her shoulder across her chest to her waist and then cascaded in a waterfall to the floor, creating a billow of sequined froth at the hem. Her hair swept up in curls away from her face, revealing glittering chandelier earrings. She doubted she'd ever looked this fancy even in all her years of theater. It was all too much, and she didn't think she could muster up the courage to walk down the red carpet.

A knock brought her away from the mirror and her glittery panic.

"Who is it?"

"Mace."

She hesitated to open the door, unsure what his reaction would be, and she momentarily wondered if she didn't answer the door whether he'd go away and she could just go home. She knew that wouldn't be the case.

Timidly, she finally opened the door and stood before him. He was braced on the doorframe with one arm, looking at his lapel and the striped handkerchief that, no doubt, someone else had placed in his pocket for him. As the door swung open, his eyes traveled from his lapel across the threshold and took in the sight of Annie's dress from the floor all the way to her face. His eyes widened, and a breathy "Wow!" fell from his lips.

"Thanks, I think," she said, letting her uncertainty show in her voice.

"What do you mean? You just walked right out of my imagination. You are stunning, Annie."

"I just feel out of place and, oddly enough, very fragile."

Mace smiled widely and offered his arm. "The cameras will love that. You just hold tight to this all night."

As they rode in the limo, Annie kept feeling like she was sweating and the glands in her throat were swelling. *This is terrible*, she thought. *I shouldn't be here.*

They exited the limo, and another whirlwind swept in, one of flashing lights, endless poses and smiles, and thirty-second blurb interviews. Then everything slowed as she spotted Chuck and Leo. She thought she had glimpsed them earlier but hadn't been still long enough to be sure. Then suddenly, Leo was beside her. His hair was cut short, and he was clean-shaven. His tux looked foreign on him, but it was obviously tailored just to him. The girl on his arm was not the lookalike actress. This girl was new and looked more like a tailored accessory than a real girlfriend. The three men shared hugs and handshakes as if they were the oldest of friends, which added to Annie's feelings of displacement. Several times Leo caught her eye and seemed to almost say something to her, but he never spoke to her directly.

Annie kept searching the crowd for Chuck, who tried his best to get to her, but he was either blockaded by the press, other producers, or Mace himself.

Soon they left the afternoon heat and glare of the California sun and stepped into a private theater. Annie gripped Mace's arm tightly, both for the cameras and for her own reassurance.

"You can go back to the hotel whenever you're ready. We'll just wait until the lights go down," Mace whispered into her ear as they entered the auditorium.

"I'd like to see your name on the big screen, and then I'm ready." Annie knew the cameras weren't on here, and she wondered what made her say that. The smile her words produced on Mace's face told her it was the right thing to say.

"I have to do press and premiere parties, but I can come get you later. We'll celebrate."

The lights went down in the theater, and Annie forgot to see where Chuck had been whisked away to. Mace slipped his fingers through Annie's, and she let him hold her hand, wondering what was for the cameras and what was not. A black screen revealed the words Annie knew he had waited a lifetime to see: "A Mace Harlen Film."

It made her smile out of pride for him. Then, as quickly as they'd seen it, he slipped her out of the back of the theater.

"I'm so happy for you and proud of you, Mace."

"Annie, this is all for you. You story is going to be out there now, and it's going to change people, just like it changed me. None of this would be possible if it weren't for your helping me push my broken down mess out of the road."

"That fateful morning..." Annie teased and slipped free of his hand, a strange warmth spreading across her cheeks and shoulders. Butterflies flitted in her chest, and she touched the base of her neck and then fussed with her hair out of nervousness, knowing she was flushed.

"I don't know if it's this night or if it's that dress, but I feel like I need to kiss you," he said with a smile on his face, "but I'd better get back inside."

Annie tucked herself back in the limo, still feeling the blush burn on her cheeks. *Mace hasn't ever talked like that to me,* she thought.

In her hotel room, Annie sat on the chaise lounge, trying not to rumple her dress. She slipped off her heels and opened the journal Chuck had given her and began writing.

It's so strange...my story is out there for people to see now. What will happen because of my story? Have we put giant targets on our backs? Tonight was glamourous, but I felt like I was in a parade or a spectacle show at a fair. Mace doesn't mean to, but he has switched from self-absorbed to highly determined. He doesn't quite see me the way Chuck does, but it's entirely possible...

A knock at the door interrupted her writing.

Laying the journal on the bed, she hurried to the door to open it. Chuck stood in her doorway looking suave in his tux. His mouth broke into the typical wide smile that Annie was both accustomed to and comforted by.

"Hey," he said as he invited himself in.

"Hey." She smiled to be able to see him finally and talk to him. "That was crazy."

"Yeah, these things are pretty nuts. How are you?"

"I'm doing okay." Annie shrugged. "Mace sent me back here to wait on him. I guess we're going out later."

Chuck avoided her last statement, unbuttoning his jacket and pushed the sides back so he could put his hands in his pockets. He surveyed the room and landed on the journal.

"Are you writing?"

"I was, yes."

"About me?" he teased.

"You're in there some," she said airily. "What are you doing here? Don't you need to be at the parties?'

"I made my appearance. Plus, I wanted to see you. I could never catch you."

"I know. Mace had me velcroed to his arm."

"You look stunning tonight," he admitted. "I didn't get a chance to tell you that."

"Thank you, Chuck," she replied, noticing that he seemed to be withholding something else.

"Are you ready to go?"

"Go where?"

"Well, I'm actually here to take you to Mace," he confessed, avoiding her eyes.

"You're here to fetch me again?" she snapped a little.

"If it helps, I volunteered. I wanted to see you."

"I don't know if I'm more irritated at you or Mace." She huffed slightly while sitting down to put her heels back on. "Doesn't that seem wrong, Chuck? You volunteered to pick me up so that you could see me and take me to have dinner with another man!"

He strode toward her as she stood up from the chaise. He put his hands on her waist and brought her closer.

"Nothing about this seems right," he started, and then he realized she was even easier to kiss in her heels. Feeling the spark in his hands, he released her. "I'm sorry, Annie. This wasn't fair. I was feeling jealous, I suppose."

"Listen, Mace might be caught up in the moment tonight, but he doesn't have real feelings for me." *At least, I don't think he does*, she silently admitted.

"I don't think he's just caught up in the moment. I told you when I first met you that you got to him."

Annie put her hands on her hips, but before she could retort anything, Chuck continued.

"Maybe he's the one you are supposed to be with. Maybe you—"

Annie interrupted him, "Look. Before you say stuff that you'll regret, let me say that the only thing I know for sure is that I'm supposed to take care of those boys at my house, and I'm supposed to teach high school students about theater and life. Beyond that, it's all a mystery. I can't pretend to know what God is up to, so don't you either."

Chuck sighed. "Are you ready to go?"

Annie frowned. "Yes."

They rode in the back of the limo as far apart as they could. When they arrived, the driver opened the door, but before Annie stepped out, she reached over and put a hand on Chuck's knee.

"Chuck, thank you for coming to pick me up. It was good to see you. You look really handsome tonight."

"Thanks," he muttered.

"Would you like to talk again after I get back?"

He crossed his legs, knocking her hand off, and looked out the window. "No. I don't want to hear how it goes."

Spurned, Annie got out of the limo and moved toward a party of servers waiting to usher her inside to Mace.

"You are on to something, Mace. I think there's more to that story than people know," Annie spurred on subtly.

"Probably." Mace shrugged.

"Did you know that Martha Grady founded the Martha Grady Foundation because she was raped when she was just seventeen?"

"I think everyone knows that," Mace said, trying not to sound too pretentious.

"Yes," Annie paused, setting down her glass, "but no one knows the rapist was Mr. Grady himself."

Mace involuntarily dropped his fork, mouth agape. His eyes searched Annie's face. She nodded silently to confirm what she had said was true. His mind raced in a figure eight pattern of questions, but he couldn't seem to make sense of any of them long enough ask them. Annie leaned across the white linen cloth as if to say something private.

"Also, those mysterious notes you were getting—they were from Martha herself."

Mace squinted at her, oblivious to the waiter who walked over to retrieve Mace's fork. Annie quickly waved off the waiter. Mace had clearly forgotten the rooftop and the stars or the city below. He just squinted at her until he slowly articulated, "But she died…"

Annie shook her head. "She's very much alive."

Mace fell back against his chair. "I knew about Nigel and Randy, but this? This is a game changer."

"I know. She'd hoped you'd say that."

"Hold on. You know all this from Martha herself?"

Annie nodded and began to explain what had happened in Chicago and her long talk with Martha.

"Why didn't I know about all this?"

Martha's words, "*You'll tell him when it's right,*" echoed in Annie's head, but she shrugged and smiled. "You were busy being a visionary."

And I was jealous, he admitted in his head, thinking back to the morning he came by Annie's hotel room and found Chuck asleep with her. *Oh! That must have been the night she called Randy for a ride. Then she met with Martha, and I sent Chuck to pick her up. She probably told him then,* he realized. *She would have been upset, and Chuck was there for her.*

"I'm sorry I wasn't there for you," Mace said, but before she could respond, his phone rang. *Typical*, he thought. It was Lithgow.

"I'm sorry, Annie. I'll just be a minute," he said as he stepped inside the nearby stairwell.

Annie thought about Chuck's harsh words in the car but remembered all the times he had been there for her. She wasn't sure what was happening, but she was overwhelmed by the night's events. She stood, leaving her linen napkin on the table and sipping the last of her wine. She took advantage of her moment alone to explore the rooftop view of the city below. The city was bright and glowing, and the busy sidewalk looked as though it was bouncing or dancing. She was glad to be up here alone, away from the madness. A chance breeze flowed through her dress and reminded her of the ridge behind the ranch. She closed her eyes and imagined she stood on red clay and not a high-rise rooftop. Once, long ago, she had been a city girl, but now she ached to get back to Texas plains country.

Her eyes flew open with a start when she felt Mace's hand on her back. His palm was hot even through her dress. She turned her body toward his as he stood beside her. She was surprised by the look of wonder in his eyes as he looked at her.

The attention Mace paid her now, away from the cameras, felt strange to Annie. She wondered, again, how much had been a show for the cameras and how much had been real.

"I want to hear more about Martha." Mace took her hand and inched a step closer to her. "But not this night and not with you in that dress, Annie." His words made her pulse race. "It's you, Annie. I can't help it—I'm going to kiss you."

Annie looked up in his deep cornflower blue eyes, desperately trying to not look at his mouth. "Tell me, oh visionary Harlen, how does this end?"

He took a step closer, still holding her hand but tucking it behind her, somehow pinning her against him.

"A true visionary knows how the movie will end but can still captivate you in a single moment so that, briefly, you don't even care how it ends. The sheer beauty of the moment will entrance you forever—no matter how the movie actually ends." His smooth, low voice and the heat from his body made Annie feel like she might just slide right out of his embrace. Her face flushed as he leaned in closer. As she felt his breath on her lips, she realized he had never kissed her before.

As his mouth met hers, the streets quieted, her heart slowed, and the city lights dimmed as her eyes slid shut. The breeze stilled, and her spinning mind was silent for a brief but shining moment.

Later that night, back in her hotel room, Annie untangled her hair with one hand and cradled the phone with the other.

"Sam, tonight was beautiful, it was shallow, it was infuriating, it was delightful, and it entranced my very soul to the point of not caring, which I don't like," Annie rambled.

"Annie, dearie, I'm glad you called." Sam acted as though he hadn't heard what she was saying. "I need to tell you something."

Annie desperately wanted to ask him why men couldn't just use their words. Why were they always using their lips? But it didn't seem like the right question or the right time. "What it is Sam? You seem on edge."

"It's about Colby."

Annie's chest tightened, and her mind spun clockwise and then did one somersault. She fought for control against her worst-case scenarios just to hear what Sam said next.

"It's his grandpa. He signed over his rights last night and somehow…"

"What Sam? What happened?"

Sam's voice thinned out and got raspy for a moment. "He managed to kill himself. I don't know how. They didn't tell me." He choked up, paused for a few breaths, and then seemed to gain control and return to normal. Annie hated being so far away from him. Then her thoughts circled above Sam, and she realized what all of it meant.

"He signed over his rights to whom?"

Sam sighed heavily. "To you, Annie."

Relief and heaviness collided over Annie and came crashing down on her heart. The worst-case scenarios faded away into smoke and dissipated as a new thought arose in her mind. This thought had been implanted by Chuck and then was left to birth itself. God had taken away her chance of having another child, but He had given her another boy.

"Have you told him?" Annie asked.

"Well, you know how it is. He's old enough that the officers tell him first, and then we get it secondhand. He's pretty torn up. He needs you here. I need you here." Sam's voice trailed off after his last confession. Sam rarely admitted needing anything. Annie's heart clenched, feeling a yoke of guilt weighing on her shoulders that she was gallivanting in a fairytale out in L.A. while Colby's world was crashing down and Sam was left to deal with it.

"Sam, I'm so sorry. I shouldn't have come. It's all been silliness anyway. I'll be home as quickly as I can."

It was quiet for a moment. Annie wondered if he'd fallen asleep, but then, quietly and sounding out of breath, Sam whispered into the phone, "Annie, I just don't think my heart can take anymore."

"I know, Sam. I'll be home soon, and we'll get through this together—you, me, and the boys."

There was another deafening pause as he struggled to answer through an even more strained voice, "Annie…it's my…heart."

Thud. It sounded like a body hit the floor on the other end of the line, and then the phone echoed as it skittered across wood floors.

Annie screamed into the phone, as the echo seemed to trail on and on. She screamed not caring who could hear her and hoping someone would. She began to sob.

"Sam?"

His silence confirmed the fear seizing her stomach and squeezing the breath from her lungs. She kept her cell phone to one ear and frantically used the room phone to dial Mace's room.

"Mace!" she yelled without letting him respond. "I think Sam is having a heart attack!"

"I'm coming!" he yelled into the phone.

Annie listened for Sam on her cell phone, but there was only silence. Sobbing, she fell on the bed, her body convulsing trying to breathe.

In ragged breaths, she prayed aloud, "Please, God, save Sam. Let Colby find him in time. Please, God." She repeated it through her sobs, not knowing anything else to pray.

Seconds later, Mace was in her room, on his phone shouting orders. "Get someone over there now. He's in the house. So are the boys. He's having a heart attack."

He didn't hug her, scoop her up, or even speak. He just began grabbing her clothes and throwing them into her suitcase. Bewildered, she watched him through mascara-matted eyes. Soon, a second set of familiar arms, covered in blonde hair, did scoop her up. It was Chuck. He carried her as Mace grabbed her suitcase and finally talked to her.

"Randy and the ambulance are on their way. We've got a helicopter standing by. We'll be there soon, Annie. Hang in there."

"Please, God," she started again but then paused. "At least let me get there in time to say goodbye."

As they jammed themselves tightly into the helicopter and lifted off, Annie felt a certainty settle over her. Sam was going to die, with or without her. She felt God tell her it was time for him to come home. Still, she ached to say goodbye. Tears escaped silently as the rotors roared above her. Unable to stop them, she buried herself in Chuck's chest and let waves of anguish take her under.

Chuck clamped his lips together and closed his eyes, feeling tears of compassion escape while Annie fought the emotional storm in his arms. Mace turned away and forced himself to look out the window.

"What if I'm not even there and he—" she uttered but couldn't finish.

"Shh." Chuck tried to calm her. "Try to relax. We'll be there soon."

She took a deep breath and tried to slow her hysteria.

Chuck leaned his head against hers so that his mouth was near her ear and whispered, "I'm so sorry for what I said and for the way I acted. I'm so sorry."

She nodded but couldn't speak. After a while, resting against Chuck and feeling the worst had passed, she did her best to compose herself and unbury her face from Chuck's chest. She took a hand from Mace and a hand from Chuck. Mace turned back toward her at the touch of her hand.

"No matter what happens," she gulped, "Thank you."

31. A FUNERAL AND COBBLER

Dense fog loomed and filled the air with such a fine mist that gray seemed to fall lightly all around. The trees and grass beaded with glassy drops of somber sky. As the beads filled and grew heavy, they fell sorrowfully to the ground.

"Even the sky is sad, Mom," Sammy said, walking hand in hand with Annie.

Annie's tears fell softly like the misting rain as she replied, "Yes, Sammy. Even the sky is crying today. Even the sky will miss Uncle Sam."

Annie was dressed in a slim black dress and Sam's black boots. Her hair was swept up in a messy bun and secured with a flower pin that had belonged to her mother. Chuck and Mace followed Sammy and Annie, with Colby trailing two paces behind them.

"I know it's inappropriate on a day like today," Chuck said in a low voice to Mace, "but I've never seen her look more beautiful."

"I know," Mace agreed.

As they approached the burial site, Mace nudged Chuck's arm. "Look who's here."

Chuck followed Mace's eyes to the gravesite where Leo stood, looking down at the casket, hands tucked in his pants pockets, pushing his suit coat back. Annie pulled Sammy close and halted. Mace and Chuck pulled up along either side of her, sensing her unease.

"Are you okay?" Mace asked.

"Yes, but I don't think we'll stay long. Maybe stay close."

Feeling like bodyguards, Chuck and Mace hemmed Sammy and Annie in with their protective presence. Colby brought up the rear and stood slightly straighter as they continued toward the site.

As they approached, Leo moved his gaze from the casket in time to see Annie and her stoic line of men walking toward him. Annie swayed against the gray horizon like a willow. He'd never seen her look more beautiful or more broken. Leo took three steps back and faded into the small crowd filtering around the casket.

Pastor Baker was normally a bold and passionate speaker from his pulpit, but as they lowered one of his dearest and oldest friends into the ground, his words were soft and tender.

"Friends, my heart does not grieve for our friend Sam because although he is absent from his body, which we lay to rest, he is present with our Lord. My heart in its humanity grieves for myself, for I will miss Sam. My heart also grieves for his loved ones. Annie, Sammy, and Colby will go on even though he is not with them, but life will change. Sometimes I resist change, but I know that our Lord is faithful and does not change. So we thank Him for His excellent care of Sam in heaven, and we trust Him to fill in the mighty gaps Sam's departure has left in our lives."

Annie nodded in gratefulness to Pastor Baker and paid no mind to the tears that tumbled down her cheeks. Sammy hugged her waist and buried his face in her side. Annie reached behind her for Colby's hand, and the three of them went to the casket. Together they lifted the saddle that Sam had loved and rested it on top of the black casket.

They each took turns saying goodbye. Sammy hugged the saddle and whispered something to the casket. Colby patted the saddle and said, "Thank you." Annie bent over the casket and kissed it, embraced the saddle, and said aloud for everyone to hear, "Lord, tell him I'll see him later."

Chuck and Mace joined the three as the casket was lowered into the earth.

Leo watched as the two men hugged Annie and the boys, and his stomach clenched in regret.

The rain began to fall steadily from the darkening clouds, and Annie turned to Mace, grasping his hand.

"Would you take us home?" Her eyes pleaded more than her words did.

He nodded and took her by the waist, leading her away from the crowd. Chuck opened an umbrella and shielded her from the sky's thundering sorrow.

She leaned into Mace as if to silently say thanks, and she said quietly, "I know Sam hoped this day would be a sunny, bright celebration, but I wasn't ready for that. I just wasn't ready to celebrate. It is sort of sweet the Lord let it be gray…because I feel gray." She leaned her head on Chuck's shoulder, and she felt heavy as if she might fall on him. He stopped and stabilized her by her shoulders.

"Mace, carry her. She's exhausted. I'll get the boys."

"No," she protested, "I can make it."

"Ok—if you're sure," Mace said while looping her arm through his so he could at least help her toward the truck. Chuck took Sammy's hand and nodded for Colby to follow.

Leo watched them move away, his eyes burning as he held back the need to run after Annie and his regret stinging worse than ever.

Mace felt Annie's shallow breaths, and she leaned heavier against him with every step. The rain was cool and dense on her face, but she made no move to wipe the water from her cheeks or forehead.

"There's a party at the house, you know," Sammy mentioned as they arrived at the truck and Mace sat Annie in the passenger's seat.

"Is she going to feel up to it?" Colby said, concerned and protective.

"I'm going to be just fine," Annie muttered. "Just get me there before everyone shows up. I need a minute alone."

"Then we're on our way," Mace said, buckling his seat belt and closing his door. Everyone piled in, and they headed home.

Later that day, Annie sat on the end of Sam's bed, staring at his lonely room. His faded jean jacket still hung on the doorknob of his closet. His slippers still waited at the side of his bed. Annie slipped her toes into their soft, plush interiors, remembering when she gave them to him two Christmases ago. He'd made jokes about them that day, but he'd worn them every day since.

She'd finally run out of tears, and what was left was a deep, resonating ache that couldn't be comforted by raw tears.

"Sam," she said aloud, "You said that God would never leave me alone, but I sure feel alone without you here. How do I raise Sammy and Colby alone?"

Sam's Bible lay open on his bedside table with his glasses perched on top. Annie scooted over and pulled it into her lap. It wasn't opened to a chapter or verse. Instead, just the inside cover lay open, where a handwritten note was scrawled:

> *Annie girl—*
> *I tried to think of something profound to give you for*
> *your birthday. Everything I learned, I learned between*

> *these pages. His profound is my profound. Happy birthday.*

Annie closed the Bible and clutched it to her chest. Tomorrow was her birthday. Sam had left the Bible for her, not knowing that he wouldn't be here to give it to her.

"I still have all your profound wisdom. I won't be alone."

In the doorway, Mace paused and then quietly cleared his throat to let her know he was there. He couldn't help but take in the beauty of the softly lit room, subtle streams of light emerging through the clouds and glowing behind the linen curtains. Annie sat on the edge of the neatly made bed, hugging a thick brown leather Bible. She met his gaze as he leaned on the doorframe, her face soft and her eyes full with a fragility he'd never seen before. Everything about her was captivating in this moment.

"Tomorrow," she started, sounding like a child in her vulnerability. "Tomorrow is my birthday."

"It is?" Mace knew he sounded appalled. *How is that even fair, God?* He fired silently up to the ceiling.

Be still.

Mace hadn't heard the voice in so long. He instantly froze, not wanting to jinx it, even though he knew that was mixing superstition with the supernatural.

Sorry about the unfair comment, he thought back.

Be still and listen.

Okay, sorry. I'm listening, Mace thought.

Annie hadn't noticed Mace's frozen posture and the distraction in his eyes while he dialogued internally. She stared at the book she now cradled like an infant.

"In a way, I'm glad it's my birthday. I know that sounds morbidly ironic, but Sam would have told me, I'm sure, that God planned this so I'd have to celebrate. Also, I'm starting to think Sam knew he was close to the end."

"What do you mean?" he asked, her comment reminding him he was supposed to be listening to her.

"The last piece of advice he gave me was that God had the right to take everything away until it was just Him and me…but even if He did, I'd never be alone. I think Sam knew God was close to taking him home. He knew he was my crutch, spiritually speaking.

Now, it's just Jesus and me. All I have left is this Bible to get me through, and that's just the way He wants it."

Mace came over and sat next to her on the bed. He didn't have eloquent answers or funny quips to lighten the mood. He just sat next to her and listened to her tell stories and reminisce about Sam. Something stirred inside him as he listened, and he knew what he needed to do…but today was not the day.

After a long pause, Annie closed her eyes, so Mace lightly touched her arm. She smiled faintly and nodded.

"We should go. I hear the boys downstairs."

"Sammy says he has a surprise for everyone. I actually came to get you."

"But you stayed to listen instead. Thank you, Mace."

He nodded and offered her his hand to help her stand from the bed. Downstairs, they found Gus, Dale, and Tom all hovering around crockpots and poker sets.

"Boys, you know you didn't have to bring food. That is what the ladies of the church have been doing all week," Annie said, laughing and pointing toward all the casserole dishes stacked all over the kitchen.

"We thought about what Sam would want at his party, and it was poker, spinach dip, peach cobbler, and those little sausages you can poke with a toothpick. So we brought those."

"And by we, we mean the ladies of the church," Tom joked.

"I knew you didn't make cobbler, Dale!" Annie said playfully, feeling lighter just by being with them.

"I learned from the best." He poked her in the ribs and said, "Martha Stewart."

"Dale!"

"What? She's got a good daytime show."

"Give me that cobbler. I'll make you my own."

"No, you won't," Tom said. "Sammy said he's got something for all of us in the den."

"Yeah, he's waiting on you," Chuck chimed in.

Everyone filtered into the den where Sammy stood in front of the TV.

"Mom, sit here," Sammy said, ushering her to Sam's recliner. Annie hesitated and then sunk down into the worn leather chair.

"Remember Mace got me that camera for Christmas?"

Annie nodded.

"Uncle Sam told me I should just start messing around with it. So I did. And then Colby helped me put this together. I wanted everyone to see it."

Annie smiled at Sammy, thinking he was so brave to show everyone whatever he'd been working on and so sweet to take their mind off their sadness for a while. Chuck dimmed the overhead lights, and Sammy pushed play.

The next half hour revealed scenes of obscure angles of Sam sneaking cookies or belly laughing from the recliner at a show. It showed interviews with him about horses, the ranch, and God. It was filled with funny little sayings he'd spout off with a straight face. It was his prayers blessing the food at dinner. It was him, snoring on the couch and reading the paper on the front porch in his robe and slippers. The final scene before the screen faded to black was of Annie and Sam at the table together, drinking coffee while sitting side by side quietly.

Everyone laughed and cried at the same time. Joy mixed deeply with their sorrow as they enjoyed lost moments of Sam, captured by young Sammy.

Annie jumped up from the recliner and hugged Sammy so tight he yelped. Then she knelt down in front of him, not caring that everyone was watching.

"I've never seen anything so wonderful in all my life. Thank you for showing us the way you saw Uncle Sam."

A chorus of praise rose behind her as everyone else agreed with her. She looked over and motioned for Colby to join her.

She hugged both boys and then pulled away. "You are both so talented. Uncle Sam would be sad he missed this." She paused, feeling the weight of her statement. "But he'd be glad it was all about him."

Everyone roared with laughter.

Over poker sets and cobbler, they swapped stories about Sam and laughed about the years together. When it was late into the night, Sam, Dale, and Tom said they needed to wander home. Chuck refused to leave Annie and decided that he and Mace should stay at the house, so they headed to the guest room. Annie put Sammy to bed, checked on Colby in the barn, and then curled up tightly in the recliner. She watched Sammy's movie over and over until she couldn't hold her eyes open any longer.

Annie awoke to the sound of tires crunching up the gravel drive. She uncurled from the recliner, her spine pinched and her hips aching. Stretching as she went, she made her way to the kitchen to look out to the driveway to see who might be coming. To her surprise, she saw Leo's old truck inching toward the house, unsure and skittish.

Quietly, she crept out the front door, pulled on her boots, and walked into the middle of the drive, wondering what she was going to say.

Leo put the truck in park, left it running, and slowly got out of the cab, watching Annie the whole time. *What am I here for? What can I possibly say to her?* He asked himself.

Her face asked the same thing, *What are you doing here, Leo?*

He crossed his arms and looked down at the gravel, hoping to find the words to say before he looked at her again, but she spoke before he could fight his way through his own thoughts.

"Thanks for coming yester—"

Leo interrupted her before she could finish. "Don't," he barked. "Don't thank me for coming. I can't help but feel like I should have been here."

"Why, Leo?"

Words formed faster than he could say them, and he rushed them trying not to lose them. "I...I am plagued with such guilt, Annie. I shouldn't have left. I shouldn't have walked out on you or Sam or Sammy. If I hadn't left, I would've been here, and maybe I could have saved Sam. I could have gotten to him in time."

"Leo!" Annie gasped softly.

"I kept thinking yesterday, 'Look what I've done.'"

Annie stood her ground and didn't move closer. Although the habit of hugging him was pushing at her, she refused. Her heart broke for him, but he had also broken her heart.

"Leo, you've got to stop this."

Leo stepped back with a defensive glared growing in his eyes, "What do you mean? I'm trying to say I'm sorry."

"You still think everything is somehow your responsibility— that everything hinges on how well you perform. You don't hold anyone's destiny, Leo. If you had been here, Sam still would have died if that's what God had planned. Don't you see that?"

"I could have saved him!" he shouted, unable to hold back. After the words escaped, he stumbled back against the truck, catching himself.

Annie's face never changed. She watched him hang his head in shame after yelling at her, and a small empathetic smile crept along the corners of her mouth.

"Leo, it's time for you to find out what you think about God."

He looked up at her with a strange expression as she continued, "It's time for you to figure out the man He means you to be. All this time, you've been the person you thought I needed you to be, which fed into your feeling you had failed me somehow. Now, you're caught up in thinking about who Sam needed you to be and how you think you failed him. You don't need all that on your shoulders. It's too heavy. You don't have to save the world, Leo. Someone's already done that."

He looked away from her, out to the western pasture. He stared at the horizon, forcing tears to dissipate and the lump in his throat to go down. He unfolded his arms and shoved them deep in his pockets, just as she'd seen him do a million times. He looked back at her, and she saw in his eyes a transparency and vulnerability.

"I know you're right. To be honest, I don't know what I think about God anymore. I am sorry, Annie, for all things I've done that have hurt you." He paused, thinking to himself, *It took hurting her to show me that I wanted to love her the right way...but it's too late for that.* "I'm sorry, too, for not seeing that you were right last year. Maybe I have loved you since the beginning, but not in the right way. I can see that now. Maybe now you can move on from what happened."

"Leo, you were once a part of this family. There will always be a place for you here."

"Thanks, but those boys need people around who know what they think about God."

"I won't disagree there."

"Well," he said, pushing off the truck and taking a few steps toward her. "I suppose this is goodbye then."

Annie shook her head and smiled at him softly. "I tried telling you goodbye once, and it didn't take. I won't ever say it again to you, Leo. I'll tell you that you're forgiven. I'll tell you that you are always welcome, and I'll tell you that we'll pray for you. We'll pray you find what you're looking for and someday come home. But I won't say goodbye."

Leo shrugged and laughed through his nose while tears threatened his eyes again. "Can I at least hug you one last time?"

Annie wrapped her arms around his waist and looked up into his pained face. "As long as you promise it won't be the last time."

Leo melted at her touch and buried his face in her hair, relishing the smell. "You're not making this easy, Annie."

"I never have, Leo. If I made it easy to walk away, you would have done it years ago."

"Maybe so." He pulled away slightly but then swept her hand up to his lips. He kissed her hand lightly, and Annie couldn't help but revisit memories in flashes. Though now, instead of blushes and butterflies, she felt gratitude. She thanked God for such exquisite memories with Leo that would endure a lifetime even if they were the last.

She gave him a big smile and pushed away.

"Have a great trip, Leo."

He left.

Annie stood in the driveway for a long time, watching Leo's truck kick up dust as it drove away. As the dust began to settle, she heard footsteps on the gravel behind her. She turned to see Mace coming toward her with a cup of coffee.

"Morning," she said as he handed her the cup.

"Morning...and happy birthday."

"Thanks! Also, thanks for the coffee. I need it."

"Was that Leo?"

"Yes." Annie smiled, knowing he had to have been watching from the kitchen window.

"Everything okay?"

"I think so."

"You guys back together?"

"Mace, we were never together—not really—and we're not together now. He's gone off to find his way."

Mace laughed but then could see she was serious, and he sucked his laugh back in to say, "What does that mean?"

Annie shrugged, taking a sip of coffee, and then said, "I told him that he needs to figure out what he thinks about God, and he needs to figure out who he is without trying to save the world all the time."

Raising his eyebrows and nodding, Mace merely said, "Oh."

As soon as a small, comfortable silence fell between them, Mace remembered the certain urging he'd felt last night. He knew now was the time to tell her.

Even as he thought about turning to her and starting to speak, Annie shook her head as a sliver of a smile eased at the right corner of her mouth.

"You're leaving too, aren't you? Martha told me you'd be important. You've got stories to tell." She smiled at him.

Mace shook his head, not knowing exactly what to say but letting words tumble out anyway. "I can't help but feel I've made a mess of things. If only I'd caught on sooner, maybe you and I would have gone differently." A tear escaped the corner of his eye before he could look away. "What if I can't do this? What if it's too big, Annie? These aren't the stories I wanted to tell. Selfishly, I wanted to tell the ones that sell, and…I wanted our story to end differently."

She started to reach up for the tear that rolled down his face, but Mace caught her hand. He brought her palm to his lips. Annie closed her eyes at the touch of his lips on her skin. She wondered if she was weak to feel this way or if it meant she had feelings for him. When he withdrew, she looked at him, and without asking again, Mace nodded.

"I hear you saying our story is over," she said softly, "but I always knew you had such great untapped purpose to find."

Mace let out a laugh.

"That night," he started as he intertwined his fingers with hers, "Gosh, that night! When I was stuck in your truck with you, you said that very thing to me—that there's something we're all meant to do. I know now what that is." Then as the bottom line of resolve hit him with a heavy thud, he grew still until, finally, he nodded his head. "I think, Annie, I fell in love with you along the way."

"You did?" she asked, surprised as his confession and thinking he had a funny way of showing it up until that kiss on the rooftop.

"Yes. At first, I wasn't going to tell you, thinking it would be easier, but now I think you need to know that I'm in love with you." His heart beat so loud he couldn't take it any longer. "And forgive me, I can't help myself."

He kissed her, perhaps for the last time. Her tears were salty on her soft lips, and her breath was sweet as it escaped. He finally released her but lingered near her lips just to breathe in what was left of their moment.

"I have stories to tell, Annie. It's in my DNA. Not to make my name famous—but to make God's name famous. Do you see?"

Annie could see he felt passionate as he conveyed his words with animation. At that moment, Annie felt both swelling pride and bitter devastation.

Mace continued, "We could make a difference in the industry. We can shed light on all the injustice. We can expose lies. We can bring them out of the shadow. And lies can't live in the light."

"We?" she asked.

"Chuck and I," Mace said, fueled with passion about making a difference. "We are going to do big things. As much as I wanted to write myself into the end of your story—and trust me, I tried even though it just didn't fit. For the first time in my life, Annie, I might just do the unselfish thing. I know it's your birthday, so I debated about telling you now. I know this is not how love stories work. A man doesn't declare his love as he's saying goodbye. And trust me, half my body and brain are telling me I'm an idiot right now. I am saying our story is over, but that doesn't mean I don't love you."

Annie nodded slowly. She reached up and traced his face. She felt it was ironic that the first time Mace had been utterly vulnerable with her was when he was saying goodbye.

"Mace, I will always treasure the memories that we have together, and I hope we can always be in each other's lives. You came here a stranger, but you became a friend who was there for me through some of my toughest times. Somewhere in the middle, I think I started to fall for you too, and I am thankful for that. For all of it." She snickered a little. "Love! What a funny birthday present."

Maces smiled sadly. "If I had known we would have so few kisses, I would have kissed you long before L.A."

Annie smiled, thinking back to that night. She knew that she might always love to close her eyes and remember that dress, the dinner on the rooftop, and Mace's kiss. She thought back to Mace's words from that night, *"Entrance you forever, no matter how it ends,"* and she realized that he had known even then.

"When will you go?" she asked, turning back toward the house and starting to walk. Mace followed.

"We have to leave after dinner tonight. We have a flight out at 11."

"Then let's enjoy my birthday, and the future will come at 11."

"Well said. I also want to celebrate Colby's pending adoption. We won't get to be here for the real thing, and I want to celebrate how God brings people together," Mace said, thinking of Colby but also of himself.

"Absolutely, but I think I need to be alone for a little while."

"Don't worry about us. We'll enlist the boys and take care of everything."

In the barn, Annie threw her leg over the saddle and settled in. As she gave Cadillac a little kick, she heard Sam's voice in her head, "*Go be alone with your Maker.*" They walked along the barn and almost passed the house when Colby and Sammy came running onto the back porch.

"Bye, Momma!" Sammy shouted. Colby waved and studied her expression, concerned.

"I won't be gone long. Just going for a ride. Everything is all right." She said the last part to put Colby at ease. He nodded and put his hand on Sammy's shoulder.

"We'll see you at the party!" Sammy shouted again excitedly.

They waved her off as she spurred the horse into a lope down the trail. Ranch life wasn't something she'd always known, but now, the rhythm of a horse was something she loved and needed. She clicked her mouth, and the horse took off. Her hair bounced on her shoulders as they galloped across the pasture, and Annie thought about how much she loved the wind in her hair. Sweat rolled down the horse's neck as he pushed harder, hooves pounding the earth with such force that it drove Annie's thoughts up to the surface of her mind.

What are You doing, God? What do You want from me? I've been through hell. You've taken my parents, my youth, my womb, Leo, Sam, and now Mace and probably Chuck. I don't understand. What else do You want from me? I've told my story. I put it out there for everyone to see, but while I was doing that, You took Sam. I didn't even get to say goodbye. What now, God? What else do You want? I don't think I have anything left.

She and Cadillac climbed over hills and raced across open plains. Once Cadillac began breathing heavily with exhaustion, Annie finally slowed. Steering the horse toward the creek that ran along the tree line, she jumped down, scooped a palm-full of cool water, dumped it down her neck, and splashed another on her face. Letting the reins hang down under Cadillac's neck, Annie removed the saddle and blanket to let him cool down. He drank from the creek as Annie rubbed his neck. Once he moved to graze nearby, she sat down on the grass and leaned against her saddle. She looked up to the wide sky and the bright clouds floating above her.

I guess You're not going to answer me today, and I suppose I can't make You. Truth be told, I just needed to get out here and clear my head, but I still want to know...why did You have to take Sam? He's the one who kept me in line and told me what to do. How am I supposed to raise two boys on my own and run a ranch and a theater?

Cadillac moseyed over toward her and nuzzled her. Annie patted his face and rubbed his jaw. Wildflowers painted the landscape with purples, yellows, and reds, and they swayed in the breeze. The sun shone through the tall grass, and it glowed. Annie didn't expect to hear all the answers from God, but she felt His presence.

I guess nature doesn't have to be told what to do, does it? Animals don't question You on what season it is or why their life goes the way it does. Poppies don't shrink back because tomorrow the sun might scorch them; they bloom anyway. A mustang doesn't hide because it doesn't know what's on the other side of the hilltop; it runs wild and free anyway. Her thoughts paused. *That sounded like something Sam would say.* The thought made her laugh, and Annie knew that she could go on. *My feelings are all confused, but just like Sam said, Your plans, Lord, are usually bigger than how I feel. I think I begin to see what You're doing. You're silent today because You wanted me to see that I already know what the answer is. You and Sam have both already given me what I need.*

She saddled Cadillac and started her ride home, knowing she would be okay.

The entire town came out to the Arrow Theater for Annie's birthday party. Mandy made a huge cake, and Max catered his hoagies and onion rings. There was a live band on stage, dancing in the aisles, and fireworks on the roof. Annie had never been more impressed with Mace and Chuck than at what they managed to pull off in one day's time.

As night bloomed above them and the fireworks smoldered out, Annie gathered everyone's attention.

"I just want to thank two of the most generous and wonderful men I know, Mace and Chuck, for throwing me this birthday party. Even more importantly, I wanted to celebrate Colby Woods. I will officially adopt him a few months from now." Her voice dropped a little as she continued. "I wish Sam could have been here to see what Mace's film is bringing to light. I wish he could have been here with all of you—he loved a good gathering," she said with a laugh and tear-filled eyes. "Mace and Chuck, we're so glad you came into our lives. None of us knows what the future looks like, but we welcome it, and I am thrilled to welcome and celebrate it with Sammy and Colby, my boys."

The eruption of cheers filled the night sky. Colby rushed Annie with a hug that engulfed her, and she was overwhelmed with joy.

"Thank you. You took me in and called me your own, just like Jesus. Thank you."

Annie's heart had never felt as full as when she surveyed her friends and her family and celebrated with wonder whatever was to come.

"Colby, thanks for helping clean up." Annie poked her head into his room after she had put Sammy to bed. "Mace and Chuck are about to leave. Do you want to say goodbye?"

He launched off the bed and followed her. Mace and Chuck were loading their bags into the back of the truck as she walked out from the barn.

"Their helicopter is landing in the back forty. I'll drive them out and be right back."

Colby nodded and went to hug Mace and said, "Thanks for everything, Mr. Harlen. Thanks for taking care of my mom."

Mace shot a glance to Annie, surprised that Colby had referred to her as his mom, and she was beaming. Mace hugged Colby and then shook his hand.

"God has great plans for you, Colby. Maybe they involve being my intern when you graduate. Your work with the movie and Sammy showed real potential."

Colby's eyes widened, and he immediately looked to Annie for approval. She winked and shrugged.

"We've got plenty of time to talk about the details." Mace smirked at her for already being protective of Colby.

Colby turned toward Chuck and hugged him as well. "Thanks, Chuck. You're one of the greatest guys I know."

Annie patted his arm as he walked past her to the barn. "See you in a minute."

Annie and the two men piled in the truck and bumped along the dirt path out to the back of the pasture. A solemn silence hung between them in the anticipation of goodbyes. As she put the truck in park, they heard the helicopter descending right on time.

She turned to them and shrugged. "Well. Shall we?"

"Yep. Perfect timing." Mace said, sliding out first and walking to the back of the truck to grab the bags. "Chuck, can I have a minute? Can you take these to the helicopter? Then you can have your goodbye?"

Chuck looked at Annie, grabbed the bags from Mace, and walked toward the helicopter, pleading with a God he barely knew to tell her how he felt.

Annie walked around the bed of the truck and stepped close to Mace, her hair whipping around from the whirring blades. She gathered it in her hand, and she realized, here they were again, in a field with a helicopter with Mace leaving.

Mace squinted, searching her face, knowing she had questions.

"You told me in L.A. that you didn't know how all this would end, but you did, didn't you?" She talked loud over the roar of the helicopter.

He took a step closer so she would hear him. "I was still trying to write myself in. See, all along I thought maybe we were the story. Even when I was fighting it and angry at God about it, I thought it was the story of the famous guy and the hurt girl—a 'what are the odds of him meeting her' plot line. Then I realized that the plot was bigger than that, so I needed to write myself out. Or maybe I was never in it to begin with…" he said, trailing off.

"It's not so much a write out as it is paths crossing and then diverging. God just has a new plot line for both of us."

"Yes. You and I had a purpose, but we weren't the story."

It's yet to unfold, Annie thought as Mace hugged her, kissed her goodbye on the cheek, and promised to call when they arrived in L.A.

As Mace released her and turned to leave, he couldn't help but feel a surge of inner peace, knowing he was doing what was in his DNA to do, even though he knew he was leaving a fraction of his heart in Texas.

Annie watched him duck against the wind from the blades as they sliced through the night air, but her eyes traveled past Mace to Chuck as he walked toward her with determination.

Something inside her stirred, kicking up memories and sending them fluttering in her stomach as she watched him approach. His height soared above her, and she could see in his eyes that he was holding himself back.

"You once told me that everything felt stolen because God said you weren't the man I needed. Do you think that could ever change? Like maybe He just meant you weren't ready at the time?" She paused and then shook her head. "Or maybe I was the one who wasn't ready?"

"Maybe...I still don't know."

Feeling a mysterious hope swell inside her, she stepped toward Chuck, coming toe to toe with him.

"What if I told you that I wasn't sure of this ending?" she said, shouting above the engine and the blades as they competed for attention. "This ending where you leave on that helicopter. What if I thought you are what I need and that I wanted to be with you? You've been there for me the whole time even when you couldn't have me. Don't you think that means something?"

"Don't do this, Annie. You know if you said that, I wouldn't get on that flight."

"Don't get on that flight, Chuck."

Chuck hadn't kissed her since that night at the bakery, and he didn't know if he should now, but he wanted to. Every fiber of his body tingled with anticipation and the adrenaline of restraint. He pulled her into his chest and wrapped her tightly in his arms, her body touching his, sending lightning through him.

"I have to leave…for now. I just think I'm not who I need to be yet. I have to finish this with Mace. We've started something big here."

"What if—" she started and then stopped herself.

Chuck kissed her temple and whispered in her ear, "Then I will honestly love you for the rest of my life from far away."

With sudden resolve, Annie felt Sam's words reverberate through her mind: *God's plans for you are bigger than the way you feel. Men and women have greater purpose on this earth than falling in love.*

She knew it was true.

Three men had confessed their love to her, but all three were seeking God's path for their lives before seeking her love in return. Three other men already had her love. One of those men had loved God above all and gone to be with Him, and two young men still needed to be shown how to love God more than anything.

EPILOGUE: TIRAMISU
PENUMBRA, SIX MONTHS LATER

As I typed the words "The end," the phone beside me rang.

"Hello?" His warm, mellow voice in my ear made finishing that much more gratifying.

"What are you doing?"

I crossed my legs and hoped that the goofy grin on my face didn't show in my voice. "Actually, I just finished a little writing project."

"Oh?" he said, excitement oozing from his masked coy tone. "What's it about?"

"Well, I wrote a screenplay."

"Do tell. Don't withhold from me."

"It's sort of a funny little thing about a female baker, looking for the perfect man. She is a Lucille Ball type, lots of funny moments, food flying around and memorable quips."

"And does she find the perfect man?"

"Well, she finds love. He's neither perfect nor expected, which makes it perfect."

"And, pray tell, what is this masterpiece called?"

"Tiramisu for Two," I managed to say without giggling, though his silence led me to believe that he was grinning from ear to ear.

I couldn't help but smile as he went on to talk poetically about the triumphant, heart-wrenching stories they were hearing and the dangerous, heart-pounding adventures they were having as they traveled the world.

"It all sounds wild and unreal," I said, amazed at the changes in him since we first met.

"We're having the time of our lives. I can't wait for you to see the stories we're getting to tell." He was passionate about his new life direction, and I could feel it ignite me like flint. "We have news from Martha as well."

"Oh?" I said, surprised that he would speak of it as if it involved me.

"We'll talk about that another time. I don't have much time now."

"Okay," I said, suddenly anxious about seeing him again. "Be careful out there."

I could hear a smile in his voice as he answered, "We are. How are you all? How are the boys?"

"They are good."

We spoke as if no time had passed, but we caught up on the past few months with baseball and the newest show that my theater program was doing. His voice had the same bold quality it had always had, but now it possessed a fresh maturity.

"Well," he paused, "We've got to end this conversation somehow. I've got to hop on a plane."

Just like six months ago, a part of me ached for a different ending. Now, just like then, I didn't want it to end, but the ending seemed inescapable.

"It was good to hear from you," I said, not fully masking my disappointment.

"I'm glad you are writing, Annie. I hope you keep doing that. I'd love to read what you've written."

"Okay!" I blurted, increasingly aware of what I really wanted to say but knowing it wasn't fair to say those words, considering our conversations about our feelings for each other six months ago.

"Well, it's been delightful."

"Yes, as always," I agreed, though I was screaming in my head that this wasn't going the way I wanted it to.

"We'll talk soon."

There was no "I love you. I miss you. It's good to hear your voice. When can I see you? My heart aches for you." We had been reduced to keeping in touch and catching up.

I sighed. I knew it was futile for me to wish for more at this moment. I was running a ranch and raising boys. He was traveling the world and making movies. Both of us were fulfilling our purpose, both doing hard things...just not together.

I was aware, right then, of the very real pleasure in our reality. It was enlightening, confirming, and inspiring. I knew I needed to embrace the newness of what we were, without losing hope for whatever was to come.

"I'll talk to you soon, Chuck..."

THE END

NOTES ABOUT *WHERE THE SHADE ENDS*:

*Penumbra is not a real town. It is a fictionalized town even though it is modeled after several towns in my home state as well as towns in Texas.

*This book was always going to be called *Where the Shade Ends*, but when my grandmother, Nancy, told me that the title was the definition of the word "penumbra," I decided it should be the name of the town.

*The Gradys are not a real family. They are not a fictional representation of any family. They are purely my imagination.

*The theater in Chicago is modeled after a gorgeous theater abandoned now in the south side of Chicago, the Royal Theater. Its blue and gold Persian interiors are a sight to behold, and it is a shame that no one gets to enjoy it anymore.

* Lou Malnatti's Pizza is a real place in Chicago. It has the best pizza ever. When in Chicago, eat Lou's!

*The Signature Room is a very real and very spectacular restaurant at the top of the John Hancock Building in Chicago.

In this book, I have fictionalized accounts that deal with rape and companies that profit from pornography. While this story is fiction, many people's stories are not.

The devastation that pornography causes to relationships, hearts, and minds is very real. You can read more about it on the websites listed below.

Fight the New Drug is a non-religious, non-political, and non-profit organization that is creating a movement against pornography.
www.fighthenewdrug.org

Life Star is a network that provides information and services to those who have been affected by impulsive sexual behaviors such as porn.
www.lifestarnetwork.com

The National Sexual Violence Resource Center has learning courses as well as lists of regional or state organizations that help sexual violence victims.
http://www.nsvrc.org

On average, nearly 300,000 Americans are victims of sexual assault each year. RAINN provides information, networks of counselors, and hotlines to call.
https://rainn.org/get-information

These organizations have not compensated me for mentioning their websites, but they have given me permission to reference them.